Alandra didn't speak, but merely wound her arms around Nicholas's neck to pull his mouth to hers in another kiss. Without disturbing their kiss, he lowered her to the soft feather mattress, then positioned himself beside her.

Nicholas knew he should halt this insanity, but passion alone was ruling him. He was a man, not a saint, and she was so incredibly sweet. What would she feel like beneath his questing hands? He had to know.

"Alandra. Sweet, sweet Alandra."

Gently tugging at her dress, he smiled at her sudden movement to cover her exposed flesh. For all her attempt at seduction, she was after all a modest young thing, yet instead of cooling his desire, her shyness fired him to a passion he had hitherto never felt.

"Do you want me to stop?" he whispered huskily. "I'll go no further if you tell me nay."

MIDSUMMER NIGHT'S DESIRE
Kathryn Kramer
Two-time Winner of *Romantic Times* Reviewers' Choice Award

Midsummer Night's Desire

KATHRYN KRAMER

LEISURE BOOKS NEW YORK CITY

A LEISURE BOOK®

July 1992

Published by

Dorchester Publishing Co., Inc.
276 Fifth Avenue
New York, NY 10001

Printed in the United States of America.

To my uncle, Howard E. Vickery, a consummate actor whose love of the theater inspired me. You are gone now, but not forgotten. The joy that you brought to others will be your epitaph.

To a very special lady, my aunt, Patricia Ferris Vickery, whose interest in my work and unfailing enthusiasm inspires me.

And last, but certainly not least, I want to thank Lydia Paglio for using her expertise once again in helping me mold this story.

Author's Note

The forty-five year period from 1558 to 1603, the reign of Elizabeth I of England, is considered to be the English renaissance. Such names as Christopher Marlow, Ben Johnson, Edmund Spenser, and William Shakespeare are associated with that time of fruitful literary achievement of dazzlingly brilliant poetry and the emergence of unsurpassed theatrical masterpieces.

Elizabeth Tudor was an intellectual, theologian, poet, musician, a lover of hunting, dancing, pageants, and great plays. At the age of twenty-five she came to the throne and issued in the Golden Age of theater. Six years after her coronation, a baby was born who would become a man of renown in his own right. His name was William Shakespeare, perhaps the most remarkable storyteller the world has known, the ultimate writer of romance. Shakespeare first came to London to become an actor and though his talents for writing were soon put to use, he continued acting, often playing character roles in his own plays, such as the ghost in *Hamlet*. Not only was he a playwright, poet, an actor, he was also a shareholder in acting troupes and theater buildings.

The established actor in Shakespeare's day enjoyed more social acceptance than had ever been exhibited before, with the exception of ancient Greek times. Drama was the source of entertainment for all classes of people in sixteenth-century England, and was the most popular event in London. Therefore, good actors were in great demand and could make a living touring the villages or joining acting companies.

The theater was a magical world where a man could enter another time, another place, and assume a new appearance. It was considered highly improper to enter the acting area without masks. Thus it is in this story that when a young nobleman finds himself in danger, it is to the theater that he flees to hide his true identity. Embarking on the greatest adventure of his life, he meets the woman of his heart where he least suspected to find her.

Act One: A Dangerous Intrigue

England 1597

"Give me that man
That is not passion's slave and I will wear him
In my heart's core, ay, in my heart of heart."
Shakespeare, *Hamlet* act 3, scene 2

Chapter One

Torches and tapers blazed brightly, casting a magical glow on the great hall of Whitehall Palace. In the far corner, on a raised dais, musicians filled the air with melodious songs as brightly colored, heavily bejeweled, elaborately dressed lords and ladies moved gracefully about the gigantic room.

From her perch high above the dancers, leaning over the crowded gallery which crossed the hall like some heavenly bridge, the young dark-haired Alandra Thatcher watched in awe, her brown eyes wide in surprise. She had heard her father speak of the court, but never in her wildest imaginings had she envisioned anything like this! It was like a gathering of brightly colored birds or gilded butterflies, flying and bouncing in time to the lilting rhythm.

"And there is the queen," she gasped aloud, riveting her eyes upon that stately personage. How magnificent she was, dressed in all her finery, standing straight and proud. Clothed completely in white, her jewels shining in the light of a hundred flames, she looked to Alandra like an angel or fairy queen. The large transparent veil wired about her shoulders did indeed form wings, and her golden-red hair twinkled with pearls and gems. So this was Elizabeth Tudor, she who had been triumphant over all her enemies and had defeated the Spanish Armada, and had brought unity and peace to England.

Alandra watched as the queen moved among the crowd, whispering to this nobleman or that lady, casting particular favor now upon a tall, blond gallant dressed in gold and green. She knew it was Lord Owen Stafford for her father had babbled on and on about the man, describing him in great detail. This lord was partially responsible for Alandra being at Whitehall tonight. He was giving a masque for the queen's pleasure and had hired Alandra's father to stage the lavish spectacle. She thought, with not undue boasting, that Murray was the finest scene designer in all of London. Did not Master Shakespeare himself make use of her father's talents? And now the scenery, costumes, and other effects for the masque would be viewed by Her Majesty. Was it any wonder that at this moment her heart swelled with pride?

The world of the theater was the only life that Alandra had ever known. She had been raised among actors, costumers, and writers, and for just a moment she wondered what living at court would be like, to dress in silks and jewels, to wear lace and to smell of lavender. The dream was cruelly shattered as she looked down at her own simple garments, the dress of dullest orange cloth with its black, laced corset binding in her tiny waist. The only resemblance she bore to those whirling about below was the white ruff she wore at her neck and wrists. Her dark tresses had

no pearls, no ornamentation at all, except for a few
wildflowers she had plucked.

Ah, well! She sighed. 'Twas a beautiful fantasy, but
one she would never experience. Even so, she could
not help wonder what it would be like to have a man
stare at her as boldly as a dark-haired man now stared
at a woman dressed in pink. As if to devour her, she
thought. Was it any wonder, handsome as he was, that
the golden-haired beauty unabashedly returned his ardor, sweeping across the room to join him? As they
stood talking, they created a perfect portrait of mutual
adoration, until the illusion was shattered by Elizabeth's appearance at their sides. As high above them
as she was, Alandra heard the queen's harsh words.

"Are you waiting to talk with me, *madame*?" The
queen's tone was scathing as she looked the blonde in
the face. "Well, speak up!"

"I but wanted to compliment Your Majesty on her
dress. It is most becoming."

"My dress? My dress!" Elizabeth's eyes traveled
from shoulder to hem and back again, surveying the
radiant vision of the woman before her. "Insufferable
bitch to try to outshine your queen!" The other woman's gown surpassed Elizabeth's but even more eye-
catching was her youth and her voluptuous curves.
"Go to your chambers and remove that gown at once.
It offends me."

"I will not!" The queen's young rival was adamant.

"You will do as I say!" The queen's gaze moved to
where the handsome nobleman stood. "Do not think
I have not seen you looking cow's eyes at him, madame. Must I remind you of your marriage vows?
Leave immediately."

For a moment it appeared that Elizabeth might well
strike the woman who had angered her, but the queen
used restraint. As the object of her anger quickly curtsied and obeyed, leaving the hall, Elizabeth watched

her go. She then turned to the dark-haired nobleman.

"I warn you. Have no more dealings with that woman. It is I who have raised you up and I who can cast you down. Remember that when the night chases away the day." Turning on her heel, she walked away with a rustle of her full skirts.

What had that golden beauty done to so inflame the queen's ire? Alandra wondered. Why was she so angry? It was a puzzlement, but none of her business, she supposed. She could never hope to understand what emotions led these beautiful people. Did these godlike creatures feel the same desires as simple folk? Were they in truth as mortal as other men?

"Alandra!" Murray Thatcher intruded on her musings. "There you be, girl. I've been looking all over for you." His voice was tinged with annoyance and concern. "Come, I need your help in putting the finishing touches on the scenery. The masque will be starting ere another quarter hour has passed. Come, come, daughter."

"I'm sorry, Father. I did not mean to concern you. It's just that I wanted to see for myself what these noble lords and ladies were about."

Her eyes were bright as she turned to face the gray-haired, bearded man who stood with his arms flung out. He looked to be an unpretentious individual, haphazardly dressed in a doublet and trunk hose that were sadly out of fashion, and his brown felt hat slightly askew, but Alandra knew what genius he possessed.

"And the gleam in your eyes reveals that you have seen them. Vain jackanapes that they be. Such an ungodly throng as might ever be assembled," he grumbled. "Ambitious, fawning monkeys."

"I think they are beautiful, especially that man down below dressed in a wine-colored doublet. He has angered the queen, though I do not quite understand why. How could she ever be in an ill temper when someone so handsome was near her?" Seeking to steal one last glance, Alandra leaned so far over the balcony that she nearly toppled from it. But Murray's strong hands rescued her.

"Careful. Careful, I say." He clucked his tongue as he followed the line of her gaze. "Nay, they are not beautiful, for beauty is as beauty does!" He shrugged his shoulders. "But think what you will. I have sheltered you, and perhaps now it is time you learned the ways of the world." Pulling her by the hand, he hurried her along. "But hasten to the banqueting hall with me. We've no time. No time."

There was a flurry of activity going on inside the huge room as Alandra and her father entered. The room had been left in havoc by the quickly departing guests, anxious to follow the queen to the great hall. Cups and tankards littered the floor as well as the tables. Liveried servants, clad in the Tudor green and white, hurried to clear them away. A thin little man swore beneath his breath as he lit torches and tapers, granting Alandra only a nod as she passed by him on her way to the stage. At last the servants vacated the hall, leaving Alandra and her father alone.

"The scenery looks beautiful, Father, but then I knew that it would. Perhaps, however, the grove of trees should be moved just a bit to the left so as not to block the shepherd's hut from view."

At his nod, Alandra nudged the creation of wood, paste, and paint aside. The masque tonight was to have a pastoral theme, and the curtains, backdrops, and sets had been painted to give the semblance of an open field.

From her place upon the stage, Alandra looked out at the hall. Tiers of seats had been set up along the sides and across the back of the hall, upon which the lords and ladies would plant their noble bottoms. The royal dais had been placed far back in the room so as to provide the best view of the stage and to leave room for the dancers. There would be three grand masquing dances and as always, all who participated would be masked. Several of the ladies and noblemen had been given parts in the evening's entertainment.

"Let me make a test of the hoisting gear. It would not do to have a noble lord fall flat upon his prat!"

"Most certainly we would not want that," Alandra said as she stood patiently while her father attached a rope with a hook at its end to the back of her dress.

Giving a tug on the rope, he pulled her high above the stage as if in heavenly flight. From her position in the air she caught a glimpse of the elegant golden-haired woman she had seen before. The lady had just entered the room, dressed in a gown of brown and honey which was far more demure than her bright pink one. Even the dull color, however, could not hide her beauty, and she would have drawn a lusty man's eyes, no matter what she wore. But when her high-pitched voice reached Alandra's ears, Alandra thought that her speech did not match her looks.

"That witch! That jealous old witch!" she was shrieking to a tawny-haired man in black. "To shame me so before the crowd. All because her beauty has long since dimmed. She seeks to make a moth of me. A plain and colorless thing."

"Plain, Morgana? I tell you nay. That is an appellation that will never be attached to you." The man could not hide his smile.

"T'was she who arranged my marriage to Lord Woodcliff, but I will not let her win. I am not a pawn or a reward for those she seeks to favor. Let her frighten the others with her frowning mouth and tantrums, but she will not have mastery over me! I will yet be victor, and Sir Nicholas Leighton is just the man I need to do my bidding."

"I urge you to caution, niece. Sir Leighton is no fool. You will make no puppet out of him."

"Caution? Only a bold soul attains that which is highly desired, and I will have my way in this. More than all the riches of this world I want to be rid of my old, doddering husband. And by God's nightgown, I will be!"

Casting a glance over her shoulder, the blonde seemed unnerved to see Alandra dangling way up in the air, looking down at her.

"You there, *girl*. What are you about? Who are you?"

Morgana Woodcliff had no sooner spoken than Murray, now satisfied with the workings of the hoisting gear, suddenly slackened the rope, returning Alandra to the floor with a thud. Somehow Alandra managed to regain her footing as the noblewoman eyed her with cool disdain.

"Answer me! Are you perchance spying?" The voice was a shriek.

Alandra was astounded by such an accusation and mortified to have caused this woman's wrath, a lady she had admired from afar. "No, mistress," she managed to say as Morgana approached the stage. "I am here with my father." She pointed toward Murray who was now down upon his knees examining the trap door of the stage, unaware of the woman's accusation. "I am the stage master's daughter."

"A stage man's daughter!" Morgana cast Alandra a contemptuous glare. "Well, see that you do not rattle off your tongue or it will bode ill for you. Do you understand? Forget what you may have heard."

"Yes, mistress."

Alandra did not understand at all. The woman's words had meant nothing to her. Why then had Alandra's presence been cause for such outrage? Watching the lady leave the room, she pondered the matter, trying to make sense of what she had overheard. It remained a mystery. These silk-and-satin-clothed lords and ladies certainly were a strange lot. Perhaps her father was right in his appraisal of them as vain jackanapes. And yet the memory of the dark-haired nobleman made her hesitate in forming so rash an opinion. Something about him had drawn Alandra's interest so much so that she could not push from her mind the way he walked, the angle at which he cocked his head, the power and strength which emanated from him. He was the kind of man a young girl dreamed about. Handsome. Tall. Well-muscled. Gallant. What she would not have given to be the recipient of just one of his smiles. Thus thinking, she sighed, leaning against the open door.

The sound of shuffling feet brought Alandra quickly back to reality. Looking up, she saw a throng of laughing revelers coming her way. It was as if her daydreams had conjured up the very man she had been thinking about for he was among the crowd, not more than a few feet away. Alandra swallowed nervously, certain the pounding of her heart was loud enough to reach his ears as he swept past her.

Merry-go-up, he was even more handsome up close than he had been from afar. Transfixed, she stared at him, realizing suddenly that as he had passed he had touched her arm. That brief caress had warmed her, set her flesh afire with a strange tingling. She couldn't think, could barely breath as she smiled expectantly, waiting for him to look at her. Instead, he did not even offer her a cursory glance. He had not even noticed her. Had she really expected that he would? Yes. Disappointed, she pursed her lips.

"What is the matter with you, you bold strumpet? Bow your head. Are you so busy ogling that you do not see the queen is near?" A sharp-featured noblewoman elbowed the plainly garbed stage master's daughter out of her way. "You should be with the other

servants in the kitchen, not mingling with your bet-
ters!'' she hissed in Alandra's ear.

Heeding the rebuke, Alandra ducked into the shadows, watching as the lords and ladies streamed into
the hall to view the masque.

She was such a fool, she thought. A simpleton to
have let herself dream even for an instant. Alandra
stared down at the fabric of her skirt that she clutched
in her hand. The drab linen was a reminder of what
she was not. She would never be one of them. There
was no use in letting such an illusion take flight. She
was as out of place here as a chicken among peacocks,
and yet for just a moment....

Quickly, she put such a thought from her mind. It
was not wise to flit into such imaginings. She was what
she was and she was proud of that. She was Alandra
Thatcher, Murray's daughter. It was enough. She
would not give the nobleman another thought. Squar-
ing her shoulders and holding up her head, she walked
through the door, firm in her determination.

Chapter Two

The air was pungent with the fragrance of spices and perfume as the lords and ladies moved from the great hall to the banquet room. From the tip of her red bewigged head to the hem of her voluminous skirt, Elizabeth Tudor looked every inch of royalty as she swept by the others.

"Your Majesty!" Each man and woman she passed was cautious to show the utmost deference.

The queen enjoyed perennial adulation; in truth she insatiably savored it, surrounding herself with handsome men who vied with each other to be her favorite. Thus the position of queen's favorite was often a tenuous one, for Elizabeth was quick to anger and glaringly surly when crossed. Was it any wonder then that Nicholas Leighton felt the prick of apprehension as he followed the tall, thin, red-haired monarch into the hall? She had berated him because of Morgana and he could not risk angering her again.

The queen's procession passed through the line of groveling courtiers reminding him anew of the perilous position he found himself in, all because Elizabeth had looked upon him with a favorable eye. The court was filled with ambition, jealousy, and intrigue, and even now he could feel eyes appraising him, wondering what must be done to send this latest favorite toppling from his lofty pedestal. Well, he would fool them, he thought. He would not give these vultures reason to rejoice. He was ever Her Majesty's faithful subject. He would not fall from grace! The climb had been too arduous for him to slip now.

It seemed to be a never-ending march past doublets and gowns, but at last Elizabeth reached the far side of the room and seated herself gracefully upon her high-backed chair despite the hindrance of the wheeled farthingale beneath her gown. Motioning to the place beside her, she said but one word, "Nicholas!"

The cloud of momentary disfavor had been lifted, and Nicholas once again enjoyed the sunshine of Elizabeth's attentions. *How like the queen*, he thought. She often lost her temper but soon regained control of herself and replaced frowns with smiles.

"I am honored, Your Majesty," he murmured, and he was. Nor did the honor go unnoticed by those assembled, he noted.

But, the taste of victory was as bitter as ashes in Nicholas's mouth. There was another whose company he sought, but being by Elizabeth's side would keep him from seeking Morgana out. Still, one could not say no to a queen, especially after the anger she had openly displayed only a few moments ago toward the woman she considered her utmost rival. Nicholas reminded himself again and again that he must be wary despite his desires.

"I can still bedazzle them even after all these years

as queen, Nicholas," Elizabeth stated proudly.

Quickly, his eyes appraised her, and he thought how she looked undeniably awesome dressed in all her finery. She seemed at that moment to personify the glory of England. Though she was in her sixties, her face sprinkled with wrinkles, the bloom of her skin long since gone, he could still see a hint of the woman she had been in her youth—Gloriana.

Elizabeth read her young gallant's thoughts as his eyes swept over her, and she wished with all her heart that she were that younger woman again. She was old and knew it well, though she buffered the truth by pretending. If just for a little while she could fulfill her dreams by sitting at this handsome young man's side, then she would be content and could imagine that she was beautiful once again.

Ah, Nicholas, she thought with a sigh, wondering what might have passed between them if she were still in the spring of her years.

Brushing wistfully at her ruff, Elizabeth's gaze swept over him with the keen eye of a connoisseur. Nicholas Leighton was just the kind of man she was always drawn to. He was tall, six feet in height with a strong, well-muscled body that bespoke of a man used to exercise. His wine-colored doublet and trunk hose emphasized the strength of his frame; his oyster-hued nether hosen clung tightly to his well-formed legs. The stark white of his ruff contrasted sharply with the blue-black of his hair, hair that was thick and had just a hint of natural curl. As was the fashion, Nicholas Leighton wore a mustache and a beard, but even this facial covering could not hide the chiseled perfection of his face or the strong chin which told the queen that this was a man who was not easily bested.

Nicholas was the antithesis of her other current favorite, Owen Stafford, who was as fair as Nicholas was dark. They were a study in contrasts in temper-

ament as well, as different as day from night, the sun
from the moon, the light from the darkness. Nicholas
was a bold man, an adventurer who relished action.
Owen Stafford was a courtier who was more prone to
wield a pen than a sword. Right from the first Stafford
had been jealous of Leighton's manliness and bravado,
and it had made for a very amusing game. Even now
Elizabeth could see Stafford's eyes flashing fire at his
opponent, and her mouth curved up in a smile, cher-
ishing the rivalry. It made her feel omnipotent, fur-
thered her longing to be desired. To fuel the
competition between the two handsome gallants, Elizabeth gestured to the golden-haired Lord Stafford.

"Come closer . . ."

"Yes, Your Majesty."

Nicholas watched as the haughty, lithe-framed, el-
egantly dressed nobleman hastened to the queen's side
as soon as he was beckoned, sweeping low in a graceful
bow. For just a moment he felt a prick to his self-
esteem, felt threatened by the gloating smile upon his
rival's lips. How he loathed the man. His dislike of the
vain, arrogant popinjay was intense and all for good
reason. From the moment Nicholas had set foot in
Elizabeth's court, Owen Stafford had made it obvious
that he was Nicholas's enemy. He had babbled vicious
rumors, made Nicholas the butt of a hundred jests,
and in all ways tried to have Nicholas banished from
court. Only by his intellect and a reasonable measure
of good luck had Nicholas survived. Now Nicholas was
seated on the queen's right while Stafford took a position on her left.

"I believe Your Majesty will be pleased by my little
masque," Nicholas heard Stafford say. As Nicholas
turned his gaze to Stafford, the smile upon the blond
lord's lips gave him sudden cause for alarm. Why was
he grinning like the cat that ate the sparrow? What
mischief had been planned?

"I hope 'twill be a brief one. I am overly tired and wish to retire to my chambers," Elizabeth retorted, stifling a yawn. "I have danced myself into weariness."

"I do not think you will doze when you see the entertainment I have prepared. You will, I think, find it most stimulating." Stafford nodded his head to the spot across the room where the custumed and masked revelers waited. "Most stimulating indeed."

"Then let the masque begin!" the queen declared.

With the beating of the timpani, the masque was unraveled, beginning with the courtier dancers, those carefully costumed and masked aristocrats. Perhaps nothing suited the courtiers' love of intrigue and admiration for personal cleverness as did the masque, Nicholas thought. More often than not these guileless-appearing performances hid a sinister intent, making light of court scandals or secrets. He wondered who was to be the victim of tonight's masque.

The theme seemed innocent enough, depicting the scene of a shepherd tending his fields. Nicholas noted with amusement that the satin garments that the young actor wore were hardly appropriate to such an occupation, but then costumes were always lavish and flamboyant. Owen Stafford was a man of incomparable wealth who could well afford the extravagance.

The stage was a swirl with color—reds, blues, yellows, and greens—as the dancers began the main dance, accompanied by the torchbearers. Stafford had chosen to give a double masque so that the dancers were equally balanced between men and women, giving Nicholas something lovely to look at. Twirling and whirling, the young women passed by him with a smile. Though professional actors had been hired, the masque used a minimum of dialogue, for no speaking was really needed. By gesture and mime, the story unfolded quite clearly.

A dancer, dressed in pink, joined the shepherd on

the stage. Only a fool would not have recognized that this young woman was portraying Morgana, the wife of Lord Woodcliff. Nicholas sat up in his chair with a start, clenching his jaw in indignation and alarm. Morgana was overly fond of pink as the entire court knew. The dancer wore a long flowing blond wig that seemed to give further hint to her identity. Another indication was the well-known fact that Morgana's ancestors had made their fortune in the wool trade as merchants.

In white, obviously portraying sheep, several male dancers joined the pink-clad dancer on the platform. Following the young woman about, they watched as she took the staff from the shepherd's outstretched hand. At court it was jested that Morgana turned even the fiercest lion into a lamb.

Nicholas could not hold his tongue. "What foul infamy is this?" he growled, looking Lord Stafford's way.

"Silence, Nicholas, I find this interesting." The queen's jealousy of the lady in question made her appreciate the portrayal. "I would see more."

In an unmistakable pun of Morgana's marriage to an old man, another actor joined the dancers. Bewigged with gray hair, bent over and stooped with old age, he maneuvered his way to where Morgana's impersonator stood. To dispel any doubt as to the actor's identity, the Woodcliff coat of arms, a bear upon a shield of blue and gold, was embossed upon his back. From behind the curtained area of the stage came the sound of thunder. The dancers mimed an argument and quarrel, proving theirs was a most stormy union.

He watched as another actor entered the stage via a trap door. Dressed in black, the dancer obviously depicted the villain of the scene. Apprehension gripped Nicholas, for he knew what was coming. Owen Stafford had somehow learned of his secret meetings with Morgana and using the masque sought to make that knowledge available to the queen.

"The bastard!" he swore beneath his breath. "The vain, pompous, evil bastard." God's blood, he would be ruined. All that he had worked for so long would be for naught and all because of one man's spite.

Reaching for his sword, the darkly costumed man danced about with the weapon as if in combat. Nicholas was certain that everyone present would know at once that this dancer was supposed to be him. He was known as the finest swordsman at court. It was because of his valor in Ireland that he had been knighted. Seeing the queen glance his way, he knew that she recognized the identity, too. Raising her brow, she looked at him in question.

"I know not what buffoonery this is, Your Majesty. I would suggest that Lord Stafford is suffering from sun fever," Nicholas answered quickly.

"Yet I have seen you with the lady. I have given you fair warning." Her answer was a breathless hiss as her jealousy was inflamed anew.

"I am innocent of any wrongdoing. In all ways I strive to please and obey my queen." There seemed to be nothing that he could say to cool her anger. Nor did the continuation of the action upon the stage help him.

The pink-and-black-garbed dancers were entwined in a slow passionate dance that left little to the imagination. From behind a shrubbery of wood and paste, the male dancer procured a set of deer's horns and walking to where the gray-wigged dancer stood with his back turned toward the pair put the horns upon his head.

A gasp hissed through the crowd. Sympathetic eyes turned to look at Lord Woodcliff, an aged man creaking with gout, who managed to stand proudly for a moment before he stormed from the hall. Having been

in his time a bold and fearless fighter, one who had
secured Elizabeth's claim to the crown, it was no great
wonder that the compassion in the throng was for the
respected nobleman. Hostile eyes turned toward Nicholas, accusing and condemning. In that one moment
his self-control snapped. Bolting from his chair, he
grabbed Lord Stafford by the front of his doublet.

"Apologize! To me, to Lord Woodcliff, and to the
lady," he snarled. "I will allow no man to do as you
have just done."

"Apologize? For telling what is true?"

"It is *not*."

"I say it is, and now there are many others who know
it as well. You follow after the lady like a hound after
a bitch in heat. It is obvious to all."

Their quarrel became heated and intense, culmi-
nating with Nicholas drawing his sword. "By God, you
will right this wrong or rue the day you were born!"

Lord Stafford drew his own sword, his face a mask
of concern, for no one would want to face Nicholas
Leighton in combat much less when he was angered.
With a whimper, he whispered, "Your Majesty . . ."

Elizabeth quickly stood, coming bravely between
the two men. "I will not have this! I will not! You will
not pursue this foolish quarrel in the queen's presence.
This is not a jousting field, my lords." She cuffed both
men across the face as was her custom when angered.
"Out of this hall! Both of you. Until your tempers have
cooled. Then and only then will I speak further about
this matter."

As if nothing had happened, the masque proceeded,
and Nicholas nearly collided with several of the
masked and costumed performers as he strode from
the hall. He was consumed with fury to have been
made the butt of such a lewd tale. Surely the queen
would hear him out and listen to his avowal of inno-

cence. She must! After his anger cooled, he would seek
the queen out, and if he were careful in his reasoning,
he might well turn the tables on Lord Stafford. That
was his only thought as he ran headlong into a young
woman standing in the shadows. The many costumes
balanced precariously on her arm flew every which
way, littering the hallway. Hastily, she bent to pick
them up.

"I'm sorry, I didn't see you. Here, let me help you."
Nicholas was not so enraged that he forgot his manners. Stooping, he picked up some of the costumes and
handed them to her.

"I—I should have been watching where I was
going."

The voice was muffled as the young woman took the
clothes from him and retrieved her bundles, tucking
them securely under her chin. Her cloud of dark hair
fell in disarray, hiding her face, yet Nicholas could
have sworn she was staring at him. He felt the heat
of her gaze. At another time he might have paused in
conversation or at least offered a smile, but not tonight. The sting of his humiliation was too fresh in his
mind.

"Yes, you should have been more careful," he said
instead. *Women*, he thought. Were they not the plague
of a man? With a shrug of his shoulders, he hurried
away, walking up the stairs to his chamber.

"So, here you are, at heel like the queen's boon
hound." The voice was shrill. Blocking his way, Morgana stood poised upon the steps. "I would have hoped
that you might have sought me out as we planned."

Tall, achingly lovely, with eyes as blue as a summer
sky and hair of lightest sunshine, she was tempting.
Enough so to entice a saint. For a moment Nicholas
nearly forgot himself until he vividly remembered the
embarrassment he had recently suffered.

"Have you not caused me trouble enough, woman?" he growled.

"I?" Morgana buried her face in her hands, collapsing in a flood of tears.

Damning his temper beneath his breath, Nicholas touched her shoulder gently, promising that he would do his best to set things to right. Not only his name had been slandered.

"We must . . . talk . . . tonight in my chambers," Morgana managed to say between her sobs.

"In your . . ." Each time she caressed him with her eyes it became more difficult to keep his wits about him, yet in the wake of what had happened it would be a foolish and scandalous thing to do. "Morgana, we must use caution," Nicholas spoke slowly, trying to maintain his calm. "God's teeth, but what you suggest would bring the walls down upon our heads!"

Her voice was scornful through her tears. "Do you think I fear my husband, a wizened old man, who is thrice my age? I tell you, sir, that I do not."

"The queen, woman, the queen! You know she loathes scandal."

Seductions had to be circumspect, for Elizabeth would brook no stain upon the reputation of her court. Had she not banished the Earl of Pembroke for getting Mary Fitton with child? How much angrier would she be were Morgana to flaunt her longed-for liaison with Nicholas, particularly now that it had been brought to light? Nicholas had to convince her to give up this mad scheme.

"The queen. The queen!" she chided. "An aged, bewigged old harridan who has never had a man in her bed. What does she know of love?" Her eyes flashed fire as she cast him a petulant frown. "I only know that I love you, that I must have you. Wouldst you sentence me to a life of loneliness without you just to please Elizabeth?"

"Morgana . . ."

Even after what had happened, and though his reason told him to send her away, he could not keep his loins from stirring at the sight of her, so elegant and feminine. A seductress if ever there was one. The soft swell of her bosom rose above the square neckline of her bodice, the stomacher that she wore emphasized her small waist.

"Oh, what I would not give if I were free." Morgana's hands moved toward him imploringly, then fell to her side. Her voice at first but a whisper had grown shrill and louder in volume. "*Free* of the bondage to that old man. Free to marry you."

"Marry?" It was the farthest thing from his mind. "Let us have no talk of marriage when you *are* wed."

"But not for long were I to have my way." Morgana's beautiful face was distorted by her expression. "Nicholas . . ."

Several men and women passing by raised their brows.

"I repeat, Morgana. We both stand precariously on the brink of destruction." The situation was steadily becoming more and more uncomfortable. What had he gotten himself in to? "We must *not* talk here."

She pursed her lips and thought for a long drawn-out moment. "Then meet me at ten o'clock at The Black Unicorn," Morgana said behind her hand, obviously pleased with her plan. "The inn across the Thames."

He knew the inn in the area of the theaters and the bear-and-bull-baiting arenas. A place of mischief and thievery. Hardly a place for a lady. He opened his mouth to protest, but before he had the chance, Morgana had run to her own room and slammed the thick wooden door.

Chapter Three

A sudden wind chilled his body as Nicholas took leave of the bargeman and stepped ashore. Looking over his shoulder into the darkness, he carefully ascertained that no one had followed him, then made his way to the inn. He knew it was a three-story, half-timbered whitewashed building with a thatched roof and boxed windows that overlooked the Thames, but tonight he could see only the light of the lantern fires from the windows.

The sounds of drunken laughter, singing, and boisterousness carried on the wind told him that the inn was filled with patrons. The huge wooden sign had come off its hinge and was banging against the outer wall as Nicholas approached the door. Once the inn had been splendid, but now it was run-down, its roof and support beams rattling from decay. He wondered again why Morgana had chosen this particular inn and appeased his apprehension by reasoning that in her

way she had been wise. There would be far less chance
of meeting any of the courtiers in such a place. But
thieves were another matter and Nicholas rearranged
the pouch of coins under his doublet.

Opening the creaking door, he found himself face to
face with a man of enormous girth who beckoned him
inside. With a flaming red beard and a patch over his
eye, the man looked like a pirate but seemed cordial
enough. With a gap-toothed smile, the innkeeper
showed him to a table in the corner of the taproom.
It was murky inside and smelled of grease, sweat, and
smoke from the kitchen fires. Stale wine and ale assaulted his nostrils. This was definitely not the kind
of place to meet a lady, and he resolved to get this
meeting over with quickly and then send Morgana
home.

"What you be needing, lovey?" The shapely young
tavern maid quickly accosted him, making it very
clear by her expression that more than serving drinks
was on her mind.

"A tankard of ale!" he replied curtly, waving her
away. He had enough on his mind without having to
worry about escaping from an amorous serving
wench.

"Are you sure that will be all?" Lifting her skirt well
above her ankle, she gave him a view of her shapely
leg.

"Yes!"

Startled by his gruff answer, the girl dropped the
hem of her skirt then quickly scurried away.

Having at last accustomed his eyes to the dim light,
Nicholas let his gaze roam over the contours of the
room, searching for any sign of Morgana's slim form.
Seeing no sign of her, he supposed that he was early
and thus settled himself back on the bench. The rushes
on the floor were in dire need of changing, and the
room recked with foul odors, but at least he was shel-

tered from the wind. For the time being, he was comfortable and content.

Wisely, Nicholas had changed his garments before setting out for the inn. He wore an olive-green doublet with plainly cut sleeves and a sleeveless jerkin of brown leather with a standing collar. Thigh-high brown boots were fastened by straps to the waist of his buff-colored trunk hose and underdoublet. Attached to the belt on the left side, he had worn his sword just in case there was any trouble. He looked very little like a nobleman now, but then it was not his purpose to attract attention. He did in fact blend in well with the chattering crowd of apprentices and sailors. Few of the patrons had noticed one more man in their midst.

"Your ale, sir." Still hopeful of his attentions, the barmaid lingered just a moment or two after setting down the tankard. "Anything else?" Nicholas shook his head, though he did give her an extra tupence. "Thankee, sir." Sauntering off, she gave him a bold wink over her shoulder.

"Have I reason to be jealous, Nicholas?" Morgana's voice came from out of the darkness, startling Nicholas for the moment. He had not seen her come in. "Are all women helpless before your charms?"

"Morgana!" Turning around, he saw her swathed in black to blend with the night. A hooded cloak covered her fair-haired head.

She placed her index finger to his lips, her voice lowering to a whisper. "We must hurry! There is little time. I have procured two horses from the hostler here. We can ride to Hereford, Northampton and on to Scotland."

"What?" Run away with her and throw away everything he had worked so hard to attain? No woman, no matter how lovely, was worth such a price. He looked at her incredulously. "Are you mad?"

Her manner was overtly seductive. "No, I am in love." Winding her arms around his neck, she looked deeply into his eyes. "I cannot live without you, Nicholas. I won't." Her intonation rivaled any actor's. "If that means running away with you, then I will do it. I will do it most gladly."

Standing up, Nicholas stared at her, torn between astonishment and anger. "So that is why you wanted me to meet you here." And he had so foolishly been acquiescent to her whims.

"Precisely. Owen Stafford's prank has made me a marked woman. But even if it had not, I would have made the same decision." Standing on her tiptoes, she pressed her body closer to his. "Oh, Nicholas!"

Nicholas felt his resolve weakening, but as he noticed two ruffians looking their way, he stiffened and drew away. The brown-haired man's eye had been scarred so that he had a perpetual wink and the other man was missing an ear. He recognized the extremely unpleasant characters, Will Frizer and Tom Banter. Thieves. Swindlers. Worst of all cutters, hired murderers, who for much less than a shilling, would slit any man's throat.

"Let's get out of here," Nicholas rasped. "We can talk outside."

Quickly, he took Morgana by the arm, trying to lead her toward the door. Instead of obeying him, she clung to him tightly as a wild-eyed man pushed his way into the room.

"God's breath, my husband!" Morgana's cry was shrill with fear. "He will kill me, Nicholas! He has threatened as much." Artfully, she hid behind her would-be lover's muscular frame.

The room thundered with Lord Woodcliff's anger. "You foul this place with your wantoness, wife! Didst you think I would not guess your intent and follow you?"

Morgana sought to explain, but her shrill voice was little more than a frightened gasp.

"And now my eyes see the truth for myself. You are caught in the act of a tryst with your lover." Furling his brows, he turned flashing eyes upon Nicholas. "Stand aside, sir. I will have my wife."

"I will not let you harm her." Nicholas's gentlemanly instincts were instantly aroused. "She is innocent of betraying you."

"Innocent?" Lord Woodcliff snorted in indignation. "It is a word that ill suits her. But have no fear. It is not she who tempts my sword, but you." To emphasize his intent, Edward Woodcliff drew his blade.

"Edward, no!"

Nicholas echoed Morgana's words. "No, Lord Woodcliff, I will not duel with you. There is naught that you must avenge. Your wife and I have done no wrong." He would not be goaded into drawing his sword against this man. He had acted foolishly before the queen, but he was calm now.

"Then I call you coward!"

Nicholas flinched but he did not move. Edward Woodcliff had once been a great swordsman, but now he was an old man. It would be an ill-matched contest. Let him rant, let him rage, Nicholas would not draw his sword. "We have no quarrel. I will not fight!"

"Then nevertheless I will draw your blood and mark you for the milksop that you are!"

Lord Woodcliff lunged and only by the grace of God was Nicholas able to duck out of the way in time. Even so, he was determined to keep to his word not to draw his sword. Using an old wooden stool, he blocked the other man's blows again and again. It was like a comic dance, a dastardly grotesque pantomime of sword thrusts and parrying. Tankards were spilled, tables overturned, as even the fiercest onlookers hurried to get out of the way. The quarrel had soon reduced the room to shambles.

Morgana cried out as her husband drove Nicholas up against a wall. The look in his eyes boded no mercy. "Edward, please. I beg you. Don't kill him." Her frantic cry distracted the old lord just long enough for Nicholas to pull free and with an oath, he drew his sword.

Little more than a blur, sword clashed upon sword, as the two men fought. Lunging blindly, Lord Woodcliff drove his sword point into an overturned wooden table. Drawing back, he intended to free his weapon and to lunge at Nicholas again, but the blow never came. Instead, his lips formed a grimace of agony.

"Lord Edward?" In confusion, Nicholas looked at the elderly man, not fully comprehending what had happened. He watched wide-eyed as with a heavy thud the old lord tumbled to the ground.

"Is he dead? He is . . ." Morgana's voice was a breathless shocked whisper, yet she did not rush to her husband's side.

Nicholas did, only to have her words proven true. Edward Woodcliff was indeed dead. "God's bones!" Nicholas threw his sword to the ground. "He is dead!"

As crowded as the room had been, it now suddenly became empty as those who had witnessed the ghastly scene fled.

Nicholas thought he was alone, then he heard something behind him. Looking over his shoulder, Nicholas fastened his eyes upon the intruder in stunned surprise. It was Lord Owen Stafford.

"So in just one night I am removed of two rivals," he said callously, nudging at Lord Woodcliff's body with the toe of his boot. "How obliging of you, Sir Nicholas."

"You bastard!" Nicholas started to retrieve his sword, but saw that Stafford had not come alone. Two soldiers of the queen's guard moved forward like trained mastiffs to guard Stafford. The expression in the men's eyes clearly showed that they marked Nicholas as guilty. Searching the room for Morgana, Nicholas saw at once that she, too, like the others, had disappeared.

"Lord Woodcliff found you with his wife and you killed him. It is as simple as that. Every lord at court knows of your hot temper, it is, I fear, one imperfection, Sir Leighton. Even the queen witnessed you draw your sword in the hall."

Never in all his life had Nicholas ever hated any man as much as he loathed his enemy now. "You stink of treachery, Stafford," Nicholas accused, knowing at that moment he could not let himself be taken prisoner, not by Stafford. If he were, there was every chance he would never live to place his case before the queen. He had to reach his estate in Sussex and gather his supporters, then he would present himself at court.

"Take him. Arrest him!" Stafford commanded.

Overturning a wooden table, Nicholas used it to block their path then boldly threw himself against the mullioned windows. Bruised, shaken, and suffering from cuts and scratches from the splintered and shattered glass, Nicholas nonetheless was free, at least for the moment.

"Follow him! Don't let him get away." The sound of shouting and the trampling of feet told him clearly that he was still in danger. Picking himself up from the ground, he used the moonless night as a cloak and stealthfully made his escape.

Chapter Four

The night air was hot and stifling in the tiny room, made even more so by the lack of ventilation. Alandra lay awake for a long, long time, tossing and turning in an effort to sleep. But she found that it evaded her. If only the room had a window, she thought. There was a cool wind blowing outside, but she could not enjoy its refreshing breath. Windows were for those patrons with shillings jingling in their pockets. Her father was not a wealthy man by any means, thus they had been given only small, cramped rooms in the inn. Rooms that matched her father's purse.

"A pox on that stingy innkeeper!" Alandra swore in irritation, using the curse that always caused her father's rebuke.

Having been raised around men, with none of the gentling influence of a woman, she was perhaps a bit rough about the edges, as her father said. As to that, Alandra had not a care. Be she unladylike in her manner, she was what she was and determined to be accepted for that. Yet tonight when the dark-haired nobleman had bent down to help her pick up the costumes she had dropped, she had known a momentary wish to be soft, feminine, and most of all beautiful. If only she could have thought of something clever to say to keep him at her side, to charm him.

No! She had vowed not to think such thoughts. A man such as that, a titled lord, was far beyond her position. It did no good for her to dream. A man of that one's ilk would give her no more than a glance. Hadn't he proved that tonight when he had so discourteously dismissed her? He had thought she was a nobody and why not? She was a foundling who did not even know her real name.

Alandra felt a deep emptiness as she remembered that moment when she had learned the truth. She had been eight years old, and inquisitive as children are at that age. Putting into words the questions that had troubled her for so long, she had bolstered up the courage to ask Murray why she had no mother.

At first he had hemmed and hawed, avoiding the subject, but her persistence forced him to answer her truthfully, as he tried his best not to shatter her world. He confessed that she was not his real daughter but a child whom he had found along a well-ridden road in a handwoven basket. Alandra's cries had alerted him to her presence, and he had stopped his wagon to have a look at the wailing child. He then had quickly decided that she would belong to him.

A castoff! A child nobody had wanted. Left at the side of the road like a bag of refuse. The revelation had stung Alandra to the quick, despite her attempts to hide it. Who were her parents? Why had she been given up? Thrown away? Because they were too poor to care for her? Or was there another reason? One which she would never know? The questions deeply troubled her, coming back to haunt her whenever she allowed herself to think about them.

Though Murray had always treated her well, Alandra often felt isolated, alone. She was bothered by the feeling that she didn't belong. Not really. Nor would she ever know who she was or where she came from. But, she was not so unappreciative that she didn't realize that Murray had raised her as tenderly as if she had been his very own. For that and a hundred other things, she was grateful.

Kicking off her blankets and bed linens, Alandra rolled over on her back and putting her hands behind her head looked up at the ceiling. She was content and very happy in her way. Indeed, she knew there were countless other young women who would have joyfully traded places with her. Traveling with the acting company was far from dull, so there was no need for her to complain. There were always new people to meet and new towns to visit. The townspeople and villagers viewed the theater folk as something akin to celebrities, as in truth some of the Lord Chamberlain's Men were.

Alandra was proud that such men as Richard Burbage, the acknowledged greatest actor of the company, Robert Armin, a celebrated clown, and Master William Shakespeare were numbered among her friends. How many other young women could make such a claim? It was just that she felt something was missing from her life, that which made one's heart feel light and gay.

Until tonight she had been confused as to what her heart yearned for, but now she knew. She wanted a man to love her so very much that he would risk the queen's anger for *her*.

Closing her eyes, she thought of the dark-haired nobleman again. How could she help it? What woman could ever forget his face? She could remember the line of his eyebrows, the finely wrought shape of his nose, the crisp thickness of his hair where it waved against his temples. He had been so close to her, so heart-stoppingly near. Would she ever meet such a man again?

Turning over on her stomach, Alandra remembered what she learned from watching the pantomime of the masque tonight, that the handsome raven-haired nobleman and the golden-tressed woman were lovers. That knowledge unleashed a puzzling new emotion within her breast. Strange that only seeing the two together could spark such jealousy.

Well, I will not let myself think of it any longer, she thought irritably. Someday a man would love her just as fiercely as her elusive lord what's-his-name desired his pink rose. He would love Alandra just as passionately, so much so that he would put his devotion in a sonnet. It was such a delicious thought that she laughed, bringing lines of poetry to her mind.

Alandra's artful musing was harshly interrupted by muffled shouts, curses, and the sound of trampling feet outside her door. The jumble of sounds drifted disturbingly to her ears. Bolting from the bed, she pressed her ear against the door in an effort to determine what was going on, but she could only hear snatches of conversation.

"Killed 'im deader than a doornile, 'e did. Roight in the back. I saw the 'ole thing, I did. But I ain't ne'er about to tell. Someone's 'ead is gonna role, and I don't want it to be mine."

"The 'ole plice is swarmin' with guardsmen and such. Poor bloke, 'e will be caught afore the cock crows in the mornin'."

"So who cares? Do you think the likes of him would care about what happened to one of us? No, I say."

"But he didn't stab him!" A woman's voice shrieked

high amid the baritone voices of her male companions. "I saw for myself what happened."

"But only a fool would tell! You don't know the way of these noblemen, Bessie. Speak up and your own neck will be encircled by a noose."

"But....but I saw ...I heard ..."

The voices all spoke at once in agitated quarreling so that Alandra could understand no more. She could discern, however, that someone of importance had been killed right within the walls of the inn's taproom. How ghastly! How frightening, and yet murder was common in this area of town. Feuds and vendettas were familiar, violent occurrences. There were bodies aplenty floating in the Thames.

Nevertheless, bothered by what she had heard, Alandra said a hasty prayer for the dead man's soul. She supposed it had been a matter of thievery. Some poor devil down on his luck, with the look of a pauper about him, had quarreled with a wealthy nobleman over a shilling or two. A fight had broken out, and in the scuffle the affluent lord had been slain. Alas, for the poor man accused of the crime! Alandra could not help pitying him, for his fate would most likely be an unpleasant one. Closing her eyes, she whispered a prayer for that man as well.

Returning to the narrow, lumpy bed, Alandra tried once more to sleep, but there were too many distractions mingling with her dreams. The wind which had been fierce earlier but had died down, now gusted again, adding to the tumult. A large tree outside the room set its many branches in rhythm with the gale, tapping against the outer wall. The noise grew louder and louder, so clamorous that at first Alandra did not notice the knocking at her door until an annoyed voice echoed it.

"Alandra! Alandra, are you in there? Open this door! Open this door, I say."

There could be no denying that it was her father who called her. His raspy voice was one of a kind so wrapping a thin beige cloak about her nightdress, Alandra hurried to comply with her father's command. The dimly lit corridor was now deserted, but even so her father's next words were whispered.

"Get your belongings together, daughter."

Deep frown lines creased his brow, the blue eyes which stared back at her were dilated with fear, and his trembling fingers pulled at his beard in agitation.

"What has happened? Father, tell me!"

Taking his arm, she drew him into the room and closed the door.

"A man has been murdered tonight."

"I know. I heard the gossip through the door. But what has that to do with us?" The fear that her father had been somehow involved made her own hands quiver.

"Calm your fears," he said a bit more gently, sensing her alarm. "We are not in any actual danger, it is just that I do not want to become involved in a matter of this kind. I suppose like all the others I am a coward, but what if someone were to recognize us as having been at the palace tonight, of witnessing all that went on there? They might suppose we were aware of what happened here as well. Our being here might very well be construed as being overly suspicious! God help us if they thought we were involved in some sort of plot."

As if his words had exhausted him, he plopped down on a wooden stool near the bed, wringing his hands in the manner he always affected when he was nervous. "Someone killed a nobleman, one who was at Whitehall this very night."

"Who, Father? Who was killed? Tell me."

For a moment Alandra dreaded that perhaps it was the dark-haired nobleman. Oh, what a loss if that one's heart had permanently been stilled.

"Lord Woodcliff, advisor to the queen and well renowned through the realm. The entire courtyard is in an uproar, searching for his assailant."

"Lord Woodcliff?" She suddenly remembered. "The *old* man."

Murray looked at her with an amused smile upending his frown. "Have a care, daughter. Lord Woodcliff was a man of but a few years more than myself. By God, I hate to think of myself as aged. Advanced in years perhaps. . . ." He shrugged his shoulders.

"But who did the deed?"

"I do not know nor do I care a farthing! I've already packed the wagon so that we may leave this place before we learn more than we want to know."

Standing up, he walked in two long strides to the door, pausing to look back at her before he opened it. "Meet me in the courtyard."

"But won't our hurrying away make us the target of suspicion?"

"We will have to take that chance." His brows shot up as he suddenly grinned. "We are theater people. Has it not been said many times that we are unpredictable and eccentric? In all probability we will be allowed to pass. We will just insist that we are giving a performance early tomorrow morning."

Forcing a laugh, he walked through the door, slamming it steadfastly behind him, leaving Alandra to her meditative silence.

Chapter Five

Hidden behind a large rainbarrel, Nicholas could hear the sound of running feet and curses. Cautiously, he peered out. The inn's square courtyard was the scene of total pandemonium. The night's events had drawn a curious crowd who hovered about the guardsmen, like moths to a flame, chattering their questions. They seemed oblivious to the surly behavior of the armed men as they thronged the courtyard, trying to find out what had happened. Nicholas blessed the guests from the inn, every one, for creating confusion. For the time being, they were hindering the process of his being found and seized.

How strange, he thought, that those who had witnessed the tragic events in the taproom were scurrying away, fearing to become involved, while others were attracted to the excitement. What unpredictable creatures men could be!

"Unpredictable and treacherous," he mumbled be-

neath his breath as the sight of Owen Stafford came
into his line of vision.

It was obvious by his frantically waving arms and
shouted expletives that the scheming lord would leave
no stone unturned until he found his quarry. Bile rose
in Nicholas's throat at the thought. He was trapped
like a fox by that yelping hound, and there was nowhere that he could go. All the exits were guarded.

Standing frozen in impotent fury, his eyes surveyed
the three-storied inn's buildings which formed a rect-
angle around the courtyard, leaving only the heavens
above unobstructed. Escape would be difficult if not
impossible. To make it even worse, there would soon
be broadsides nailed to every tree and post in London
and the surrounding countryside proclaiming him to
be a hunted man. Even if he could break free of the
inn's boundaries, his fate was precarious. Stafford
would waste no time in implementing his plot. How
easily a trap had been sprung. Too easily.

To find a secure place to hide was his only desire at
the moment. But where could he go? Where would he
be safe from detection? If he could reach one of the
upper galleries which led to the bedchambers without
being detected, perhaps he could hide there for a time.
He quickly put that thought from his mind, however.
His fleeing figure would be illuminated by the torchlights now being lit in the courtyard.

How could he escape these wooden walls? Only reason tempered his impulse to act rashly and recklessly.
He could not go far without being apprehended. What
then was he to do? Indecision goaded his frustration
until his eyes lit upon a brightly painted wagon at the
upper end of the courtyard. It was hitched to two
horses and ready for travel. How thoughtful of the
owners to leave it unattended. How convenient! If he
could reach the open end of the wagon without being
seen, he might yet have a chance of escape. But how

was he going to get there without being seen?

Although the wagon was shrouded by shadows, Nicholas knew that he could not take the chance of his movements attracting attention. He needed to create a diversion. His chance came when the wind, which had been whistling through the roof tiles and shutters, blew out several of the torchlights. Hurrying, he fumbled about for a large rock and took aim, hurling it at the roof top several feet away.

"He's on the roof!" someone shouted as all eyes looked in that direction.

Stumbling through the darkness, Nicholas headed in the opposite direction, darting in and out between crates and barrels as he made his way toward his intended hiding place. Upon reaching the wagon, he pushed aside the curtains behind the wagon seat and climbed inside, pausing a moment. Feeling relieved that no sound of pursuit seemed to follow him, he smiled, but he knew he was not safe. Not yet. He might still be caught.

"Never!" he breathed. Somehow he would outwit them. Covering himself with a large piece of canvas, he moved his lips in a silent prayer, a prayer that was seemingly answered as the minutes passed by in silence. Nicholas became quite pleased with himself, certain now that Owen Stafford would search for him in vain. How sly he had been to hide himself right under that bastard's nose. He would prove himself more than a match for Lord Stafford. That vain popinjay would expect him to use bravado, would no doubt think him fool enough to try to escape on horseback. Instead, he would use subterfuge.

In all probability the wagon would soon be wheeling its way out of the courtyard, toward some unknown destination. Nicholas didn't really care where that was as long as it was far away from here. He would go as far as the owner of the wagon would take him.

By that time the search would have died down some-
what, he reasoned, and he would have time to plan
his next course of action. Stafford be damned! No man
trifled with Nicholas Leighton.

It was surprisingly comfortable inside the boxed-in
wagon, and Nicholas whiled away the time by looking
around him. The sides were paneled, the semicircular
top covered with ornamentation both inside and out.
It was much like a house on wheels. The top was made
of painted canvas, stretched over wooden hoops.
Added wood to the top and sides made it completely
weather-proof. The back had two large hinged doors
for easy loading and unloading, the front had curtains
which were drawn to give a small measure of privacy.
Whoever had built the wagon had done so with a loving hand. For the moment he felt safe.

The complacent security he felt was soon threatened, however. The sound of men's angry voices and
tramping feet passed by the wagon. Fearing discovery,
Nicholas clutched his sword, prepared to go down
fighting. Then he heard a raspy voice arguing.

"I have seen no one," said the voice. "Would that I
could help you but I can not."

"A man was murdered here. Lord Woodcliff by
name."

"A tragedy to be sure, yet I knew the man not at all.
As you can see by my garments I am but a simple
man."

"Why are you in such a hurry to leave?"

"I am by trade a player, a member of Lord Chamberlain's Men. You have heard of them, have you not?"
A grunt was the answer. "We are giving an early-
morning performance, our last in London. I am at the
moment on my way to meet with Will Shakespeare,
a playwright and actor of great renown. We are to
begin our summer tour to Sussex and Kent."

Sussex and Kent! Nicholas could not have been

more blessed, for Sussex was his own destination. This wagon offered him a haven from those who sought him, and at the same time he could sneak onto his own lands without anyone being the wiser. Traveling with such a group as these players would keep him safely out of sight. Who would notice him amidst such gaily garbed men? It would give him time to think and to plan. Somehow he would clear his name and regain his favor with Elizabeth.

"Shakespeare?" a grumbling voice was saying. "The name means naught to me. Ha. Actors. Playwrights. A scurvy lot if you must know. A blight on the good name of London, I say. Better to let 'em be on their way. A troublemaking bunch if ever I saw one. No wonder the mayor wants to close all the theaters down."

"I beg your pardon." The man with the raspy voice was obviously annoyed. "My players and I have spotless reputations. We bring joy to the crowds."

"Your kind brings together thieves and whoremongers and contrivers of treason who corrupt innocent minds. The brethren of the city should be in church, not joining in lascivious gawking." Nicholas thought that this man was in all probability a Puritan, for his words and opinions said as much. They had always been enemies of those whose work was in entertaining others. An interfering lot.

"Aye, you are right, Ned. They are instruments of the devil." A second man added his voice to the matter. "Get you gone, we have had enough trouble here."

Nicholas thanked the men silently for such a command. It seemed that just this once bigotry and narrowmindedness had won the day. He held his breath in anticipation, exhaling in relief as he felt the floorboards bounce and sway as the movement of two people jostled the wagon while they settled themselves on the front seat.

"We'll be leaving then. Don't want to stay where we are not wanted, don't you agree, Alandra?"

"Let them pass through!" a voice ordered.

The swaying of the wagon soon proved the occupants had hastened to take advantage of that dictate. Thanks be to God that the guardsmen had not thought it necessary to search the wagon!

Nicholas was exhausted, and the rocking of the wagon as it moved along the bumpy Southampton roadway toward London Bridge nearly lulled him to sleep. Closing his eyes, he listened as his companion travelers mingled their voices in conversation. He heard the familiar raspy male voice and paid little heed, but the melodic voice of a woman caused him to listen intently. Low and soothing, so different from Morgana's shrill tone, the voice charmed him and made him wonder about the woman's appearance. Would her looks match the voice? If so, then she would have the face of an angel! Despite the danger he was in, he found himself besieged with curiosity, wanting a glimpse of the woman's face. Remembering how Morgana's high, grating voice was ill-suited to her looks, he decided that this one would most likely be as ugly as a hag.

"I told you 'twould be a simple matter, daughter. They were as anxious to rid themselves of us as we were to be allowed to go. Puritans! I loathe the lot of them. They have caused us nothing but trouble. Stirring up the mayor and aldermen against us, threatening to have all the plays in London discontinued and every theater in London pulled down about our heads. If it wasn't for good Queen Bess, God bless her, I fear they would make good on their words."

"Never, Father. Never!"

"Oh, but they would if not for the queen. As it is, they have done their damage, sending a letter to the Privy Council, making a list of misfortunes the city is enduring by having actors in its midst. They speak of us as if we were naught but mice or rats, by God. Purge the city of us indeed. Because of *them* Will has planned a longer tour than usual so that we will be gone until the furor dies down."

"Oh, but in a way I am glad. I love the countryside in flower. Just think of all the places we will visit and the many people we will meet. And we will be among our friends. Can we ask for more than that?" There was a lilt of laughter in the woman's voice, charming Nicholas anew.

"Leave it to you, Alandra, to view the matter with an optimistic smile. Ah, girl, that's why I love you so. Could any man have been as blessed? We will speak no more about this matter of the Puritans."

The young woman was a cheerful wench, Nicholas thought with a grin. He heard her humming a tune and was overcome with the curiosity to have a look at her. Maneuvering himself toward the front of the wagon, he pushed aside the curtain just an inch and peered out, startled by the vision that met his eyes.

Hair a dark, rich shade of brown framed a perfectly lovely face, of which he was afforded only a view of the finely molded profile. But as she turned her face toward her father, Nicholas saw long, thick black lashes shading cheeks as pink as the petals of a rose. Never had Nicholas seen such soft, unblemished skin or such full, sensuous lips which seemed to have been made just for kissing. She was beguiling, entrancing, yet with a look of innocence. A flower just ripe for the plucking. She was a tempting morsel and Nicholas could not help thinking how much she teased his appetite.

"Perhaps this journey will not be as tedious as I had first supposed," he whispered to himself, leaning against the side of the wagon to let his fantasies take flight.

His musings were sharply put to a halt as he re-

membered that it was his lusting after another woman
that had been his ruin. Had he not the sense of a goose?
Had he not learned a lesson tonight? Women could at
times be nothing but trouble. If he were wise, he would
keep his distance from this one no matter how pretty
she might be. Besides, he did not plan to remain with
these people for very long. At the first opportunity he
would procure a horse and ride full haste to his lands.

The sudden jolt of the wagon wheels jarred him, and
reminded Nicholas that he had been in one position
too long. His arms and legs were cramped and stiff,
and without a second thought, he stood up, trying his
best to stretch his aching limbs and bring back the
blood to his feet and hands. Unable to stretch to his
full height, lest he bump his head on the top of the
wagon, he contented himself with a stooped posture
as he more closely took inventory of his surroundings.

The wagon was filled with a hodgepodge of wood
and pasteboard set pieces. Trees, rocks, arbors, and a
throne or two were scattered about, and there was
even a large monstrosity painted to resemble a castle
turret. There were boxes and crates of costumes folded
carefully so that they would not even have one wrinkle.
The sight of such garments reminded Nicholas of his
plight. He could not stay dressed in his own doublet
and hosen, for although he had changed clothes before
going to the inn to meet Morgana, he knew these garments would be described on the handbills and broadsides that were circulated. Surely he could find
something in the boxes of clothing to wear until he
could manage to find more suitable garments. He busied himself searching through the meticulously folded
costumes and was so intent in his exploration that he
did not see the eyes which peered through the curtains
of the wagon, widening in surprise as they caught sight
of him. Nor did he hear the sharp intake of breath.
Only when he felt the impact against his skull did he

realize the danger and by then it was too late. Reaching out, groping against the all-encompassing darkness which engulfed him, he knew total helplessness as he slumped to the floorboards.

Chapter Six

The sputtering flames of an oil lamp illuminated the pale face of the man sprawled on the floorboards. "Merry-go-up! I think you have killed him, Alandra!"

Her father's words filled her with fearful consternation. Alandra hurried forward to examine the man she had just hit from behind with a shovel. Hovering over him, she breathed a sigh of relief as the rise and fall of his chest proved that he was still breathing. She had not killed him, but had rendered him senseless, at least for the moment.

"He was rummaging through the costumes. I feared he was going to steal from us so I—I hit him," she hurried to explain. "It was a reflex reaction. I did not mean him serious harm."

Quickly, her eyes roamed over the stranger as her father held the lamp aloft. There was something disturbingly familiar about him, though she did not want to believe what she saw. It couldn't be! Her eyes were

playing tricks on her. Or were they? Anxiously, she
looked into the man's face, taking in his tousled black
hair, the curve of his brows, the high, chiseled cheek-
bones. His full lips were parted as he drew in a shallow
breath, but she seemed to remember that mouth
frowning.

"Dear God. It is him," she breathed.

"Ah, now, now, now. I would have done the same,
child. You acted to protect me and our belongings."
Murray smiled fondly as he prattled on. "You are always my guardian angel, Alandra." He set down the
lamp and hurried to smooth back his daughter's hair,
a gesture he had used to soothe her since she was a
little girl. "Who is he do you suppose? And what is he
doing in our wagon?" His gray eyebrows shot up in
question.

Alandra didn't answer. She was too perplexed by
her own questions. Though this man was dressed in
travel-stained and torn garments of drab, coarse cloth,
she felt with certainty that this was the same man she
had seen in the banqueting hall at the palace, the man
who had bumped into her. The nobleman! But what
could he possibly be doing here? As if to find the answer written on his face, she leaned closer to scrutinize
him carefully. The profile, the mustache, the short-
clipped beard showed beyond a doubt that it was the
same man.

"What are we to do with him?" Murray's voice
echoed with concern, but he did not seem to realize
that he had glimpsed the man before. But then, Alandra reasoned, Murray had not seen him up close as
she had.

"I don't know," Alandra answered peevishly. Certainly an unconscious nobleman was a serious com-
plication. "Let me think the matter out."

Murray paced up and down woefully. "We can not
throw an unconscious man out on the street, can we,

daughter?" He shook his head. "Nor do I want to take
him back to the inn when we had the devil's own time
getting away." Picking up a large stick of wood in case
a weapon was needed, Murray hovered over their unexpected "guest." "We know not a whit about him. He
could be a thief on the run. He might be dangerous."

"There has to be an explanation!" Alandra exclaimed. There had to be a logical reason for his being
here, though she could not think what that might be.

"Yes, indeed there does but...but..." Murray's
eyes widened as a thought came into his head. "Why
...why it's possible that he's the one who killed Lord
Woodcliff! It would answer why he took the liberty of
climbing aboard our wagon."

"A fugitive?" The scandal at court came quickly to
mind. It was an interesting theory, but one she
shrugged off. Alandra was too coolheaded to jump to
conclusions. "We must give him a chance to explain
why he is here and what he was doing, Father. He will
tell us when he opens his eyes."

"Tell you what?"

Nicholas heard their conversation through the haze
of his awakening mind. His head throbbed, but he
forced himself to open his eyes. For a moment confusion dazed him, but as he reached up to touch the
knot at the back of his head, he remembered that
someone had hit him and his gaze sought out the culprit. Gray eyes met enormous brown ones, and he
sensed immediately that the girl had struck him. Her
guilt shone clearly in the lustrous copper-hued depths.

"You! You nearly cracked my skull."

His heated stare scorched her. "You're lucky I didn't
do worse than that," she answered, fighting to maintain her composure. Oh, he was an arrogant one.
"What are you doing in our play wagon?"

"I obviously didn't enter so that I could be so callously struck!" Nicholas lashed out, wincing as he rubbed the bump on his head.

"Here now." Murray folded his arms across his wide chest. "Don't you be blaming my poor daughter for the knock to your noggin. There are robbers and ruffians roaming about. A body cannot be too careful." His narrowed eyes appraised their unwelcome guest as he tapped the stick of wood against his shoulder in warning. "Which brings us to why you *are* in our play wagon. Tell me that if you can."

The scowling old man's anger cooled Nicholas's own. He was after all an intruder in their midst, and if the truth were told, he knew their wariness was justified. Still, he couldn't trust them with the truth. There would no doubt be a reward for his capture, and even the most honest of men would often turn betrayer for the jingle of coins. Tensing his jaw, he mumbled a lie. "I had not the money to pay the innkeeper for my lodgings."

"Had not the money?" Alandra was taken aback in surprise.

"I thought that by hiding in your wagon I could escape the old pirate's wrath. I have no liking for Ludgate Prison."

Alandra was baffled at the untruth, but her father clucked his tongue sympathetically, having himself been in a similar predicament. "Old Quincy does charge too much for his rooms. It would serve him right to get his comeuppance! I fear The Black Unicorn has seen better days." For a moment he lapsed into the past. "Why, in my youth there was not a grander inn in all of London. But it seems that buildings, like people, soon show signs of age." Offering his hand, he helped Nicholas to his feet. "But just what is your trade, my good man? Are you without coins because you are out of work?"

Nicholas nodded his head, thinking quickly. "I'm an

actor by trade." It seemed a reasonable fabrication. If he held to this story, perhaps the old man would let him travel along with him, at least until he was far enough out of London to be safe.

"But I saw—" Alandra was startled by such a blatant falsehood. She stood gaping at him, waiting for him to show some sign that he remembered seeing her at the palace. No such recognition came.

"An actor? An actor. Merry-go-up, it is a small world." Murray was delighted.

"An actor trying to escape without paying his bill, you say. But where are your clothes?" Alandra asked heatedly. "Did you bring your bags?"

"I hardly had time to pack," Nicholas countered. This young woman was going to be trouble. Women who thought overmuch always were.

"Ha!" Alandra wanted to let him know right from the first that she wasn't being taken in. Not for a moment. "Father, he's a liar. He—"

"Fate has dealt you a lucky blow." Murray laughed merrily, not hearing his daughter's accusation. Nodding his head in her direction, he added, "I think I can be of help to you. I dabble in acting myself you see, though making scenery is my profession."

"Father...I..." Alandra thought to warn him of this man's deception, but Murray merely winked at her conspiratorially, obviously having taken a liking to the dark-haired man.

"With whom did you serve your apprenticeship? Pray tell me, for I might know the man. I have worked with some of the greatest actors of our time."

"Apprenticeship?" For just a moment Nicholas was at a loss for words, but recovering his wit he blurted out a name, one he had heard several times at court, bandied about by those who were patrons of the arts. "Alleyn. Edward Alleyn."

"Edward Alleyn!" Murray was very impressed, for

the actor was known as one of England's best. He was a member of the rival Admiral's Men and had created Marlowe's Faustus and Tamburlaine upon the stage.

"I studied most diligently with him," Nicholas lied blatantly.

Alandra was outraged by this handsome rogue's duplicity. "Why then are you not with the Admiral's Men now?" she asked, hoping to trip him up. Seeing that now he was tongue-tied, she smiled, seemingly daring him to answer.

Nicholas thought quickly. "I had an argument with another actor, and since he was more established in his profession than I, I bid the players *adieu*. I seek to find another company."

How easily lies tripped from his tongue, Alandra thought with ire. To this moment he had not uttered one word of truth. He was no actor, that was certain but he did seem to share their talent for pretense and chatter.

"You had an argument?" she asked warily, wondering what game he was playing. What had he done to necessitate such false statements? Or perhaps this was the first word of truth he had spoken? Certainly, she had seen his display of temper at court when he had quarreled with Lord Stafford.

"Yes, an argument. Over a woman," Nicholas said sourly, remembering the cause of his plight. "Most regrettable episode."

"A woman?" Alandra queried, looking at him with derision.

Of course it would be over a woman. He was a philanderer, a man who undoubtedly played loose and fancy free. Just as he had with that poor old lord's wife. No doubt this man had charmed many women. Perhaps the golden-haired woman she had seen him with was not the first nor the last to offer up her heart.

"But we stand here spewing forth our words with

ne'er a thought to our manners," Murray said quickly,
doffing his hat. "My name is Murray Thatcher, and
this fair flower is my daughter, Alandra." He looked
at Nicholas in expectation.

"Nicholas." Nicholas damned his stupidity as soon
as the name was out and quickly amended, "*Christopher* Nicholas."

"Ah, Christopher." Murray liked that name. "Like
my good friend, Christopher Marlowe, God rest his
soul." He shook his head sadly. "But then, of course,
you would have known him, too. He was a star in the
heavens until his untimely demise. I'll always think
there was much more to the story than was told." He
lowered his voice. "His death was no accident. I think
it was murder."

"Father, that has not been proven." Alandra feared
for her father to bandy such accusations about, lest
the wrong ears hear him. It was well known that Christopher Marlowe had been a spy against the Spanish,
as well as a poet and playwright. She did not know of
this nobleman's thoughts on the matter. Nor that he
wasn't a spy himself for that matter.

"It's all right, Alandra." Nicholas spoke her name
like an endearment and smiled as he saw her flush.
She was a lovely wench and he was determined to win
her favor. "I've often thought the same thing myself.
But you are right. We had best not speak of it."

"As you say, Mister Nicholas." She feared to look at
him, lest her eyes give her away. She wondered if
Christopher Nicholas was his real name and found
herself doubting it. Why should she believe him when
everything else he said was obviously such a lie? Actor
indeed! He most likely did not even know the upper
stage from the mid-level and would soon prove himself
to be a novice.

"Call me Kit." Nicholas found himself liking his new
name. It sounded very dashing, he thought. Kit Ni-

cholas. Yes, it sounded very fine indeed. Mischievously, he offered her a bow, amused by her pretense of not liking him. He would soon have her singing a different rhyme. If there was one thing he knew well, it was how to attract women, and he needed her good will.

"I prefer to ... to call you Christopher." Alandra's tone of voice bristled with indignation. Worse yet was the frustration she felt when her father asked the man to join them. "Father, you can't! He's not who he claims to be. He's not! And even if he were, we can't let a stranger travel with us."

Frantically, she tried to get her father's attention, hinting at Murray's own previous suspicions that this man might well be Lord Woodcliff's killer. Alas, Murray ignored her. It was all too apparent that he was totally taken in by the scoundrel's duplicity.

All right, Alandra thought, she would hold her tongue for a while, but she would keep an eye on this nobleman. Besides, it might prove intriguing to watch him continue with his masquerade. Being an actor was not such an easy profession—as this Christopher Nicholas would soon find out.

Chapter Seven

The Thames glittered like silver in the moonlight as the play wagon rattled across London bridge on the way to the Mermaid Tavern. Murray had not spoken a total falsehood to the guardsmen at The Black Unicorn Inn. He was to meet William Shakespeare at the first light of the dawn, though no play was to be staged. The tavern was to be the players' point of assignation, and from there they would form a caravan and take to the road.

"I'll introduce you to Will Shakespeare and put in a good word for you, though I have no doubt that he will let you come with us. A fine-looking gentleman like yourself will be most welcome in our midst. It will attract the ladies." Murray grinned as he looked at Christopher Nicholas. Wedged between Alandra and the handsome gentleman, he held the reins tightly. "Perhaps we can find suitable transportation for you. It's a bit uncomfortable for all of us to ride together."

"I don't mind," Nicholas said quickly, casting the man's lovely daughter a sideways glance. "I like the view from here."

Besides, it was most fortunate that he was not sitting in a room at the Tower or at Ludgate at this moment. He would have been behind locked doors if Owen Stafford had had his way, or worse yet he'd be dead. Now having changed his soiled garments, donning a blue tunic, gray hosen, black cape, and a blue velvet hat that Murray had informed him had been worn in the performances of *King Richard III*, he felt more at ease and less recognizable. Hopefully, he would not suffer that ill-fated king's doom.

"I don't suppose Alandra minds either, do you, daughter?" Murray nudged his daughter good-naturedly. "She's so used to putting up with all of us older men that a fine-looking younger gent in the group will be most stimulating. Isn't that so, Alandra?"

Alandra didn't answer, she was too perturbed for words. This Christopher Nicholas, or whatever his name was, was far too sure of himself already without her comments adding to his self-confidence. No doubt he expected her to hurl herself into his arms at the very first opportunity. Certainly, the bold way he was looking at her told her so. Had any woman ever told this bold swain no? She doubted it. Was it any wonder then that he was so cocksure?

Furthermore, although she had strongly advised against it, though she had told her father of her suspicions regarding this interloper, Murray had insisted on keeping his word and letting the "actor" ride along with them. Usually, Murray listened to her intuition, but he had shrugged off her apprehensions about this newcomer. God hope, they would not come to regret it.

Looking at him beneath her thick lashes, she as-

sessed the nobleman. Why was he lying? What had he
done to make himself a fugitive? He had been so anxious to change his garments that that in itself had
heightened her suspicions. But just how dangerous
was he?

"I don't think your daughter is certain that she likes
me, but I'll win her over," she heard him say.

Alandra quickly looked away when she realized he
had caught her staring. Oh, he was comely all right
as well he knew and no doubt thought that the reason
for her intent gaze. Worse yet, he had a definite charm
about him that made it difficult for a woman to keep
her wits about her. Rogue that he was, he seemed the
answer to a maiden's prayers, the perfect choice for a
lover. But while she might have been interested in him
before, she firmly convinced herself that she had no
designs on him now and warned herself to be on guard
against his using his charm on her.

The narrow cobbled streets were lit by lanterns set
on posts, and Alandra busied herself with counting
them as the play wagon passed. It helped to take her
mind from the handsome stranger sitting so perilously
close to her. From time to time she could sense his
eyes on her but in haughty stubbornness she refused
to glance in his direction.

London was a city of loud noises, even in the dark
hours of the morning. The sound of horses' hooves,
coach and wagon wheels clattering against the cob-
blestones, the loud voices of rosy-cheeked milkmaids,
and sellers of newly gathered cresses, shattered the
illusion the soft glow of the lanterns cast upon the
roadway. Surrounded by a medieval wall, London was
a jumbled, cluttered city as the early-morning light
would soon reveal. Gabled houses were crammed together, furtive alleyways teamed with crime, yet it was
the place that Alandra and her father called home.

The site where Alandra had grown from a child to a woman.

With the exception of the brief yearly players' tours, Alandra had rarely been outside the stone walls. The world of the theater had nourished her, and she had been well content, yet as Alandra had put her childhood years behind her she longed to see more of the world. Observing the brightly bedecked nobles and ladies at Whitehall had caused her to be all the more anxious to be out of her cocoon. The world was hers, waiting to be conquered. Was it therefore surprising that she was filled with expectation now? There was a sense of freedom when the players were on the road that Alandra did not feel in the city. Freedom, romance, and adventure seemed to beckon her like a bright new toy.

"We're about to undertake the most extended tour we've ever made," Murray blurted, feeling nervous about the silence between his daughter and the black-haired man. It wasn't like Alandra to be so quiet. "The work will not be as stimulating as in London, but somehow we'll make do. We always have. 'Tis not our first summer tour nor will it be our last. Course now, no new plays can be given. We'll have to rely on works we've done before, and those will have to be cut for country playing."

"Yes, of course. The plays will have to be cut," Nicholas answered, trying his best to sound well informed.

Nervously, Nicholas pulled his cap farther down on his head, hoping it would shadow his face. It made him ill at ease to be traveling through the city streets when Stafford's men might be searching for him. Though he had suggested to Murray that he ride inside the wagon, the man would not hear of it, insisting that Nicholas ride up front where it was more comfortable and where he could breathe in the early-morning fresh air. Nicholas could not take the chance of arousing the old man's suspicions by insisting that he hide.

So far, all had been well, for it was still dark at this predawn hour. Most of the Londoners were still abed and those out in the streets seemed to be paying little attention to the wagon. If anyone did show undue attention, Nicholas reasoned, he could easily dart behind the curtains and out of sight under some pretense or other.

"Are you familiar with any of Master Shakespeare's plays?" Murray was asking now.

Nicholas had seen an enactment of Shakespeare's *Romeo and Juliet* at court recently, a play he had thought far too morose for his tastes. He disliked tragedies. "I am familiar with some of his works."

"Good. Good. It will make it all the easier for you to learn your lines. But having studied with Edward Alleyn, you will have no trouble learning your roles."

"I will have no trouble at all," Nicholas said with boastful pride. Indeed, he doubted that being an actor was a troublesome task at all, though he was not concerned with whether it was. He would be long gone before the matter was put to a test.

The wheels of the wagon clattered along Watling Street, and soon the tavern hovered in sight. "Ho! There we are, The Mermaid." It was a needless observation, for the wooden sign with the painted mythological beauty proclaimed that they had reached their destination.

Nicholas was the first one from the wagon. Before Alandra had even the slightest idea of his intention, his hands were closing about her waist as he helped her down.

"I can manage quite well by myself!" she said sharply, pulling away from his grasp.

Murray was shocked again by her blatant rudeness. "Alandra!"

Alandra bit her lip then managed to say, "Thank you, Mister Nicholas."

"Mister Nicholas. Mister Nicholas, indeed. I'll soon have you calling me Christopher."

Nicholas was undaunted by her aloofness. She had spirit and he liked that. The more she scorned him, the more intrigued he became. Too bad he would not have time to get to know the pretty chit better. It might have proved amusing. The wench would have led him on a merry chase, but he would have captured her. Watching her well-proportioned form with apprecia-tive eyes, he followed her toward the tavern door.

The loud sound of voices halted Nicholas in mid-stride. Seeing three guardsmen mounting their horses near the stables, he pulled his hat down and gathered the cloak tightly around his body. He had forgotten for a moment that he was a hunted man, but would not have such a dangerous lapse of memory again. Until he was safely on the way to Sussex, he must be on his guard and block from his mind any other thoughts that might distract him, including Murray Thatcher's daughter. Stroking his beard, Nicholas re-alized that this thatch of hair must be removed at the first opportunity, for it all too clearly gave away his identity.

"Oh, don't wait for me, Christopher." Murray waved Nicholas on, thinking his pause to be courtesy. "I'll care for the horses and be in directly."

Nicholas glanced warily at the three soldiers, fearful that the old man's voice might have caught their at-tention, but they were too immersed in chatter to no-tice him. They in fact did not even look in his direction. Nicholas rather suspected that they were in their cups and breathed a sigh of relief as he pulled open the tavern's portal.

The interior of The Mermaid was dimly lit. The fire in the hearth had burned to embers; only a few candles illuminated the room. Even so, Nicholas noticed the man standing in the corner of the tavern immediately. There was something about him that commanded attention.

"Alandra!" The man's eyes sparkled with gladness at seeing her, and for a moment Nicholas stiffened. What was this man to her? That she hurried to the man's side with a joyful smile added to his unease, though he chided himself that it was none of his concern.

"We missed you while you were back home in Stratford, Will. It's always so dull when you are gone."

"But each time I come back you have grown more beautiful. Perhaps I will write a sonnet to proclaim how lovely you are. Would you like that, my lovely dark lady?"

Nicholas let his eyes roam over the man, studying this gentleman who brought forth Alandra's unguarded affection. He was older than Nicholas, in his mid-thirties perhaps. Of average height and build, he was dressed in garments that were fashionable but somber, as if, unlike many men who shared his profession, he did not want to attract undue attention. The man's brown hair was worn nearly to his shoulders. The hairline which was beginning to recede made him appear much older than his years. Like Nicholas, he wore a mustache and clipped beard.

"Write a sonnet for me? Oh, would you, Will? I would be so honored. No one has ever written any poetry for me."

"But they should, Alandra. They should. You are the kind of woman who will soon steal many hearts. You have always had mine." The piercing brown eyes beneath thin, highly arched brows focused on Nicholas, eyeing him up and down appraisingly. "And who might this be?"

Nicholas introduced himself. "My name is Chris-

topher Nicholas. I assume that you are William Shakespeare."

"I am."

The intense scrutiny unnerved Nicholas, but at last
Will Shakespeare smiled.

"If you are a friend of Alandra's, then you are likewise a friend of mine."

"He's *not* a friend! We've only just met," she murmured, purposefully keeping a cautious distance between the handsome young man and herself. "Tonight
in fact. He wants to join the players."

"Ah, I see. So you are an actor."

"He *proclaims* himself to be," Alandra replied
curtly, hoping Will would throw the scoundrel out into
the street, even though her father was taken in by him.

"Hmmm." Will looked from Alandra to Nicholas
and back again, then raised his brow. "We have actors
aplenty in our company—"

"Just as I thought!" Alandra cast the would-be actor
a triumphant glare. "I guess you'll have to find another
acting troupe to make use of your *great* talent!"

Nicholas' pride was stung. Besides, he needed the
protection the players would afford him. "Please re-
consider. I am quite good and would add much to your
company."

"Ha!" Alandra retorted with a toss of her head. She
looked toward Shakespeare, hoping he would cut the
braggart down to size.

"Perhaps we might be able to use you," he said,
looking at the newcomer once again.

Alandra couldn't believe her ears. "But, Will . . ."
She would have to have a talk with him at the first
opportunity.

Shakespeare's decision was firm. "We will give him
a chance to show how useful he can be. And before
you receive any major roles you must read for me."

"Thank you. I will be satisfied with whatever you

decide," Nicholas said with a slight bow. He couldn't help but wonder that if he was called upon to act what that would entail. Surely he could handle it if need be. How difficult could it possibly be to memorize a few sentences and to move about a stage? Besides, he intended to be with the actors only as long as he needed to be. Why should he worry?

"Good. The company will be doing two of my plays. *A Midsummer-Night's Dream* and *King John*. I will think on the matter of what to do with you."

The door behind them creaked as someone entered the tavern. Instinctively, Nicholas sought the shadows as he cast a furtive glance over his shoulder, fearing that he might be recognized. He dare not forget that danger lurked in every corner of the city. Much to his relief, however, it was only Murray.

"Has Alandra introduced you to Christopher Nicholas, Will?" The gray-haired man sauntered over to where the two men and his daughter stood.

"She has," Shakespeare answered, raising his brows in Nicholas's direction.

In that moment Nicholas sensed that the playwright suspected he had a secret. The dark, meditative eyes seemed to be conveying a silent communication making Nicholas uneasy. If the man suspected something, could he be trusted not to be overtly curious? Nicholas had to take that chance, for at this moment he had no other choice. He only hoped that this Will Shakespeare would not prove to be a thorn in his side.

Chapter Eight

A cloudless sky hovered above Kent like a bright blue canopy as the wandering parade of actors traveled along on the first leg of their journey. The winding roads twisted and turned, crisscrossing through the countryside like a huge chessboard. It was a beautiful area of meandering brooks, rolling hills, and meadows etched by watercourses, woodlands, and pasturelands. Cattle and thickly fleeced sheep grazed peacefully. Along the North Downs, villages were perched on hillsides, and the woods were packed with bluebells and primroses, already in bloom.

Though only a few miles from London, it was a world quite apart from that city's sprawl. There was a fresh country smell mixed with the scent of blossoms, so different from the fouled city air. More than one member of the acting company could be seen breathing in the fragrance or appreciating the soft breeze which stirred through their hair. These same light winds could grow tumultous and at times swept across the weald to drive the many windmills which dotted the landscape.

Despite the beauty of the countryside, however, Nicholas was in any but a contented mood. The journey had been tiresome. The rest of the theatrical company had arrived at the inn before the first cock's crow. When all were assembled, they left The Mermaid to pass along Weston Road on the outskirts of London and then beyond.

It was a parade of gaudily decorated wagons, mounted horsemen in brightly hued garments, and a laughing and jabbering throng of less finely attired men, walking beside the wagons. Once again Nicholas was on foot, though in a better mood after his rest in Murray's wagon. In an effort to further disguise his appearance, he had hastily shaved off his beard, using a razor he found among the costumes.

Nicholas studied this group of actors, musicians, and stage men with whom he would be journeying. Most of them seemed to be a happy and lively group, even though touring was said to be not as comfortable or as profitable as playing in the large London theaters. Only a few serious complaints had been made. As for Nicholas, it didn't matter where the procession headed or in which inn they stayed. All he wanted was the strong, muscled flesh of a horse beneath him and he would be satisfied.

He thought of obtaining a mount, fantasized about his escape, and when John Heminges rode up to him, he requested a horse.

A stocky, seldom smiling man of strong opinions, who seemed to have authority to speak for the company, Heminges answered, "Only the leading actors ride on horseback. Hirelings such as yourself are expected to walk alongside the wagons."

"Walk!" Nicholas clenched his jaw in outrage. He

was not used to being treated in such a highhanded manner. Oh, that he could tell this conceited buffoon a thing or two. Heminges seemed to be a haughty individual if ever there was one, he thought sourly.

Standing with his hands upon his hips, Nicholas sputtered and fumed in barely suppressed anger as Heminges rode away, but there was nothing that he could do, lest he destroy his cover. He could hardly tell them that he was a nobleman, not after concocting his prior story. Still, it irritated him to see the lovely dark-haired Alandra's smug smile.

"What do you find so funny?" he growled, kicking the dirt as the wagon passed by him.

"That it is unfortunate that you did not bring an extra pair of shoes. Those will be quite worn by the time we reach our destination," she said haughtily.

"God's whiskers, I did not intend to trudge alongside a scurvy wagon like some apprentice or fledgling boy."

He looked with ire upon a group of young men who had been hired to take the young women's roles in the plays. Nicholas knew that the women were never used as actors to avoid fierce rivalries and jealousy in the acting companies. Therefore they were forbidden to enter the acting profession.

"To think that I am being treated like these callow youths who cannot even grow a beard."

"You did not think you would be asked to walk?" she asked innocently.

Of course he didn't, Alandra mused. He had thought them to be so stupid that they would put a horse at his disposal. Well, he would soon learn that the actors were not as lame-brained as he supposed. He wanted to be among them, then let him abide by their rules.

"Of course I didn't think that!" he sputtered in answer. To be quite truthful, her cockiness was getting on his nerves. That and the way she studied him, as if she knew something he didn't know that she knew.

"Why, Mister Nicholas," Alandra said with feigned sweetness, "one would nearly suppose that you fancied yourself to be a wealthy merchant, alderman, or nobleman. Well, be that as it may, only an actor of renown would warrant a horse in this procession."

"Indeed!" His eyes strayed to the foppish young men assembled and frowned at the thought of being thought of in the same vein as they.

Alandra noted his scornful look. "I do wonder what you will look like in a skirt."

"Me. Dress as a woman?" To play a woman's part was unthinkable, no matter how minor the role, even in his current predicament. "By God, never! If I am asked to act the role of such a fair flower, I will quit before I begin."

"You should have thought about that before you weasled your way among us," Alandra shot back, then couldn't help saying, "but don't fear. It takes great talent to take a woman's role. A skill I doubt very seriously that you have."

"Oh, is that so!" She was infuriating. For a moment he wished he really was a serious actor so that he could make her eat her words.

Women complicated the lives of a troupe, he'd heard it said, and now he could testify that it was true. Certainly, Alandra Thatcher was trouble. But what was she doing in this company? Was she not most obviously female? And troublesome at that! He put that question into words, then waited for her reply.

"Me? I'm different!" She protested.

His question disturbed her, for it brought to mind her apprehension of what was to happen to her now that she had become a woman and was no longer a girl. A few of the actors had made an unwelcome comment or two of late. "Why, I've been with them since before I could walk and talk. They are my family! Besides, I do not take part in the plays but only assist my father," she said quickly, lest he get any ideas of stirring up trouble.

"But you are a woman and women can ere be the plague of men." Nicholas spoke from experience.

His comment angered her. Handing the reins to her father, Alandra cast him an impudent scowl, then retreated inside the wagon.

"Don't think too harshly of Alandra," Murray said behind his hand, coming quickly to Nicholas's rescue by offering him a ride in the wagon.

Nicholas quickly took the old man up on his kindness, jumping up and sitting beside the stage man's girth.

"I thought her to be as soft as a rose, but she does have a thorn or two," Nicholas grumbled, folding his arms across his chest.

"My fault, that! She was raised around men and knows nothing of a woman's wiles. Spirited as a young colt, she is, but I have an inkling that you are the one to tame her."

"Me?" he asked, surprised. She showed no liking for him at all, made it a point to glare at him in fact. "I want naught to do with her. She has done nothing but scorn me. And to think I envisioned an angel when I heard her speak. Seems to me there is a hint of Beelzebub in her manner."

"Have patience."

The old man's grin softened Nicholas's mood, for who could stay angry when in this jolly gentleman's presence. Nicholas had already developed a deep affection for the man, knowing full well that if Murray had been able to procure a horse for him he would have. Right from the first the old man had befriended him.

"As to your position in the company, give it time,"

Murray continued. "All these actors who now sit their mounts so proudly once walked beside a wagon as you must do for the time being. A young man like you who has fulfilled his apprenticeship under such a fine actor as Alleyn will soon be making more than five shillings a week. I wager you'll soon have a horse to ride, too. Methinks it will be only a matter of time."

It didn't matter, Nicholas thought. As soon as they reached Faversham or perhaps even before, he would obtain a horse and ride to his own lands. Beg, borrow, or *steal*, he would have a horse. Were it not for the fact that the town crier was proclaiming his supposed crime all over London, he wouldn't have come this far with such a motley group.

Walk be damned! Did these actors think themselves deserving of respect because they had distinguished themselves in their professions or because they had all recently been granted coats of arms? Well, he was a knight, by God. How he wished he could throw that in their faces. And as to the dark-haired wench, he wanted nothing to do with her at all. She had shunned him all along the cobbled pathway toward the outskirts of the city and now seemed to relish his humiliation.

Pulling his cap down over his eyes, Nicholas reflected on Alandra's reaction to his gestures of camaraderie. He had smiled at her from time to time, trying to thaw the frost between them, but she had only smiled at the others, never at him. He had sensed her eyes watching him nonetheless, staring at him when his back was turned, studying him with her pensive gaze as if trying to look into his very soul. Her searching eyes unnerved him, threatened his composure, and made him wonder just how much she knew of him. She seemed to be challenging him in some way. Saucy wench, what was she up to? Nicholas felt certain he would find out soon enough.

* * *

The company did not even take time to stop by Maidstone, a marketing center, but passed right by. They hurried through orchards and hop gardens, pausing only once or twice, so desperate was Shakespeare to make good use of time and distance. The entire company heaved a huge sigh of relief when at last the setting sun turned the thatched roofs of the squat village cottages to gold. They knew at last that the first day's journey would soon end.

"We'll pass this village by and go to Boughton Monchelsea on the ridge and there bed down at the inn," Nicholas heard Shakespeare say.

He acknowledged Will's words with a weary nod. Having climbed off the wagon, once Alandra took her place by her father, Nicholas had walked the last few miles and he was totally exhausted. Not at all in a jovial mood. Tired and cranky in fact. His feet were painfully blistered, his shoes filled with gravel, the muscles of his legs achingly sore. The knot at the back of his head was a painful reminder of how easily he had been taken unaware. With each step he had taken along the rutted road, there had been only one thought reverberating through his mind. He had to get a horse! Somehow. Someway. Tonight when all the others were sleeping he would make his move. It was necessary for his survival.

Nicholas had already formulated a plan that would help him clear his name. It would be much too dangerous to ride brazenly through the portals of his own castle, lest Owen Stafford entrap him. He would ride as far as he dared and to Bodiam then from there he would send a message to his younger brother who was tending to Nicholas's duties on the estate during his absence. James was a most capable young man. A bit too scholarly perhaps to suit Nicholas and not inclined to fighting, but most loyal when the need arose. De-

spite the difference in their ages, there was a special
bond between them that even danger could not disa-
vow. Together they would rouse Nicholas's supporters
and withstand any army Stafford raised against them.

In the meantime Nicholas would send a message to
the queen, requesting an audience. She must hear
from his own lips what had really happened at The
Black Unicorn and of Lord Stafford's imperious treatment of him. It was not up to that pompous lord to
be his judge and jury! Surely Stafford envisioned himself as having far more power than he really did. Well,
he was to soon have his comeuppance.

Surely by now Morgana would have come to her
senses, he thought, and spoken to the queen in his
behalf. Let Stafford argue with that! Nicholas had
Morgana as an eyewitness. Lord Woodcliff had come
at him with a sword. Clearly, it was a matter of self-
defense. At least that thought eased his mind. But he
had to have a horse, had to get to his estates. His entire
plan hinged on finding transportation.

Nicholas's eyes scanned the town as the players entered the village green. It was a small hamlet slumbering in the fading light of the sun. The market square
was flanked by half-timbered cottages and shops.
Across the stone bridge that spanned a trickling waterway was an old church whose steeple looked as though
it dated to the time right after the Normans' invasion.
It was the inn, however, that held his eyes, a brown-
and-white, three-tiered building which sprawled in-
vitingly at the foot of a steep hill. Unlike most struc-
tures of its kind, the stables were not enclosed within
the confines of the courtyard but a safe distance away.

Had Nicholas designed it himself, it could not have
been more perfect for his needs. If he were careful, it
was possible no one would even miss him until morning. By then he would be safely away.

"God's bones!" he exclaimed, the corners of his

mouth tightening into a smile. It was all going to be so incredibly easy. All he had to do was to wait until the others were asleep and then make his move.

With the exception of the players, only a few other travelers sought the quarters of the inn and they were safely ensconced in the taproom, drinking their wine and ale.

Standing inside the doorway, Nicholas watched and waited.

"You've got that sparkle in your eyes. I know what you are thinking."

Nicholas was startled as Murray came upon him. "You know what I am contemplating?" How could he, unless the little old man could read minds?

"You are nearly as hungry as I, but I've been told the food is good here."

"Food?" Nicholas sighed in relief. "I'm famished."

That was not a lie. Following Murray to a table Nicholas took a seat beside him. It would be a good idea to eat all that he could while he had the chance. Once upon the road he might not have the chance for a proper meal. So he indulged himself, taking little time for conversation.

After a hearty meal, the members of the Lord Chamberlain's Men departed one by one to their rooms, Murray and Will being the last to leave. Lingering behind, Nicholas watched stealthfully as the lights in their rooms were extinguished, leaving the inn in darkness. Gathering the folds of his cloak close about him, he moved toward the door with all the furtiveness of his desperation.

Chapter Nine

Like the others in the group Alandra was bone-tired,
yet even so she was unable to sleep. Why hadn't she
revealed to Will everything she knew? Why hadn't she
voiced aloud her suspicion that Christopher what's-
his-name may have killed a nobleman of the court?
Why hadn't she told Will that at this very minute the
newcomer was being sought? Why hadn't she shouted
out a warning?

Will had known Alandra since she was a little girl,
and she had always confided in him. He had taught
her to read, had tutored her for a time as a favor to
Murray who had wanted his daughter schooled. Out
of their acquaintance a deep friendship had blossomed
and second only to her father, Alandra trusted Will
more than any man she knew. Why then had she kept
silent?

What if Christopher Nicholas *had* killed Lord Woodcliff? Her father had mumbled such a suggestion when

he first had laid eyes upon the intruder in their wagon. Than the scoundrel had charmed him with his tale of being an actor. What if it were true? What if he had killed that poor old lord in cold blood so he could run away with his wife? It made sense, did it not? Certainly, it would be a good reason for him to pretend to be an actor. The traveling players offered him a perfect way to escape.

She should turn him in! If he were wanted by the queen, and if he were found among the players, they could all be in trouble. Will deserved to know that. It was her duty to tell him. Why hadn't she then?

Rising from her bed, she hurried to dress and opened the door of her room. She would go talk to Will and put the matter to him. He would give her good advice. Hadn't he always? Alandra did in fact feel more at ease just knowing she was going to tell Will all that she knew. As she stepped through the doorway, however, she spotted Christopher down the hall.

What was he up to? So, he couldn't sleep, either. Or was there more to it than that? Was he a sleepwalker? She doubted it.

Hastily, she stepped back, ducking behind her door and peeking out so that he would not know that he had been spotted. Why was he acting so strangely? With his mantle pulled about him, he was glancing hurriedly from side to side as if he were afraid of being caught in some foul deed. He was acting so secretive. What could he be about? Alandra decided to follow him and find out.

Nicholas whirled around, searching the shadows. He could have sworn he heard something. He didn't see anyone, but he was doubly cautious as he ran down the stairs and pushed through the front door. He raced toward the stables, which loomed before him in the moonlight, goaded on by the thought that now he'd have a precious horse and would enact his escape.

Slipping through the opening, he pulled the door shut and caught his breath while waiting for his eyes to adjust to the darkness.

It was quiet, only the nickerings and pawing hooves of the horses disturbed the stillness. Nicholas did not hear any human sounds. Unlike the larger towns where a hostler cared for each horse in wistful expectation of a large tip, here each owner was responsible for his own mount's care. The stable was deserted. So much the better.

He dared not light even a candle, lest he attract unwelcome attention, thus Nicholas chose the nearest horse he came to, a dark animal that would blend with the night. Working in total darkness, he lifted a bridle from its peg on the wall, quickly untangling the straps of the reins. Calming the horse with soft words, he slipped the headstall over the ears, then pressed the bit against the animal's mouth.

"Be quiet, don't give me away," he crooned, adjusting the straps and buckles with a deft hand. He was tempted to ride the animal bareback but feared if he did, it might warrant undue attention. Fumbling about for a saddle, at last locating it, he swung it upon the horse's back. Bending down, he fastened and tightened the saddle girth.

Nicholas had not had time to arm himself properly, but he had taken a dagger which had decorated a wall in the inn to use with his sword. He had been tempted to procure a pistol, but he rarely used such a weapon. They were cumbersome, unreliable, and inaccurate at best, thus he had satisfied himself with the two shining blades. A man on the run needed arms that he could count upon to protect him—and money. Thank God, he had taken his purse when he had gone to meet Morgana.

He would be in constant danger, and he would have to be cautious, for there could be travelers on the road who might raise an alarm. Hopefully, if he were seen, he would not be recognized this far from London. Still, he wanted no keen-eyed sheriff-following on his heels.

Nicholas knew Stafford would head for Nicholas's estates, but if fate were with him, he would arrive before that bastard found him. Stafford had no way of knowing that he had already escaped from London, so perhaps there was a chance. And even if there wasn't, it would be far better to go down fighting.

"Quietly now," he breathed as he led the horse from its stall and out of the open stable door. "We have a journey to make, you and I."

It was this sight that met Alandra's eyes as she walked down the thickly foliaged path, following the trail she had seen Christopher take. His broad shoulders and height gave him away despite the shadows. Christopher Nicholas was stealing a horse! She would have had to be a fool not to have known what he was doing.

"The villain!" she gasped softly. She was stung with anger. He was a thief! Despite the kindness her father had displayed, Christopher was stealing from the acting company. It was but one more crime to be added to his guilt. A liar, a thief, and most likely a murderer, too. For how could she doubt that now?

Alandra watched in outraged silence as he climbed upon the animal's back. Two thoughts then meshed in her brain, the loss of the horse and more importantly that Christopher was fleeing. Well, she wouldn't let him go! He wouldn't get away with this.

Without another thought, Alandra hurried to the stables and mounted Pedant, one of her father's horses. Riding bareback, she followed in pursuit. Heedless of any danger to herself, she knew only that she had to bring Christopher Nicholas back!

Chapter Ten

The great hall of Whitehall Palace echoed with the sounds of laughter, the buzzing of voices whispering the latest gossip, and the chatter of politics, as well as grumblings of a more serious nature, concerning Lord Woodcliff's death. And Elizabeth was outraged.

"Look at her, the unrepentant, adulterous slut!" The queen's fan fluttered in an ominous tempo as she expressed her ire to Lord Burghley, her white-bearded friend and councilor. Wearing his usual black garb, the caps of his wool coif cap pulled over his ears, he always looked as if he were in a state of mourning. He was the queen's wise old owl whose wings had been clipped by illness and old age.

Burghley squinted as he looked at the subject of his monarch's dismay. He clucked his tongue sympathetically. "Now, now, do not be too hard on her. She is young and—"

"Young and with the morals of a dockside whore, I

would warrant!" Elizabeth snorted indignantly, more than a bit miffed that Burghley too had been taken in by the "Widow" Woodcliff's charms. "It is upon her head that my poor dear Lord Woodcliff's death should be placed, no matter who wielded the sword."

"Upon her head?" Burghley started to say something but thought better of it. There were times when silence ruled the day.

"I want you to keep an eye on her, Cecil! I do not trust her. I would have to be a dim-witted fool not to know she is up to something."

"Yes, Your Majesty!" he said humbly.

Burghley, who was affected by that "unhappy grief in the foot," as he called his gout, hobbled along beside the queen as she moved toward the object of her ire.

Although the Widow Woodcliff wore black, she displayed anything but an attitude of mourning. Instead, Morgana coyly positioned herself at the center of a throng of crooning, attentive men, basking in the glow of their affection as she artfully made use of her supposed grief. Her admirers quickly scattered, however, as a frowning Elizabeth swept into their midst.

"Get you gone!" she commanded, shooing them away like chickens. "I would speak with this...this woman alone."

In confusion, Lord Burghley started to leave, too, but the queen grabbed his sleeve. "Not you, Cecil. You can hear what I have to say." Elizabeth's eyes closed to slits as she assessed her rival, as radiant as ever even dressed in the dark somber hue. The black velvet made her hair look all the more golden, her eyes a more pristine shade of blue, and emphasized the fairness of her skin.

"You wish to talk with me, Your Majesty?" Morgana's demeanor was demure as she dutifully bowed her head.

"Where is he?" Elizabeth snapped. Lord Stafford

had told her that Sir Nicholas Leighton had vanished, and she suspected Morgana was to blame. It angered the queen that Nicholas hadn't sought her out to throw himself on her mercy.

"Where is who?" The blue eyes widened with innocence.

"Your lover. Sir Nicholas!" Elizabeth's gaze was unwavering as she waited for any facial expression that the young woman knew her handsome courtier's whereabouts, but her face was as stony as a statue.

"I have not laid eyes on him since that wretched masque!" Morgana said, adding quickly, "and he is *not* my lover."

Elizabeth smiled slightly. "If that is true, then I at least can credit him with some good sense." Then, she became stern again. "I warn you, madame. If you are hiding him or shielding him in any way, you will rue it."

"I tell you I have not seen him!" Morgana clenched her hands tightly together. Did the queen know that she was at The Black Unicorn that night? Was she toying with her? Had Stafford babbled that information about? She couldn't be certain.

Slowly, Elizabeth circled the object of her irritation. "Haven't seen him you say," she said softly. Oh, but the little baggage was good at lying.

"And won't, Your Majesty," Morgana declared, looking straight at Burghley in an obvious attempt to win him to her side. Certainly, she was peeved at Nicholas for refusing to run away with her and for so thoroughly disappearing without even one word to her.

Elizabeth folded her fan, touching the tip of Morgana's nose with it as she said, "But what a pity. Then you will not be able to warn him that right at this very moment Lord Stafford is laying a trap for him."

Morgana's icy hauteur faltered for just a moment. "A trap?"

Lord Burghley put his finger to his lips to gesture silence, but Elizabeth blurted it out.

"A cleverly worked-out scheme that will bring our wayward ram back into the fold where he can be questioned about your husband's murder and exactly what happened that night. Exactly what happened!" Elizabeth laughed softly. "Surely you want to see justice done."

"Of course," Morgana answered quickly.

Inside, Morgana was seething. How she hated the interfering old witch! And feared her as well. Anxiously, she waited, relaxing only when the queen walked away. She watched as Elizabeth and the old feeble lord moved across the room. At last when their attention was diverted by a handsome courtier, Morgana made her move.

Speedily and furtively, she sought out a man to do her bidding. "Find Nicholas. Move heaven and earth if you have to, but find him or all is lost."

Chapter Eleven

The moon glowed like a golden coin in the velvet-black sky, shining its mist of light upon the horseman traveling up the rocky, pitted road. Nicholas rode at a furious pace with the intent of reaching Biddenden by daybreak. He was near exhaustion. All that he had suffered since his scuffle with Lord Woodcliff at the inn seemed to be catching up with him for his body pricked and pained in a dozen different places. But he was determined not to pause or to rest even for a moment.

I will not be daunted, he thought clenching his jaw. *I will reach my estates or know the reason why!*

He had been riding hard. The flanks of the horse heaved in rhythm to the hoofbeats and he felt each pulsation. The stallion was lathered. There was foam on the animal's neck and spittle dripping from its jaws. This and not his own misery at last forced Nicholas to slow his pace. He had never been one to ride a horse to death.

"All right. All right. I'll give you at least a rest, big fellow. You've been a friend to me this night," he said at last, reining the horse toward a grove of trees.

It was deathly silent except for the howl of the wind, and Nicholas gathered his cloak about him, only now aware that he was chilled. Hot mulled wine would be a welcome boon when he reached Biddenden, but he could not afford to rest there overlong. A few hours perhaps and then he must be on his way again. It would be risky business to travel during the day, but he must chance it if he wanted to reach his estates. His own lands! Oh, how they had been on his mind as he had traveled the roads. He could nearly visualize the stonework and tall towers of his home as he closed his eyes.

Hoofbeats! Nicholas thought he heard the faint clopping sound as the wind hushed to a breeze. He listened more closely. Yes, he heard the sound distinctly now. The thought that he might have been followed quickened his breath with alarm. He knew well the dangers which lurked behind the bushes in the dark of night, from thieves, robbers, and the like. Or worse yet, it could be someone who had recognized him at the inn and thought to claim a reward.

He would have to count on the element of surprise to thwart his pursuer. If he wanted to ascertain his own safety, he would have to strike first and ask questions later. The hunted would become the huntsman with one fell swoop. Nicholas prepared himself for the inevitable meeting as he waited for the other horseman to catch up to him.

As Alandra rode, she scanned the road ahead of her, seeing no sign of Christopher Nicholas. She had lost him. But how could that be? Where could he have gone? He must have continued on down the path, she reasoned, for there were no other roads crossing this way. Clinging to Pedant's mane, wishing now that she at least had a bridle, she put her heels to the animal's flank and urged the gelding on.

But the horse was misbehaving again, used to pulling a wagon but not accustomed to carrying a rider. Alandra had to concentrate on controlling the animal, for he suddenly seemed intent on galloping back the way they had come. Spiritedly, the horse reared up, its front legs pawing at the air. "If you do not want to find yourself in a stew, you will cease such tomfoolery," she hissed in the horse's ear.

As if responding to the threat, Pedant raced like the wind across the wide, marshy meadow toward the trees with Alandra hanging on for dear life.

A satyr-like figure exploded into Nicholas's view as rider and mount raced over the grass-carpeted ground. With a violent oath, he gave chase, anxious to rid himself of this nuisance who threatened him. He'd find out just why he was being followed, by God. Digging his heels into the stallion's side, he shot away after the disappearing horse and rider.

Nicholas's mount was more powerful in his strides, thus it was more than a match for the other animal. Swiftly, the stallion closed the distance between the horses as Nicholas muttered curses beneath his breath, bemoaning each precious lost moment when he should have been traveling the road to Biddenden.

Alandra heard the soft trod of hooves, and turning to look back over her shoulder, she recognized the rider. She had caught up with Nicholas! Or at least he had caught up with her. As he rode up beside her, she started to call out, but before she could even utter a squeak, a large, strong arm reached out to grab her. Dodging his grip, Alandra started to tumble from her horse.

Instinctively, she reached out, trying to grasp at anything that would shield her fall, but her hands caught nothing but empty air. Suddenly, the hard earth rose up to greet her. The fall left her bruised and gasping for breath and as she lay upon the ground, she was covered by her captor's body, held immobile by his strength. She could only lash out at the man who was nearly crushing her.

"You'll think twice before following another hapless victim!" Nicholas said angrily. "You young scoundrel."

Alandra opened her mouth to curse him, but words would not come. She was too winded. Her heart beat painfully in her breast, she couldn't breathe, and for one agonizing moment, she was certain she was about to die. Instead of weakening her, however, that fear brought forth an inner reserve of strength, and she struggled more fiercely.

"Stop fighting or I'll throttle you within an inch of your life. You're lucky I didn't take a sword to your bloody hide, you sneaky little rogue." Catching the pummeling fists with his hands, Nicholas soon subdued his captive. "Why even now I should..." A glimpse of the huge brown eyes looking up at him stunned him. "By God. You!" he managed to say at last, gazing at the face reflected in the moonlight.

Alandra somehow forced herself to speak. "Yes, it's me!" she croaked hoarsely, staring defiantly up at him.

"What in the name of God are *you* doing upon the road at this time of night? 'Tis hardly in good sense to take a midnight ride." His face was dark and impassive, yet he set her wrists free and moved an arm's length away from her.

"I was following you!" Quickly recovering her strength, she sat up. "That is Will's horse that you stole. Did you think that no one would discover your foul deed?"

Her accusation took him by surprise, rendering him speechless again, yet he glared down at her. How dare this chit of a girl speak to him that way. It irritated him, particularly since Nicholas found himself in a quandry as to what to do with her. He was incensed that she had so thoroughly hindered his plans.

"You, sir, are a thief!" Alandra continued her tirade, thinking his silence was caused by shame. Standing up, she brushed herself off, trying to recapture at least a shred of her dignity. "But I intend to see that you return to the inn to face your just punishment. Will has great need of his horse."

"I am *not* returning!" He couldn't. Not now. Not ever. "And as to the horse, I would not have *borrowed* this stallion had I not great need of him." Nicholas felt his temper flair and tried valiantly to control it. Damn his intolerable temper! It would do little to aid him in this instance. "When I resume my journey, it will be to go north and not east."

Damn, why did her frowning little face so enchant him? She was an infuriating, interfering, haughty little witch. He tried not to notice her thickly lashed brown eyes, her delicate straight nose with a delightful tilt at the tip that was now thrust so piously in the air, or her generously curved mouth that challenged him to taste its sweetness, even though it was censuring him with each word she spoke.

"But you must return!" Alandra was incensed. "I will not go back without you."

Nicholas put his hands on his hips. "You must, for most assuredly I won't go. Besides, for you to go back in defeat will teach you not to go meddling in another's affairs."

Nicholas knew as soon as the words were out of his mouth that he would not allow her to do such a thing. It was much too dangerous for a young, pretty woman to ride about the countryside at night alone. All sorts of vagabonds roamed the night. That she had come this far without being molested was a blessing. What's more, he could not allow her to go back and tell the others what he had done. Yet what was he to do with her?

"I ought to strangle you!" At that moment he wanted to.

Alandra jumped back. It was dark and they were all alone. Even so, she said with bravado, "Do and my father and the others will hunt you down like a dog. Do not be fooled by my father's jovial nature or by Shakespeare's calm. Harm one hair on my head and you will rue it."

Nicholas grumbled beneath his breath. The only alternative was to take her with him, and that thought caused the bile to rise in his throat. What a gallant fool he was when all was said and done. It had been his chivalrous nature that had gotten him into one predicament when he had not wanted Morgana to have to wait alone at the inn. Now that same gallantry was about to be his undoing again.

A myriad of emotions coursed through Alandra's veins, yet she handled herself with a grace and behavior that would have made the actors' proud, masking her apprehension. "You, sir, if you have a thimble's worth of honor in your veins, will make amends for all that you have done."

"I will not go back!" Nicholas said again.

"Then if you insist that I go back without you, I will do just that," she said softly.

Oh, she would stir up a hornet's nest when she got back. The entire countryside would be up in arms. They would capture this noble ruffian and hang him for the horse thief that he was. Slowly, she walked to where Pedant grazed as peacefully as if the midnight collision had not occurred.

Nicholas had to admire her pluck and spirit as he

watched her approach the mount. Most females would
have been shaking in their shoes, or using tears to get
their own way. He thought suddenly that there was
much more to this pretty young woman than he had
first realized. But he read her thoughts in her expression and cried out. "Oh, no!" In just a few steps he
caught up with her. "I will have to take you with me.
It is the only way."

Perhaps she would be a blessing in disguise. Yes, he
thought, she might make his journey a less harrowing
one. Stafford would not have alerted the surrounding
countryside to *two* travelers. They could pretend to be
man and wife. It would be a most clever ruse, and one
that could prove amusing.

"You think I would go with you? Ha! You might
well be far more dangerous than any miscreant I might
encounter." How did she know he wouldn't carry out
his threat and strangle her along the way?

His gray eyes were unrelenting. "You have no other
choice. If I have to tie you to the horse or drag you
behind me, you will accompany me, Alandra."

So, now he had added abduction to his list of crimes.
"Drag me then." Planting her heels firmly in the dirt,
she refused to budge.

"All right!" Taking off his belt, he looped it over her
wrists, then tugged her toward Shakespeare's horse.

Alandra was astounded that he would actually carry
out his threat. "What a vile bastard you are!"

Nicholas shrugged her insult off. "You leave me no
choice, madame!" As he yanked at her bonds, he heard
a jingling clank and looked down to see his money
pouch at his feet.

"A thief twice over!" Thinking he had robbed the
money from the troupe, she was even more determined
to bring the wrongdoer to justice.

Nicholas quickly retrieved the money pouch. "The
money is mine," he said, showing her the pouch.

"That may be," she said sarcastically, thinking the worse of him. He was still a horse thief, kidnapper, and philanderer. Was he also a murderer?

"But if you come with me willingly, you have my word that you will come to no harm."

Alandra reassessed the situation. Clearly, he was determined to make her obey. If she did not, then she would obviously suffer for it. So be it then, she would pretend to give in to his wishes, at least for the moment.

"I'll go with you," she said softly, even going so far as to manage a smile. Oh, yes, she would go, but he would regret taking her with him in the end.

Nicholas was pleased that she had conceded to his wishes so easily. "Good!" Loosing his belt from her wrists, he led her to her horse and reached down to encircle her waist, helping her to mount. "Come, we must hurry. Already I am behind the schedule I have set for myself."

"Of course. We must hurry . . ." she echoed, her mind whirling with schemes and plans.

"But remember that if you are going to travel with me, then you must learn to keep pace."

Without another word, he slapped Pedant on the rump, sending the horse galloping down the road, guiding his own horse close behind.

Chapter Twelve

Biddenden was a beautiful village sleeping in the sun, with weavers' cottages and a fine medieval guildhall with seven gables. Yet by the time Nicholas and Alandra reached it a few hours after daybreak, she hardly noticed its appeal. She was having second, nay third and fourth thoughts about the wisdom of what she had done. Where had her boldness brought her to now? Her foolish bravery? She was being abducted. He was not her prisoner as she had desired, but she was his. For no matter what could be said about her situation, that was exactly what she was. Though she had cleverly tried several times to escape, she had been caught again and again. Clearly, Christopher Nicholas had eyes in the back of his head!

The journey had been grueling at best. Alandra's backside ached, and every muscle in her body throbbed when at last they reached the door of the inn. She had traveled for longer periods of time, it was true, but not upon a horse's back. Now, after over nine hours of clenching her thigh muscles to Pedant's ribs, she was in agony. Though she had longed to rest along the way, Nicholas had forced her to go on.

Sleep and worry clouded her brain. What would her father think when he found she was not in her room? He would be fitful, frantic, overcome with worry and concern. How could she have ridden off without at least leaving him a note? Had she scribbled at least one brief line, her father would have attempted to find her when she didn't return. As it was, Murray and the others would have no idea as to where she had disappeared. But then in her bravado she had never envisioned that she wouldn't be back before dawn with Christopher Nicholas in tow.

Silly fool that she was, she had really expected him to return with her when she had set out upon the road. So much for being the hero of the day! But that was water under the bridge. She still had not figured out what Christopher was up to.

Just where was he going? And what did he intend to do once he got there? Would he take her back to Boughton Monchelsea when he had accomplished his goal? She had to believe that he would, that everything would turn out all right, or face the danger of breaking down in a fit of disappointed and angry weeping.

"It's a decent inn at least," Nicholas said as he leapt off his horse and came quickly to her side to help her dismount.

He was always the perfect gentleman, she could not fault him there. Polite, charming and as wily as a fox, no doubt. "I have enough coin for us to eat, and to rest a bit. Then we'll take to the road again."

Before Alandra could protest, he had caught her around the waist and lifted her down from the horse's back. Such a simple gesture yet she was so startling aware of the heat of his hands. Her breath caught in her throat and her whispered "thank you" sounded hoarse and strangled. If only he wasn't such a black-guard!

"Are you all right?" His voice sounded genuinely concerned.

"Yes!"

It was a lie, for her heart was pounding so erratically that she thought surely it was about to take flight. Hastily, she surveyed the scene, hoping to alert some-one as to her plight. Alas, she saw but one old man, and he ignored her frantic waving.

"Oh, no! We'll have none of that!" Angrily Nicholas wrapped his arms around her, holding her struggling body. "I'd hate to have to harm someone because of your foolishness," he hissed in her ear.

She hadn't thought of that. Her efforts to enlist aid would have to be more subtle. "I was merely being friendly," she countered, thinking fast. So far there was one thing that worked to her advantage. Chris-topher did not know that she knew about the old lord's murder, or that she suspected him of having done the deed.

"Well, don't be too friendly!" Nicholas wasn't fooled, but he didn't want to press the matter. Still, it emphasized to him how diligently he would have to keep his eye on her.

Alandra jerked away from him only to find that her legs would not support her. Her knees buckled, and she would have fallen if he had not reached out to steady her. She had to clutch his arms for balance, absorbing his hard, warm strength. It was a clumsy embrace but an embrace just the same, and as he bent his head, she was suddenly aware of how vulnerable she was to a kiss. Would he be such a rogue as to take advantage of the situation? Her hands trembled at the very thought. But the kiss did not come. Instead, Ni-

cholas cupped her face with his hand and looked deep
into her eyes.

"I know this journey has been difficult for you, Alandra. I'm sorry for your discomfort. Perhaps someday
I can make amends."

Her hair was a mass of tangles as it fell in wild
abandon about her shoulders, framing her oval face
with haphazard curls. Her unforgettable beautiful
brown eyes stared back at him with obvious apprehension and he found himself wishing that things
could be different. Another time, another place and he
might well have tasted her sweetness. But his survival
was all he could allow himself to think about now.

"My . . . my father . . ." she breathed, her dark eyes
opening wide as she thought once again of how worried Murray would be. Moreso had he known the danger she had thrust herself into.

"It is most regrettable that I cause him concern, but
there are things in this life, Alandra, which cannot be
helped. I would not willfully have caused him to worry
had there been another way."

Despite his resolve, his eyes caressed her face, lingering on her mouth which held his rapt attention.
Poised only inches from his own, it was enticingly
inviting, but he was not the kind of man to dally with
a young woman who was probably a virtuous maiden.
He had caused Murray Thatcher enough trouble without bedding the man's daughter. It would be a treacherous way to repay the old man's kindness. Nicholas
pulled away, though his gaze rested on the rise and
fall of her breasts.

"You will allow me to send a message!" She had to
let Murray know that she was safe. The players would
have to continue their tour without her, and hopefully
if she was clever, they could read between the lines.

"No!" Messages were often intercepted. He could

not take a chance on her initiating his capture. "There will be no missives allowed!"

Alandra was adamant. It was her only hope. "But I must!"

"You will do as I say." Nicholas was brutally reminded that his life was in danger. This was no casual horseback ride through the weald, no lover's tryst. He was wanted for murder and faced a gruesome fate if he were caught. There was much more at stake than a father's concern for an unruly daughter. "You should have thought of your father before you followed me!"

Alandra was stung by his rebuke. How dare he act as if she were at fault for this vile situation! He was the one who was the wrongdoer. "And you should have considered the kindness you had been shown by my father and the others before you turned thief!"

"A man does what he must do! I had to have that horse."

Their bickering threatened to cause a stir, and Nicholas cast a wary glance over his shoulder. The courtyard was deserted now, but he knew from experience that it would soon be swarming with servants. He could not take the chance of angry words being exchanged between them again, lest they arouse suspicion. Likewise, he had to get her inside before she willfully attracted attention and brought someone swooping down on him.

"No matter what you think of me, hold your tongue," he ordered sternly.

Nicholas could not take the chance of leaving Alandra alone. Though he was exhausted, he knew he would have to sleep with one eye open, lest this small slip of a girl decided to do something foolish. She could bring the whole countryside down about his ears. He could imagine Owen Stafford's delight if he was cornered by some overzealous sheriff and imprisoned for being a horse thief.

He took Alandra firmly by the arm and led her to the stables. He kept her safely in his sight as he cared for the horses. Two days, he reasoned, then he would be upon his own lands. He would have his brother, James, escort this comely wench back to her father, and then he would be done with her. As to being a thief, as she called him, he'd send a bag of gold with her to more than compensate for the use of that *playwright's* flea-ridden horse. Nicholas Leighton always paid his debts.

Silence stretched between Nicholas and Alandra, each lost in their own thoughts. Alandra called herself a fool a dozen times over for coming this far with Christopher Nicholas. She should have tried harder to get away, even if she had to thump him soundly on the head again. She fantasized about having him at her mercy. What she wouldn't have given to have him slung over Pedant so that she could bring him back to Boughton Monchelsea.

Just what is this man capable of? she wondered. How did she know he would not strangle her if she proved a nuisance? Because he gave her his word that she would not come to harm? Ha! What good was the word of a thief and a liar?

Alandra at last broke the silence. "I'm tired and thirsty." Slowly, Alandra worked her way toward the door. "I'll go on ahead and meet you inside the inn."

Nicholas was on her in an instant. "Stay here! I'll be finished in good time, mistress." He bowed mockingly. "I don't want you going anywhere without me, madame."

"I can well imagine!"

Turning up her nose, she held her head aloft. Angrily, she walked back and forth, nearly wearing a hole in the earthen floor.

Lifting the saddle from his mount, he flung it to the ground. "I never trust a woman's anger, and you are perilously angry with me right now. That makes you doubly dangerous, you know."

"I have reason." Her tone was curt. Why even try to be civil? He didn't deserve politeness after what he had done.

"Yes, you are justified," he conceded. He hated strong-arming a woman, but he had to keep her from sounding an alarm. "But so am I. I have reasons for doing what I do."

"I know how to keep a secret," she said firmly.

Oh, no, he wasn't going to tell her, though just like all women she was as curious as a cat. "I suppose you can keep a secret, but you will not be privy to mine!" Taking note of the stubborn manner in which she stiffened her back, he added, "I cannot tell you." How could he, when he wasn't really certain about what had happened himself? It had happened so fast. All he knew was that Lord Woodcliff had goaded him into a fight, despite his vow not to draw his sword. There had been a clash of swords, then suddenly the old lord was dead. To save his soul, Nicholas couldn't even remember dealing the death blow.

"You mean you won't tell me!" His very silence only deepened her suspicions.

"If I did, I would involve you in something that you are far better ignorant of."

"Oh?" Then he was guilty of the worst, she thought.

"But do not judge me too harshly. Things are not always what they seem." Brusquely, he rubbed the two horses down.

"No, indeed not," she countered.

She was about to tell him what she thought of the whole situation, throw her suspicions in his face, when she noticed a large piece of parchment nailed to the stable door, which she had not noticed before. Slowly, she walked toward it, hastily scanning the large letters.

It was a broadside announcing Lord Woodcliff's death and offering a reward for any information about his murderer. The description matched what Christopher had been wearing when she had first seen him in the back of the play wagon. The gray eyes, the dark hair, the beard he had worn, his height, proclaimed Christopher Nicholas to be the wanted man. Now, she knew why he had been so anxious to leave London. He *was* a murderer!

Waiting until Christopher's back was turned, she yanked the missive from the door and quickly folded it up, but not before the large letters of a name registered in her mind. Nicholas Leighton. *Sir* Nicholas Leighton. Sticking the paper down the front of her bodice so that she could show the broadside to the members of the troupe, she knew it was a name she would not forget.

Chapter Thirteen

The inner courtyard rang with the sound of women's laughter and the chatter of men as the workers of the establishment went about their day. Alandra heard one of the kitchen maids telling a story as she and Christopher walked by. She slowed her steps in order to listen to the tale of the Biddenden Maids who had lent fame to the village since the twelfth century. It was said that the two sisters had been joined together at the hips since birth, a frightening omen. For thirty-four years the two women had never been free of each other's company. But their tragedy turned into prosperity for the town when at their death they had allotted twenty acres of their land to aid the poor. In gratitude, their portrait had been painted and hung in the guildhall for all to see.

"I feel a bit like those poor unfortunate maids," Alandra whispered beneath her breath.

Surely Christopher—or Nicholas Leighton as she

now knew him to be—hovered as close to her as if they
too were joined together like the ill-fated twins. She
felt his warm breath upon the curve of her neck as
they entered the front door of the inn, and she cast
him a dour look. Oh, how she wanted to make an
outcry of his guilt, but now that she knew beyond a
doubt that he was dangerous she kept quiet. The
thought of having some poor innocent person's death
upon her conscience made her doubly cautious.

Reaching down inside her bodice, she secured the
handbill. How did she know he would not murder her
were she to prove an inconvenience? She had to be sly
in the timing of her revelation of his guilt. But the
time would come! Then she would get even with him
for his highhanded treatment of her.

The memory of whisperings she had heard through
the door of The Black Unicorn came to her mind. There
had been a woman speaking with the man, saying
vehemently that the man accused was innocent, that
she had witnessed the deed herself. Could it possibly
be? No! As the broadside scratched against her breast,
she was reminded of all of Christopher's sins and
pushed the possibility of his innocence away.

"I'm going to speak with the innkeeper." Nicholas's
whisper jolted her from her musings. "Speak not a
word or you will rue it."

She swallowed an angry retort as they sought out
the innkeeper, a gray-haired, short little man with an
ever-growing bald spot atop his head. As he welcomed
them with a genuine smile, Nicholas invented the
story that he and Alandra were newly wed. The blush
that stained her cheeks seemed to corroborate his
story. When she opened her mouth to speak, she was
quickly silenced by a gentle poke in her ribs.

"Recently married. How charming. How delightful." The innkeeper's smile widened, and he insisted
they be given the second best room in the inn for the

price of a lesser one. "Come, I'll show you the way."
The appraising glance he gave Alandra seemed to say
that he envied her husband. A stern look from Alandra
told Nicholas he had best keep his hands to himself,
no matter what untruth he had instigated.

It was musty and smoky inside The Red Lion Inn,
and though Nicholas's garments were begrimed, no
one seemed to notice. It was a gathering of various
social classes, a diversity represented in the clothing
of the guests. Immersed in conversation, intellectual
and otherwise, few of the inn's guests seemed to notice
the man or the young woman at his side.

Following the rotund form of the proprietor up the
wooden stairway, Alandra grew more and more nervous. Christopher had killed once. How did she know
that he would not kill again? Kill her! Certainly, it
would make it easier for him, but then again he needed
her. Her very presence insured his safety. A lone trav-
eler was being hunted but not one who had a wife. He
knew it! How sly he was!

Christopher, she thought crossly, was not even his
name. Touching the broadside, she remembered anew
the glaring black letters. This arrogant nobleman had
kept many things secret, but it was about time he
made her privy to at least a few facts about himself.

"This room will be perfect," she heard him tell the
innkeeper, thrusting a shilling into the man's outstretched hand.

"Please make certain that no one disturbs us. I believe you take my meaning, eh, my good man?" He
punctuated his question with a bold wink at the innkeeper.

A hearty chuckle was the other man's answer as he
took his leave, closing the door behind him.

Alandra seethed with anger. He had told his falsehood without even one thought for her good name. "A
pox on you for such audacity!" she swore, casting her

eyes uneasily at the four-poster bed along the far wall. Share a room she might, but she would not share a bed. "Imagine telling that kind old man that we are wed."

Nicholas sought to placate her. He wasn't in the mood for a tirade. "It seemed the only way," he answered calmly.

At least he could assure their privacy and keep them above suspicion. At the same time it would afford him the chance to keep her safely within his sight. He swore an oath as he fumbled at the laces of his doublet, anxious to strip it off. The offending garment was coated with the road's dust and his sweat. Opening the window, he hung it over the sill to air before tomorrow's journey.

Alandra eyed him warily as he took off his boots. "The only way?" she asked softly, her eyes darting from Nicholas to the bed and back again. A strange quiver danced up her spine. Of all his sins was he a rapist as well? If so, he was in for a surprise if he thought her to be an easy target.

"Do not look so uneasy." Nicholas had noted the direction of her eyes. "Your virtue is safe with me."

Wearily, Nicholas plopped down in a chair, too exhausted to argue any further.

Taking a deep breath, she resigned herself to the situation, determining to make the best of it. What else could she do?

While Nicholas rested, Alandra walked around the room. It was decorated most becomingly with wall hangings, a small oak table, and matching chairs. A comfortable room. A stone hearth gave promise of warmth if it became necessary to start a fire, though on a warm night such as this one, she doubted it would be necessary.

Mullioned windows looked out over the courtyard, and she could see the bright flames of the lanterns down below, looking like fireflies in the distance. Reaching the window, she put her index finger against the glass. The scene below looked so peaceful, yet she knew instinctively the flurry of excitement that would erupt were it known a wanted man was at the inn.

"Where are we going from here?" she asked, staring out the window as if she could see his intended path through the dark wisps of the night.

"To Cranbrook, then south to Bodiam," he answered, stretching his long muscular limbs.

Alandra could not help watching him out of the corner of her eye. What a magnificently proportioned man he was, broad at the shoulders, trim in the waistline. His arms and legs gave proof of his strength, yet she knew his hands could be gentle.

"To Bodiam?"

"I have urgent business there. I go to see my brother."

"Your brother." Was he a liar, a murderer, and a thief, too? She wanted to ask but thought better of taunting him. "And just how do I figure in your plans?" It was a question she had to ask no matter how she feared the answer. Would she be locked up? Held against her will?

His eyebrows furled into a frown. "Shouldn't you have asked yourself that question before you came flying after me? You have injected yourself into my scheme, mistress, but I will see that you are escorted back to your father and the others." Wanting to change the subject before another argument ensued, he asked, "Are you as hungry as I am?"

"Probably hungrier. I think I could well eat a whole side of beef without even washing it down with ale. Shall we see?"

Nicholas had closed his eyes and looked tolerably serene, but he opened his eyes quickly as she started for the door. "Where are you going, girl?" He was on his feet in a flash, blocking her way.

"Downstairs so that we may sup. Was that not what you intended?" She glared at him, sending sparks from her dark brown eyes.

"We will have supper sent up to us."

Opening the door, Nicholas made his wishes known to a chambermaid coming down the hall, and in no time at all the oak table was overloaded with a veritable feast which they ate with great relish. Roast gull basted in honey, bread, fig pudding, and an assortment of vegetables and fruits were appreciatively devoured. When at last the empty plates and goblets of wine were pushed aside, Alandra gave in to her need to know more about this dark-haired nobleman. For the time being, all ill will was cast aside. Perhaps if she pretended to be friendly, it would allow her to take him unaware. Her father had always said that you could attract more with honey than with vinegar.

"You mentioned your brother. What kind of a man is he?"

After the complete silence, the abrupt question seemed to startle Nicholas, but he answered her inquiry with a slight smile. "A lad about your age. Eighteen years old." A spark of happiness came into his eyes. "Sharp of mind and ready of wit! A youth of whom I am most proud."

"Is he much like you?" Heaven hope that he was not. She envisioned a younger version of Nicholas somehow. Another philanderer and ladies' man.

"My brother is red of hair, a trait he acquired from my maternal grandmother. He is lithe of form and wields not a sword but a pen."

Closing his eyes momentarily, he thought of happier times when his family had been together. He prayed they would not be punished for his supposed crime. Surely Elizabeth would remember the loyalty the

Leightons had always given her. Where were his younger sisters now? Mary. Jane. He supposed they would each be in their nurseries, singing lullabies to their newly birthed babes. Jane in Norfolk and Mary in Suffolk. Always a seafarer, his father had taken Nicholas's mother across the seas to view for herself the colony in Virginia he had established for the queen.

"What of you, Alandra? Have you any siblings to share your hearth?"

"No!" Her answer was short and clipped as the old questions came to her mind. Again and again, she had tried to tell herself that her ignorance of her past did not matter, yet now she believed it did. It made her feel so empty inside not to know the truth of her birth. "That is to say that I don't think so." Did she have siblings? If so, had they been kept or also dropped along the road like unwanted kittens?

"Don't think so?" Nicholas was puzzled.

"Murray is not my real father you see," she said averting her gaze, "though I could not love him more if he were. He...he found me and raised me as his own. I have not an inkling of who I am." Strange how she found herself freely telling him the story of Murray's finding her in a basket and of her childhood. But then, what did it matter? "I've tried to push any wonderings out of my mind, but every so often I think about who my parents were. Perhaps a merchant couple or tradesman and his wife." Her eyes filled with sudden tears. "It is frightful to think that they abandoned me."

Nicholas raised his head to look at her, and a softness came into his eyes. "I'm sorry, Alandra. I had no idea."

How very wrong he had been when he had imagined Murray as a widower raising his motherless daughter. Come to think of it, though, he should have seen that they bore no resemblance. Was it possible that he might have been wrong about other things as well?

Suddenly he wanted to believe that Alandra would never betray him. He needed desperately to confide in someone and wanted it to be her. Little minx that she was, he was fiercely attracted to her. Strange how quickly she was capturing his heart. If only he could trust her, could trust anyone with his secret. But alas, he could not! Especially her, for she was a woman.

Bitterly, he remembered how quickly another woman had turned on him when there was danger. Morgana had only been concerned with saving her reputation, and had left him to face his punishment alone. As if it had not been her foolishness that had gotten him into this mess in the first place!

He had to be wary, cautious, as silent as a mime. And yet, were this another place, another time, and, if he was not in such perilous danger, he might well have wooed Alandra Thatcher as she so justly deserved.

But there is danger, lurking around every corner, he thought, shaking his head. He must not forget that fact, no matter how winsome the wench might be. He watched her actions vigilantly as she settled herself against the pillows upon the bed, nestling into their softness. She soon closed her eyes, completely exhausted from the journey. Curled up among the blankets, she looked so achingly lovely that it touched his heart. If only she had not become enmeshed in his troubles.

"You seem to arouse tender feelings in me, Alandra," he whispered, walking quietly to the bed. He felt protective of her, but not to such an extent that the sight of her did not spark his desires. It would be best not to put too much temptation in his path, he reasoned.

For a long moment he stared down at her, mesmerized by her peacefully slumbering form. She was so lovely, he mused, moving his eyes almost tenderly over her thick dark lashes, her slightly uptilted nose, her generous mouth. That he had been harsh with her he well knew, for his apprehension and the danger he was in had made him afraid to trust anyone. She had asked him if she was to be his prisoner, but as his gaze slid slowly over her slim body, he knew the answer. She was not his captive, but if he were in her company much longer, he might well be hers. Pulling a blanket from the foot of the bed and spreading it out on the rush-strewn floor, he purged himself of such thoughts, trying to seek his own slumber. But tired as he was, sleep was a long time in coming. A very long time.

Chapter Fourteen

Alandra dreamed a frightening distortion of voices and pictures. She was being chased down a long dark tunnel. Looking over her shoulder, she could see a man's shape steadily closing the distance between them. He reached out, his fingers brushing against her hair. Nimbly, she ducked out of the way, yet he kept coming. An all-consuming panic surged wildly through her veins. She had to get away!

He was going to kill her, murder her, because of what she knew. He'd murdered the old lord and now he was going to kill her, too. And there was no one who could save her.

Her pursuer was laughing, an infernal sound. She tried to evade his grasping arms, but suddenly she couldn't move. She was on a treadmill, slowly losing ground. She wanted to scream, but no sound would come. The only sound at all was his damnable chuckling. She would soon be cornered and he knew it! But she kept going, stubbornly running.

Then all of a sudden the floor gave way, and she was falling, moving in wild, spasmodic gyrations, tumbling down, down, down.

"Wake up! Wake up! We have no time to waste."

Distant sounds penetrated Alandra's dream as she was roused from her deep sleep by Nicholas's command. Her eyes flew open to see him standing over her. Remembering the dream, she shrieked and pulled away.

"Hush!" Nicholas didn't want her voice to bring everyone running. Reaching down, he covered her mouth with his hand, keeping it there until she quieted. "You must have had a nightmare."

Yes, Alandra thought. *One about you.* Her heart was beating wildly. It took a long moment for her to steady its tempo. Then all that had happened came flooding back to her in a torrent of memories—her late-night ride, their frantic journey across the countryside, the early-morning sojourn at the inn. Shivering, she remembered bits and pieces of her dream.

Nicholas watched her, charmed by the sight. Her dark brown hair curled about her face in a most enticing way, framing her face like some nymph or woodland sprite. Though he was loathe to admit it, he had strong desires for the girl.

"As soundly as you slept, I had my doubts about you," he said softly.

"Doubts?" Had she called out in her sleep? Could he read her mind? Did he know she feared him? Alandra's eyes darted nervously around the room. She hated being at his mercy.

How could she have allowed herself to sleep? It had been her plan to wait until he slumbered, then to unlock the door and to make her escape. Instead, she had obviously fallen asleep first and lost her chance to get away. Fool. She was a fool. Ah, but she had been so tired. Yet she would not lose heart. There would be another chance.

Unaware of what she was thinking, Nicholas was in a mood to tease her. "I feared the fairies had bewitched you into a hundred years' slumber. You have a most melodious snore."

"I never snore!" Alandra was indignant. He was purposely provoking her. "I do not snore," she repeated, "but you certainly did. Loud enough to wake the dead." She wouldn't let him know she had slept the entire time. Let him wonder.

"You were too immersed in your own slumbers to hear me. If your accusation is even true," he countered, wondering what game she played.

She appraised him quickly, noticing that he had donned his doublet and had thrown his cloak over his arm. Clearly, he was in a hurry to depart and didn't want to waste any time.

Not wanting to be the cause of a rebuke, she rose from the bed, smoothing the wrinkles in her dress as best she could and running her hands self-consciously through her tangled hair.

"Our horses are watered, fed, and saddled. I was able to procure a bridle and saddle for you at the price of more than a few shillings. For the price I paid, one might well have thought the leather trappings, were made of solid gold. And you accuse me of being a thief! 'Twould seem to be a name more fitting the innkeeper."

"It would seem that it would take one to recognize a man of like crime," Alandra shot back. His perfidy still angered her.

Nicholas didn't want to argue, for it was an argument he couldn't win, not unless he explained all. He stared at her for a long inscrutable moment, then his mouth twisted up in a grin. "It is my hope that the bridle and saddle will make the rest of the journey more comfortable for you, for I would welcome a change in your mood. Perhaps you might think of it as payment for the use of your friend Shakespeare's horse."

"A saddle and bridle in exchange for a horse?" Her laugh was scornful. "I would hardly call that a fair trade."

So, he had already been out to the stable. His absence would have offered her a perfect chance to escape, but she had slept her opportunity away. Well, in the future she wouldn't make the same mistake.

"Alandra..." Nicholas threw his hands up in the air. What did it matter what she thought of him? And yet it did.

Alandra studied him. What was ticking inside that noble head of his? Another plot, another plan? What was he up to? That she was still alive and unharmed said something for him. And yet maybe her murder just wasn't in his plan—at least not yet. But what about after she had served her purpose? What then?

She watched as he turned his head, wishing with all her heart that she could delve into his thoughts. His gaze was locked upon her, and Alandra was suddenly, achingly aware of her disarray. She must be a mess! With sudden feminine vanity, she wished for a comb or a brush, not to mention a bath. Involuntarily, her eyes strayed to the corner where a large wooden tub rested.

"Oh, no! There is not time." Nicholas swore beneath his breath, "Women and their foolishness."

Tugging at her hand, he hurried her through the door and down the wooden steps of the inn.

"We must be on our way and quickly. Against my better judgment, I let you slumber longer than I first intended. Now we must make up for that delay," Nicholas flung over his shoulder as he pushed open the front door of the inn and headed for the two horses in the courtyard. "If my instincts are right, there is a storm coming. We must try to outrace it."

"A storm?"

Overhead the sky was cloudy but not threatening. Nonetheless, Alandra shrugged her shoulders in compliance, not in a mood to argue. Let him think what he might. Mounting her horse, ignoring her aching body, she thought only of the necessity of getting away from him eventually.

They proceeded on to Cranbrook at a furious gallop. Riding like the wind, Alandra was thankful for the bridle and saddle which did make riding easier. Grudgingly, she admired the way Nicholas sat his horse. She had never beheld a better horseman. Bending close to the horse's churning muscles with masterful ease, he looked dashing, the eptiome of a gentleman. Following suit, she mimicked him and found that by seeking a firm grip on the reins and leaning forward she was able to manage Pedant quite well.

Despite the overcast sky, Alandra preferred traveling during the daytime, for it gave her a chance to view the rapidly passing scenery with an appreciative eye. It was a beautiful countryside of rivers and broad plains, and small valleys joined by switchback roads over densely wooded ridges which rose to a high point in the distance. Before them lay a colorful panorama of thick hedges and trees which would afford many hiding places if they were pursued.

Suddenly she wished that her father and the others in the company were with them. Had they traveled on to Faversham without her? She thought not. They would most likely be frantically searching for her, fretful in their concern. Just as Nicholas was being hunted she would also be the subject of a search. In that lay her hope of quickly putting an end to this escapade.

They passed by Cranbrook without stopping, though Alandra did catch sight of its fine medieval church which had been given the honorary title of "Cathedral of the Weald." Outside the town the storm at last caught up with them. Thunder rumbled overhead with the promise of a torrent as dark gray clouds moved across the sky.

"Damn!" she heard Nicholas say, though he gave no indication of seeking shelter. Instead, he seemed determined to ride through the rain, and Alandra cursed him beneath her breath. Didn't anything stop him?

"A pox on him and his arrogance!" she grumbled, slowing the stride of her horse. Well, if he was such a fool as to push on, she wasn't. He was riding right into the tumult. Stubbornly, she stopped. Nicholas was upon her in a minute, and she realized that though he seemed to have forgotten her, he always kept her within his view. Behind his dark lashes and veiled eyes she knew now that he was aware of *every* move she made. Regretfully, she began to have doubts that she really could escape from him.

"Is something wrong?" His voice boomed as deeply as the thunder.

Shaking her head in resignation, she put her heels to Pedant, guiding him down the roadway just as the heavens opened in a cloudburst. Alandra was soon soaked to the skin, shivering against a sudden burst of wind which howled around them. Despite the storm, she was determined not to complain.

In the end it was Nicholas who sought shelter, guiding his mount to a grove of thickly leaved trees beside which stood a dilapidated woodsman's hut. By way of explanation, he nodded in the direction of the roadway which was quickly becoming a quagmire.

Alandra didn't utter a single word as he helped her down from her horse. She was shivering violently, and she sighed appreciatively as he draped his cloak over her. Nicholas noted that her face was begrimed with mud, yet despite the dirt, he thought she was stunningly pretty.

God's whiskers, but she is lovely when she turns up the corners of her mouth and shows those pearly white teeth, he thought. He felt a sudden twinge of conscience that he had been the cause of her discomfort.

"Alandra, I've been an unmitigated ass, not realizing how cold you would be in that thin linen dress. I'm sorry. It was not my intent that you should grow ill."

His eyes mirrored his concern, and for a moment Alandra thought that despite his crimes there was some good in him. Certainly, he had shown considerable regard for her comfort, first with the saddle and now this pause to wait out the storm.

"If I can find some firewood, I'll build a fire. That will soon warm you."

Then he led her inside the hut and left her to gather the wood.

There was not enough dry kindling to be found to start a sufficient blaze. Gathering Nicholas's cloak tightly about her, Alandra tried futilely to warm herself, but the shaking of her limbs would not cease.

Each quiver, each tremor was noted by Nicholas, increasing his feeling of guilt. His damnable pride, his thoughtless determination to reach Bodiam before nightfall, had prompted his actions. Yet, how could he have forgotten the dangers of catching a chill? Hadn't his young cousin, Stephen, nearly died when he had gone riding in such a storm?

"Alandra..." Drops of rain glistened on her thick lashes and brows, and he reached out to wipe them away. His finger moved over her cheek. "Let me keep you warm."

Before she had time to think or to answer, he gathered her in his arms, his mouth only inches from her

own. It was such a sudden embrace that she was
stunned. Her heart hammered in her breast, beating
in rhythm with his, as she stared up at him mutely,
her brown eyes huge. She was giddily conscious of the
warmth emanating from his body, aware of a bewil-
deringly intense tingle in the pit of her stomach as he
bestowed on her a heated gaze. A look nearly hot
enough to start a fire. Gone now was her body's chill.
The shivering that overtook her was for a far different
reason.

"Alandra. Sweet, sweet, Alandra..." He touched
her, moving his hand slowly up her arm from elbow
to shoulder as he explored, caressed. "There, is that
better? Do you feel warmer?"

Silently, she nodded.

"Good." He arched against her, cupping her face in
one hand, forcing her to meet his stare. For a long time
he merely gazed at her then with an imprecation, bent
his head.

"Christopher!" Her voice was husky as his lips drew
ever closer to her own. He was holding her so tightly
that she could not avoid his lips.

He claimed her mouth in a gentle and strangely
chaste kiss, yet one which nearly devastated Alandra's
senses.

"Let me g—" Alandra stiffened, but his mouth
closed on hers again, muffling her command.

Imprisoning her against his chest, his arms tightened, and Alandra was aware of her body as she had
never been before. Her breasts tingled with a new sensation, and though she could have denied him, she
made not even a token protest as he kissed her again,
a kiss that held far more passion than the first.

The tip of his tongue stroked her lips as deftly as his
hands caressed her body. In response, she moaned,
turning her head so that his mouth slanted over hers
and his tongue sought to part her lips. She mimicked

the movement of his mouth, reveling in the sensations that flooded through her. She wanted to feel more, to know more about this glorious new experience.

Sheltered together in the woodsman's hut, they clung to one another. Alandra wanted to savor his tender assault, relish the feel of his mouth against hers. In all her dreams she had never imagined a kiss could be so overpowering. Nicholas ignited a fire in her blood, a hunger that was not for food. Instead, a new craving teased her, one with which she was not familiar.

Nicholas's desire was not any less fierce than hers. He had known desire before, but never like this. Even Morgana had not sparked such a flame. His reaction to Alandra's nearness, to the soft, innocent mouth opening to him, trembling beneath the heated encroachment of his lips, was explosive. He shook, giving in
to a shiver that was nearly as violent as Alandra's had been. For one moment he nearly lost his head completely. His hands pushed her back slightly as his fingers fumbled at her bodice, searching for her soft flesh.

She shivered and her skin flushed as his hand rested on the full mound of her breast.

Suddenly a flash of lightning crackled nearby, bringing Nicholas instantly and disagreeably back to reality. Reluctantly, he lifted his mouth from Alandra's and drew his hand away.

"Dear God!" Nicholas groaned as he moved away from her.

The spell was broken. Alandra was horrified at how she had so completely capitulated to his advances. But then he was quite adept at lovemaking, was he not? Particularly with other men's wives! Glaring at him, she ignored the clamor in her own body and blamed what had happened entirely on him! Philanderer that he was, he had known exactly what he was doing.

"How dare you!" she rasped.

Nicholas regretted the incident. Now was no time to become emotionally entangled. Worse yet, the kiss had revealed to him that she was most definitely not like Morgana. No toy to be trifled with.

"I'm sorry, Alandra."

"As well you should be!" Frustration and rage welled inside her. How self-satisfied he must feel to know how easily he could ply his charms on her. She'd allowed him to kiss her without even a show of resistance. It was humiliating.

"I should never have betrayed my promise." He felt the tension in her.

"No, indeed you should not have." But of a certainty it wasn't the first time he was guilty of betrayal, she thought. How many times had he gone back on his word?

"God's bones, I might not have stopped with a kiss. It will not happen again." He had seduced so many women at court that he had lost count. But Alandra was an altogether different kind of woman.

"Indeed, it will not!" Her hand came up to press against her quivering mouth. She was not so naive that she did not know what he had intended. "If you ever lay your hands on me again..."

It was in that inopportune moment that he spied the handbill. Having been disturbed by their close bodily contact, it thrust impudently up between her breasts.

"What is this?"

Alandra reached for it, but she was too late. She watched in stunned surprise as he plucked it out and quickly read it.

"So you know."

"Yes, I know!" For a moment she could hardly catch her breath as she waited to see what he would do.

Now that she knew the truth she was doubly dangerous to him.

Nicholas touched his bottom lip as he eyed her up
and down. She knew. What was he to do about it?
Silence her? "This poses a serious problem."

"I'm sure it does."

Hastily, she took a step backwards. But Nicholas
caught her wrist.

"It is not what you think! I'm not a murderer!" he
explained, throwing the broadside to the ground.

"Oh, no?" Despite her apprehension, her tone challenged him. "Oh, no? Then why are you running
away?"

"I—I was cornered by my enemy, my rival. I didn't
have the chance to explain. I was caught in a situation
that boded ill for me." He clenched and unclenched
his fists as he remembered that night. "I didn't want
to see him dead."

"Not even so that you could have his wife?" Alandra
asked coldly. She vividly remembered the way he and
that haughty blonde had looked upon each other. Only
her husband had stood in their way.

"It happened so quickly." Nicholas's head began to
pound violently, and he put his hand to his temple. "I
admit that I went to The Black Unicorn to meet her
but only so that we could talk. She was upset."

"I don't doubt it!" Alandra said wryly.

"Suddenly her husband was charging at me, and
though I refused at first to draw my sword, he wouldn't
let me be. He goaded me on. We fought and—"

"You ran him through." Hearing him tell the tale,
she nearly believed him.

"I must have, though I do not remember dealing the
blow. All I know is that Lord Woodcliff fell. He was
dead." Nicholas clenched his jaw. "Lord Stafford
came rushing in shouting accusations, ready to throw
me to the wolves to further his own ambition. I fled

the inn. Looking for a way to escape, I spotted your play wagon and the rest you know."

"Aye. You ducked into our wagon thinking to make use of poor *simple* folk by lying!" And yet had he told them the truth, what would have happened then? Would they have shielded him? Or turned him over to those on the chase?

"I had to tell a convincing story, Alandra. And had you been in my place, you would have done the same. Deny it!" Now he challenged her.

Alandra stared at him. For the life of her, she couldn't say that she wouldn't have done the same thing had she been on the run. Still, she didn't completely trust him. How could she? "Let me go," she said softly. "Let me go back. You have no need of me. Not really. You could—"

His tone was curt, cutting off her plea. "I can't. Not yet. Not until I get safely to my estates. Once there, once I am among my own, I will see that you return to your father and the others. But only then."

Alandra could see that there was no changing his mind. "So, until then I am your prisoner," she said bitterly.

Nicholas smiled sadly. "I prefer to think of it as your being my companion, to make my journey less lonely and dismal, Alandra."

Abruptly, he left the hut and went to fetch the horses. Alandra bent to pick up the broadside and stuffed it back inside her bodice.

"Now, if you will be so good as to mount, we will be on our way again," he said, holding the horses' reins.

Alandra wanted to say no, wanted to tell him to go to the devil, yet for some reason she found herself climbing upon Pedant's back. What if he told her the truth? What if the old lord had been killed in a tussle? It wouldn't be the first time nor would it be the last that such a thing happened. London and the surrounding areas were filled with such incidents. Did she want Christopher to be beheaded for what had happened? Not really.

"I'll go with you," she said, turning up her chin proudly. "If ..."

"If what?" Nicholas waited warily.

"If you promise you'll return Will's horse."

She spoke so solemnly, so determinedly, that Nicholas chuckled. He'd expected her to be like Morgana, grasping and greedy. Instead, what she proposed was more than fair. "It's a deal."

That agreed, they once more set off down the road.

Chapter Fifteen

It was a wet and dirty ride to Bodiam, through muck
and mire, and they were not the only ones caught in
the storm. Several wagons and carts were stuck in the
muddy road. Soon the narrow paths became completely impassable except on foot or horseback. The
waters of the Rother threatened to rise and overflow
their banks. Despite this, Nicholas was insistent that
they continue, promising Alandra that once they had
arrived at their destination there would be a bath and
a warm fire. It was a pledge that she meant to hold
him to.

Alandra watched the road in silence, lost in her
thoughts, reliving Nicholas's kiss a dozen times or
more. Her emotions were in a turmoil, for his warm
lips on hers had awakened a myriad of sensations she
hadn't been prepared to feel. Oh, she could lie to herself and pretend she was not attracted to him, but that

would have been a lie. She was, and the acknowledgment of that truth made her realize that he was even more dangerous to her now than before. Emotions could be treacherous, could land a woman in terrible peril. Were she not careful, she might end up being putty in his hands, believing anything he told her, doing all that he said.

But it would not come to that. Alandra had her pride. Deep down, she knew he was a womanizing swain, nobleman or not. The kind of man who meant trouble to a young woman such as she who so wholly gave her heart. She was looking for love, not for a tumbling. She was no match for the other women he had no doubt known. She was not such a fool that she did not know there was much more to love than midnight trysts, moonlight, and kisses.

But there was more at stake here. Alandra and Christopher were worlds apart. He was a nobleman and she one of the common folk. Even though they had been thrown into each other's company, there was a wall between them that could never be scaled. And what of the trouble he was in? It was the kind of predicament not easily gotten out of.

Oh, Christopher. Christopher. Strange how she always thought of him by the false name he had assumed. But then, perhaps it was far better for her to call him by his alias, lest she inadvertently ruin everything by a careless mistake.

Alandra was a practical dreamer, or so her father and Shakespeare always said. She had a romantic soul blended with a mind that always bowed to common sense. Nevertheless, as she traveled, she allowed herself to wonder what might have happened if she and Christopher were equal. Were he a glovemaker's son like Will, or a genuine actor as he professed to be, she felt certain there might have been a chance for the mutal attraction between them to ignite, to blaze as brightly perhaps as a hundred stars. But he was not a glover's son. Touching the tiny bulge where the broadside rested beneath her bodice close to her heart, she was brutally reminded of that. Nicholas Leighton was a nobleman, albeit a wanted one.

Alandra watched the passing scenery with a strange feeling of loss, knowing that once Christopher had reached his final destination she would more than likely never see him again. She had not cared before, but truthfully she did now. He was an interesting man, a fascinating companion, though not a man without faults. He was stubborn, prideful. And, yes, a man who knew himself to be irresistible to women. As to the more serious sin of murder she wasn't of a mind now to judge him, not after what he had told her. Let him prove his innocence. For good or ill, she'd let him prove it.

Nicholas could sense Alandra's eyes on him. Right from the first he had suspected that the haughty manner in which she treated him was partly a ruse to hide her blossoming attraction to him. He had purposefully made use of her feelings for his own purposes. Now he was sorry. He didn't want to hurt her. She deserved better than that. Men often divided women into two groups, those who were for marriage and those whom a man used to satisfy his lust. Alandra was not the latter but a woman with brains, spirit, and virtue. The kind of woman one seldom met in London and rarely at court.

"Once this is over I'll send her back and that will be that!" he said beneath his breath. Yet at the same time there was a voice deep within him whispering that he didn't want to let her go. There was so much that he could teach her about love and life. A whole banquet waiting to be savored. Together they could— but no!

With a daughter so wondrously fair Murray would have suitors vying for her hand. Alandra would go to her marriage bed the virgin she was with only a kiss to remember him by, and Nicholas in turn would try to put her from his mind. It was true that her nearness had thrown him temporarily off guard, but that would not happen again. As soon as he met with his brother, he would do all he could to set things right again. It would be as if they never met.

Mud-splattered and weary, Alandra and Nicholas soon approached Bodiam Village at the edge of Bodiam Castle, and found a ripple of unrest flowing through the usually tranquil place. Much to his alarm, Nicholas could see armed men walking about the streets as if they expected trouble.

"What's wrong, Christopher?"

"Perhaps everything!" he answered, knowing that whatever happened he could not endanger her. She was innocent of any wrongdoing. "Alandra, leave me. Go to the castle and ask for my brother. Tell him what has happened. Instruct him to take you back to Boughton Monchelsea. Go now!"

"No!" Despite her previous hopes that he would be brought to justice, she now had a serious change of heart. The thought of his being hanged made her ill.

"I said go!" He clenched his jaw in frustration. God's teeth, but she was a frustrating lass.

"And I said that I won't!" He read gentleness and caring in the large eyes. "We made a bargain, you and I. It's not finished yet!"

"Ah, lass, lass, I'm grateful for your loyalty." That she remembered him kindly was somehow desperately important. "But you must not get involved in any of this. I should have sent you back no matter what I feared you would tell the others."

All his well-intentioned words might as well have fallen on deaf ears, for Alandra was staunch in her

determination to support him. Somehow she could
help him, she insisted. It had often been said that two
heads were of much better use than one.

"Stay here. I'm going to see what I can find out ..."
she said as she dismounted.

Leaving Nicholas behind in the barn, Alandra made
her way into the village, and mingled with the crowd.
An old woman crossing the cobbled streets of the mar-
ketplace, holding a basket of freshly baked bread aloft,
paused to reveal part of the story. The townsmen had
been put on the alert for a murderer, having been told
that the suspect would most likely be headed toward
Bodiam. It was their intent to apprehend him and so
prove their loyalty to the queen.

" 'E's the lord of the castle," the woman said, pointing in the direction of the fortress that rose nearby, a
structure of gray stone towers and turrets. "I've seen
'im myself, I 'ave. There's been a warrant for 'is arrest.
Signed by the queen 'erself."

Alandra pieced together the details of the story from
the fragments that she learned from the villagers. Lord
Owen Stafford, certain that the guilty man would head
to his own lands to raise a force of armed men, had
sent his own retainers to mingle amidst the crowd,
some disguised as tinkers, tailors, or farmers, others
boldly displaying their arms. It was a trap, the villagers said, anxious to impress her with their knowledge. The castle itself was crawling with armed
guards, all Lord Stafford's men. Alandra realized that
Nicholas's journey had been in vain. All that he had
done was to walk straight into a trap and she suspected that few of the men of the village would have
defied the powerful hand of Stafford despite their supposed loyalty to Nicholas. A man on the run had no
friends. Except now for herself, Alandra thought, casting the townfolk a disdainful glance.

She thought wryly that Nicholas would have been

better off in London where there were always those on the opposite side of the law who could be bribed to offer aid. In London the narrow, twisting streets would have given him at least a chance of escape, but in the village that prospect was much less favorable.

Hurrying back to the barn, she quickly told Nicholas what she had learned. "And so if you try to clear your name, to visit your lands, or to get your hands on any money, you'll be arrested. It is as simple as that."

"And what of my brother? Do you have any news of him?"

Nicholas had the look of a defeated man, an expression Alandra could not bear.

"For the moment he is safe, though far away from Bodiam by now. I believe they said he has gone to Norfolk." She saw the gleam in his eye that meant trouble and knew what was on his mind. "You must not contact your family in any way, for Owen Stafford is waiting for you to do just that."

His anger exploded as he thought of the snare he was in. "And just what am I to do? Roam about the country like a bloody vagabond? Turn myself into a lamb? Act the coward? I have little money left. No place to go. How long before I'm arrested as a jobless wanderer?" He threw back his head and choked out a laugh. "Imagine the jest Stafford will make of that." He did not tell her that his property had obviously been stripped from him too. For all intents and purposes he was a pauper; that was all he trusted himself to reveal. "Owen Stafford has won."

"Maybe not!" Alandra gave serious thought to the matter. "You could go back with me."

"What?"

"You are being hunted, but were you to seek out Elizabeth and tell her all, perhaps she would use clemency and—"

"No!" he cut her off. Elizabeth would be furious with

him, as much for his dalliance with Morgana as for
Lord Woodcliff's fate. Despite her age, the queen
viewed all of the men at her court as hers. It was an
unspoken rule. He had bridged that rule by showing
Morgana attention. It was enough to send him to the
Tower. Moreover, he knew Stafford. He would do
everything in his power to poison Elizabeth's mind
against his rival.

"No!" he said again. "I cannot put myself at Elizabeth's mercy. In her present state of mind, she will
show none." Nicholas closed his eyes. What could he
do? How could he make himself invisible?

"Then what?" Alandra's suspicions were beginning
to nag at her again.

Nicholas was inspired. "I could travel with the players, at least for a time."

Now it was Alandra who shook her head. "If we were
caught harboring a fugitive, it might well mean our
doom." Now that she knew he really had killed Lord
Woodcliff, and after the matter of the horse, how could
she even think of it? "My father and Will would never
forgive me were I to bring them to ruin."

"You won't. I won't!" He talked rapidly, trying to
convince her.

She did not argue, though her head whirled with
reasons why it was impossible. "How can you be so
certain that you won't bring down the very sky upon
all our heads?" she asked warily. He was no actor as
would all too quickly be proved were he to set foot
upon the stage. A clever spectator acting as a spy
might very well ferret him out.

"What better place to hide than with an acting
troupe. It will give me a perfect chance to dress in
disguise. Using the wigs, fake beards, make-up, and
costumes, I will be able to look different every day."
Nicholas was now certain that it was his only chance.
"I'll learn the acting trade so that I can change my

walk and mannerisms as well. No one will ever suspect." He smiled. "I doubt even my own mother would recognize me in one of your father's costumes."

"We're headed south by way of the coast."

"Where else could I be assured a warm room and a soft bed? What better place to hide while the authorities search for me?"

"And you would be paid a steady wage." Alandra was slowly thawing to the idea. Had Christopher not stolen Will's horse, he would have traveled with the players.

"Will is always decrying injustice, but . . ." She hesitated. Perhaps for a little while. At least until Christopher found another way. "Not a one of them would turn you in. In fact, you might make friends among our company, friends who might even be persuaded to help you. I know Shakespeare likes you. He told me—"

"You must not tell them about me!" It was enough that Alandra knew, he couldn't take the chance on letting anyone else in on his secret.

"But I must!" It was Will's company. He had a right to know. Hiding Christopher could mean trouble for them all. It had to at least be Will's decision.

"Please . . . at least for a time."

She wondered if he realized just what he asked of her—to betray the company for the sake of his safety. Yet she found herself agreeing. "All right, but at the first sign of trouble I must tell Will. Agreed?"

"Agreed." There wasn't any alternative. Certainly, she set a hard bargain. "I'll give it a try."

Grabbing the reins of his horse, he led it to the barn door only to have his worst fears realized. He could see that all of the roads had by now been blockaded. So far he had not been seen, but Nicholas knew full well that he would be recognized as soon as he left the barn. He was well known in this village, with or

without his beard. Even his fable of being newly wed-
ded would not get him out of this predicament.

"Give me your cloak," Alandra exclaimed.

"What? Are you cold again?"

"Give me your cloak!"

He did as Alandra bid, watching in amazement as
she crumpled it up and stuck it beneath the skirts of
her gown.

"I've not been raised around actors without learning
at least a few of their tricks. There are times when we
can't pay our bills, you know." She took hold of her
horse's reins. "Is there a midwife in the village?"

"She lives just outside of it."

"Just as I had hoped."

"Alandra..." Suddenly he began to fathom what
was in her mind. "Wench, you are a marvel! Pray to
God that your trickery works on Stafford's inept
guards."

Chapter Sixteen

The situation they were in seemed more like a play then reality, Alandra thought. It was like some fanciful farce or mime, though she proceeded with but one thought. She had to save Nicholas! It was a resolution that guided her on, made her force herself to be calm and to think of what must be done. First and foremost was the need to disguise Nicholas, for as he had told her, his identity was too well known in Bodiam.

Having often aided the actors in putting on their make-up, Alandra tried to remember all the tricks of their trade. Nicholas's thatch of dark hair was too recognizable, but if she used a bit of flour to turn its black strands to gray....

Searching frantically through a pile of sacks stored in the barn, she whispered a thankful prayer, hardly daring to believe her luck in finding a half-empty bag of flour in the corner. Alandra would put it to a much more important use than baking bread. Ripping open the sack, she dusted Nicholas's hair, lashes, and brows despite his protestations, then she stepped back to appraise her handiwork.

"Something more is needed," she exclaimed. "You hardly look to be an old man. But what?" The thrust of his shoulders, the tilt of his head, the proud manner of his bearing proclaimed his nobility. "Bow your head, slump your shoulders like this."

She affected a stoop and was quick to praise how easily he mimicked her. His dazzling smile, the teeth that were his glory, threatened to give him away, however. Most commoners would have stained teeth not those of a pearly hue. Even Elizabeth's teeth were said to be darkened from her addiction to sweets.

Looking around frantically for something to alter his smile, she could find nothing, not tobacco or tea or any such bounty from the New World that might have been useful. There were a few berries growing on a bush outside, and though they were not quite what she had in mind, they would have to do. Still, there was something about Nicholas that spoke of virility and strength.

"Stay behind me as much as possible. 'Tis the only way. Keep your head down and whatever you do, keep from looking any man in the eye. Let us hope they do not look too closely at you. Keep their attention focused on me," she instructed him.

To alter her own appearance, Alandra tore off the stylish ruffs at her wrists and neck. Plaiting her wavy curly hair into a braid, she pirouetted before Nicholas to gain his approval.

"I'll play your wife once again as I did at the inn. However, do not think to give out that we are newlyweds again, lest we have to explain our impetuosity," she said, rubbing the full rounded bundle beneath her skirts.

Momentarily, Nicholas found himself wishing that

what they were portraying was real. What would it be like to be married to this little wench? Never dull, surely. It would be an adventure just taming her. Hastily, he put the thought from his mind, for now was not the time to contemplate it. It was something that could never be. Alandra Thatcher would never carry his child. Their stars led them in different directions.

Alandra continued, "We will tell anyone who intercepts us that you are my husband, near crazed with fear that the child will make an early appearance. And not one midwife to aid in the birthing."

Her affectation of a woman awaiting childbirth was convincingly real, and Nicholas thought what a pity it was that she could not appear upon the stage.

Instructing him to put his hands around her shoulders as if to steady her upon her feet, Alandra led Nicholas down the pathway to the small yeoman's cottage a short distance from the barn. There she acted out her story before the startled man and his wife.

"Our first baby," she moaned, "and I so far away from my mother."

"Poor girl, and you little more than a child!" The farmer's wife cast Nicholas a chastising glance, blaming him for his wife's predicament. "A man worth his salt would never have let you stray from your own hearth when a wee one is planning an arrival." Putting her hands on her ample hips, she clucked her tongue, saying beneath her breath, "And it's not as if he's so young that he doesn't know better."

" 'Tis not his fault. The babe is early," Alandra hastened to say, relieving her "husband" of any blame. "But, pray, please allow us the use of your wagon so that I might get to the midwife before it is too late." Catching Nicholas's eye, Alandra winked at him. Seemingly everything was going well.

The farmer and his wife agreed to let them use their wagon to travel to the midwife's cottage, but Alandra had not counted upon the kindly old couple insisting they come with them.

"You might have need of me along the way, dearie," the woman insisted.

"Oh, no. No. I wouldn't want to trouble you." Alandra's eyes met Nicholas's stare behind the woman's back, acknowledging that there was nothing that they could do for the moment but accept the offer.

Securing their own horses to the back of the wagon with the explanation that they would travel on from the midwife's cottage as soon as his wife was able, Nicholas helped Alandra into the hay-filled cart. Taking his own place beside her, he questioned the wisdom of their scheme. He knew that one look at Alandra would tell the expert midwife that she was lying. The pretense of expecting a child could only be carried so far. They had not intended to see the midwife at all but to pass by her cottage. Now there seemed to be no way they could avoid it.

The road to the midwife's cottage was little more than a path that cut between hedgerows, past a cow byre and hayloft, behind a lean-to for pigs and poultry, and through an open field of blue and golden flowers. Midway to the small house, they were accosted by three guards clothed in Stafford's livery of yellow and brown.

"And where do you think you're going?" The surliest of the three demanded of the farmer, blocking the road with his mount as he spoke. "You've been instructed that no one leaves the village until that outlaw, Nicholas Leighton, is caught. Turn around and go back!"

Nicholas was afraid to speak lest his voice betray him, but Alandra was not so shy. "Please! Please!" she begged. "Let us continue. My baby is coming now and I must have the midwife to attend me." Managing a deep-throated moan, she gave vent to her pain, then quieted. "Dear sirs, wouldst you see me birth my child before your very eyes?" Holding her stomach, she groaned and lifted up her hips as if in the throes of childbirth.

"Well, I don't know ... I've been told ..."

Letting out another cry which made even Nicholas flinch, she breathed, "You have been told to watch for an outlaw. Surely you will find no such culprits here. Once more I ask, nay I plead with you, to let me continue this path, else whatever happens is on your head. Please move and let me, my husband, and these kind people move on."

Her imprecation was convincing, for the man guided his horse out of the wagon's way. Nicholas heard him say to the other guards, "A farmer, his mate, an old man, and his breeding wife. Surely Stafford would not want us to waste our precious time with such as they!"

"By God, no, and yet I would have wished to tarry were that one not with child. Such a comely wench to be married to a man so much older than herself, but 'tis not unusual. If God wills it, I'll be able to sire a child when I am his age." The sound of the three guards' raucous laughter carried in the wind as the wagon rumbled past them.

The small cottage up ahead looked deserted at first, but the appearance of a skinny, white-haired woman with gnarled hands proved that it was occupied. Something in her deep-set eyes told Nicholas that this healing woman would not long be fooled. She had the wisdom that comes with age and experience and the gift of insight as well. Already she was studying him with her all-knowing expression.

"There is something strange about you ..."

Noting the old woman's stare, Alandra quickly thrust herself in front of Nicholas. "Strange? Do not speak so. He is a good husband. A kind man."

"Obviously a fertile one," the farmer added enviously.

For the moment the old woman's attention was diverted from Nicholas as she directed her attention to the matter at hand. "How long is it between your pains?"

"How long?" Alandra couldn't even answer. The only thing she knew about childbirth was the swelling.

"Once the pain has pricked you, how many fingers can you count on before the pain starts again." The midwife waited for an answer.

"Ten . . . or . . . or perhaps more."

"Then it will be soon. Very soon."

She quickly ushered them into the cottage then walked to a small table in the cottage. She plucked up two leather pouches laying there.

Healing herbs, Nicholas thought, nervously glancing out the open doorway to the wagon. How were they going to make their getaway?

"I will need twine, a knife, and boiling water," she ordered the farmer's wife, nodding in the direction where the woman might find those necessities.

Nicholas knew they couldn't keep up this drama for long.

"Now to take a good look at you!"

Leading Alandra to a tiny bed in the corner, the old woman bid her lay down, then with a curt order for the two men to leave the room, she pressed her hands on the bulge that was supposed to be a baby. "What is this?"

Nicholas knew he had to act now. Looking out the doorway, and seeing that the guardsmen had moved far up the road, Nicholas made his move, settling the matter in his own way. Reaching for his sword hidden beneath his doublet, he brandished it threateningly. "Move and I will skewer you like a pig upon a spit!" he threatened.

"Nicholas—" She didn't want these people to get hurt.

"Alandra, go untie the horses and make ready to ride like the wind."

As she quickly followed his instructions, Nicholas reached out for the lengths of rope she took from the horses and tied the farmer to the wagon. The midwife made it a twosome.

"You will be cursed for this! You will never know a day of contentment. Always you will look behind to see if you are followed. You will die in a prison cell!" The midwife hurled abuse at his head while the farmer's wife merely looked at him dumbfounded.

Suddenly before Nicholas could slip the rope around her wrists, the farmer's wife astounded Nicholas with her agility, taking to her heels with a speed that belied her girth. Before he could move to stop her, she was running down the road, screaming at the top of her lungs to summon the guards. There was no time to chase after her, only a brief interval to mount his horse and follow Alandra down the long, winding road.

They chose first a main street, a remnant of the Roman occupation so many centuries ago, then branched off to a side road which was little more than a bridle track. The condition of the road was deplorable but that did not keep them from guiding their horses at a breakneck speed, expecting at any moment to be pursued.

As he rode, Nicholas inwardly chastised himself for his stiffnecked, stubborn stupidity. He had thought he could best Stafford, had wagered his future on arriving at Bodiam before that conniving swine, but he had forgotten that in matters of deviltry the blond-haired lord was a match for Satan himself. He had underestimated the man, but he would never make that mistake again. If he had a chance to learn from it. His deepest fear was that they would be caught and that

Alandra would suffer for aiding him. That thought, as much as his own danger, goaded him on.

Outside of Cranbrook the rain began again, a torrent that threatened to slow Nicholas and Alandra in their flight. The wind whistled in their ears, bit at their faces and, most menacingly of all, brought the sound of hoofbeats to their ears. With a feeling of absolute dread, Alandra realized that they were being followed. The look of anger on Nicholas's face told her that he had heard the noise, too.

"Alandra, follow me!"

It was not a request, but a command, and without even a pause, she obeyed, knowing instinctively that somehow Nicholas would save them.

With Alandra right behind him, Nicholas veered from the road and across the fields, dodging among the trees. They drew closer to the dense shelter of foliage where he knew they could hide themselves.

Drenched with rain, their hearts beating frantically, they plunged into the greenery and hid. Scarcely daring to breathe, they watched the men ride past them, heard their shouts, the soft plop of their horses' hooves over the mud. Time passed slowly, and then at last Nicholas felt certain that they were safe.

"And so, I have won for the moment, Lord Stafford," he whispered, knowing the sweet taste of freedom once again. He knew a shortcut to Biddenden and from there to Boughton Monchelsea. Though he knew the pathways he had chosen were not as comfortable as the way they had come, that there were no inns at which they could stay, they had to make do with the inconveniences. Every inn within riding distance from Bodiam would be suspect by Stafford and his men. He could not take the chance of being caught, nor of bringing ill treatment to Alandra.

He was still a hunted man, but somehow looking at

Alandra calmed him. She had believed in him when all others had turned away. He would remember that. Though one phase of his life had ended, it seemed suddenly as if a new one was beginning.

Chapter Seventeen

The narrow alleyway was dark, a more fitting place for a thief than a lady, yet Morgana Woodcliff walked briskly without any obvious fear. They had to be there, she thought determinedly, tugging at the dark hood of her cloak cautiously to hide the blond hair that might give her away. She had to find out what had happened or suffer for her curiosity. Surely then, it was worth braving the dirt, squalor, and danger.

Sidestepping a pile of rotting garbage, she impatiently scanned the doorways of the run-down buildings, but the only forms she saw were females. The two prostitutes stared at her as she passed by, but she haughtily ignored them. The hags might have been pretty once, she thought, before their poverty and too much drink had taken its toll, but now they were old far before their time. The fools had bartered poorly for their favors. Morgana, to the contrary, knew just how to make full use of her stunning beauty. Because of that, she had come far, and intended to make it even further up the social ladder. The queen be damned!

At the sound of wooden wheels clattering on the hard-packed ground, Morgana stealthfully ducked into the shadows. But it was just a ragman approaching, pushing his squeaking cart down the deserted alley. Morgana drew back as he passed, fearful that the dust he stirred up might soil her, then continued on her way.

Drunken laughter caught her attention. At the end of the narrow alley two men stood, waiting. One was tall, the other even taller, but it was their faces that easily identified them. In all of London there were none quite so ugly, so much so that not even the night could hide their repulsiveness. Still, they were the ones she sought, and she gave the signal she knew they would recognize.

"Why there ye be, melady." In an attempt at politeness, one of the men swept off his wide-brimmed hat. "Complimenting us by your presence."

Morgana wasn't about to waste her time with mock pleasantries. She came right to the point. "Did Stafford catch him?" These men had a network of fellow scoundrels that reached from Dover to well beyond the border of Scotland. "Well, did he?" Her heart fluttered, she held her breath as she waited for the answer.

"Catch 'im?" Throwing back his head, the ruffian chortled. "Not 'im. Not Sir Nicholas!"

"Then your...eh...colleagues warned him in time."

"Didn't 'ave time, but it doesn't matter. Some'ow 'e knew just wot to expect. I 'eard that 'e slipped through the trap as slick as a weasel!"

She exhaled in relief. "Good! Good." But that didn't end the matter. "Where is he now?"

The other ruffian shrugged. "Don't know!"

"What!" This was not the answer she wanted to

hear. Locating Nicholas was the other important part of her plan. "What do you mean?"

" 'im and the girl slipped out of the noose then just vanished." He mimicked the hand motions of a magician, opening his clenched fist and spreading his fingers wide. "Poof!"

"Girl? What girl?" She hadn't counted on this. "Some village child?"

There was an insinuating chuckle.

"Don't stand there laughing like idiots, tell me!" There was a command in Morgana's tone that quickly sobered them.

"Not a child, melady, a young woman. A dark-haired wench 'at I 'eard was most comely." Bawdily, he cupped his hands to his chest as if holding up big breasts.

"A woman!" She nearly choked on her outrage. How easily Nicholas had found someone else to take her place. "That bastard!"

"Melady, wot a thing ter say!" The shorter of the rogues made pretense of being shocked, but the venom in her gaze quickly subdued him. There was something in her eyes that made the hairs at the back of his neck prickle. He was warned that this was not a woman to trifle with.

Jealousy flowed through Morgana's blood like poison. How did she know Nicholas hadn't planned this right from the first? To make a fool of her then go running off with some little brunette strumpet? Well, he would regret this day, she would make certain of that. Oh, she would locate him all right. Some way. And when she did, she would make him pay for his betrayal.

Chapter Eighteen

Bedraggled, begrimed, and mud-spattered, Alandra and Nicholas reached the ridge at Boughton Monchelsea in record time, safe and sound despite their aches and pains. Riding both night and day, stopping only a few times along the road to rest their tortured bodies, they now viewed the village and inn like a welcome friend.

"How can I ever thank you, Alandra? Because of your quick wit, girl, I am unimprisoned and unfettered." It was the first time he had put into words his gratitude.

His appreciation should have made her happy, instead Alandra had second thoughts about what she had done. Now she was involved, his accomplice. There might be those who could give a description of her. What if it came back to haunt her someday?

"Alandra ..." He sensed her thoughts, knew she didn't trust him completely, at least not yet. Even so,

he felt relieved that at least there was a fragile camaraderie between them, and it was a beginning.

There had been few chances for conversation in their
frenzy to return to the safe companionship of the actors, yet during their journey Nicholas had been all
too aware of the young woman at his side, fighting the
feeling which threatened to consume him. Without
even looking, he had known her every gesture, the way
her hips moved with the rise and fall of the horse's
flanks beneath her, the way her bodice tightened
across her firm young breasts as she held the reins of
her mount. The dark tresses of her hair whipped
around her shoulders as they traveled, and he knew
an insane desire to ride up beside her and brush the
blowing strands from her face. But that was not the
worst of it. During the moments when they had paused
to recover their waning strength, when he should have
closed his eyes in an all too brief interlude of sleep,
her nearness had just about driven him mad. Knowing
she was lying close by, he had tossed and turned as
the painful ache in his loins had gone unfulfilled, finding it harder and harder to keep his vow not to possess
her.

Alandra sat straight in the saddle, and her dark
brown hair glinted red in the fading sunlight. Wind
swirled about her slim figure, molding the folds of her
gown against the slender length of her thighs, giving
Nicholas a tantalyzing view of her legs and the gentle
curve of her bottom. Aye, he was going to have a difficult time ignoring her soft womanly curves, but he
had to try. He would not reward her bravery and her
aid by breaking her heart, though he suspected that
she would be his if he so desired.

But I'm a broken man, he thought, *at least for the
moment. I have nothing to offer a woman but my heart.*
He had to remember that and this pretty young woman's innocence. Alandra was the kind of woman a man

married, and for the moment Nicholas had to put all
thoughts of matrimony far from his mind until he had
reclaimed his honor.

"I hope the others are waiting, for what will we do
if they have left us far behind?" It was a question that
had bothered her all along the way, for Alandra knew
how tight the schedule of a touring players' company
could be. If they had left, it would ruin all her plans,
and put Nicholas's life once again in danger.

"They will be waiting. No one leaves behind a rare
treasure, Alandra. No matter how pressing their ob-
ligations might be." *And you, girl, are a treasure*, he
thought.

His words turned out to be prophetic, for the company had indeed lingered at the inn with the hope that
Alandra would return. Gathered together in the courtyard to rehearse their lines, the players gave an au-
dible gasp in unison as they saw her ride in with
Christopher beside her.

"Alandra! Daughter! Where on earth have you been?
I've been near out of my mind with worry! Merry-go-
up, what has happened?" Murray ran forward to help
her from her horse and to gather her in a fond embrace
as soon as her feet touched the ground. "I thought . . .
I feared . . ."

"We feared you had been kidnapped or worse!" John
Heminges gave Christopher a haughty frown as if he
condemned him as the culprit.

"We've been nigh frantic in our concern!" William
Sly, a stocky, curly-haired actor, exclaimed, casting
Nicholas a look of reproof.

"The entire countryside is up in arms looking for
you!" John Lowin, another actor, called out. "What
happened?"

The players circled restlessly about Murray and his
daughter, as they sought an explanation. Only Shakespeare seemed unruffled, and Alandra could have

sworn that he somehow suspected what had occurred.

"Give the lass a chance to tell you," he said, motioning the others aside. Hurriedly, he tried to bring order to the chattering throng of performers. "Gentlemen! Gentlemen! Let Alandra tell the tale."

Bowing to his authority, they at last grew silent, though every so often they glanced askance at Nicholas.

Alandra had always been completely truthful with her companions; now she knew she had to lie. She tried to quell the guilt that surged through her as she began. "I was kidnapped!"

"Kidnapped?" They gasped in unison.

Crossing her fingers behind her back, Alandra sighed. If she was going to tell a story, it might as well be a good one, she supposed, fabricating a narration that made Christopher the hero. "But our new friend, Christopher Nicholas, came to my rescue."

"Kidnapped!" Beneath his ruddy complexion, Murray turned as white as a ghost. "Alandra, your . . . your virtue . . . has . . . has—"

"Nay! Christopher saved me just in time." She smiled at the momentary look of discomfiture that suddenly crossed Christopher's face and knew that he was remembering their passionate kiss. Meeting and holding his gaze, she continued, "I was in the stable, giving Pedant and Petruchio their nightly feeding, when someone came upon me from behind. A dark and ugly man with a scar from here to here." She traced a line with her finger from the left side of her nose to her chin. "Before I knew it, he had pulled me with him upon Will's horse, and though I struggled, I could not break free of him."

"The ungodly cur!" Heminges swore.

"The bastard!" William Sly exclaimed.

"The brute! To so mistreat our Alandra," the others

murmured angrily, casting sympathetic eyes in her direction.

"But how did you get free of him?" Murray's raspy voice asked the question they all were wondering.

Alandra told a merry tale intended to save Christopher's good name and once and for all extricate him from any guilt associated with the deed. She had screamed, she said, and their noble companion had heard her cries for help, and without thought to his own safety or well-being had taken Pedant and ridden in frantic pursuit. There was not just one man but two roguish thieves intent on villainy and mischief. They had taken her on a hellish ride to Maidstone and beyond, headed for the marshy coast near Rye. Romney Marsh, Walland Marsh, and to the Channel she suspected. She whispered that they had intended to sell her into a harem.

"A harem? A harem? Dear God!" Wringing his hands, Murray was beside himself at the possibility of what might have happened.

Throughout the ensuing minutes, she held the entire company spellbound as she recounted Christopher's timely entrance. Swinging his sword with deadly aim, he had fought both men at the same time and sent them to the ground, sorely wounded.

"He was as stalwart a hero as I have ever seen." Closing her eyes, she could almost imagined that it was exactly as she had described. "And then he escorted me safely back, through the countryside, with nary a thought of the murderers and thieves who wander about."

Opening her eyes, she met Shakespeare's pensive gaze, the brown, almond-shaped eyes searching out her deepest thoughts. She knew at that moment that he judged her story a colorful fib, but he smiled at her nevertheless.

"Bravo! Bravo, Alandra," he whispered in her ear. "I could not have done better myself."

There was an air of tension among the gathering as each actor assessed her story, at last judging it to be the magnificent truth. Alandra had never lied to them, they had no reason to doubt her, thus every one of them gazed upon Christopher with an altogether different look in his eyes. Admiration had replaced resentment and suspicion as they now welcomed him as a hero and boon comrade. It was even promised that he would be given his own horse as a reward for his courage.

"I owe you more than I can ever hope to repay!" Murray said with a tear in his eye. "I will ever be your friend."

Pushing and pulling Christopher along, the actors made their way to the taproom to celebrate with tankards of ale. They made a great show of accepting him and had Nicholas ever doubted their fellowship he had no reason to doubt it now. The very walls of the tavern echoed with their laughter and their salutes to the hero in their midst.

"To Christopher!" they hailed. "A noble, valiant man."

Then as quickly as their voices raised to a fervent pitch, they just as suddenly died down as John Heminges raised his hand to speak.

"I do not give my friendship easily, but you have earned my respect this day."

Everyone was in a riotously good mood except for Alandra who looked upon the scene with consternation. If they only knew the truth! Knew that Christopher was a wanted man. Knew that by his very presence they were all in danger. Oh, how she had sold her soul and theirs as well, and for what? A handsome nobleman's smile? His kiss? His earnest avowal that he was the victim of circumstances? What if it was a lie? What if he *had* cold-bloodedly killed Lord Wood-cliff? What then? What if circumstances forced his hand again?

As for Christopher's appearing on stage, it was out of the question. If he were spotted, they would all be in serious trouble, hard put to explain what he was doing in their midst. Though she knew the final decision lay with Shakespeare, Alandra would do her utmost to keep him out of their performances. And yet look at him now! Joining in the laughter, enjoying the camaraderie and attention, Christopher was unaware of what awaited him, Alandra thought wistfully. The actors had his full attention. He was close to letting his male ego be his ruination, as if he actually believed he had the skill to shout out verses!

"I'll have to watch him carefully," she whispered to herself. One false move, one hint that he was going to do anything at all out of the way, and she would sound the alarm. Meanwhile, she had it within her means to blackmail him into behaving himself.

Act Two: All the World's a Stage

"All the world's a stage,
And all the men and women merely players."
Shakespeare, *AS YOU LIKE IT*, act 2, scene 7

Chapter Nineteen

The world of the theater was a world unto its own as Nicholas was soon to discover. Drama was a kind of magic. It was a colorful sphere of make-believe and pretense where for a while reality was put at bay in favor of the fantasies the actors created. As for the actors, Nicholas had heard Shakespeare say that they were shadows of reality, their purpose to hold the mirror up to nature and to embellish upon what they found there.

Nicholas was able to forget his own plight and problems for a time as he delved into this new environment. Shakespeare had assigned him to be a prompter and he found himself completely absorbed in preparing for the coming performance in Faversham. Pitching in made him feel necessary and needed, as well as endearing him to the others.

Sequestering himself in the back of the play wagon from time to time with Alandra, he listened as she explained to him the elementary rules of the company, which he had to know to continue his charade. There was always a director of the troupe, called a "captain," she said. For this tour, that man was Shakespeare.

"Captain Shakespeare." He smiled at addressing the creative genius thus.

Alandra told him that the acting companies were organized on the "sharing plan."

"Sharing plan?" Nicholas was dubious. He had learned at court that men seldom shared anything. It seemed the true nature of humans was to be selfish.

"Profits as well as financial risks are divided among the members. 'Tis only fair," Alandra remarked.

"I can well imagine. Will and his friends undoubtedly get the largest share of the pie!" he mumbled, remembering the way such a matter would play with the noblemen. He looked down at her silently, his eyes raking her as he remembered the days they had shared on the road. Thinking about them now made him realize that despite the danger they had been enjoyable moments.

"Not at all." Alandra met his eyes, stare for stare. How dare he judge them when he himself was far from sinless! Realizing that the only way to win his respect was to be just as firm of opinion as he, she held her ground, coming to the actors' defense. A man like this would have little use for those who were spineless. "Not at all! Will is always most fair. After each performance the shareholders divide the money left, after meeting all expenses that is."

"Aha!" Nicholas was certain he had found the flaw in the plan. No doubt the list of expenses was padded to allow someone to put the shillings in his own pocket.

Alandra sensed his thoughts and bristled. "Heminges is a most able business manager. A fair man. The account books are open for any of the members of the company to see." She squared her shoulders proudly as she informed him, "As a matter of fact keeping the ledgers is one of my duties."

He couldn't help but smile. "Well then, it seems my finances will be in very good hands." As well as his fate.

Alandra looked at his hands, hanging loosely at his sides. Big hands, strong hands, the sort to wield a sword. But he was weaponless now and at her mercy. Were she to say but a word to the others, he would be lost. But what was the use of thinking about it? She had already made her choice. Nor could she really say that she was sorry. Having him with the players had added spice to their travels.

There was a long pause, an unnerving silence. It seemed that suddenly each was ill at ease with the other, wondering what was going to happen from here. Were they to be adversaries pretending friendship for the sake of the others, or was there the possibility of more?

"Once you have made a few shillings you can pay back the company for your use of Will's horse," Alandra blurted, taking refuge from the uneasiness of her feelings with sarcasm.

"I would repay the money now if I had it, just to see a softer look in your eyes when you look at me." Picking up a wooden scepter, he toyed with it. Damned if she didn't make him nervous at times, he who was always so at ease with the court's ladies.

Alandra sighed. "It's just that I'm uncertain about so many things, Christopher. You requested my trust, and I conditionally agreed, but there are several things that trouble me."

"Nevertheless, you will not be sorry." She had saved him. How could she think he could ever return such a debt with betrayal? "That I most sincerely promise."

Alandra sighed. "A woman who believes a man's promises is a fool!"

Nicholas smiled. "Nonetheless, I am sincere."

"Then I had best help you play at your little game, at least for a while, lest you make an unfortunate slip of the tongue." Alandra continued with the subject of the business side of things. "The expenses of the company include payments to authors, hired men, and the fund out of which the common stock of costumes, properties, and other materials are purchased. And so far we have been managing to acquire quite a goodly sum above and beyond what we spend. Entertainment is quite profitable, Christopher!"

Though not all in the company were shareholders, Nicholas followed her advice and promptly made an agreement with Will to be one of those who would risk his earnings on the venture. Thus, though he was penniless now, having spent the last of his money during his and Alandra's journey, he hoped it would not be long before he was earning a goodly sum. He had no liking for penury.

Alandra was careful to familiarize Christopher with the Company's rules of conduct and fines for their infringement. Nicholas learned that each player was to be fined one shilling for lateness to rehearsals, three shillings for lateness to a performance, ten shillings for being intoxicated during a performance, twenty shillings for missing a performance, and forty pounds for taking any company property.

"Such as Will's horse?" Nicholas asked, raising one dark brow. "Then it seems I have reason to be even more beholding to you than I first realized, mistress."

"It seems that you do," she quickly countered. "And I shall see that you repay your debt, Christopher. You're not at court now. Each among us has to earn his keep. If you are going to be among us, you'll have to work."

And work he did. He spent the next few days dedicating himself to learning as much as he could about the theater in the hope that by so doing he could manage reasonably well. He didn't want to be found out as a fraud and cast out.

Acting was not as easy as he had first supposed, Nicholas was soon to find as he watched the players in their rehearsals. What a conceited buffoon he had been to suppose he could easily masquarade upon a stage. Acting was much more than memorizing lines and phrases and repeating them. It was portraying a character in detail so convincingly that those who looked on believed the fantasy. Gestures, tone of voice, movement, all added to the performance and separated the novice from the professional. Some of the men he traveled with had been trained from childhood in this profession. How could he have expected to compete successfully?

Shakespeare decried poor players who strutted and fretted their hour upon the stage only to fail. Poor players were plentiful, and Nicholas had no liking for suffering their fate of being booed off the stage in disgrace. He had far too much pride. Besides, he just could not take the chance of being recognized were he to be so bold and stupid as to actually venture forth on this new challenge. Thank God that Shakespeare had not put him to the test yet, but Murray's faith in Nicholas's acting ability was unfaltering and therefore dangerous.

Murray seemed obsessed with bolstering Nicholas's confidence. Thinking it was Nicholas's hope to make a mark for himself as an actor of great renown, Murray was constantly speaking up in favor of Shakespeare quickly giving Christopher an important role. Nicholas quickly assured him that he was well content in being patient and performing the various tasks assigned to him as well as being a prompter. The truth was that he wished he could silence the old man. Murray's good-natured interference was going to get him in trouble.

To add to his unease was Shakespeare's keen interest in Nicholas. The "captain" of the company always seemed to stare at him with a penetrating intent that seemed to examine the workings of Nicholas's mind. Nicholas experienced a gut-wracking nervousness in the man's presence that he had never known before. He was certain on many occasions that his farce of claiming to be an actor had been exposed, that somehow Shakespeare had not been fooled.

When the company held a meeting to find out who was to take certain parts, Nicholas held his breath, for Murray had strongly suggested that he be given the role of Demetrius in *A Midsummer Night's Dream*. As it was, a young man named Howard Abbington was assigned the role in the comedy set in a fairy-tale world of Athens, Greece, thus putting Nicholas's mind at ease, and Shakespeare had stressed the importance of Nicholas's prompting Abbington in his lines. Again, Nicholas was relieved that Shakespeare had ignored Murray, for his job gave him a chance to be involved with the theater company yet at the same time enabled him to keep his distance from the audience.

The late-afternoon sun sparkled in the cloudless blue sky, reflecting on the sea of blossoms that thickly covered the trees in the orchards as the traveling troupe passed by. Birds flew from bough to bough, singing a brilliantly cheerful melody, but Nicholas's attention was diverted from the beauty surrounding him when he heard his name.

"Christopher! Christopher!" The rumble of wagon wheels announced that Murray had ridden up behind Nicholas's horse. Catching his eye, he waved joyfully. "I wouldst have a word with you."

Nicholas paused as he squinted his eyes in Murray's direction.

"I'm sorry, Christopher."

"Sorry for what?"

"That Abbington was chosen in your place to play Demetrius when we perform in Faversham. I think Will intends to groom you for a very important role. Undoubtedly, he didn't think any part in this play good enough for your talents. You'll eventually get a large part. You'll see."

Nicholas smiled ruefully. "Aye, we'll see."

Murray's face flushed as he said, "By the way, I never really had the chance to thank you properly for saving Alandra! Seems every time I tried someone was about you. But I am grateful, Christopher. I want you to know that. There be no greater man in my eyes, I'm thinking."

"Your thanks are most humbly accepted," Nicholas replied. "But Alandra was in truth the heroine, not I the hero as she described."

He smiled, thinking of Alandra. She would never know how much he looked forward to those times when they were together in the wagon. He was coming to know her, and with each day that passed, she fascinated him even more. If he did not watch out, he thought, he might well fall in love with her. He must be careful, he must guard his heart. But how? He knew her innocence had seduced him as Morgana's wiles had never completely done.

There was no artifice with Alandra. How could he not be charmed by her? She was a young woman of intelligence, spirit, and strong will. It surprised him to see that among such a scholarly group she could hold her own very well. Even Shakespeare himself often bowed to her outspoken opinions, sensing her intuition to be correct.

"Now don't be too modest, Christopher." Murray gave a deep throaty chuckle.

He'd watched the two young people as they traveled, noting the meaningful glances that had passed between them. He suspected what Alandra had not dared to hope, that this new young actor felt more deeply for her than even he realized. Murray knew he was not mistaken, for he'd seen the expression that entered Christopher's eyes whenever he gazed upon Murray's brown-eyed daughter.

Ah, young love, he thought with a sigh. All this time he had been so worried about finding a proper husband for Alandra. Now all his troubles seemed to be fading. All he needed to do was to lend Cupid a hand in aiming love's potent arrow. And he would, God's chin whiskers, but he would.

"Ah, yes. It's a hero that you be. Tell me the story again, for I don't think I could ever tire of hearing it."

Nicholas was unnerved by the old man's scrutiny. He suddenly felt uneasy and sought to change the subject before he inadvertently gave himself away and let it be known that he had been the culprit not the rescuer. Glancing toward Shakespeare, he promptly spotted the needed diversion. "How did you meet Will, Murray?"

A grin split Murray's face from ear to ear, and it was obvious that Nicholas had touched upon a welcome subject.

"I literally bumped into him."

"Bumped into him?" Nicholas was puzzled.

"I was carrying a piece of scenery I had just created. A masterpiece, if I do say so myself. Wasn't paying attention to where I was going. I came around a corner and whopped him with it." Murray laughed as he remembered. "Sent the poor lad flying, I did!"

"A bit like my first meeting with Alandra," Nicholas

said, pointing to the spot on his head where she had hit him that night in the play wagon.

"Aye. But from such an embarrassing moment was born a great friendship and a turning point in both our lives. I introduced Will to Christopher Marlow and others in the writing community, and he in turn gave me the chance to follow my heart's fondest dream." Murray sighed, his eyes glazing over as he was thrust back into the past. For a moment it was as if Nicholas was not even there. "He was such a shy, quiet man. Awkward. A bit of a bumpkin. A glovemaker's son from the country, you know, with none of a Londoner's knowledge."

"And yet he carries himself with as much grace as any nobleman." Certainly, he was proof that a man could put his humble beginnings aside, Nicholas thought. Despite his origins, Shakespeare was as sophisticated as any man at court.

"Aye, he does. Self-taught. He's learned from life itself and has used what he has observed in his writing." He couldn't have sounded any prouder had he been the man's father. "Will was just a penniless scholar but he was resolved to become a success. And he has. Now he can hold his own with any man from Oxford or Cambridge if he has a need to."

"I'm certain that he could." Nicholas didn't doubt but that William Shakespeare could well hold his own with any of Elizabeth's courtiers. "But what led him to writing?"

Once again Murray showed his pride. "Me," he stated. "He was unhappy with the actor's lines he was given, critical of the so-called guild dramas, morality plays, and pageants that were being presented at the Inns of court. I told him that if he didn't like them, he should write his own and he did." Murray sighed. "But it was a long road to success. Will began by finishing plays started by others, brightening up old plots with a fresh view. He went through a long winter, as he calls it. But talent won out."

"It seems so."

"As time goes by, his writing has become even more important than his acting. I would venture to say that Shakespeare's genius speaks for itself."

"Loudly and very clearly," Nicholas agreed.

"And perhaps the same will happen for you." Murray cocked his head. "Perhaps you might become a playwright, too."

"Me?" Nicholas threw back his head and laughed. That was one deception he would not even attempt. "No, no, I'll leave the drama to Shakespeare. I'll one day but recite what he puts down. It's safer that way."

"Safer?" Murray eyed Nicholas quizzically. "Sometimes yes and sometimes no. 'Tis the actors who bear the brunt of the audience's displeasure." He patted Nicholas's arm. "But do not worry. We will be a success from the moment we reach Faversham until the end of our tour. You will see."

"I thought I heard Heminges say that we would reach Faversham in two days' time," Nicholas said.

"Aye, that we will." Murray made a great show of smacking his lips. "Faversham is famous for its oysters. I'll treat you to supper when we arrive. Seems to me it is the very least I can do to repay you." Taking off his hat, he wiped his brow. "I imagine you are as anxious to reach that town as am I. Being on the road too long jiggles my bones. I'm not as young as I used to be, no matter how Alandra flatters me. How glad I am that you and the others are such expert actors. Makes my job easier." He whispered behind his hand, "There have been times when I've loathed playing at Faversham. It takes a lot to please that crowd. Seafarers and the like. They will not be content with less than a perfect performance. But we have no need to worry.''

Nicholas smiled. "No need at all!"

"We'll bedazzle them. Those groundlings won't make us the target of apple cores and orange peels."

"Groundlings?" Nicholas tried to hide the fact that he was completely baffled by the word.

"Groundlings! Groundlings, Christopher. Merry-go-up, one would imagine you had never seen the inside of a courtyard theater before. Ah, how I loathe those rascally knaves who don't have money for a seat and thus stand in front of the stage and gawk."

"Even in the theater it seems people are divided into classes," Nicholas replied.

"Ah, the lordlings, midlings, and groundlings. The wealthy patrons with their private boxes, the midlings whose purses entitle them to the galleries and the comfort of benches, and lastly the common man whose wages afford but a penny to spare. Enough to get them through the door to view the play from ground level and the pit around the stage. They can be, I fear, a most boistrous crowd. If an actor forgets his lines or disappoints them in any way, they can be heartlessly annoying."

Nicholas was grateful that he would not have to endure such humiliations. But the thought of a knight of the realm being bombarded by apple cores, orange peelings, and nutshells made him laugh, a deep husky sound that quickly vanished.

"But without them we'd soon be out of business, would we not? Despite the fact that they only pay a penny, they are the greatest part of our crowd after all. Those pennies add up."

"Aye, every penny adds to our coffers."

Murray shrugged his shoulders and started to ride off, but a sudden thought caused him to pause. "By the way, has Will told you that we will have a very

important personage among the crowd at Faversham?''

"Important personage?"

Lord Burghley. If he approves of our performance,
there is every likelihood that we will be asked to do
the Christmas festivities at court."

"Lord Burghley!" Nicholas's alarm showed clearly
on his face. Lord Burghley was Elizabeth's most
trusted minister, one who knew his face all too well.
More than just his acceptance among the actors was
now at stake. His very life might depend on his keeping
as far away from the feeble old lord as he could.

Chapter Twenty

The flickering light of the oil lamp cast shadows against the wooden sides of the play wagon as Alandra waited. Christopher was late, and for a moment she feared he was not coming, that he had decided that being a member of the acting company was too difficult and had decided to run away. What if he had stolen another horse and fled? How would she explain that to the others?

He would come. He would! Hadn't he surprised her with his steadfastness and determination to meld in with the others? Hadn't he tried his best? And so far he had done nothing amiss. Nothing that she could criticize. He had in fact been almost perfect. Perhaps too perfect. What if it had been nothing but a ruse?

Fretfully, she fought against her apprehension, cautioning herself to be patient. What would be would be! If he left, good riddance. His presence was a danger to them, after all. She tried to convince herself that

she didn't care a whit if he left or not, yet she knew
it was a lie. She did care. Much more than she should.
Despite her best intentions, she was drawn to him,
fool that she was.

Alandra paced up and down, waiting, busying herself by sorting the costumes into four large piles ac-
cording to size. All of them too narrow across the
shoulder for Christopher's frame. Ah, but he was a
most masculine man, just the kind a woman dreamed
about. Hard and strong and fierce!

And maybe dangerous! Alandra sensed that he had
a temper, one that he held carefully in check. But if
he let it go? Of what was he capable?

Certainly, his anger had been tested. Living among
the actors, on the move, was undoubtedly much more
difficult than he had at first supposed. Hardly at all
like life at court. And the others had expected him to
do his share. But Christopher was not a man to give
up, no matter what the challenge. And yet there was
not the intrigue here that there was at court, no temptation to use a sword to further ambition. Was it then
a fair test of his mettle as a man?

She must not forget that his staying among them
was not for love of their companionship. What better
hideaway could there be? There was no other place
where he had access to wigs and costuming and could
disguise himself and not be questioned for it. Among
the actors being masked and wearing make-up was a
perfectly normal thing to do, thus it would not be
thought unseemly for Christopher to alter his appearance and therein assure his anonimity. Forsooth,
Christopher was as snug here as a bug in a rug and
he knew it!

"Alandra . . ."

Turning, she saw him standing at the wagon's opening and immediately felt relieved. Still, she chided
him, trying to sound stern. "You're late, Christopher!"

"It couldn't be helped," he countered. "Will was in a particularly talkative mood. He and Kempe cornered me while I was watering the horses. Man talk." Talk of politics, women, and business. "I apologize." His smile was meant to charm her and it did, though she wouldn't let him know it.

"I know how Will can chatter at times. It proves that he likes you." She patted a spot beside her on the wagon's wooden floor. "Shall we begin? If you are going to be the prompter for the performances, you had best learn to do it well! Will is giving you the benefit of the doubt because you are new to us, but he'll make you prove your mettle. If you have fooled him this long, you won't for much longer. Come."

Nicholas shook his head. "Nay." He had been doing a lot of thinking lately. Murray's having told him about Lord Burghley had unnerved him, opened his eyes. Staying with the players was an unfair thing to do. He was endangering them, opening them up to trouble.

She looked at him suspiciously. "What do you mean, nay?"

"Your father told me that William Cecil, Lord Burghley, once Elizabeth's formidable councilor, is to be in the audience at Faversham. He knows me on sight! I cannot chance going with the company there, thus I have come to say good-bye."

"Good-bye? Just like that." She snapped her fingers.

"You should be glad. Once I am gone, you will all be out of danger." He watched her face, hoping for a sign that she would be sorry to see him go.

Alandra felt the blood leave her face. How easily he just tossed them all aside. "You ungrateful oaf!" Angrily, she threw a bundle of costumes on the floor.

"What?" He had been prepared for anything but this.

She fixed him with an angry stare. "Lord Burghley

be damned! That isn't why you go. From what I have heard, he can't even see his hand in front of his face. 'Tis not because of him that you want to run away.'' Folding her arms across her chest, she rasped, "Why then?" Had he just been biding his time, waiting for a moment to meet with *her*? With that yellow-haired woman? Were they planning to run away together? If so, then he could at least be honest.

Nicholas's own ire was sparked. Here he was trying to do something noble, free the company of his unwelcome burden, and she was acting as if he were doing something wrong.

"Burghley is but a symbol of what is to come. First he and then another from court, then another will be in the audience. My luck might hold out for a week, perhaps a month, but one day I might be pushed upon that stage and the game will be lost."

"You're afraid!" It was a startling discovery.

"I'm not!" He'd faced death and never flinched. "At least not for me." His eyes softened. "I fear for you, Alandra, and the others. If Elizabeth thought for a moment that you had willingly and knowingly sheltered me, she would bring down the very sky upon your head. Think, Alandra, think!"

What he said was undoubtedly true, but Alandra was not in a cowardly mood. If he left and he were caught, it might well mean his life. "We're actors, all of us! If that moment comes, we'll fend for ourselves. We have before." Her mouth softened into a smile. "In the meantime you had best learn what you are about or Shakespeare will have your head!"

Nicholas sat down, his leg brushing against her thigh as he settled himself comfortably. He tried hard to push the amorous thoughts from his mind, determined to forget that Alandra was a very desirable woman. But, by God, it was difficult if not impossible at times. He was getting more firmly hooked on the little lady with each moment that passed.

"I hasten to obey, my lady."

"Now about this matter of prompting..." she began.

Acting companies had only one full copy of each play. In this "prompt book," notes were made relating to performance—cues for sound, music, special effects, entrances, exits, and notations about properties. Luckily that copy belonged to Alandra's father which gave her valuable access to it. It was a compliment that Christopher had been entrusted with it, for the other actors were given "sides" which included only their own lines and cues. During the performances a plot or skeletal outline of the action indicating entrances, exits, properties, music, and the names of the players would be hung up back stage for quick reference.

Nicholas tried hard to listen as she familiarized him with the guidelines for a good performance, but his thoughts were elsewhere. They were alone together with only the lamp lighting the darkness. Nicholas was not immune to the provocativeness of the moment. His eyes smoldered in the dim light. Somehow he could not keep his gaze from the cleft between her breasts that showed just slightly when she bent over.

Alandra flushed as she saw where Christopher's eyes had wandered. The memory of his kiss was a bittersweet ache in her heart. A moment of madness between them brought on by their shared danger. Or had it been something more?

"I think I may have reason to be afraid, of you, lass." Slowly, he bent his head forward.

"Afraid of me?"

She thought he meant because of what she knew of him, but his eyes told of a far different reason. She had seen that look before. Passion. Desire. For her! She looked back at him and found her eyes drawn to the strong column of his throat. He had left his doublet off and the cut of his shirt exposed the flesh of his neck and upper chest.

"Sweet Alandra..." The feelings inside him had to have an outlet, and she was so very, very sweet.

He's going to kiss me again, she thought. At that moment it was what she wanted most in the entire world. Slowly, she raised her face to his in expectation.

"Alandra..." He reached out, his hand moving up to her unbound hair. His fingers bared her neck, his fingers lingering on the soft flesh of her throat. "You are beautiful."

Alandra slowly drew nearer to him. It was late, they were alone, and she was succumbing to the spell of the night. She felt his breath ruffle her hair, felt the sensation course down the entire length of her spine. She wanted to push reality away, but all too quickly she remembered that he was a nobleman. The queen's man. A courtier. A man whose taste in beauty ran to golden-haired angels. She didn't know him, not really. Would she ever?

There was a gulf between them that could never be breeched. A difference in stations that he would recall, even if she allowed herself to forget. In the end she would only be hurt if she allowed herself to dream.

"We must concentrate on other than dallying," she said quickly, pulling away.

Nicholas, hiding his disappointment, was good-natured about her rejection of him. "Ah, but you are a hard taskmaster, wench! But once this is all over, once the danger has passed and I have cleared my name, then we shall see."

Chapter Twenty-One

The great hall of Greenwich pulsated with the sound of the gay tune that floated in the air. The floor vibrated with the dance steps of the courtly revelers. Row upon row of royal portraits seemed to be smiling, as if they too were humming a tune. But Elizabeth was not in a frolicksome mood.

Though she was loathe to admit it, court was incredibly dull without Nicholas. She missed his smile, his wit, his sense of daring. It had been stimulating with Sir Leighton and Lord Stafford always at verbal sword points. Now there was really no one to take Sir Leighton's place as Stafford's rival, and she thought how that was such a pity.

As she stifled a yawn, she was overcome with boredom. Walsingham, Dudley, and so many of her other favorites were dead. Lord Burghley had retired from his active post as her councilor because of ill health and his irritating misshapen son was in his place. And now with Nicholas gone from the roster, it seemed that court would never really be the same.

Hoping to liven things up a bit, Elizabeth had moved the court from Whitehall to Greenwich, which with its sculptured yews and sumptuous gardens pleased her. She was constantly surrounded by her ladies-in-waiting, court favorites by the score, dignitaries and officials, and she moved easily and gracefully among them. But despite all the people, she felt lonely. No one cared about Elizabeth the person. Not really. But somehow she had the feeling that Nicholas had. At least once. But what was the use in even thinking about it? Nicholas was gone and wherever it was he had disappeared to, there seemed to be little chance of his returning.

Ah, but she had at least been able to enjoy a little revenge by banishing that golden-haired harpie from court. Morgana Woodcliff had been properly given her comeuppance and told to spend some time in the country, in hopes that she would have time to appreciate a period of "proper mourning." And just in case she had any thoughts of disobeying Elizabeth's orders to act like a proper widow, Lord Burghley had been told to go along with her for company. A request he had actually seemed to enjoy much to Elizabeth's annoyance. Even at his age he was taken in by Morgana's beauty, but then it was said that there was no fool like one well past his prime!

As to Lord Stafford, Elizabeth was disappointed. The angelically handsome blond man had not too subtly revealed that his looks did not match his disposition. Elizabeth sensed that he could be devious and thus was always on her guard. That did not, however, keep her from enjoying his company.

"You are to be given the honor of partnering me in my first dance, Lord Stafford," she exclaimed loud enough for all to hear as he approached. In a flash of green and gold, Owen Stafford offered her his arm as the court musicians lifted up lute, viol, brass, woodwind, and sackbutt to begin another lively tune. Elizabeth loved to dance and was known to pirouette with the energy of a woman half her age.

"You look radiant tonight," Stafford was quick to say, but somehow the words sounded hollow to Elizabeth. When Nicholas had complimented her, he had always sounded sincere.

Lord Stafford eagerly led her through the movements of a round dance, twisting and whirling through the intricate maze of steps, until they were both out of breath and dizzy. As soon as that was over, he took her hand for a stately pavan.

"So, have you located Sir Leighton?" Elizabeth asked to the soft accompaniment of the music. She knew well that he had not, but that didn't keep her from toying with him.

His pale blue eyes locked with hers, and for a moment she could see that he was struggling with his anger.

"No! The cursed, murdering bastard is more clever than a thief."

"Indeed," she replied, choosing to ignore the insult he had just paid to Sir Leighton's parentage.

"But I will capture him! On that you have my word! Sir Nicholas Leighton will be residing in the Tower ere another week is out, that I promise."

It amused the queen how everyone near them picked up their ears at the mention of Sir Leighton's name. The court seemed divided into two camps: those who believed in Sir Leighton's innocence, and a larger majority who were certain he had killed his aged rival for the sake of pure unadulterated lust. But no matter their personal view, all at court loved a good scandal.

"Then you know where he is?" she asked sweetly, playing at the game. Of course he did not, she thought, but he was desperate and that was the cause of his blustering.

"All of England has been plastered with handbills of his description as well as a detailed report of his dastardly deed. Lord Woodcliff will be avenged!" Stafford's blue eyes flashed with an ominous inner fire.

Elizabeth judged the look in her young lord's eyes and held up her hand. "I do not want Sir Leighton to be harmed. Not an eyelash, not a hair on his head." She knew it to be important to make herself quite understood. "I of all people held great respect for Lord Woodcliff. I was and still am sympathetic with his reasons for outrage. I mourn his death very deeply. But were Nicholas to request it, I would listen to his explanation."

Lord Stafford paled. "The explanation of a foul murderer?"

Elizabeth could be an intolerable shrew, but today she was in a mood to be fair. "There was an unfortunate fight. Tempers were raised and swords slashed in the air. Poor Woody was the loser. Such things happen." *Look at him*, she thought. *What a hypocrite*. He held himself up as judge and jury when she knew him guilty of more than a few sins himself.

Lord Stafford's expression was of a cobra that had recently devoured a mouse. "I fear Your Grace has not been informed of all the details." Taking advantage of the moment, he slowly and deliberately removed a piece of paper from his doublet. "Lord Woodcliff was savagely and ruthlessly assaulted from behind."

"What?" She was startled.

He thrust the piece of paper at her, savoring a major triumph. Sir Leighton was ruined! "You may read the report for yourself, Majesty. Lord Woodcliff's mortal wound was in his *back!*"

Chapter Twenty-Two

Queen Elizabeth herself could not have received a more enthusiastic greeting than did the Lord Chamberlain's Men as the wagons and horses made their way into the coastal town of Faversham. Horns blared, voices rose up in shouts as the sound of laughter and merriment followed the parade of actors and the others in the company down the neatly cobbled street in the center of the town. Even though the aldermen and Puritans had closed down the theaters in London for the summer, it was very obvious that the actors were welcomed here. London's loss was Faversham's gain, Nicholas heard more than one passerby say.

Young women and old threw flowers at the troupe until the street was covered with blossoms of red, white, blue, and gold. Wide feminine eyes blinked come-hither looks, and their smiles gave evidence that many of the youthful lasses were more than willing to share their favors with the actors.

As he rode, Nicholas reflected on his good luck at having been accepted by the players. He basked in the actors' friendship. They still considered him to be a hero. Moreover, he found himself thoroughly liking this group of men. There was a trust and confidence among them and no fierce rivalry existed. Indeed, even Heminges was not as self-centered as Nicholas had at first supposed.

Costumed for the parade in an assortment of garments Alandra had concocted carefully to hide his true appearance, Nicholas felt safe from any unfriendly eyes. Though costuming for *A Midsummer-Night's Dream* resembled the garments of the day, he wore a wig of short auburn hair and a mask which artfully hid his identity. Garbed in blue, from his trunk hose to a waist-length doublet, he was meant to be colorful and he was. His only discomfiture was caused by his ruff which seemed to prick him no matter which way he turned his head.

Most of those assembled in the procession were equally as flamboyantly dressed. As they rode, Nicholas's eyes sought each one out.

Will Kempe, decked out in green, was a thoroughly likeable man with a natural wit that drew people to him at once. Alandra had told him that the tawny-haired man was one of the greatest comic actors of the times, and Nicholas believed her. The actor's portrayal of Puck brought forth even his laughter. Moreover, Kempe was just as quick of wit out of his costumes as he was playing a role and always made the others in the group laugh.

William Sly, a heavy-set man, with a full face and the surly look of a fighter, had proven to be surprisingly graceful upon the stage. He was the perfect choice for Bottom the Weaver. Loyalty and generosity to the others in the company were his strong points. Sensing that Nicholas was short of coinage, he had even offered to loan him money, though Nicholas had declined.

John Lowin, a mustached actor with a heavy jowl and the manner of an aristocrat despite his humble family ties, was dressed in gold which fit his role as Theseus, Duke of Athens. Though he was baseborn, Nicholas realized that Lowin could have taught many of Elizabeth's courtiers the art of being a true man, for he had shown the greatest bravery during those moments on tour when things grew harrowing.

Heminges, who now looked upon Nicholas as an equal, glanced at Nicholas and waved from the head of the parade. Nicholas considered Heminges to be a reliable fellow, though a bit stubborn. But it was evident that he had business ability and was regarded with confidence by his fellows. Several members of the company had even made him executive of their estates and guardian of their wills.

Last but not least was Richard Burbage who had joined the actors in Faversham. He was a lithe actor in his early thirties who was already being acclaimed as the only actor in England who could hope to fill Edward Alleyn's shoes. Dressed in black and gold, with wings attached to his back, he was to play Oberon, king of the fairies and weaver of magic. Nicholas had been particularly amused by a story he'd heard of Burbage's womanizing. The tale had gone around London that a woman had fallen for Burbage in his role as Richard III and had extended him an invitation to visit her. But Shakespeare had overheard it and left the theater before Burbage. A message had been brought to Burbage that "William the Conqueror was before Richard III." Thus did Shakespeare win the fair lady instead.

The procession marched past the white-painted guildhall with its market stalls below the ground-floor arches, past the church with its carved stone, and

came at last to the innyard, where the company would
set up its trestle stage. Already an audience of onlookers twittered in the courtyard expectantly. Nicholas felt the same surge of excitement he always felt
before a battle and reasoned that in some ways this
would be much the same. A display of daring, agility,
and skill.

Instinctively, Nicholas's eyes sought out Alandra,
for even with all the commotion he had not forgotten
her and the many evenings they had spent together in
the play wagon. Now he was glad he hadn't hastily
run away. Everything would be all right. The play
would run smoothly, he would be safe from prying
eyes in the wings, and none would be wiser. Of all
places Lord Burghley would never suspect him to be
among the actors. His being here was coincidence and
nothing more. Nicholas knew he was foolish to have
feared.

As if she read his thoughts, Alandra smiled, and Nicholas halted his horse, dismounted, and gathering a
bouquet of brightly hued flowers which littered the
streets brought it to her side.

"For you, Alandra. Would that I could give you much
more. Words cannot express my gratitude."

He made an extremely romantic figure standing in
the bright haze of sunlight, with his dark blue hosen
hugging his long, muscular legs, and his doublet
straining as he reached up to put the flowers in her
hand. At that moment Alandra's heart skipped a beat.
She could not take her eyes from him. Transfixed, she
stared, and clenching the flowers, she tried to ignore
the strange tightening in her stomach. There was a
warmth, a glow deep inside her, the significance of
which she dared not contemplate. For one moment it
was as if they were all alone on the street. Then the
insistent voice of Will Kempe urged Nicholas to resume his position in the parade.

Watching him walk away and mount his horse without a second pause, she knew he held her heart. If Shakespeare was right, if love did make the world spin about, then Alandra braced herself for a whirling ride. Love hovered just out of reach, and despite her doubts about Christopher, Alandra was prepared to grasp it firmly, to take hold of it before it darted away. She had planned just what to say to Christopher Nicholas, had practiced her well thought-out words as diligently as he had helped Abbington rehearse his lines. Tonight she would tell Christopher what was in her heart, for she knew it was the only way. If she waited too long, if too much time elapsed, she might very well lose him and that she could not bear.

The courtyard of the inn was a cacophony of sound as the entire town prepared for the play. Merchants, beggars, traders, mountebanks, peddlers, and pickpockets swarmed through the crowds.

"Ale! Wine! If you've a thirst, I can quench it!" cried out a man selling a bottle of ale.

Nicholas quickly gave the man three pennies in exchange for a cup. Though he pretended it was to quench his thirst, he knew that his true intent was to give himself an extra bit of courage and to relax his frazzled nerves.

"Oranges, apples, nuts! This way, this way. Get them in time for the performance." As the voice called out, Nicholas winced, remembering Murray's warning. How glad he was not to be at these oafs' mercy. Heaven help the others if they displeased this boisterous gathering. Oh, how he would loathe being their target.

"Sausages! Hot sausages!"

The cry of this seller reminded Nicholas of his hunger, and he bought a long sausage which he ate as he gave his horse to the hostler. He proceeded to the area where the stage was being hastily erected by hired carpenters. It was an improvised platform at the north end of the innyard, situated so that the inn's fixed gallery might also be used as a stage.

Nicholas remembered Murray's explanation of lordlings, middlings, and groundlings, and looked up at the balcony where the obviously wealthier patrons and citizens would watch the comedy from the comfort and shelter of the building's overhang. Were an untimely rainshower to occur, they would be well protected. The actors and groundlings were not as fortunate, he thought with a wry smile. A sudden rain could mean ruin for the costumes. The starch in the ruffs would dissolve and leave them but a limp rag around their necks. Looking up at the sky, he scanned the bright blue expanse for any sign of clouds and gave a sign of relief to see that there were none.

"It will be a bit hectic and disorderly without a proper tiring house in which to change your costumes," Shakespeare was saying to the actors as he stood near the stage. He also searched the heavens for sight of an impending storm. "But you will soon become accustomed to the inconvenience. I've ordered a small curtained area to be built at the back of the stage. It should do for our purposes."

Nicholas barely heard the playwright's words, for a painfully familiar voice could be heard above the noise and the chatter in the courtyard, a woman's voice, high and shrill.

"Oh, Cecil! Cecil, you have been such a comfort. Though not even this entertainment can soothe my shattered heart. I fear I may never laugh again. To have been widowed at my young age is utterly devastating! Surely Elizabeth must realize the grief I feel. I am not the monster she thinks I am."

Nicholas's gaze was drawn to the prattling woman, afraid to believe his eyes. Dressed in a gown of mourning black, her golden hair shimmering in the sun, stood Morgana Woodcliff. Positioned by Lord Burghley's side, she was scanning the unruly crowd, at last resting her eyes upon him.

Chapter Twenty-Three

Alandra glimpsed the look that passed between Christopher and the blond beauty, and for a moment her heart stopped. It was her! Here! The Widow Woodcliff. It could be no twist of fate, no coincidence that the woman was here. For all his talk of wanting to protect Alandra Christopher had blatantly lied. He had obviously sent a message and told the woman he was with the company and where to meet him. But, Alandra wondered, when could he have sent the message and who had delivered it? Her first suspicions about why he had lied to her father were right after all. He and this shrew were partners in the crime, and now had come the perfect time for them to seek each other out.

A sudden memory of what the fair-haired lady had mumbled that eve of the masque came again to Alandra's mind. It reverberated in her ears as clearly as if the woman was just now revealing it. "I will yet be the victor, and Sir Nicholas Leighton is just the man I need to do my bidding."

Do her bidding! Had he? Was Christopher, nay Nicholas Leighton, a man so possessed by love and lust that he had murdered a man because of it?

Of course! It was all so clear to Alandra now. This woman had planned it all and Christopher had executed it.

Curiosity got the best of Alandra. She had to know what was being planned. Without any heed to her father's cries, Alandra jumped down off the play wagon and ran to the second-floor balcony where the white-haired nobleman and the beautiful lady were cozily sheltered. Ignoring propriety, she wrapped her skirt around her legs and climbed up the pole of the gallery. She sat within hearing of the woman and her old companion, just out of sight of their vision.

"That man fascinates me, Cecil. Look there."

As if she didn't know who Christopher, nay Nicholas was, Alandra thought with a sneer.

"Where?" The man's deep cough punctuating his question hinted that he was ill.

"The one who glanced up here briefly then quickly looked away, as quickly as if I had shown him my disfavor. The one clothed in blue. Do you know who he is?"

"My eyes are not what they used to be. God's blood, woman, how am I supposed to see from here?" The voice was gruff with annoyance.

Alandra heard the wood of the balcony creak and supposed the man was leaning over the railing to get a better view. *I hope he recognizes Christopher,* Alandra thought. *Recognizes him and drags him away. That would serve him right. It would serve them both right, conspirators that they are.*

"I know most of the actors. Lord Hunsdon, as you know, the first one that is, was a very good friend of mine. Extremely choleric by nature, you know. Obsessed by swearing. Could be extremely tactless. No courtier, but the queen loved him. He was her cousin, you know," the old man was mumbling. "Faithful to his friends and servants. 'Twas the burden of the Lord Chamberlain which caused his untimely death though ..."

"I don't care about all that, Cecil!" The shrill feminine voice reverberated with impatience. "Do you know that actor? That is all I care about."

Again she pretends not to know who Christopher is, Alandra thought, sniffing disdainfully at the woman's foolishness.

"Ho! I recognize Burbage. 'Tis his beard that gives him away. He is quite the painter you know, in addition to being a fine actor. Painted a portrait of my granddaughter. See there, the one dressed in black hosen and black-and-gold doublet made up to look like an angel with those wings." He laughed. "And Kempe, a goodly fellow. Might have been a jester if he had lived in times past. Dances a splendid jig. He's acknowledging us by taking off his hat. And there's Condel, Heminges and Sly ..."

"Cecil! Stop chattering so. I don't care about them. I want to know about the actor in blue!"

"The one standing next to Shakespeare?"

"Yes! Yes, that one."

There was a pause, and Alandra thought she would burst from anticipation. Now she knew what the game was. The blond witch was testing the old man to see if he recognized Christopher. It was part of her lethal game.

"I've never seen him before. Don't remember any auburn-haired gentlemen among the players. Must be new." There was another long silence before he asked, "Why? What is your interest in the man? You are, as you have so recently told me, in mourning, Morgana."

"I like the way he moves. His strength, his grace. 'Tis all! I would like to meet him. And the other actors as well," she hastily added.

"Then it can be arranged. I know the young Lord Hunsdon. I will offer up an invitation as soon as the performance has ended for all of us to sup in the inn tonight." Another long pause. "But I urge you to use caution with the actor. If Elizabeth hears of any indiscretion, she will be most unforgiving. There are those who will be ever watchful of you and will look upon any unseemly manner with a most discerning eye."

Alandra had heard enough to be forewarned. Sliding back down the pillar to the ground, she cursed the wanton lady beneath her breath. The man-hungry bitch! But Alandra was determined to undermine what the woman had planned. As soon as the performance was over late this afternoon, Alandra would seek Christopher out and invite him to her own chamber. Somehow, some way, she would keep him occupied, to make certain he was not given the chance to fly to the glittering noblewoman's arms. No matter what she needed to do, Alandra knew she must keep him entertained in her room until Shakespeare could signal her that all was safe. She would have to tell Will now all that she knew about Christopher. Oh, he'd not be running off. Not this time. Never with *her*!

The shrill blast of a trumpet put a stop to her pondering as she realized the horns and drums were announcing the start up the play. From his place amidst the groundlings, Murray was frantically waving her to his side.

"Alandra! Alandra! What be you about, girl? Hurry. Hurry. The play is about to begin. I need your help."

Everyone was running about in fact. Something had happened, something that had the entire company up in arms.

"Abbington has eloped with a tavern wench!" William Kempe, cried out. "Ran away he did this very morning. That's why he wasn't in the parade." His ribald laughter drew a stern look from Heminges which quickly silenced him.

"Ran away?" Murray's eyebrows shot up, and it was obvious that far from being disconcerted he was delighted. "Not to worry, lads. Christopher here is prompter, he practically knows the whole play. He can do it!"

"Christopher will have his chance," Heminges agreed, and his pronouncement was resoundingly echoed by the others actors.

Nicholas was thunderstruck, at a loss to think of any words he might say to change their minds as his worst nightmare came true. Take Abbington's place. Never! Before he could even open his mouth, however, he was being pushed toward the stage. No, it couldn't be. He thought of hiding, waiting out the performance.

But Murray was having none of that. "Christopher has studied with the greatest actor of our day. It's time he had a chance to prove himself. Come. Come."

Nicholas looked frantically around for Shakespeare but he was nowhere in sight. But Alandra! She would do something to save the day. She didn't want him on that stage any more than he wanted to be up there.

"Alandra!" Nicholas cried. He waited for her protest, but it didn't come.

Alandra was angry enough to see him burn in hell, but perhaps, she thought, this was nearly as good.

Nicholas felt as if his neck were already in the noose. "But—but who will aid the actors with their lines?" The prompter was always harried, preoccupied with assuring that the actors came on in proper order, that their properties were at hand, and that the scenery, pulleys, and trap doors worked.

"Don't worry, I'll do that. Just give a great perfor-

mance, Christopher," Alandra said with a forced
smile. "And, oh, Christopher," she said as he was being
led away. "Good luck!" To wish an actor that was the
ultimate wish that he would have just the opposite,
as well she knew.

Anxiously, Alandra took her place behind the curtain at the rear of the stage where she could shout out
the lines as needed. Oh, how she relished the chance
to watch him make a fool of himself. He would cause
a minor if not major uproar among the groundlings.
Conceited, philandering, roguish liar that he was, his
bubble would soon burst.

The play opened in the palace of Theseus, Duke of
Athens, and Alandra watched as John Lowin entered
from the left side of the tiring-room curtain to say his
lines.

Espousing his longing to enjoy his wedding night
with the queen of the Amazons, to be held on the first
night of the new moon, Theseus proclaimed how difficult the waiting was to be. Not half as difficult as it
was going to be for her to concentrate on the play,
Alandra thought, even now lapsing into thoughts of
what Christopher had done. He had cruelly murdered
a poor old man so that he could have that man's wife.
Involuntarily, her eyes strayed to the object of her
thoughts, and Christopher returned her stare with a
bewildered look of his own. Yet much to her disquiet
he seemed to trust her. Well, that was his mistake. She
had trusted him, too, and where had it gotten her?

It seemed Demetrius's entrance came all too
quickly. Nicholas felt his legs go weak as he stepped
upon the stage with two young actors and Shakespeare
who had suddenly appeared. Somehow, Nicholas's
limbs, though quaking, supported him, and he found
himself shouting out the lines he remembered reading.

"Relent, sweet Hermia; and Lysander, yield." He
felt hands on his shoulders, turning him toward the

audience to declare with outstretched hands, "Thy crazed title to my certain right."

Alandra stifled a laugh. Christopher was having the devil's own time, just as she knew he would. And yet as the play progressed, her jealousy and anger softened. She couldn't let Christopher ruin Will's play because she was peeved. Moreover, if he was exposed as a fraud, there could be a nasty scene. She had already put the players in peril by keeping secret about the fugitive in their midst, to cast caution totally to the winds was insanity. Despite everything that had happened, she owed it to the others to give Christopher professional aid. Acting as his lifeline, she carefully and diligently led him through the rest of his performance.

Nicholas was astounded that he didn't just sink through the stage. The play, however, did in fact run surprisingly smoothly, despite his inexperience. Having carefully watched the actors had helped him, and luckily, Demetrius had very few lines.

Nicholas too thanked God for the wig atop his head and the makeup Murray had hasily spread over his face. Having been certain he would be set upon the moment he stepped upon the stage, he began to relax, though he could not help but be annoyed at the constantly chattering crowd. He looked out to see five sailors sprawled indolently across the benches, playing at cards. Two young apprentices seemed more intent on ogling the wenches than in watching the play. All in all it was a most discourteous throng who seemed to think it their privilege to shout out comments to the actors as if they imagined themselves to be part of the dramatics. This nut-cracking, card-playing, ale-swilling noisy group of men and women.

Ducking behind the curtains after leaving the stage, Nicholas dared his first look at Morgana since he had seen her. She was chattering avidly to Lord Burghley at her side, fluttering her fan furiously in an attempt to cool herself from the heat of the midafternoon sun. Had she recognized him? Had Burghley? Remembering Burghley was half-blind, he felt relieved.

As to Morgana, Nicholas knew he would soon find out, for if she had, she would seek him out at his room in the inn. Did he want her to? He wasn't certain. Truly, she was a beautiful sight and even now stirred his desire, yet he could not forget that she had so easily deserted him when he had needed her most. Morgana had thought only of herself and the danger of being caught at the inn with him. If he saw her, could he convince her to testify in his behalf, or would she be afraid to let the queen know she had been an eye-witness?

His uncertainty troubled him. He could not take a chance on being betrayed. Morgana...How different she was from Alandra. He could never for a moment imagine the noblewoman doing as Alandra had done to help him escape. Though she was comely, Nicholas suddenly thought that Morgana's prettiness did not go beyond her face.

Morgana aroused his lust but not his love. It was his manhood that responded to her and not his heart. What then did he feel for Alandra? It was a question that plagued him, though he realized he must push it from his mind and concentrate upon his lines. If in some way he could stumble his way through this, he would be forever thankful to God!

The scene changed to nighttime in the woods near Athens, subtly suggested by Murray's wooden and paste trees and a large yellow moon which hung from the gallery of the inn midway between the rafters and the top of the tiring house. It was a play within a play, for the Athenian workmen—Bottom, Snout, Snug, and the others—practiced their own play in the forest in hope of winning the duke's favor by their performance.

Remembering Shakespeare's declaration of how he had patterned these characters after the groundlings, Nicholas could not suppress a chuckle, for William Sly, as Bottom, mimicked their gestures and mannerisms to perfection.

Most actors were musically inclined and could play instruments. During the scene with Oberon and Titania, the king and queen of the fairies played upon their instruments to add a sense of atmosphere. As he took his place on stage, Nicholas was all thumbs, his singing voice as melodious as a croaking frog, yet he managed to fit in amongst the actors reasonably well. As the play unfolded, his nervousness evaporated.

Nicholas did in fact become a bit too sure of himself as the play progressed, and that quickly brought about his downfall. He forgot a line, and the hooting and booing from the groundlings did not help him regain his composure. Nor did the gratuitous contribution of several apple cores thrown upon the stage assist his memory. In fact, his loss of temper nearly made him lose his reason entirely. How dare they!

"Lysander! Speak again, thou runaway, thou coward, art thou fled?" Alandra's oh-so welcome voice called forth the line, and Nicholas quickly repeated it, his memory restored at least for the moment.

Then Nicholas choked on another important line, when Morgana blew him a kiss from the gallery as he looked her way. He felt of a certainty now that she knew him and could not help wondering if she would reveal his identity to Lord Burghley despite the danger to her. Only by the greatest self-discipline was he able to put aside his worry and speak his closing lines of the play.

Bowing low before the crowd, the actors received their applause. When Nicholas raised his head to look at Morgana one last time, he was unnerved to see that she and Lord Burghley were no longer in their seats.

As he stood with the other actors near the stage, he learned of the invitation extended to the actors to sup with the aging queen's former councilor and the newly widowed lady. Somehow the summons boded ill, and he could not help wonder if he were walking into another trap. Or perhaps Morgana again had it in mind to run away to Scotland with him. Would he go now that she was free? Immediately, he answered no as his eyes beheld the smiling countenance of the impishly pretty dark-haired, dark-eyed young woman coming toward him.

"Christopher, you were wonderful. You surpassed all my expectations!" For the moment Alandra was caught up in the actors' jovial mood. "With the exception of a few muffled lines."

"Which you nonetheless spoke out very clearly when all was said and done," Murray said, steadfast in his loyalty and thus overlooking Nicholas's many flaws. "I am most proud of you."

It was difficult for Alandra to pretend feelings which were at odds with her true emotions, but she gave it her very best try. Without his knowing it, Christopher was being tested tonight. If he came to her room, then he was most likely innocent. If he went running off to meet Morgana Woodcliff, then there was a good chance that he was not. It was as simple as that in her mind.

Without a thought to the actors standing about, she threw her arms around Nicholas. In that moment he forgot all about Morgana as he basked in the warmth and glow of Alandra's affection and praise. Was there any woman like her? Curious as a cat, mischievous as a monkey, graceful as a swan, as unpredictable as any woman could be. She tugged at his heart.

How could he tell her no when she asked him to dine with her later in her room for a quiet celebration? Just the two of them. The little minx had saved his hide,

not once but several times. And if she had forgotten
to prompt him on some of his lines tonight, he brushed
it off as being due to the excitement of the first night's
performance. Nicholas could not help thinking that
perhaps her room would be the safest place for him,
at least until he discovered what Morgana was up to.
Casting a glance over his shoulder, he followed the
others into the inn.

Chapter Twenty-Four

Alandra couldn't have been more apprehensive, than if she had an appointment with the hangman. The time had come for her to reveal to Shakespeare what she knew about the man masquarading among them. Worse yet, she would have to tell him that she knew all along that Christopher Nicholas was an imposter. She had known, and yet blatantly gone along with the lie and in so doing had risked the theater company's well-being. Betraying Will's friendship, she had entered into a deceit nearly as abominable as Christopher's.

Taking a deep breath, she knocked on Will's door. He opened it immediately, and she could tell from the expression on his face that he had been expecting her.

"Come in, Alandra." Though he seemed in a remarkably pleasant mood considering Christopher's flawed performance, his eyes were hard. "I was expecting you."

Alandra wished that she could read Shakespeare's mind. Usually, the playwright had mobile, flexible features perfect for acting and eyes that revealed his emotions, but he was maintaining complete control of his expressions so that his thoughts were unreadable now.

"I—I have something to tell you, Will. Something I should have told you before." Alandra swallowed hard. Being with the players was the only life she had ever known. Now, if that was his decision, Shakespeare could cast her out with but a word.

"About your friend, Christopher Nicholas." He poured her a small glass of whiskey. "I think you might need this."

She refused at first, but suddenly needing fortification, put her hands on the glass and guided it to her mouth. She swallowed once and choked on the harsh, fiery liquor.

Shakespeare shook his head. "Ah, Alandra. Alandra..."

Alandra caught her breath, staring as he filled a glass for himself. "He's n–n–not who he says he—he is..." she stammered, making her confession.

"Aye, I know! He all too soon gave himself away."

The eyes watching her were unreadable, yet at least he didn't show anger.

"You know?" She was startled by his revelation.

"And have for some time." His expression was carefully controlled.

"But you didn't say a thing!" Alandra thought to herself that she should have known a man like Will, one with such deep roots in the theater, couldn't be tricked into believing Christopher Nicholas's story.

"I didn't say anything because I wanted to see just what he was about. I was curious as to why he would pretend to be something that he wasn't." He took a drink of his whiskey in long, measured gulps.

"You thought it was some kind of game..." Alandra

cast her eyes down to her shoes. Will had known, but never supposed it was as serious a matter as it was.

"He did not rescue you, did he, Alandra?"

"No!"

"I thought not. Would you care to tell me the real story? I have a feeling that you are fairly bursting to talk to someone." He settled his thin, long-legged frame into a chair.

"He took your horse, Will. Stole it! I followed after him. It is as simple a tale as that." She frowned as she related the story of their clamorous late-night meeting, of his determination to take her with him, of his near capture in Bodiam, and their clever ruse to escape the borders of that town.

"At first I was little more than his prisoner, but later on when he was in the direst trouble I helped him of my own free will. I had come to believe his lies, and that he might be innocent you see. And I had to save him. I could not let him be imprisoned for a crime he said he did not commit!"

"And just what was that crime, Alandra? I have a feeling it was something that cannot be easily righted." His eyes entreated her to confide in him.

There had never been any secrets between Alandra and Will. Since she was a little girl she had told him everything and he had given her his advice. She would have trusted him with her life. How then had she so woefully betrayed him?

Reaching inside her bodice, Alandra retrieved the handbill she had purposefully tucked away again. She placed it in Shakespeare's hand. "This will tell you all. Christopher Nicholas is Sir Nicholas Leighton, wanted by the queen and God knows who else for the murder of Lord Woodcliff, one of Elizabeth's advisors."

Shakespeare's eyebrows shot up as he read the

broadside. "I sensed him to be a fugitive, but not anything like this!"

"I was suspicious of him, right from the first. I saw him at court, you see, and knew him to be a nobleman. I tried to tell my father but for some reason he refused to believe me. He likes Christopher."

"And Murray is at heart a kind old soul."

"Father and I were at the inn. In trying to get away from Lord Stafford's men, Christopher, or Nicholas, hid out in our play wagon. I hit him over the head, and when he woke up, he said he was an actor." She laughed bitterly. "Actor. Ha! He proved today that he is not."

Will crossed his legs. "Actually, his voice is of a soothing timbre, his pronunciation sharp and well defined. Being a nobleman, he has been gifted with a certain grace of movement and stately carriage. Were we to teach him how to make use of these attributes—"

"Will! He's wanted for murder!" Surely Shakespeare wasn't saying he could stay. Besides, Alandra didn't want him to. Not now. Not after seeing that Woodcliff woman!

Shakespeare pulled at his gold earring. "So he is!" His eyebrows furled. "And that does make it a most serious matter."

Alandra's tone was scornful. "I believed him. I believed him when he said he might have killed that old man in the heat of combat because I wanted to believe him."

Will studied the broadside intently again. "And how do you know that he wasn't telling the truth?"

"Because—Because that—that woman was here in the audience tonight. Lord Woodcliff's wife, the one Christopher was having an affair with. It was the scandal of the court!" She couldn't keep the jealousy out of her voice. "No doubt they were co-conspirators and plan to fly off together."

"Ah, so I see. Because she is here, you suddenly choose to see Christopher as a villain. But what if he is not? Then you greatly wrong him."

Clutching her hand to her breast, she closed her eyes. "Oh, how I wish I knew for sure! The uncertainty is tearing me apart. There are times when I truly think him innocent and again times when something in his look makes me doubt it."

Shakespeare clucked his tongue, and in that moment Alandra knew that she could fool anyone in the world, but not him. He could read her feelings for Christopher like an open book.

"Do you care so very much for him?" Will's piercing eyes bored into hers.

"I do. Fool that I am. But how can I care for a man who would do such a thing to another?"

"Even the greatest scoundrels have those who love them." Shakespeare shrugged. "Besides, things are not always what they seem, Alandra. The gallows are full of men who are innocent."

"He's not!" But even now she wished with all her heart that he was. Even if he ran away with that woman, she didn't want to see him executed for murder. Not Christopher.

"This broadside declares him to be a nobleman, Alandra. That changes a great many things." His voice was soft. "I have no need to ask if you love him. Your eyes tell the tale."

"Oh, Will! I lost my heart when he kissed me." Twisting and turning her sleeve, Alandra unconsciously tied it in a knot. Realizing her mistake, she hurried to undo her mischief. "But what does it matter? After today, knowing what you know . . ."

Though Will usually nourished her fantasies, his voice was stern now. "I will not lie to you. His traveling among us is risky. And were I to find out that he has done what is proclaimed, I would not hesitate to turn him in. But somehow my instinct—and I believe that I know people well—is that there is more to this matter of Lord Woodcliff than is being spoken. And if there is the slightest chance that Christopher is innocent, I would move heaven and earth to help him."

"But the queen!"

"Would likewise want to know the truth. I have no fear of her. She is basically kind and merciful and mingles tenderness with her blows."

Alandra could hardly believe her ears. Here she had been so certain that Will would be furious and now he was saying that he would shield Christopher.

"But as to your affections, I would not see you risk a broken heart. Mine was broken once long ago and I still feel the pain." He reached up and touched his chest as if something inside tormented him. "Be careful, Alandra. I am certain he is a gentleman, that he would have no intent of hurting you, but the lords and ladies of the realm can often be like selfish children, playing with hearts as if they were toys, then cruelly casting them aside."

"I know." Alandra sighed. "I've told myself a hundred times just what you speak of, but every time we are together, my heart outwits my head and I find myself longing for his touch. I want to taste of paradise, if only once."

"As did I once . . ." Sadly, he shook his head. "But as to the matter of your young man, what are we to do?"

"I've invited him to dine with me tonight, to test him you see." Angrily, she stamped her foot. "Oh, I hate feeling so confused. Perhaps I would be better off if he did run away with her, then at least I would be quit of him."

"And be of little use to us because of your pining."

Shakespeare tugged a lock of her hair. "I wish I had fairy magic to aid you. Were I Oberon, I would bid Puck to sprinkle magic flower juice in yon lord's eyes so that he would return your love." He paused, adding hopefully, "But perhaps after all such artifice will not be needed. You are delightfully pleasing to the eye, Alandra. If given the chance, perhaps true love will come about and you will find him to be the perfect prince you at first thought he was. Then you will have your handsome nobleman."

Alandra had been taught to believe in happy endings, and Shakespeare nearly made her believe that her handsome nobleman would have his good name restored, would return to his castle in Bodiam and would take her with him. It had to happen that way, she told herself. All her dreams had to come true.

She sat on the arm of her chair as she and Will conspired.

Chapter Twenty-Five

The flames in the wall sconces had burned down before Alandra heard footsteps outside her door. She had begun to believe that he would not come, and her spirits had plummeted as visions of Christopher and the golden-haired lady had danced inside her head. A mixture of jealousy and apprehension had filled her, a fear that she might never see him again, that willingly or not he had ridden off with that tantalizing creature.

"Alandra! Alandra!"

The sound of knocking accompanied Christopher's voice, scattering all her fears. Casting a quick glance at her reflection in the mirror, Alandra tried to still her trembling hands. Now that the moment was at hand, she was assailed with nervousness, wondering if she would have the fortitude to do and say what she had planned.

"Alandra, are you in there?" His voice was sharp

with impatience. "Open the door. Don't play coy with me, lass, I'm nigh onto starving."

Without further hesitation, she opened the door. "Then by all means, sir, enter."

She gestured with a wide sweep of her hand toward the feast spread out upon the table; roast swan in orange sauce stuffed with almond dressing; pigeon pie; plates of steaming vegetables seasoned with herbs; a small loaf of bread; and an assortment of fruit—apples, plums, and pears. Two empty glasses seemed to be awaiting the bottle of wine that Nicholas had brought with him. Pushing quickly into the room, he soon had them filled.

"My lovely young prompter, you certainly saved my skin today." Handing her a glass, he grinned. "To the Lord Chamberlain's men and to us." He clinked his goblet against hers in a toast.

Alandra's voice was soft, but she looked him in the eye. "To the Lord Chamberlain's men and to you, Christopher."

"I was apprehensive about how I had done but Will Kempe, Lowin, Sly, and even Burbage congratulated me on my fine performance. It seems I have proved myself as an actor." He suddenly roared with laughter. "The two young actors who played Helena and Hermia have even asked me if I would coach *them*. They said 'twas obvious that I had studied with Edward Alleyn and wanted the chance to benefit from my experience. What a fine jest that is!"

Alandra did not join in his laughter, fearful Christopher's ego would be inflated to the danger point. He had somehow managed to avert a total disaster, but he was far from being a good actor.

"Do not get too puffed up with pride," she admonished. "You were lucky this time. Next time it might be different!"

Nicholas's amusement sobered. "Your friend, Will, had words of caution for me, too, but he did say that he thinks me to be a natural at acting, despite the mistakes I made today. And any word of praise from him is a welcome boon." He ran his hand over his clothing. "As a matter of fact, 'twas Will who lent me this fine array of garments, knowing I had none of my own." He slowly turned around so that she could admire his clothes. "He is much longer of leg than I and slimmer in the shoulders, but it is by half a goodly fit, and I am beholding to him for his kindness."

Alandra let her eyes appraise him. The candle and torchlight emphasized the planes of his chiseled features, the mystifying depths of his gray eyes. In Will's black satin doublet and matching knee-length breeches, he made a dashing figure, though she suspected Will's true purpose in giving him these garments had been to ascertain that he would blend with the others in the company and not draw undue attention to himself.

"Will has ever been a most generous man and one with whom I would trust my life. He also seeks to be your friend." Alandra took three long gulps of her wine, letting it warm her.

"Then from this day forward it is friend he shall be."

Crossing his arms, putting one foot up on a large stone of the hearth, he freely gazed at her, comparing her in his mind to Morgana. She looked especially pretty tonight. Her gown of thin gray wool with a yoke of white pleated lawn dipped in a v, exposing just a teasing view of her breasts. Her hair was also different, he noted, drawn atop her head in a style that was currently fashionable at court. It emphasized her long, slim neck and the perfection of her features. The open, standing collar and farthingale of her dress had been copied from the noblewomen.

He's staring at me, Alandra thought, *as if my nose has suddenly turned upside down*. Yet there was a gleam in the depths of his eyes. Oh, but she wanted him to think that she was pretty.

"Shall we eat, Christopher?" Walking across the room as gracefully as she could, she took a seat at the small, round table.

"Eat?" For just a moment he was dazed, but he quickly recovered and remembered his manners. "As you wish, my lady." With a slight bow, he sat in the chair opposite her.

Ah, what a beauty she would be dressed in the finery of Queen Bess's hall, he thought. She could well rival any woman there, even Morgana. Her eyes alone threatened to enchant any man who gazed too long into their depths. Yet she was totally unaware of her own loveliness and this added immensely to her charm. Pray God, she never grew whining and conceited like some of her sex whom he had known. A troublesome lot.

He looked away from her to concentrate upon the food so appetizingly placed before him. Although he was hungry, he hardly tasted the delicacies that passed his lips. He was just too fascinated with her.

A cocoon of enchantment enclosed them and as if they moved in slow motion, they noted tiny details about each other—gestures, expressions, posture, even sighs. The room was strangely silent as the meal continued. Both Nicholas and Alandra were ill at ease, floundering for something to say, vitally aware of each other in the dimly lit chamber.

Nicholas abruptly stood up and walked to the fireplace to start a fire, not because it was chilly but for something to do. He watched as it flared. "Alandra ..." He shifted from foot to foot, his eyes straying to the large featherbed that loomed like an inescapable temptation. Had she been another sort of woman, she'd be lying on that mattress on her back by now.

"Yes, Christopher?" She waited expectantly, uneasy that he might have come to make a confession. Perhaps all was not as rosy as she supposed. It was true that he had come here and had thus passed her test, but the matter didn't end there.

"The food. It—it was delicious," he blurted.

He'd hardly eaten a bite. "Yes, it was..." *Oh, Christopher talk of anything but the food. Tell me how soft my skin is, or that my eyes sparkle in the firelight, or that my lips remind you of the petals of a rose.*

"I must admit that I've enjoyed my stay here at the inn. And with the actors." *And with you,* he thought but did not say.

Sitting down on the hearth stones, he stretched out his lean, muscular legs, managing to look far more at ease than he felt. He regretted having put the log on the fire, for it was suddenly getting much too hot in the room. He tugged at the ruff around his neck, wishing he could rip it off.

"And they with you." She didn't want to talk about Will and the others at all. "Christopher?" Looking at her goblet, she longed for another glass of wine, anything to give her courage. "I can never find the words to tell you how much I've enjoyed the time we've spent together..."

Nicholas was discomfited to find himself wanting to kiss her, to hold her. Though he fought his desire for her, he could not help but think of how she had felt in his arms, how soft her mouth had been when he had kissed her before. He was drawn to her like a moth to candlelight.

"And now we are together again. Alone." He returned to the table and tried to finish his food, but he just couldn't eat.

"Alone," she whispered.

Their eyes met and held, conveying a silent message.

It was Nicholas who looked away. Dragging his fingers through his hair, he frowned. "I—I must leave now that we have supped!" he said a bit too sharply, feeling the sudden need to get away. Though they had often been alone in the wagon, there had been others close by. Now they were totally isolated within this room and that knowledge was too enticing.

"Leave? So soon?" Alandra's disappointment showed in her eyes. Was he going to *her* then?

"We'll be doing *King John* in Rye and I thought to get an early start on reading the play." He was uncomfortable in his lie.

"Bring the pages here."

He shook his head. Shoving his half-empty plate away, he stood up, deciding to tell her the truth. "No, that's not true. You're just too tempting, Alandra. The truth is that all this time I've been struggling with the fact that I desire you. Very much."

His forthrightness stunned her, and she dropped her spoon.

"Being here alone with you like this brings out my carnal nature, I fear." He headed for the door but paused to look back at her. "I realize how difficult it would be to stop with a kiss."

"Perhaps I wouldn't want you to stop, Christopher." There, she had said it. The truth was out, and she was relieved that she had spoken what was in her heart. "I keep thinking of the rainstorm and the way you held me close. I liked it when your lips touched mine. I want you to kiss me again." She paused, waiting for his response, then rambled on. "If that is a brazen thing to say, then I am sorry. But truth is truth."

Her honesty was like a fresh summer breeze bringing a smile to his lips. "Then it seems we are both of like mind. What then are we to do?"

In the fathomless depths of his eyes, she saw a stirring of passion that drew her to him. Slowly, she walked across the room.

She stroked his arm, and her touch was his undoing. All the passion he had kept so carefully controlled now burst forth. Compulsively, he moved close to her. His fingers traced along the line of her jaw, the contours of her face, then lightly he touched her lips.

"God's blood, lass, what you do to me."

Her head whirled in a dizzying awareness of him as he captured her slender shoulders in his hands and drew her close against his chest. The length of his hard, muscular body felt hot against her own as he lowered his head to press his lips to hers. His kiss took her breath away. It was infinitely more pleasing than she had remembered. His tongue touching hers tasted of the wine they had sipped. Returning his kiss with unrestrained abandon, she felt desire spread languidly through her body. It worked its way up from her knees to the top of her head. A warm, tingling feeling. She did not want him to stop, but wanted this to be the moment she had dreamed about.

Anxiously, she waited to see what was to come. Moonlight and kisses was all she knew of love, though she was aware there was much more to it than that. As a child she had listened to the actors' ribald stories when they thought she was abed, yet hearing about lovemaking and experiencing it were not the same at all. Definitely not!

Nicholas's kiss went far beyond a mere touching of lips. His tongue searched the contours of her mouth in a gentle, exploring caress that intensified her newly found passion. Hesitantly at first, then with an increasing measure of boldness, she mimicked the gentle exploration of his lips and tongue, helpless against the powerful tide of passion that consumed her, a quivering sensation that shot through her body as she felt his hand slide down to cup her breast.

How long he kissed her, she did not know, having lost all knowledge of time. Her world was in his arms, his nearness her only reality. Wrapping her arms around him, she ardently embraced him, pushing away her modesty, her fear, as her senses clamored for him. His kisses. How she liked his kisses.

Lifting his mouth from hers, Nicholas stared down into her flushed face, his breath coming quickly between his parted lips. He was totally ruled by his emotions, having the devil's own time resisting the temptation she presented. For all her tender years, she was most definitely a woman, one who affected him as few women ever had. She was warm and responsive in his arms, yet her eyes held the look of trusting innocence. He would have to be the world's most insensitive bastard to take advantage of her now.

"Christopher?" she protested softly as he drew away.

"I told you that I would not be satisfied with kisses," he said harshly.

"I know..."

"I am a man, Alandra, not a beardless boy. What I'm thinking now might shock you, for my words of love are not for a maiden's ears." He gently touched a stray curl. She was so damnably young! "I doubt you know much of passion."

"I know what I feel when you kiss me, touch me," she breathed, more than slightly piqued that he might think of her as too naive. "I know quite well what it is you want to do. I'm not a child."

Her lashes dropped to veil her eyes in a manner he found to be most beguiling.

"What you want is what I want, too. I want you to change me from a maiden to a woman." Could she have put it to him more straightforward than that?

The heat of his body was steadily climbing. Nicholas swallowed, trying to calm himself. "Alandra, lass, you cannot realize the whole of it. I want to take off your clothes, to touch you, learn every secret of your body. I want to caress your breasts, to feel the warmth of your hands touching me." He pulled her up against him, showing her what male arousal felt like and he felt her shiver. "I want to be so deeply sheathed in your softness that we are like one being. That's what I want at this moment, but I will not take your virtue." He took a step back. "That's a gift for the man you love."

"I could love *you*! I was attracted to you the first moment I saw you. But then, I was afraid."

"And well you should have been and should be now." His protectiveness resurfaced, warring with his desire. "I can only hurt you, Alandra."

She didn't speak, but merely wound her arms around his neck to pull his mouth to hers in another kiss, a kiss that deepened as he carried her to the bed. Gently, without disrupting their kiss, he lowered her to the soft feather mattress, then positioned himself beside her. Desire was like a fever, and she reveled in the sensations flooding her body. At last her dreams were going to come true. Christopher was going to make love to her.

Nicholas knew he should halt this insanity, but passion alone was ruling him, an ever-growing ache that would not abate without fulfillment. He was a man, not a saint, and she was so incredibly sweet. What would she feel like beneath his questing hands, naked and writhing? He had to know.

"Alandra. Sweet, sweet Alandra."

Compulsively, his hand closed over her breast to begin a slow, leisurely exploration. Gently tugging at her dress, he bared first one breast then the other, smiling at her sudden movement to cover her exposed flesh. For all her attempt at seduction, she was after all a modest young thing, yet instead of cooling his desire, her shyness fired him to a passion he had hitherto never felt.

"Do you want me to stop? It is your decision, Alandra," he whispered huskily. "I'll go no further if you tell me nay."

With the trust of a child seeking to learn to walk, she took his hand and drew it again to her breast, giving him his answer.

"Then so be it!" If this was what she wanted, then, God's blood, he would fight his feelings no more.

Dropping his head, he kissed the valley between her breasts, then caressed each soft mound with his lips and tongue, teasing the peaks until she gasped aloud. Alandra had suspected his lovemaking would be wondrous, but she found her imagination had fallen far short of the reality. Every place he touched her sparked with fire.

Nicholas's mind whirled in confusion. Despite the fact that he was experienced with women, he felt as if he were going to make love for the very first time. Indeed, he had tumbled tavern wenches, chambermaids, and women of nobility whose virtue had long ago been taken, but Alandra was his first innocent. He wanted to make what happened between them beautiful for her, but suddenly he felt apprehensive, cautioning himself not to push her too hard or too fast and break the fragile spell that was woven around them tonight.

Slowly. Move slowly, he told himself, pulling the bodice of her gown down around her waist, savoring the smooth, golden flesh that his ministrations had exposed. He was awed by the loveliness of her soft, velvet skin, the firm young breasts that rose to meet his caress. He savored the expression that chased across her face, the wanting and the passion that were so clearly revealed. Though his soul might well be damned for all eternity, he wanted to complete her initiation into womanhood. He strained at the fastenings of his doublet, anxious to remove that constricting garment. He wanted to feel the softness of her breasts against his naked chest, wanted to....

A loud knock upon the door startled Nicholas. His eyes were hooded and unreadable as he watched Alandra sit up on the bed, trying to cover her exposed breasts.

"Who is there?" she asked, cautioning Christopher to silence.

" 'Tis Will, Alandra. I wanted to tell you that all is well."

It was their signal, and Alandra swore softly. Will couldn't have picked a worse time to intrude. Nevertheless, she called out, "Thank you, Will." She waited for him to go away, fearing what he might reveal, but though she listened, she did not hear his retreating footsteps.

"His timing is atrocious! Tell him to go away," Nicholas whispered in her ear.

Teasingly, he tugged at her hands, exposing her breast. He stroked and caressed the nipples of her breasts in a motion that was exquisitely erotic, and Alandra moaned low in her throat.

"The coast is clear," Shakespeare continued, waiting for her reply.

Nicholas swore beneath his breath as Alandra thanked Shakespeare once again. He rolled her over until she was lying beneath him. Stripping off his doublet, then tearing at his shirt, he shuddered as their bare flesh touched. His lips took hers again in a hungry urgency, his breathing becoming hard and labored.

"The she-wolf has gone, Alandra."

Wrinkling his brows in a frown, Nicholas pulled away from Alandra. "What is this talk of a she-wolf?" he whispered. For a long moment he stared into her eyes.

Before Alandra had time to answer, to warn him that Christopher was still in the room, Shakespeare mumbled against the door, "I fear the lady was sorely disappointed, for I told her plainly that the handsome young man she so fancied was elsewhere occupied. Thus, she consoled herself with Burbage, who is himself a quite charming rogue, though she asked many questions. I tried my best to fully satisfy her, making up a splendid tale. Do you want to hear it?"

"Yes. *Tomorrow*, Will." She was anxious for him to go away, and loathe to have him discover the nearly naked Christopher in her room. Making love to him was one part of her plan she had not revealed to Shakespeare, though she knew he would understand. "I am already abed."

"Then good night, Alandra. Sleep well, knowing your young man to be safe, at least for the moment."

This time there was the sound of booted feet on the wooden floor as Shakespeare at last walked away.

"So that is what this is all about!"

There was a hint of anger in Christopher's voice, and Alandra could barely bring herself to look at him. How could she reveal to him her jealousy of the woman she knew he desired? Or of her certainty that they were in cahoots?

"A woman seemed dangerously interested in who you were and I feared—"

"You found out about Morgana being here."

That he could speak *her* name after what had passed between them sorely wounded Alandra. Flushing with embarrassment, she fumbled with the bodice of her gown, covering her bare breasts.

"Yes, I found out. I saw her with my own eyes and I knew I had to keep you out of her clutches." Her tone was defensive as if she had done something wrong. Uncertainly, she met his gaze. His face was cold and implacable, without even a hint of the desire once etched there.

"Her clutches?"

"I thought perhaps that you and she . . . killed him and . . . tonight was a test!" she blurted.

"A test?" Nicholas was angered that Alandra once more doubted him.

"I—I thought it to be no accident that she was in the audience."

"Well, it was!" Who was she to take it upon herself to decide whether or not he should see a woman? This episode tonight was more in keeping with Morgana's temperament than Alandra's. "And so you made certain that I was preoccupied."

"I'm no fool, Christopher." Oh, how his reaction wounded her. " 'Tis obvious to see even now how taken you are with her." He didn't deny it and that made her heart ache anew. "I—I only wanted to make certain you were careful."

She wanted to say more, anything to shatter the suddenly hostile silence that was growing between them. The words stuck in her throat.

He looked utterly disappointed. "I had thought you to be without wiles, but clearly you have played a clever game, Alandra. One which nearly cost you a great deal."

Rising from the bed, he hurriedly dressed. He reached the door in five quick strides, yet his hand paused on the latch as he turned back to look at her, frustrated by annoyance. Not at her but at himself and what he had nearly allowed himself to do, despite his vows.

"You should have told me what you were about. Why didn't you? Why this masquarade of desiring me?" he demanded angrily.

"Think what you will, Christopher," she hurried to say. "If you look into your own heart, you might be willing to admit the same could be said of you." *I still want you, that has not changed*, she thought.

He dared not look into his heart for fear of what he might discover. He was too fond of this winsome imp. He was perilously close to feeling an emotion he was unprepared to feel, thus he forced himself to turn away from her again.

His voice was gruff as he fought to hide his passion. "We will forget this ever happened, Alandra. You have my promise that I will not forget myself again, no matter how tempting the provocation. If you will not guard your virtue, then I will. I owe it to your father."

Without another word, he left the room, leaving Alandra to stare after him in dismay.

Chapter Twenty-Six

The Lord Chamberlain's Men took little time to savor their triumph in Faversham. After two more performances they moved on to Rye, a lively old walled town along the coast. The company's performance in the small medieval town was even more successful than those at Faversham, due in no small part to the fact that Christopher's presence on stage was absent, for which Nicholas was grateful.

As to his relationship with Alandra, it was fragile at best. As the players moved from town to town, Nicholas put more and more distance between himself and the stage man's daughter. Stung by her constant suspicion of him, he had made a promise to himself not to be tempted by her again. But, oh, at what a price! The threatening peril of his own contentment. Alandra Thatcher had become an obsession, no matter how vehemently he tried to deny it.

By daylight she attracted his gaze; at night she

haunted his dreams. He was taken by the wench, even
more so now that he had come so close to making love
to her. The entrancing vision of her bare breasts hovered before his eyes whether he was asleep or awake.
So beautiful. So perfect. Nicholas wouldn't have been
a bit surprised if every man in the company was able
to read his desire as plainly as the road which guided
them southward, beyond the North Downs. Dover was
the site of the famous white cliffs, yet Nicholas noticed
little of the scenery as his eyes were focused on another
splendor riding on the wagon beside her father. She
was an enchantress with the most beguiling eyes.

And an infuriating stubbornness, he thought bitterly.
Was she going to condemn him as a villain of the worst
kind every time her mind gave in to suspicion? How
was he going to convince her that he was not a devious
kind of man? A man who would coldheartedly murder
another for the sake of lust or ambition?

Anger was a barrier he hastily erected between them
to still his longings, to keep her carefully out of his
reach. And all the while the truth was he wanted
naught but to run to her, to gather her into his arms
again, to finish delightedly what they had begun.

"To take her virtue," he muttered, reminding himself once again that he was a much better man for
leaving an innocent young woman alone. A tryst between them was not meant to be. He had to accept
that and thus put Alandra out of his heart and head.

As to Morgana, Nicholas had heard the story from
Shakespeare the next morning. She had not known his
identity after all, but had merely been tempted into
wanting a dalliance with the handsome actor. Shakespeare had taken Morgana aside, had fabricated a
story that the actor in question was very happily married and at the moment enjoying a private supper with
his doting wife, one who was exceedingly jealous and
prone to violent moods. Morgana had responded by

leaving the inn after barely a half-hour's time, insisting her duty to the poor aging Lord Burghley called her away.

So much for her avowals of undying love! At first Nicholas's ego had suffered, but now he was relieved. It was over once and for all. The spell Morgana had cast on him had been broken. Nor would she ever know that her eyes had been drawn to him. He was safe from her chattering tongue, rescued by a beguiling young lady.

Alandra. He tried not to look at her, but, God's eyebrows, how she drew his eyes again and again. He relished the sight of her, and yet at the same time it caused him pain, an agony of unfulfilled longing. Never before had being honorable made him so unhappy.

If only he had not been so cleverly seduced by Morgana and proven himself to be the greatest of fools! But he had been and had lost everything because of it. He was naught but a fugitive now, a man pretending to be a struggling actor. A man who had lost control of his destiny. Once he had been the most eligible man at court, now he was nearly a pauper. A man on the run. The target of Elizabeth's anger. A man who might very well be caught and spend the rest of his life in the Tower—or worse yet be executed. Hardly the perfect prospect for a lover.

But what if he could clear his name and regain his favor at court? Become Sir Nicholas Leighton again? Instead of solving his dilemma, it only complicated the matter. The bitter truth was that he could never offer Alandra more than a scandalous union. Mistress never wife! Elizabeth would never approve of one of her noblemen marrying a young woman who had neither title nor fortune. The queen would be unrelenting in her scrutiny of any woman he chose as his bride. Alandra was, as she said, a young woman of humble origins, and thus in the end Elizabeth would rudely refuse him his wish, just as she had with her other courtiers. Alandra was too fine a woman to be put through such an indignity.

"Stay away from her! For once in your life think with your brain and not with your loins, Nicholas. For the love of God!" he whispered beneath his breath. Quickly, he looked away from Alandra, lest he be enticed from his better judgment by large brown eyes and a dimpled smile.

"Have you been to Dover before?"

"I beg your pardon?" Nicholas suddenly realized that William Kempe had ridden up beside him as he muttered to himself.

"I asked if you had ever been to Dover?"

"Never!" Why he lied, Nicholas didn't know. What harm would there have been in mentioning one previous journey? Even so, Nicholas was on his guard.

"I don't really know much about you, Christopher. You never talk about yourself," Kempe was saying now.

Nicholas stiffened. A man on the run couldn't take the chance of becoming too friendly, especially when he had to keep looking over his shoulder, fearing that someday he would be recognized and the cocoon of safety he had woven around himself would crumble.

"There isn't much to tell," Nicholas said defensively. "I'm afraid, if the truth were told, I am a very boring fellow."

"I doubt that. There is something about you that tells me you are very adventurous." Kempe seemed determined to break through the shell Nicholas had erected around himself. "That you might have even been a soldier at one time in your life. Were you?"

"Most assuredly not!" Nicholas realized he had spoken a bit too harshly. Kempe was probably only trying to further their friendship. He had no reason to be suspicious. "At least not in real life," he amended. "But I've played soldiers on the stage."

"Aha! I'm not a bit surprised. You have the strength and build to play such parts. Not like me." He rubbed his hand over his ribs. "Too thin."

They rode on for a long time before Kempe spoke again. "I'm looking forward to Dover. Aren't you?"

"Aye, I suppose." Because of his mood, it was difficult for Nicholas to sound too enthusiastic. The trip was becoming tedious, and he longed for the simple luxuries of life. Being constantly on the move was beginning to get to him.

"Dover has a regular local audience so we will have no worries of attracting a crowd there. It is always full of travelers." Kempe was obviously trying to lift Nicholas's sagging spirits. "You have a treat in store. I'll show you around. Dover has many attractions, from the great castle frowning over the town from its position high up on the clifftop to the ships riding at anchor, a reminder of the queen's victory over Spain nearly ten years ago when two galleons of the Spanish Armada were wrecked on the nearby Goodwin Sands."

"Ah, yes . . ." Nicholas remembered that victory very well, having taken part in the battle.

Looking out across the shortest route between England and the continent, it was rumored that on a clear day one could see the coast of France from atop the white cliffs. If only he could view it with Alandra at his side. Without realizing it, he turned his gaze in her direction.

"You can't keep your eyes from her."

"What?" Nicholas damned himself for being so careless as to give himself away.

"You are quite taken with her." Kempe reached out to pat him on the shoulder. "Don't be embarrassed. Certainly, the two of you would look very good together. She's a pretty and saucy young woman."

"She's not for me! She's too young and inexperienced. And I am not the marrying kind!" he said emphatically while he recalled the way she had felt in his arms. Night after night he had tossed and turned, remembering.

Kempe's grin was devilish. "Is any man truly the marrying kind?" As they passed a farmer's daughter along the way, he threw her a kiss. "Ay, but the women in Dover. I'll take you with me to one of the taverns when we get there. You'll see."

Alandra heard Kempe's words as the wagon passed by. Let Christopher go! What care she? Tavern wenches were more in keeping with his taste, were they not? As well as aristocratic shrews! She didn't care a whit what he did!

An easy thing to pretend, yet the truth was she had thought often about that night when he had caressed her. His fingers had brought forth fire wherever they had touched her, causing her body to ache with suppressed passion even at the memory. She was assailed by bitter disappointment that she and Christopher had not made love. She sensed that no other man would ever arouse within her the fierce, all-consuming emotions that he had.

Even looking at Christopher stirred her. Unable to resist glancing at him out of the corner of her eye, she noted that he had removed his doublet and had rolled up the sleeves of his white linen shirt. The cords of the neckline were loosened to reveal a wide expanse of his bare chest, tanned now by the sun. His black hair, longer than it was when first she saw him, brushed the lace of his collar as he threw back his head to look up at the sky. Alandra was overcome with the uncontrollable urge to call out to him, to flirt openly with him. Only her pride kept her from such an action. She would not go to him; he would have to come to her. That was the secret of an interesting woman, or so she had heard Will say. The unobtainable was always the most desirable.

As to his coldness toward her, she found it deplorable. He had been acting surly, angry that she had suspected him once again. To her way of thinking, he deserved no apology. She had done him no wrong in desiring him or in saving him from the clutches of that yellow-haired witch. Why then was he acting like such a cur?

"Alandra! Keep the wagon on the road!"

Murray's screech alerted her, and pulling at the reins, she guided the horses back to the center of the path.

"Alandra. Girl!"

Murray's face was grimaced in a familiar expression. It meant he was about to give her a lecture. She was all too aware of his scrutiny as he climbed through the curtained opening to sit beside her.

"I'm sorry, Father. The sun was in my eyes."

Murray cocked his head. "The sun or Christopher Nicholas's face?"

She opened her mouth to protest but thought better of it. Murray could read her like an open book.

"Speaking of Christopher, what is wrong between you? He doesn't hover around you anymore." His tone was that of the utmost disappointment.

"Nothing is wrong. I just think it's time he got along on his own. After all, he did study with one of the greatest actors."

Murray took off his hat and wiped his forehead. "Yes. Yes! I suppose so."

Alandra sought hastily to change the subject. "*King John* was a most appropriate drama to choose for England's southlands, don't you agree? Will told me the Magna Carta was signed at Runnymede in Surrey."

Murray was not to be so easily distracted. He got right back to the subject he wanted to talk about. "He is a strong man, a fine man, one suitable in every way for you, Alandra. I had feared you'd never meet your match, a man worthy of you. I was just certain no man would be able to curb your willfulness, but the moment I first laid eyes upon him, I knew. I knew he was the one!" He nudged her in the ribs. "And you were taken with him, too. Admit it!"

"All right, I was. To tell you nay would make a liar of me, but—"

"It's time you found a husband, girl. With little dowry I had cause to worry, but an actor is a perfect choice. I will but give him my share in the acting company in lieu of money. 'Twill be perfect. Perfect." He chuckled at the brilliance of his carefully thought-out plan.

Murray's laughter brought only a frown from Alandra. If only her father knew the truth, he would have no cause for humor. Christopher Nicholas was a nobleman who would want much more by way of a dowry than a poor stage man could ever offer. Worse yet, he was a nobleman on the run.

"Please, Father, let's have no talk of marriage. It is unseemly and untimely."

Marriage? Ha! Remembering his dalliance with Morgana Woodcliff, Alandra turned up her nose. That was the last thing she would ever do—marry a philanderer! Sharing her husband with other women was out of the question.

"Untimely? Untimely? To the contrary. The sooner the better." Murray clucked his tongue. "Now that you are blooming into womanhood, it is time we found you a mate. You've got to settle down, daughter. Have a home of your own. You can't go roaming about with a ragtag band of men forever."

"It's not a ragtag band of men!" Alandra was quick to defend the actors, even to her father. "And—and I enjoy going with you. Surely there is not one among the actors who would deny me."

Or would they? She was a woman now and she knew the rules. For a moment she panicked, and the old insecurities came back to haunt her. A foundling! One whose own parents had abandoned her. A child no one else had wanted.

" 'Tis the only kind of life I know, being in the theater." How could she be certain she would fit in anywhere else?

"Aye, I know."

Her apprehension turned to anger. "Who has been grumbling?"

"Heminges!"

"Heminges?"

She should have known. As a father of fourteen children, a man who was active in parish affairs, he had always been a thorn in her side, insisting the life she led was no life for a girl-child. It was not the first time he had posed a threat to her freedom, and Alandra clearly suspected it was prejudice on his part. His disdain clearly proved what he thought of those who had no relatives and thus no one of importance to protect them.

"What has he said?"

"That this will be the last summer you should be allowed to go tour. He says a woman as lovely as you will invite trouble for us sooner or later."

"Trouble!" Alandra's temper was sparked. "A pox on him! Will has a say in the matter. He will side with me." When trouble brewed, it was always Shakespeare and her father who took up for her.

"But he might be outnumbered. After all, the other wives, lovers, and daughters are left behind. Heminges is quite a persuasive and stubborn man." Murray tried to soothe her, but Alandra was not to be calmed.

"Heminges is as gossipy as an old woman. He should mind his own business. He should—"

"He cites your abduction as an example." Murray's eyes darted from Alandra to Christopher and back again. "I will agree with him on one matter, daughter. A woman needs a man to protect her, a young, strong man. I am old. You need a husband, Alandra. And you know whom I would see you choose."

"Well, you can put a certain prompter out of your mind. Besides, Edward Alleyn be damned, I sincerely doubt that Christopher Nicholas will ever be an actor of renown."

"Alandra, be reasonable." Murray threw up his hands in agitation. "Oh, if only you had been raised by a woman, you would have learned how to use a woman's wiles. You would have Christopher eating out of your hand . . ."

She would talk on the subject no longer, despite her father's urgings. Yet she could not chase away her own fantasies. Her eyes strayed to Christopher as they traveled, wondering what it would be like to belong to him, imagining.

The sting of the sea wind stung her cheeks, announcing the actors' entry into the channel port. Alandra set aside her ponderings to enjoy the panorama. Dover lay at the end of the North Downs and ran upland along the valley of the Dour, the river from which it got its name. It was a bustling port, once the walled Roman town of Dubris, the headquarters of the Romans' northern fleet.

From whichever direction it was approached, a powerful castle loomed over the town, four square and forbidding, full of weapons. Beside the steep road that led up to the castle was an ornate gun nicknamed "Queen Elizabeth's Pocket Pistol," an ornately carved and decorated cannon which had been given to the queen by the Dutch. But it was the sight of the cliffs towering over the western fringes of the town that left Alandra breathless.

"Awesome, wouldn't you say, Alandra?" Shakespeare took note of Alandra's surprise as he rode up to greet her.

"Completely!"

"And even more so when approaching from the Channel. A coastline whose role for centuries has been to present the first line of defense against invaders."

Instructing a startled Murray to take the reins, Will swept Alandra up in his sinewy arms and deposited her on the saddle in front of him, just as he had when she was younger. "I want to show your daughter some of the sights," he said to Murray, but whispered in Alandra's ear, "there seems to be something you would like to tell me. Am I right?"

Only Will would understand her predicament. "Yes. I've made a mess of everything, Will."

Shakespeare chuckled low in his throat as he guided the horse toward the cliffs. "Now, suppose you tell me what has happened."

Alandra took a deep breath and began. "Christopher was still in my room when you came to my door, Will. We came close to making love. But then I spoiled the moment with my suspicions, and he left quickly, as if I had set his pants on fire."

Shakespeare smiled. "Perhaps you did!"

Alandra blushed. "He told me that he will not come near me in that way again, that he will guard my virtue because he owes it to my father." She sighed. " 'Tis my maidenhead that stands between us." She pointed at the cliffs. "Though it might as well be yon mighty hills."

Though Will took her on a short tour of the area, she hardly even noticed her surroundings she was so miserable. "He wanted to make love to me, Will. There was no denying that. And he would have, had you not come upon the scene."

"Then let us be thankful that I *did!*" Will's voice held a tone of scolding. "You are not some strumpet to succumb so easily to love's delights," he said more gently. "Your Christopher has judged you to be just what you are. The kind of woman a man marries."

"So he will not touch me because I am an untried maid, and yet he can never marry me because I am not his equal!" Alandra said sourly. She had never been so disappointed in all her life. She had been so certain that the romantic Will at least would understand, would goad her on to fulfill her desires.

His voice was as impassioned as if speaking some of his own lines. "You must find a husband among one of your own kind!"

"An actor?" she asked sarcastically.

She assessed the actors in the company. They were either too young or too gray in the beard. Too fat or too thin. Too tall or too short. The comely ones were either married, with a wife and children awaiting their return, or of an effeminate nature, preferring their own sex. Was it any wonder she was unmarried?

"Or a tradesman, perhaps?" she demanded.

"Yes, Alandra."

"And never give vent to my love for Christopher."

Shakespeare's nod of agreement broke her heart.

"Thus am I doomed to unhappiness, and all because of my virtue. Damned then be that thin strip of membrane that keeps me from experiencing the greatest of joys!"

Shakespeare shook his head sadly. "Or greatest of sorrows if you lose it unwisely!"

"But you write about young lovers and always in the end a loving heart conquers all! And it can, Will. It can."

"In stories, Alandra. Not in real life. I myself have

never experienced true love, but let a moment of passion ruin me." Shakespeare hung his head. "Think you that I love my wife? Then I tell you clearly that I do not. The theater is not only a way of expression for me but a means of escape ..."

"Escape?" So it was true then what she had heard whispered that Will's wife was a scold. Alandra was shattered by the revelation. Poor Will! And she had been so certain that he held the whole world in the palm of his hand.

"Be careful, Alandra. Do not let infatuation blind you. Life is fact not fantasy. You cannot forget that, for Christopher is a hunted man, one who now has a large reward upon his head."

Pulling a broadside from his doublet, he handed it to her, revealing the true reason for his scolding mood. Indeed there was, as Will said, a handsome price on Sir Nicholas Leighton's head. Worse yet was a written statement, said to be taken from eyewitnesses, of what had happened that fateful night at The Black Unicorn.

Alandra stared at the ink-stained paper in her hand in disbelief. Christopher had claimed that Lord Woodcliff's death had occurred while they were engaged in hand-to-hand sword fighting. This account was at severe odds with what he had told her.

"He said the old lord was killed during a fair fight. Fair fight! But a sword wound in the back? In the back!" she exclaimed, stunned.

Angrily, she asked Will to return her to her wagon. Let Sir Nicholas Leighton explain this if he could!

Chapter Twenty-Seven

Voices chattered, howled, and shouted with excitement. There was a goodly crowd at the inn, come to see the players. Hawkers sold tobacco, apples, nuts, and pamphlets to the spectators. The courtyard was noisy, made particularly so by the boistrousness of those Nicholas now knew were groundlings.

"It seems our reputation has preceded us, Christopher," Murray called out as he stretched his solid bulk.

"Aye. Let us hope they are pleased," Nicholas added. He knew by now that there was no counting on decent or orderly behavior from such an audience. He wondered how the actors could remember their parts when they had to compete with the nut-cracking noise, the raucous jokes, and the gratuitous contributions of fruits and vegetables from these oafs.

"They will be. It appears to me that they are of good humor already." Murray grinned at Nicholas.

"No doubt because they are already in their cups.

It looks as if the ale has been flowing freely." He sniffed. It smelled like it, too.

Pushing through the crowd, Nicholas headed for the tiring house. There he found the young lads who were to play the female roles struggling into their gowns, blauts, and kirtles. Stifling a chuckle, he was thankful that he was not of such tender years. He was, as Murray said, too wide in the shoulders to play any of the women's roles.

But he had also not been given any more male parts, either. Perhaps because of the mistakes he had made as Demetrius, he thought. Not that Nicholas was complaining. Having suffered on the stage once in a lifetime was enough for him! He was content to leave the soliliquies to the actors.

But Nicholas didn't escape totally unscathed for this performance. One of the young men assigned to take the part of the ambassador had taken ill, thus Murray, frantic as usual when something went wrong, hastily thrust a costume at him.

"We'll make it fit!" he insisted, letting a seam out here and there where Nicholas was large, taking a tuck where Nicholas was thin.

An ambassador, Nicholas thought, *a non-speaking part and thus safe.* Donned in a wig, mustache, and beard, he thought that the part did suit him well, if he did say so himself. He made a most noble Frenchman. And even though the costumes were woefully out of style, it did feel good to wear silks and velvets again, if only for a short while. The soft cloth of the red shirt, the smooth gold tunic, even the hosen and mantle felt splendid against his skin. The colors were rich and heraldic. But most of all he enjoyed wearing a sword at his side again. Vanity prodded him, and he found himself relishing the thought of Alandra seeing him thus.

Alandra. He parted the curtains of the tiring house

to look for her and was surprised to see the prompter's spot vacant. Where was she? Nicholas's head swiveled as he searched the crowd for her. Hurriedly, he sought out Murray. "Where is Alandra?"

"She's not with me!" Murray's expression showed his own displeasure. "But do not despair. She'll be here. My daughter has never missed a performance."

"Then where is she?" Nicholas felt ill at ease without her. Vulnerable. She brought him luck!

"She said that she had to take care of some business. I saw her talking to the proprietor of the inn." Murray jumped as the trumpet announcing the start of the play sounded. "She'll be here."

"Christopher. Christopher. Come on. We must make our entrance." Burbage and Armin tugged at his sleeve.

Though he was decidedly nervous even though he didn't have to remember any lines, there was no way out for Nicholas. Quickly, he plopped the long-haired, gray wig upon his head and followed the other actors.

Out of the corner of his eye, Nicholas saw Alandra in the prompter's usual place and felt that he could now relax. She was his good luck charm, he thought. What's more he could trust her. Though she knew a secret about him that could destroy him, she had kept it to herself. For that he could credit her. If she doubted him from time to time, well, under the circumstances, he thought she could be forgiven. Yet when their eyes met, he saw that she was glaring at him. Nicholas was unnerved. What had happened now to annoy her?

All he could hope was that one day this mess he had gotten himself into would straighten itself out. Then he would have to return to court and all of this would be just a memory.

Feeling slighted by her reaction to him, Nicholas turned his attention to the stage, watching the actors' gestures, listening to the flow of language. He was magically transported to another time, when John and not Elizabeth ruled England. As he watched and listened, he became absorbed in the flow of words. Shakespeare was a genius, there was no arguing that. He had earned Nicholas's respect as a playwright, actor, and as a man.

Nicholas was actually beginning to like the theater. It was fun!

He particularly liked this play, *King John*, with all its pomp and pageantry. It was well written, well casted and well acted. Maybe at some point, despite his dismal performance as Demetrius, he could convince Shakespeare to give him a part. He'd talk with Will about it. With Murray's and Alandra's help, he might actually be able to succeed.

Take on a role? He was planning his future as if he thought he was going to be with the players for a long, long time. Would that be so bad? Looking over at Alandra, he suddenly wondered what would happen if he never returned to court. What if he mastered the art of acting and made a new life for himself? A life that included Alandra? What then? After all, he had heard that the leading actors, those who earned great fame, often earned a lion's share of the profits. Celebrities on the stage were rewarded with public idolatry. Certainly, he could learn a great deal from Shakespeare.

Stay among the actors. It was an interesting thought. Become Christopher Nicholas, member of the Lord Chamberlain's Men. What would Shakespeare say?

Undoubtedly, Will would be agreeable. He was a gentle man, consistent in his courtesy, incapable of taking serious offense. Never boastful. For all his talent, he was modest, always sharing any praise for his plays with the actors. Little by little Shakespeare was gaining Nicholas's trust. Certainly, Will had made an effort to be friendly. But what would the playwright think if he knew Nicholas was a fugitive? A wanted man? Just how friendly would he be then? And the actors? What would their opinion of him be if they found out he had lied to them all?

And what if someone recognized him while he was performing and had him arrested?

Sadly, he looked over at Alandra. A man couldn't live a lie, even for the sake of love. He didn't belong here and in truth there really wasn't any place for him.

Nicholas's eyes left the actors for just a moment as he scanned the crowd. How many people were there sitting in the galleries, standing on the ground? More than a thousand, Murray had guessed. An odd gathering. People who would never rub elbows ordinarily. Lordlings, midlings, and groundlings. Butterflies, moths, and caterpillars.

Suddenly Nicholas felt as if all the blood drained from his face. His fingers tingled, his heart froze in his chest. He forgot all about the play, the audience, and where he was, as his gaze focused on a scar-faced man. Something clicked in his head! A memory tucked away in the back of his mind until now. He remembered that rogue was at The Black Unicorn that night. As being near Lord Woodcliff the night Nicholas's world had been torn apart. He seemed to remember now seeing that man flee after Lord Woodcliff's death.

"You. Frizer!" The words passed through Nicholas's lips before he could think.

Looking about frantically, Will Frizer took to his heels, pushing through the crowd as he sought a means of escape.

Years of habit took hold. Deftly, Nicholas reached for the sword at his side, forgetting it was little more than a toy. Raising it threateningly, he leaped off the stage, heading for the man he thought might be his only salvation. He had to question him. If he could make Frizer tell what he had seen that night, Nicholas might clear himself of guilt in Elizabeth's eyes.

Nicholas kept his quarry in sight as he pushed and shoved through the crowd of groundlings, but they, thinking his actions to be part of the play, did little to assist him. They hooted and hollered their approval but stood their ground, forming a human wall between Nicholas and Frizer.

"Let me pass! Fools, move out of the way!" When they didn't oblige him, Nicholas took matters into his own hands, aiming his fist at one well-girthed paunch. With an *oomph*, the man staggered backward. Nicholas's knee brought another groundling to his knees, his elbow yet another.

Quickly, Nicholas pushed through the opening, hoping to corner Frizer before he could get away. *God's whiskers, don't let him disappear*, Nicholas thought. The man might be his only chance.

Nicholas moved stealthfully until he was ten feet away from Frizer. So close. So very, very close.

Will Frizer's eyes met Nicholas's and the look there was so malevolent that he was stunned. Nevertheless, Nicholas pleaded, "I must talk with you. Wait!"

Frizer lunged, his knife nearly ripping the shoulder of Nicholas's doublet.

"Who are you?" Frizer shouted. "Why are you after me?"

Nicholas didn't answer, instead he lunged, playing with the cutter at his own game, but Frizer was fleet of foot. In a pattern of pushing, ducking, and jumping, he quickly put Nicholas at a distance as he fought desperately to escape the inn's courtyard.

He can't get away! Nicholas thought desperately. If he did, Nicholas might never find him again. He hurled himself forward. "Catch him. He's a thief and a hired cutthroat!" he shouted.

As the crowd gasped in surprise and fascination, Nicholas gave chase.

Chapter Twenty-Eight

Nicholas had never moved so fast in his life! Willing his legs to take long, swift strides, he followed closely on Will Frizer's heels as the ruffian dodged and darted through the crowd and away from the innyard. Pushing over rain barrels, vaulting over anything in his way, Nicholas ran until his lungs threatened to burst. Yet the rogue managed to stay just out of his reach.

Changing his tactics, Nicholas used a shortcut and cut across the cutter's path as he headed across the cobbled street. Nicholas almost caught up with his quarry, but then a rickety hay wagon rumbling out from an alleyway came between them.

Nicholas was exasperated as he watched the rogue disappear from sight. Bloody damn! Where in hell had the bastard gone? Two darkened streets led out of the square, like a *Y*. Which one had Frizer taken? Nicholas chose the path to the left.

Once away from the inn and the crowd, the streets

grew silent. It seemed that most of the residents of Dover were attending the performance. Shops had been locked behind their heavy shutters, the cobbled streets had only a few passers-by. Glancing warily from side to side, Nicholas tightly gripped his sword as he pushed onward.

He came to a haunt for sailors, a dingy, stinking narrow street that overlooked the ocean. Taverns dotted the landscape, and boats and ships were as plentiful as fleas on a dog. He wandered about, eyeing the old decaying brick warehouses warily. He had to be careful, lest he be taken unaware. Something about the area raised the hackles on his neck. It was just the sort of place where a rat could hide amongst those of his own kind. And it was undoubtedly here that Frizer had gone.

Nicholas was on guard as he walked. He was rewarded for his tenacity as he at last spied Frizer among a group of men who were lounging near a signpost. Now that he was among his companions the ruffian made no attempt at running. Instead, he grinned evilly as if welcoming a confrontation.

Nicholas realized at once that he had walked into a fox's lair. These were rough and rugged men with a look of cruelty in their eyes, wearing serviceable blades under their short cloaks. One of them, a red-haired man whose touseled hair hung to his shoulders, laughed softly.

"A pleasure it is seeing ye here, old man," the ruffian said, addressing Nicholas whom he assumed from his gray wig to be of advanced years. "I have need of some coins and I have suspicion yer purse might well be bulging!" The burly thief placed his hands upon his thick thighs, his cold dark eyes squinting against the light of the sun.

"I have no money pouch." Nicholas had no quarrel

with these men, nor was he in the mood for a battle when he was so outnumbered.

"Then we will find another way for ye to pay the toll to use this road." The red-haired man took a step forward, scoffing at Nicholas's rapier.

Frizer boldly pushed the man back. "Nay, Robert. He chased after me. This one is mine. I would take my revenge," he loudly informed his companions. "But ye can take yer turn with him when I am through."

Nicholas was outnumbered ten to one. Usually one to stand his ground and fight, he broke into a run. Only a fool would take a chance on being killed. He wanted to catch Frizer it was true, but not at the expense of his own life. Then his name would never be cleared. The sound of pounding boot soles sounded close behind him.

Weaving in and out, making use of his strength and agility, Nicholas easily outdistanced the men chasing him, but his escape was cut short. Several two-storied buildings loomed in his path, forming a wall at the end of the dark alley. Now he would be forced to fight.

"Aha! Now I have you." The voice behind him rang with malicious triumph. "I'll cut yer throat and teach ye to chase after me."

Turning, Nicholas was relieved to see that only four of the ruffians had followed him. Far better odds than fighting the whole gang.

"Cut my throat? I think not!" Nicholas's eyes blazed as his swordsman's instincts took hold. In one agile movement, Nicholas sprang forward, his sword poised and ready for combat. He swung at his nearest attacker and had the satisfaction of seeing the man stagger and fall. "Next!"

The red-haired man rushed at Nicholas's back with a dagger, trying for a quick, crippling blow to Nicholas's right side, but Nicholas whirled and parried just in time. He felt their blades collide and lock.

"I'll take him off yer hands, Robert, if ye can't handle him alone ..." Frizer unleashed his own sword, attacking Nicholas on the left.

The third man rushed forward, but Nicholas thought fast, spinning to smash his fist into that man's face before he could draw his sword. The man staggered back, lifting his hand to his bloodied mouth.

The sound of sword on sword rent the air as Nicholas fought two men at one time, swinging his sword fiercely. Everything seemed to happen simultaneously, registering quickly in his mind. He no sooner felled one than the third man rose to take his place. He did not dare take his eyes from the swish of the quick-moving blades, but though the men were aggressive and brutal, they were no match for Nicholas's experience.

"Who are ye? Where did ye learn to fight like that?" Frizer demanded, amazed.

With a grace that belied his height and strength, he kicked Frizer's weapon aside as if it were naught but a stick. "It seems you thrive on attacking aged prey, Frizer! Well, I am not yet gray and grizzled."

Nicholas struck out. Screeching in pain, Frizer shuddered beneath the impact of the sharp steel piercing his flesh. He reared back, his face suffused with anger as he threatened, "Ye bloody old bastard, ye'll be sorry for this!" Scrambling wildly to retrieve his sword, he muttered a violent string of swear words.

"And you will be sorry for your sins." Nicholas struck out again, this time bringing forth a trickle of crimson from his adversary.

Gone was the cutter's fierce bravado. Like a wounded beast, Frizer slunk away, making his escape around the corner of an alehouse. Nicholas started to pursue him, but as he moved, he was tripped by one of the other rogues lying on the ground. Together they rolled over and over as they grappled. Nicholas had his hands full, battling with first that man and then another, but in the end he was victorious, watching as the men turned coward and fled just as Frizer had done.

Nicholas had no time to congratulate himself. Hastily brushing himself off, and wiping the blood from his face and hands, he hurried off in the direction Frizer had taken. This time, however, Frizer had truly vanished without leaving even one trace of where he might have gone. The gathering darkness acted like a cloak to enfold him, hide him.

Damn! He was somewhere in this hellhole! But where? Nicholas searched and searched but in the end had to admit defeat. Will Frizer was gone. He might just as well try to find a shilling in a hayloft. But Frizer was here somewhere. Tomorrow or the next day he'd find him. Some way! He had to! He'd come back to visit the innyard again and again until he did catch him.

It was late when Nicholas returned to the inn. There he found the actors gathered together at the table, eating, drinking, and enjoying their favorite pastime of all: talking.

"Nicholas, you had best hurry and take your share while there is still food aplenty." Shakespeare gazed Nicholas's way with a mysterious, all-knowing look. "I fear we have eaten the poor innkeeper out of house and home. The sea air no doubt." Will wiped his mouth with the hem of the tablecloth. "The pigeon pie is delicious, by the way."

Nicholas was famished. He didn't need any prodding to unleash his appetite. Fighting always did that to a man, he supposed. Plopping down in a chair next to the playwright, he relished the dishes set before him. "The pigeon pie is, as you say, excellent." He expected a scolding from Shakespeare but true to form, Will made light of Nicholas's actions.

"You held the audience spellbound, Christopher. It made the audience feel as if somehow they were part of the action," he said. "So much so that I just might add that scene to the play."

Shakespeare didn't ask any questions, but Nicholas had the feeling that somehow Will knew what had prompted the sudden chase.

"The man I went after was witness to a great wrong." Nicholas felt the need to explain, lest Shakespeare think ill of him. "I had to catch up with him."

"And it looks as if you did," Heminges said dryly, eyeing Nicholas.

"Aye, and most obviously he was the loser in the skirmish," Kempe said with a grin. Grabbing up a large towel, he threw it at Nicholas. "Your face is streaked with blood and grime."

Nicholas looked at Murray. "I was set upon, but I promise you I did not put your sword to shame. As battered as I may look, I can tell you that the other men look far worse." It took but a few moments for him to realize that Alandra, who usually hovered near her father, was nowhere in sight. Where was she?

Shakespeare seemed to read Nicholas's mind as he said, "She is in her room. Something is deeply troubling her. Something methinks only you can explain." His voice dropped to a whisper as his eyes swept toward the stairs.

Nicholas followed the man's line of vision. Ah, but Alandra looked stunning, as she descended the stairs. Usually one to dress in more subdued hues, tonight she wore a dress of bright green, the full skirt just clearing the ground as it floated over a farthingale. Her hair was worn long, unencumbered by braids or fastenings, bedecked with a wreath of tiny flowers.

There was something strange in her expression. Something that made his blood run cold. Still, in front of the others she pretended cordiality. "Christopher!

Forsooth, but you did make yourself the topic of conversation. No doubt the merchants' wives will make your performance the center of their chattering for days to come. But the audience was delighted. Will says you enlivened a dull part of the play."

"That he did," Will agreed. "Today's performance was out of the ordinary."

Nicholas saw their eyes meet, and the look there seemed to send some secret signal. What was going on?

"Aye, I'm just full of surprises," he answered. "As are you." He wanted to ask her right then and there if she had let Shakespeare in on his secret, but the room was full.

One by one, however, the actors left the room, leaving only Murray and Kempe behind. At a signal from Murray, Kempe did not tarry, and followed Murray up the stairs. It was as if Murray sensed Nicholas wanted to be alone with Alandra.

Alandra was incensed with him, but, nevertheless, she dipped the end of the tablecloth in a half-empty mug of ale then brushed at a cut on his forehead. "You're wounded."

"A scratch and nothing more." He tried to sound gruff, but, dear God, her touch was like heaven. Even the sting of the ale was soothed away. It took all his will power to pull away from her but somehow he managed.

"And what of the other man?" Alandra asked coldly. "What happened to him? Is he lying in some gutter somewhere, a sword wound marking his back?"

Nicholas was taken aback. "Of course not!"

"At least then he has fared well. Better than some who have crossed your path."

She started to leave, but Nicholas grabbed her arm. "By God, just what do you mean by that?"

Their eyes fought a frantic duel. Alandra tried to get

free of him, but he held her fast. He wasn't going to turn her loose until she told him what she had meant by her jibe.

"Confess, Nicholas," she hissed in his ear. "Tell me the truth for once!"

"The truth about what?" Realizing that he had raised his voice, he quickly softened it. "What is wrong with you? What have I done to spark your ire. Tell me!"

"You said Lord Woodcliff died in a fair fight," she whispered, barely controlling her outrage. "But the word is out that he was stabbed mortally in the back. In the *back*, Christopher!"

"What?" His face paled as he realized what she had said and its implication. "Oh, no!" Once again something, some revelation, sparked in his mind. He remembered the frenzy of that night, how he had briefly turned his head to look at Morgana, how all of a sudden Lord Woodcliff was falling. He hadn't remembered dealing a blow. Perhaps he hadn't. "It was someone else!" The truth hit him forcibly. "Someone else must have killed him and left it for me to take the blame."

"Oh, of course!" Alandra said with sarcasm, yet the look on his face tempered her anger, a look of surprise that he had not the acting talent to feign.

Though she had vowed not to listen to his lies again, to avoid this murderer as carefully as if he had the plague, she did not argue as he tugged at her hand.

"We must talk." When she did not answer, he said, "Please! If you have any feelings at all for me, Alandra, you must hear me out. But not here." Someone could enter the room at any moment.

"All right," she agreed, "I will go with you but first know this. Will Shakespeare knows about you. If anything happens to me, he will know exactly where to look!" There, now let him try to harm her, she thought.

"He knows!" Nicholas held the look of one totally betrayed. Even so, he wanted her to hear him out.

Chapter Twenty-Nine

The moon was full, a large glowing ball in the black sky. It was a night for lovers, Nicholas thought as he took Alandra's hand and drew her out to the courtyard. How ironic, for it seemed the conversation that was to pass between them was to be far from that shared by lovers.

"Christopher!"

He put his hand across her mouth, wanting to have the first say. "I have made many mistakes in my life. There are those who might call me stubborn, prideful, a bit of a rogue where women are concerned, head-strong, and like most of us foolish on occasion." His hand moved from her lips to her chin, then trailed softly to her throat.

They stared at each other, two dark silhouettes against the curtains of the stage. Nicholas's face was stony, his expression difficult to read. Was it any wonder then that a knot squeezed in the pit of Alandra's stomach? She had actually come to think that she knew him, but did she?

They were well out of sight of the others. Were he to put both hands around her neck and squeeze, he could permanently silence her. He was already wanted for one murder, what would keep him from doing her in, too? For the first time in a long while she was truly frightened. He talked about fools. Surely she was the greatest fool of all to have come out here alone with him.

Look at him, she thought, *his legs are braced slightly apart as if preparing himself*. For what? His graceful, muscular body was taut, his hand as strong as steel as it moved along the column of her throat. It was true that she could scream, but in the time it would take for someone to come to her aid, she could suffer.

Staring down into her wide brown eyes, dilated black in the darkness, Nicholas was stung by the emotion he read there. At the moment she was terrified of him, was looking at him as if he were some devil or beast. He had to make her listen! Even if he never saw her again, he couldn't stand to have her think him capable of such a loathsome thing as a cowardly murder.

"Alandra!"

His voice startled her out of her mesmerized lethargy. She had to get away. Now before it was too late. With that intent, she turned and picked up her skirts to flee, but Nicholas reached out to stop her.

"Let me go!"

Thinking only to halt her flight, Nicholas's grip on her shoulders was punishing. "I will, but only when you have heard me out." He pushed her up against the wood of the stage, blocking her escape. "Look at you. You are trembling. God's blood, but it tears at my heart for you to think that I would ever do you harm, Alandra."

"I don't know what to think anymore . . ."

"I love you, Alandra!" The words were out before he even realized he had said them.

"Love . . ." He didn't know the meaning of the word. "Let me g—"

Nicholas's mouth came down on hers and smothered the *o*. He had to prove to her how deeply he cared for her and this was the only way he knew.

His kiss was fierce, taking her breath away. He held her lips captive to an assault that was unlike anything Alandra could ever have imagined. She tried to twist her face away, but he wrapped his fingers in her thick hair and jerked her mouth back to his. She could feel the hard, warm length of him against her, heating her own body with a fire that made her burn. But still she struggled against him.

His hand slid over the curve of her hip, pressing her firmly against him, as his teeth gently nipped at her lips. Then melding his mouth to hers once again, he kissed her deeply, as if in this one moment he could rob her of her very soul she thought. And well he did! It was like stepping into another realm, a place where only feelings reigned. And her feelings were all too potent.

When at last he pulled away and she could stare back at him, Alandra looked deeply into his eyes, determined to delve into his soul as he had tried to do to her. What she read there warmed her heart. He did care about her.

"I didn't kill Lord Woodcliff! I didn't, Alandra. I know that now."

For good or for ill, her heart ruled her brain and she found herself believing him, undoubtedly because she wanted to. "Then who did?" she asked.

"That man I chased after today is the key. He knows. He was there." He clenched his jaw. "Or perhaps it was he who did the deed, at Stafford's urging no doubt.

That ruffian is known to be a hired killer." He began mumbling, as much to himself as to her. "We were fighting. I was trying to go as easy as I could because I knew of Lord Woodcliff's frailty. He was once the very best swordsman in the land, but time robs a man of his prowess."

Closing his eyes, he tried to conjure up the scene. "Woodcliff was lunging blindly at me, angered to the point of carelessness. I remembered Morgana saying something to me and I turned my head only for an instant. I saw the curtains move out of the corner of my eye, but thought nothing of it at the time and yet ..." He paused.

"What happened then?"

"I looked back at Lord Woodcliff, and seeing him topple in a heap on the ground assumed that my sword had slain him. But ..." He remembered Will Frizer taking to his heels. Why? And Stafford, how had he so conveniently entered upon the scene?

"You are telling me that you didn't kill him, Christopher, and I want to believe you ..." Even so, it was a story that stretched the imagination.

"Alandra, I cannot lie to you and tell you that in the heat of combat or in defending my queen I have not caused a man's death, but when it comes to honor I swear to you that I have never used my sword to bring about murder! I am not that kind of man! If Lord Woodcliff was struck in the back, as you say, then there is some other explanation than that I killed him. I would never strike a man from behind. Never!" His voice was impassioned in his defense.

Just as Nicholas had drawn on his memory for aid so now did she. She remembered pressing her ear up against her door at The Black Unicorn, trying to hear what was going on outside. At the time what had been said hadn't meant a thing to her. Now it did. "But he didn't stab him!" a woman's voice had shrieked. "I saw for myself what happened..." A witness! But who? Alandra couldn't remember the woman's name, but perhaps she would. Somehow she had to.

"Alandra, do you believe me?"

"Yes," she breathed. Trusting was part of loving, how then could she do otherwise but believe what Christopher had told her?

"At least I have that!" At the moment it seemed the most important thing in the world. There was a price upon his head, he might be betrayed and set upon at any moment, and yet at least he knew that at last Alandra believed in him. "But what am I to do?" He felt so weary, so tired of it all suddenly.

"There is nothing that we can do," Alandra whispered. She touched his dark hair, brushing it back from his face. "Except find out *who* did kill Lord Woodcliff."

Chapter Thirty

The inn was quiet. It was well after nightfall, and most of the players and members of the household were abed. Alandra, however, couldn't sleep. Silver light from the moon streamed in through the open shutters, illuminating her face as she sat at the small dressing table in her chamber. How many strokes of the brush had she passed through her hair? A hundred? A thousand? She had lost count. All she could think about was what had happened tonight.

Tossing the brush aside, she touched her fingers to her mouth, remembering Christopher's passionate kiss, his avowal of innocence. He had said that he loved her, and though she wanted to believe him, she thought it more likely that his declaration was an outburst spurred on by the moment. He was in serious danger and no doubt knew her to be his only friend, the only one he could turn to. But love her? She ached to believe it, and yet reality nudged at her thoughts, pushing aside her dreams.

She frowned into the polished metal mirror. What would happen if Christopher was able to prove his innocence and reclaim his courtly renown? Would she still be the apple of his eye, she the girl who didn't even know who she really was? A nobody! She who had been left by the road like discarded refuse, abandoned by her own parents. If only she could reclaim her past, learn who had given her up, then perhaps she could set aside the ghosts who haunted her. But she didn't know and probably never would.

So much had happened that she didn't really know what to think anymore. Life had been so simple before Christopher, nay Sir Nicholas Leighton, had come into her life. If Alandra had not been totally happy, at least she had learned to appreciate some contentment among the actors. She had felt as if she nearly belonged. Now all she could wish for was to be something that she wasn't. Something she could never be. Someone *he* could love.

Rising from the chair, she threw herself down on the bed, tormented by her thoughts and dreams. She was being selfish, only thinking of herself. If she really loved Christopher, really loved him, she'd want him to be happy. And that happiness could only come when he was back where he belonged. He was a nobleman, not a prompter nor an actor, as out of place among the players as she was at court. If he was innocent, and she believed now that he might very well be, then he deserved to take his rightful place beside Lord Stafford. Thus, somehow, some way, she had to think how to help him.

It was hot in the room, and though Alandra threw open the shutters, she was uncomfortable. It was such a beautiful night! The branches on the trees seemed to beckon her, motioning her to join them. Realizing that a breath of air was just what she needed, Alandra opened the door to her room, tiptoed down the stairs, and left the inn.

The air was sweet with the smell of flowers, and the leaves of the trees looked like black lace against the sky. Night birds trilled. The world was a beautiful place when all was calm. Taking a leisurely stroll, she appreciated the sights, smells, and sounds, while she tried to sort out her thoughts and feelings.

How terrible it would be if she had been accused of something hideous and knew she was innocent of the condemnation. But one thing she was sure of. She had to do everything in her power to help Christopher.

Alandra thought she heard a twig snap. "Christopher?" Looking around, she expected to see him, but no one appeared. Again she heard a noise. "Who's there?"

Suddenly she was grabbed from behind. "What are you doing! She struggled against her assailant. "Take your hands off me this instant!"

"Not until I get what I have come for!"

Alandra's head snapped around, and she recognized the man holding her. It was the hostler, a man whose constant staring at her might have bothered her when first she arrived had not her thoughts been so undividedly on Christopher.

His eyes swept over her with a hunger that made her cheeks burn, as if he knew what she looked like unclothed. Alandra uttered a gasp as his sour-smelling mouth descended upon hers and his tongue forced its way into her mouth.

Alandra quickly drew away from him. "Leave me alone, you great oaf!"

"Oaf, is it? I think you are not as naive as you would have me think. I saw you kissing that man here, near this very spot tonight. You know what I want to do. I

want to sample that which lies between your legs."
He laughed, grabbing her.

"Then you will be taken to toll for such boldness,
sir," she said as she struggled to free herself.

"By who?" The hostler threw back his head and
laughed. "Everyone in the inn is asleep. We are all
alone!" He tightened again his hold on her.

Alandra stared up at the man, her heart pounding.
She was all too aware of the dark sky. It was late and
as he said, no one was about.

Thrusting back her shoulders, she refused to be in-
timidated, but she knew she had to escape this devil.
She had to run as quickly back to the inn as she could.
She darted out of his arms, but the hostler was upon
her in an instant.

"Do not think you can escape me now that I have
you all to myself. Ah, no, no, no!" His hands captured
her shoulders. With a mumbled oath, he dragged her
up against his chest.

Alandra fought back, trying again to break his hold
on her, but her hands were ineffectual against his
strength. "Take your hands off me!" she shouted.

The hostler merely laughed at her. His mouth moved
to mere inches from hers as he muttered, "No! And
there is little that you can do to fight me off, so why
not just enjoy it, eh? I know what you people in the
theater are like. I am a most skillful lover as you will
soon see." He pressed his mouth hotly against her
throat as if he would devour her.

Furious and frightened, Alandra screamed in outrage and fought in deadly earnest. She would never
give herself to this brutish man. Never. "Let me go! A
pox on you if you don't!"

He muttered words that were unfit for a woman's
ears, words that she knew to be obscenities about the
act of lovemaking.

"I tell you again. Leave me be!" Bringing one knee

up, she intended to aim a blow at his manhood, but he moved aside and rendered her assault harmless.

"Do that again and I will make you regret it," he threatened.

"Please! Please!" Alandra pleaded softly.

The hostler's eyes glinted with a spark that went beyond mere desire. A look that turned Alandra's blood to ice water. He was enjoying her fear as if he felt a sense of power at her helplessness. Oh, how could she have ever been so stupid, so careless as to walk about in the night?

The hostler was like a man possessed as his hands tore at her bodice. He was far too aroused to be deterred by her efforts at defense. His hands seemed to be everywhere, bruising and burning. Alandra's dress was torn from her shoulder, and she cringed as she felt his fingers fondling her naked breast. Suddenly she was naked from the waist up.

"Ah, you are lovely! Well worth the wait!"

His hand slid up her thighs, pushing the hem of her gown around her waist, and she panicked. He was going to rape her, and there seemed little that she could do to stop him! She felt nausea rise in her throat.

Christopher, please come! she prayed. But he didn't, and she realized there was no one to defend her but herself.

Chapter Thirty-One

Nicholas fidgeted as he sat at the inn's large table. He drummed his fingers nervously and tapped the toe of his boot against the floor. Usually calm and composed, he was a bundle of nerves and more than his dire predicament was on his mind. Ah, but it had felt so right to hold Alandra in his arms, to kiss her. Why had he let her go? It was the last thing on earth that he had wanted to do.

He imagined what might have been. His fingers would have wandered gently along her collarbone, moving to the softness of her breasts. He would have pushed her down upon the sweet-smelling grass and pulled her close against his sun-browned body, while kissing her with enough force to suck the breath from her. He would have stroked her naked breasts, then slid his hands lower, lifting up her skirts, touching her secret place, arousing her untried passion as he whispered words of love. He should have kissed and caressed her until she was too inflamed to plea for restraint. Then he would have been between her naked thighs and....

Nicholas pressed his fingers to his eyes, trying to block out the unsettling image. He was lusting after her, as he never had for any woman. And yet that desire was tempered by a much gentler emotion. The question was what to do about it.

He paced up and down, back and forth, trying to get her image out of his heart, his mind, but his walking about did him little good. He needed to cool down, needed the calm of the cool night air. Hurriedly, he flung open the inn's back door and sought the solitude of the night. And yet surprisingly enough it wasn't completely quiet. The shriek of a nightbird suddenly unnerved him.

A bird? By God, no! It was a woman's cry, he heard it distinctly. Someone was in trouble. Quickly, Nicholas headed in the direction of the sound.

Uselessly, Alandra's fists beat against the hostler's back, but there was nothing she could do to push away his crushing weight. She could feel him pressing his loins against her, and tensed as she glimpsed him fumbling with the fastenings of his trousers. The man was determined in his quest.

This can't be happening! I won't let it! her mind screamed. She heard the sound of cloth tearing as her garments were ripped and tugged away from her body. "No!" Her outcry was shrill. "Let me go!" No man would force her against her will, and stiffening her spine, Alandra fought with every ounce of her strength. She went half-mad, fighting to escape, kicking and lashing out with her fists.

Nicholas bounded through the trees like a wild animal. "Let her go!"

Alandra had never heard a more welcome sound than Christopher's voice. After aiming a kick at the hostler's shin, she uttered a cry of relief and rolled away from him.

"Sir, you are interrupting a matter that is none of your business," the hostler sneered.

"Alandra is my business!"

Though the man was strong, Nicholas came upon the hostler in a fury, lifting him up by his leather doublet to meet him eye to eye. "You bastard! I ought to—" He smiled slightly as he saw that the man's face was crisscrossed by scratch marks. "But it looks as if Alandra has already marked you."

"I have never seen such a hell cat! The pleasure was not worth the price!" The man's look was vibrant with hostility as he looked Alandra's way. "You are welcome to her."

"She is not yours to give." Nicholas trembled with rage as the realization of what had almost happened swept over him. He raised his fist in challenge.

"I will not fight you."

Nicholas thrust the man from him in disgust. "Good, for by my faith, you are not worth fighting." His eyes were gentle as they touched on Alandra. "Did he hurt you?"

"I am unharmed. All that is bruised and battered is my dignity." She covered her breasts with the remnants of her torn and tattered bodice.

"Good. For had he dishonored you, I would have had to kill him!" As if to add menace to his threat, he touched his sword. "As for you, you bastard, get out of here now, before I change my mind and skewer your liver on the tip of my sword."

Without a backward glance at Alandra, the hostler ran in the direction away from the inn.

"Alandra. Oh, Alandra!" She looked so young, so vulnerable. In three quick strides he was at her side, gathering her into his embrace. "Are you all right?"

"Yes! I fought him ..." She snuggled against him.

"You made a good show of bravery!" He brushed the hair back from her face with an aching tenderness, then lifted a strand of her hair that had tumbled over her breasts.

His touch was healing, his fingers strokes of velvet as he caressed her. Alandra felt warm and protected. "Christopher..." There were so many things she wanted to say.

"Hush!" His fingers were gentle as he touched her lips. "Let me talk." Nicholas took a long, deep breath. "I love you, Alandra!" There he had said it again, something he had never said to a woman before. But having revealed his feelings, he felt lighter of heart, as if in admitting it to her, he had finally come to terms with the truth himself.

"Oh, Christopher!" Alandra had dreamed of hearing him say those words. Now he had, twice in one night. All through her ordeal tears had burned her lids, but she had somehow managed to hold them at bay. Now they filled her eyes.

"Alandra! Love!" Her tears unnerved him. He couldn't stand to see her cry. "Don't!" He brushed at the moisture that trickled down her cheeks, his eyes touching on her full breasts which he longed to reach out and fondle.

Slowly, his mouth came down on hers, engulfing Alandra in the familiar sensations his lips always brought forth. Pressing her body closer to his, she sought the passion of his embrace. She craved his kisses with a warm sweet desire that could no longer be denied.

"Alandra!" He spoke her name again in a breathless whisper as he drew his mouth away. He had tried to stay away from her. By God, he had tried. But he was only flesh and blood, and he wanted her now with a fever that stirred his blood beyond all reason. Yet that fire was tempered with gentleness, and he felt a warmth in his heart as well as his loins. "I don't want to hurt you. Never that."

"I know. I also know that we come from two different worlds and that someday you will have to leave me. I am prepared for that, Christopher." The words hurt as she said them. "But in the meantime we could share such happiness."

"Alandra, I wish..."

Now it was her turn to silence him. "There are things that are beyond our control. You were born to walk amidst nobles, I to be among plainer folk. I have accepted that. What I can't accept is living my life without knowing what it is to be loved by you, in fact as well as words."

"I have never wanted anything as much as I want you now, Alandra. Never!"

She could feel his growing desire, giving proof to his words. "Then make love to me, Christopher. I want you so. Make me a woman."

How could he refuse when it was what he wanted, too?

The moon's soft light shone down upon them as Nicholas lowered her slowly to the ground. The night was warm with only a hint of a breeze, and the night birds serenaded the lovers.

There on a soft bed of grass he cradled her in his arms, sheltered beneath the outflung branches of two, entwining trees. They clung to each other, oblivious to everything but the sheer heady desire that consumed them.

Nicholas kissed her eyelids, the curve of her cheek, and her mouth with all the pent-up hunger he had tried to control for so long. His tongue gently traced the outline of her lips and slipped in between them to stroke her tongue. "Your mouth tastes so sweet," he whispered "and you are so soft..."

He felt her tremble beneath him and opened his

eyes, mesmerized by the potency of her gaze. He found himself trembling, too, with a nervousness that was unusual for him. Anticipation, he supposed. Eagerness. Desire. The thought that this achingly innocent woman had never had another man filled him with a wrenching tenderness. He would make it beautiful for her, this much he vowed.

Slowly, leisurely, Nicholas stripped the remnants of her garments away, like the petals of a flower. His fingers lingered as they wandered down her stomach to explore the texture of her skin. *Like velvet*, he thought. "You are so beautiful."

She glowed under the praise of his deep, throaty whisper. "Am I?" The compliment pleased her, made her more sure of herself in this quest to experience the unknown.

"Very..." He sought the indentation of her navel, then moved lower to tangle his fingers in the soft wisps of hair between her legs. Moving back, his eyes enjoyed what his hands had bared. "Do you have any idea how much I want you?" He took her hand and pressed it to the firm flesh of his arousal. Then he bent to kiss her again, his mouth holding hers captive.

Twining her hands around his neck, she clutched him to her, pressing her body eagerly against his chest. Christopher, her Christopher. She had spent so many nights dreaming that he would make love to her. Alandra tried to speak, to tell him what was in her heart, but all she could say was his name, a groan deep in her throat as his mouth and hands worked unspeakable magic.

Nicholas breathed deeply, savoring the spicy scent of her perfume, which engulfed him. "So much wasted time," he murmured. "But now I'll make up for it." His head was bent low, his tongue curling around the tips of her breast, suckling gently.

Raising up on his elbow, he looked down at her, and

at that moment he knew he'd put his heart and soul in her hands. Removing his doublet and shirt, he pressed their naked chests together, shivering at the vibrantly arousing sensation.

"Alandra . . ." Her name was like a prayer on his lips.

The warmth and heat of his mouth sent a sweet ache flaring through Alandra's whole body. Growing bold, she allowed her hands to explore his firm body. He was so perfectly formed. His masculine beauty hypnotized her, and for a moment she was content to stare. Then with a soft sigh, her fingers curled in the thick springy hair on his chest. His fingers lightly circled in imitation of what he was doing to her.

His lips nuzzled the side of her throat. He uttered a moan as her hands moved over the smoothly corded muscles of his shoulders. "Ah, how I love you to touch me . . ." he gasped as if his breath was trapped somewhere between his throat and stomach. He couldn't say anymore. The realization that she was finally to be his was a heady feeling that nearly made him dizzy as he brought his lips to hers. Such a potent kiss. As if he had never kissed her before.

In fact Nicholas had the feeling that he was doing everything for the very first time as he made love to her. She was the only woman he would ever love. Burying his face in the silky soft strands of her hair, he breathed in the fragrant scent of her hair once more and was lost to any other thought.

Closing her eyes, Alandra awaited another kiss, her mouth opening to him. She loved the taste of him, the tender urgency of his mouth, as she enjoyed the seemingly endless passionate onslaught of his kisses. It was if they were breathing one breath, living at that moment just for each other.

Desire writhed almost painfully within his loins, and Nicholas had never wanted anything or anyone as much as he did her at this moment. It was like an unfulfilled dream just waiting to come true.

Nicholas cupped her breasts. Lightly, he stroked them until the peaks sprang to life under his touch, the once soft flesh now taut and aching. His breath caught in his throat as his gray eyes savored her. *No longer forbidden fruit,* he thought. Now she was his. Bending down, he worshipped her with his mouth, his lips traveling from one breast to the other in tender fascination. His tongue curled around the stiffened peaks, his teeth lightly grazing until she writhed beneath him. He savored the expressions that flitted across her face, the wanting and the passion for him that were so clearly revealed.

The night air caressed Alandra's skin, and the stars hovered above them in the sky like candles. *My bridal chamber,* Alandra thought moving in sensuous fascination against him. Her hands crept around Nicholas's neck, her fingers tangling and tousling the thick waves of his black hair as she breathed a husky sigh. How wonderful it was to be loved! She caught fire wherever he touched her, burning with an all-consuming need.

She shivered in his arms, and fearing it was from the night air, he gathered her closer, covering her body even more tightly with his.

"I want you so . . ." she whispered.

"Landra!" A shudder racked through him as he pushed her away just for a moment. Quickly, he stood and stripped off his remaining clothes, and Alandra took her turn to appraise him. The image of his broad, bronzed shoulders, wide chest, flat belly, and well-formed legs would forever be branded in her mind.

Kneeling, he enwined his fingers in her dark hair, pulling her face up to his. He kissed her again, his knowing, seeking lips moving with tender urgency across hers.

Then they lay together kissing, touching, and his

hands did such wondrous things to her, making her writhe and groan. Every inch of her body caught fire as passion exploded between them in wild oblivion. He moved against her, sending waves of pleasure exploding along every nerve in her body.

"Christopher... love me..." she breathed.

His hands caressed her, warming her with their heat. Sensuously, his fingers slid down the velvety flesh of her belly, moving to that place between her thighs that ached for his entry.

His swollen length brushed across her thighs. Then he was covering her. His gentle probing ignited a sweet fire curling deep inside her as spirals of pulsating sensations engulfed her.

She felt his maleness at the fragile entry to her womanhood, then the pressing of that delicate membrane. Every inch of her tingled with an intense arousing awareness of his body. There was only a brief moment of pain, but desire pushed it away. Alandra was conscious only of unbearable pleasure as he began to move within her.

Nicholas groaned softly, the blood pounding thickly in his head. His hold on her hips tightened as he took her. She was so warm, so tight around him, that he closed his eyes in agonizing pleasure as he moved back and forth, initiating her fully into the depths of passion and love.

Instinctively, Alandra tightened her legs around him, certain she could never withstand the ecstasy that enslaved her body. It was as if the night had shattered into a thousand stars, bursting within her. She was melting inside, merging with him into one being. As spasms overtook her, she dug her nails into his back, whispering his name.

A sweet pang shot through Nicholas, and he closed his eyes. Even when the intensity of their passion was spent, they still clung to each other, unable to let this magical moment end. They touched each other gently, wonderingly.

"What a passionate wench you are." He nibbled playfully at her ear.

"Am I now? And are you not pleased?"

"Aye! But not surprised."

Nicholas was not taken unaware by the passion she expressed. He had sensed that she would be a woman to whom the culmination of desire was like a whirl-wind, and she was all that he could have asked for, all that he wanted. Indeed, she made love with the same carefree, honest, loving spirit with which she lived.

Cradling her against his chest, he lay silent for a long, long time as he savored her presence beside him. His hands fondled her gently as she molded her body so trustingly to his. *If only I could keep her with me forever,* he thought, *and never let Elizabeth, Owen Stafford or the ambitious court of England intrude.*

Nicholas realized that for the first time in his life he was truly happy. Money and power were said to be the most important things on earth, but he knew differently. Without someone who really cared, life was hollow and made of a man a shallow creature. Alandra made him feel alive!

Don't go back. Stay with the actors. The idea was so tempting. But could he just give up his past with no regrets? As he leaned his chin against Alandra's soft, fragrant hair, he was almost persuaded to do so.

Chapter Thirty-Two

The moon was beginning its downward descent when Nicholas and Alandra reluctantly made their way back to the inn, laughing and talking uninhibitedly, like two mischievous youths returning from a misdeed. Indeed, it had been a nighttime tryst that neither would ever forget, a joyful, passionate joining that caused them the greatest happiness and not even a moment's regret.

So this is love, Alandra thought realizing that nothing could have prepared her for this breathtaking ride on a world spinning out of control. She had never realized just how incomplete she was without Christopher until the moment she had known the glorious satisfaction of Christopher's making her his. He had made her want to blend herself with him until they were flesh of one flesh, heart of one heart, inseparable from that moment on. Now she was a woman and no longer a girl.

"Are you as content and happy as I am?" Nicholas asked.

Alandra felt her heart skip a beat as Nicholas tugged at her hair. "Doubly so," she answered. She paused to look regretfully from the direction they had come. "I wish we could go back. 'Twill be a special place to me from now on. Enchanted."

"Any place will be enchanted when we are together, Landra. Our love will make it so." Just looking at her brought forth his desire. Nicholas wanted with all his heart to go back to the tree-shrouded meadow and make love to her again, but unselfishly he thought about Alandra's reputation. If morning came and it was found that she was not in her room, she would be the victim of cruel gossip. Heminges was always grumbling about women being trouble. He couldn't take the chance of Alandra being targeted for serious rebuke.

They walked the rest of the way in silence, the looks that passed between them saying far more than words could ever tell. Nicholas knew that from this moment on Alandra would be branded in his heart, his soul.

The innyard was silvered with the moon's muted radiance, but luckily the interior of the inn was dark, without even one candle to illuminate the windows. Nicholas's arm draped possessively across her shoulders seemed perfectly natural as they walked. She was his. From this moment on she would always be in his heart.

Alandra paused to look up at the sky, letting her breath out in a long, deep sigh. "I'm so happy, Christopher! I never knew that it was possible to feel like this."

"Nor I!" He felt as if the years had been swept away, and he was but a boy again. He gazed intently at Alandra, wanting to engrave every detail of her beauty upon his memory—the arch of her brows, the upward tilt of her mouth, the way the moonlight danced upon her dark brown hair.

Alandra inhaled deeply. There was something magical about her surroundings. The grass seemed to sparkle with diamonds, the branches of the trees were entwined as if embracing, and the breeze seemed to be humming a love song. She wouldn't have been a bit surprised to see the fairy folk that Will wrote about dancing in the darkness. She felt light of heart. Carefree. Perhaps it was always that way when one was in love.

Nicholas pulled her to him. "Alandra! Alandra! I've waited for you all my life." His lips grazed her forehead, brushing gently along the heavy brush of her dark lashes, teasing the line of her jaw, then caressing her neck. "I don't want to let you go!" His emotions caused his throat to tighten, making his voice very husky. "I want to make love to you again and again."

"And I would have you love me again, sir, now that I know to what delights you can take me!" Alandra arched against him in sensual pleasure, her hands sliding over the muscles of his arms down to his firm stomach.

"Oh, how you tempt me." Nicholas's eyes moved up to the loft where the hard wood was covered with a soft bed of straw. His strong fingers stroked and fondled her breast as he struggled with his longing. "But you will be a bit sore after tonight, Alandra." Especially since they had made love a second time, a mating even more passionate than the first. "I want to be the most considerate of lovers." He playfully touched the end of her nose. "But tomorrow night...."

"Tomorrow night!" The words made her tingle as if a gentle wind caressed her.

"And the next and the next..." For an endless moment he held her against him, then as if fearing to test his resolve, he let her go. "Come, Landra. It grows late, and as much as I regret it, we must return to the others."

"Aye."

They held hands as they opened the thick wooden door. Nicholas tiptoed in, determined to protect Alandra's reputation at all costs. He looked cautiously about the room before he was satisfied that she could enter.

"Deserted! Everyone is still abed," he whispered.

Alandra paused to listen then as she moved, she tried to tread lightly so as not to set the floorboards creaking. But each step seemed to explode in the silence.

Nicholas led her to the stairs. "And so I say to you, good night, my lady."

Their fingers moved over each other's faces. She lifted her arms to encircle his neck, hardly daring to believe that he was hers now. "I will always belong to you," she said softly as she clung to him, her breasts pressed against his chest, wishing they didn't have to say good night.

Nicholas buried his face in the dark cloud of her hair. "Tonight as I lay in my bed, I will be thinking of you and how you should be beside me. Oh, how I wish ..."

"As do I ..." Dare she even imagine that someday they might pledge their troth to each other as man and wife? Somehow after tonight anything seemed possible. Perhaps if one wished hard enough, dreams could come true.

Her body arched against his as he caressed her. His fingers seemed to be everywhere, touching her, setting her body ablaze with desire.

But Nicholas was a man true to his word. He repeated the word, "Tomorrow."

"If I can wait that long. Now that I know what I have been missing, I feel the need to make up for lost hours, Christopher."

"And indeed you shall if I have my way. But off to bed with you now."

Mutely, Alandra nodded, a mischievous smile trembling on her lips. She leaned against him, outlining the shape of his mouth with her fingertips. "And are you doubly certain you do not want to join me there? 'Twould seem to me that a featherbed would be much more accommodating to lovers than the hard ground."

"Aye, 'tis soft. But the feathers tickle my nose." He patted her on the behind. "Now off with you, wench. You must learn to obey me."

"Obey, is it?" Deliberately, she rubbed up against him, smiling as his reaction to her nearness proved how much he desired her.

Nicholas groaned and reached for her, but Alandra laughed softly and danced away from his grasp. "Tomorrow." Blowing him an impudent kiss, she disappeared up the stairs.

Nicholas stood there for several minutes after she had gone. A smile lit up his eyes and for a moment he was tempted to follow her, to change his mind about making love to her in her room. Then with a shrug of his shoulders, he turned away.

Chapter Thirty-Three

Muted rays of sunlight fluttered through an opening in the inn's shutters. From beneath the window the sound of the first cock's crow reminded Alandra all too jarringly that morning had come. She stretched her arms and opened her eyes as her hand made contact with solid flesh. Christopher. Last night he had come, making good on his promise of "tomorrow." Now his arm lay heavy across her stomach, the heat of his body warming hers as they lay entwined.

The sound of his steady breathing made her heart pound wildly. A flush of color stained her cheeks as she remembered the words she had said, the things she had done. Closing her eyes, she remembered that moment vividly when he had knocked at her door three times in signal, and she had opened it to him giggling like a naughty child. His kiss had silenced her laughter, growing deeper as he wooed her with his lips.

Her senses had responded to him immediately. Beneath his hands and mouth, her body had come alive, and she had been lost in a heat of desire that she had never believed possible. His hands against her aching breasts had warmed her through the fabric of her gown. Never had she removed her garments so quickly or so frantically. A pain had formed so taut in her belly that she had feared she would explode with wanting him.

Undeniably she had been bold last night, but caring about him so deeply had made her brazen. It seemed a wanton lived inside her body, an ardent woman who responded unashamedly to Christopher. Despite the heat of their passion, however, he had been gentle with her, hurrying nothing, taking his time. He had savored her body, his fingers sliding over her skin so tenderly that she had tingled with a prickly fire. But when he had touched the softness between her legs, she could wait no longer. Arching upward, straining against him, she had parted her thighs, and he had entered her so smoothly, so easily that she wondered if she were dreaming. But 'twas no dream. The heated lovemaking that had followed had been too gloriously real.

"Lover ..." she whispered.

Once Alandra might have thought the word to have a tawdry ring to it, but feeling as she did about him, she couldn't believe that the passion and joy they found together was wrong. She couldn't help feeling happy and content. Life couldn't get any better than this.

The world was a much happier place when two people were in love. Love was intangible, yet Alandra thought at times that she could nearly reach out and touch it. It seemed to enfold her, warm her. The feelings that stirred inside her breast for Christopher were certain to plunge her into turbulent waters, and yet wasn't he worth the risk?

Determinedly, she shoved aside the misgivings that entered her mind and clung to her optimistic feelings. She did love him. Right now that was the only important thing. Her mind, her heart, the very core of her being, longed for him.

The moments she spent with Christopher were the most blissful and contented of her life. Just being with him made her smile. The hours seeming to fly by as the sweet harmony that had first blossomed between them now flourished. There was a romantic side to Christopher that deeply touched her. When she was with him, she felt special. He said over and over again that there was just one "Alandra" and that she belonged to him.

Rising on one elbow, she looked at him now with aching tenderness. He looked so much younger and vulnerable when asleep, not at all like England's foremost swordsman. He snuggled up against her, his powerful body sprawled across the bed as if he didn't have a worry in the world. Touching a lock of dark hair that had fallen across his brow, she felt just as protective of him as he felt of her. She would help him prove his innocence and would never let anyone harm him. No one!

Above all she wanted to make him happy. And it certainly seemed as though she'd succeeded. His face had the calm peace of a contented man.

"Christopher loves me!" she whispered, and that thought brought a smile to her lips as she again stretched languorously. To Christopher she had given her heart, completely because with him she was incapable of holding the tide of her feelings in reserve. Though she longed for a firmer commitment from him, wanted with all her heart to be his wife, his love was enough for now. Whatever happened she would never be sorry for what had passed between them. It would have been far more unsettling if she had never experienced the ultimate joy of his love.

Leaning forward, she touched his mouth lightly in a kiss, laughing softly as his lips began to twitch.

"Alandra?" Nicholas cherished finding her cradled in his arms, her mane of dark hair spread like a cloak over her shoulders. He felt an aching tenderness and drew her closer. "Good morrow, fair lady. What a welcome surprise."

"For me as well as for you." She snuggled into his arms, laying her head on his shoulder, curling into his hard, strong body. "I trust you slept well, without the feathers of the bed and pillows tickling your nose," she said with a laugh.

"Aye, I slept very well. Such enjoyable activity as we partook of last night made me sleep like a babe." He did in fact feel quite warm and content. He belonged with Alandra, there wasn't any question of that now.

His hand moved lightly over her hip and down her leg as he spoke. Weeks of frustration and worry just seemed to have melted away. She was his! At last he had come to know the glorious sweetness of her body. Oh, but her body had been pure heaven, her genuine outpouring of love a precious gift. Whenever they were together, she made him the happiest man alive.

"I'd like to wake up every morning and find you next to me," he confided, nibbling at her ear lobe playfully. But he was not sure just what destiny had in store for him. He wanted to hide out from the world forever, but could he? Despite his smile, there was just a hint of a furl to his brow. "Alandra . . ."

"Hush!" She didn't want to spoil the morning by letting reality intrude upon her dreams. She knew what he was going to say, that he wanted so much to marry her but couldn't ask her now when his future was uncertain. "We must content ourselves with the moments that we do have."

"Then come here, temptress." He reached for her as a primal growl purred in his throat. He kissed her, and pleasure jolted through him. As she arched her body and sighed, he knew it to be the same for her, and her response gave him a heady feeling. He had been able to bring her deep satisfaction not once but several times during the night.

Nicholas moved his hands over her body, stroking lightly. With reverence, he moved his hands over her breasts, gently and slowly, until they swelled beneath his fingers. He outlined one rosy-peaked mound, watching as the velvet flesh hardened.

Alandra closed her eyes to the sensations she was becoming familiar with now. Wanting to bring him the same pleasure, she touched him, one hand sliding down over the muscles of his chest, sensuously stroking him.

"And to think I sought to protect you from that hostler when it seems I really should have protected you from myself," he whispered in her ear.

"I don't want to be protected from you. We were meant to be together, Christopher."

Their eyes met and held as an unspoken communication passed between them. He was ready for lovemaking and so was she. In a surge of passion, he rolled her under him. Then they were rolling over and over in the bed, sinking into the warmth and softness. Alandra sighed in delight at the feel of his hard, lithe body atop hers.

A flicker of desire spread to the core of her body. Being with Christopher aroused every emotion she had ever known. She was passionately in love, recklessly so.

"Alandra, my love ..." he said, his voice thick with desire. Slowly, sensuously, Nicholas let his hand slid

Kathryn Kramer

up her thigh, his fingers questing, seeking that most intimate part of her. His legs moved between hers and pressed to spread her thighs.

Alandra moved her body against him, feeling the burning flesh touching hers. He inflamed more than just her body. Indeed, he sparked a flame in her heart and soul.

Caressing her, kissing her, he left no part of her free from his touch, and she responded with a passion that was kindled by his love. Her entire body quivered and she would never get tired of feeling Christopher's hands on her skin, of tasting his kisses.

Boldly, she explored Nicholas's body, and his flesh was warm to her touch, pulsating with the strength of his maleness.

As her fingers closed around him, Nicholas groaned. "Alandra!" Desire raged like an inferno, pounding hotly in his veins. His whole body throbbed with the fierce compulsion to plunge himself into her sweet softness, and yet he held himself back, caressing her once more, stroking her, until he could tell that she was fully prepared for his entry. Her skin felt hot against his as he entwined his legs with hers.

"Love me. Love me now," she whispered. Her frantic desire for him was nearly unbearable. Her body arched up to his, searing him with the heat of her passion. Warm, damp, and inviting, she welcomed him as he entered her.

Writhing in pleasure, she was silken fire beneath him, rising and falling with him as he moved with the relentless rhythm of their love. They were spiraling together into the ultimate passion. Climbing together. Soaring. Sweet, hot desire fused their bodies together, yet there was an aching sweetness mingling with the fury and the fire. They spoke with their hearts and hands and bodies words they had never uttered before in the final outpouring of their love.

In the aftermath, when all their passion had ebbed and they lay entwined, they sealed their vows of love with whispered words. Sighing with happiness, Alandra rested within the cradle of Nicholas's arms, happy and content.

"I love you." Nicholas placed soft kisses on her forehead. She mumbled sleepily and stretched lazily, her soft thighs brushing against his hair-roughened ones in a motion which stirred him again. "That was pure heaven. Shall we try it again," he breathed mischievously.

A loud pounding at the door interrupted their pleasure.

"Bloody damn!" Nicholas's oath was muffled by Alandra's hand.

Rising from the bed, she cast a worried look in the direction of the sound.

"Alandra?"

"What is it, Father?" Alandra did her best to sound sleepy.

"Open up! I've got something important to tell you!"

"By God!" Nicholas rasped. He had no liking for being found stark-naked in Murray's daughter's bed. This was not the place, the time, or the way, to announce that they were lovers. In consideration of Alandra's good name, he had done his utmost to be discreet.

"Come back later, Father." Alandra looked at the door then at Nicholas, then back at the door again. "I want to go back to sleep."

"Sleep? It's morning, Alandra."

"Aye, so it is." Alandra was always an early riser. To try to send her father away would only pique his suspicions. Undoubtedly, if she insisted she wanted to stay abed, Murray would think her ill and bring some tight-lipped physician to see her. "Give me a moment. I'm coming."

Nicholas gave Alandra a regretful look. Groaning, he bounded out of bed, his ardor cooled. Hastily donning his hosen, trunk hose and doublet, he searched around for a hiding place. The bedroom was sparsely furnished with but a small table, one chair, and the bed. Escape through the window? Alandra's room was on the second floor and overlooked the courtyard. There was too much risk of his being seen. It would be best to wait out Murray's visit, but the only spot able to accommodate Nicholas's large body was underneath the wooden bed frame.

"Alandra! What is taking you so long, girl? I'm standing out in the hallway in my nightshirt."

"I'm coming!" Raising on tiptoe, Alandra quickly gave Nicholas a kiss on the cheek. "I'll get rid of him as soon as I can."

"Be about it quickly. I have ere been an impatient lover." He patted her on the behind, then with a grumble, got down upon his knees as if in prayer.

Taking a deep breath, he managed to squeeze under the bed and lay there as silently and unmoving as he could while Alandra shrugged into her nightgown and crossed the wooden floor to let Murray in.

"Merry-go-up, daughter! Wait until you hear what has happened."

Pushing through the door, Murray walked into the room, granting Nicholas a look at his knobby knees as he passed by the bed.

"Tell me!" For a moment Alandra panicked, fearing her father had something to tell her about Christopher. What if someone from court had learned he was in Dover?

"Our moneybox has been stolen." Murray shook his head woefully. "One of the young actors apparently broke into Heminges room and made off with it during the night."

"What?" She let out a long sigh of relief. "Is that all?"

"By God, child!" Murray's shout was like hearing a tabby cat roar.

"I only meant that it might have been worse. I feared at first that some tragedy had befallen us. But money is only money after all."

"Only . . ." Murray was rendered speechless, then he sighed. "I suppose that you are right. Our health, our well-being, is much more important. But woe is me. Woe is me."

Alandra was nervous as her father approached the bed, wondering if there were any telltale signs of the amorous activities that had occurred during the night. Certainly, the coverlets were in disarray.

"We will all have to be most circumspect with our shillings," Murray warned.

But Alandra wasn't really worried, and said, "We will quickly fill the moneybox again when we go back to London."

"But that's just the point. We can't go back!"

"Can't go back to London?" If her father thought that bit of news would disappoint her, he was wrong. It gave her more time with Christopher. Besides, until they found out who killed Lord Woodcliff, he would be in the utmost danger there.

He hurried to explain. "Ben Jonson has been arrested."

"Another seditious play?" It wouldn't be the first time their friend had been taken into custody. Nor was it serious. Playwrights often suffered such indignities when they wrote something with which one of the noblemen had a quarrel. Was it any wonder Shakespeare was cautious?

"He killed a man in a swordfight."

"No!" The reminder of Nicholas's plight came back to haunt her.

"Yes!" Murray sat down in the chair near the foot of the bed, nervously tapping his toes against the frame. "He's written to Will of his intent to plead benefit of clergy. Scholars are allowed such, as you know."

"I know." If only Christopher could have made a pledge of being scholarly, he might not have had to run.

"Aye. If you ask me, old Ben will be exonerated, but meanwhile things couldn't be worse for us." He paused to reflect on the matter. "What happened stirred up those Puritan troublemakers again. The theaters are still shut tight, and it looks as if they will remain so for quite a while." Murray clucked his tongue in annoyance. "We won't be returning as soon as Will had planned."

"Then where do we go?" Alandra found herself wishing that they could remain in Dover, a town which already held such precious memories.

"That's why I'm here. We will most likely head in the direction of Bath. Will is having a meeting to decide. Undoubtedly, we will have to move on quickly. This inn is very expensive, and now most of us have little funds. Thus the meeting. I knew you would want to sit in on it."

"A meeting!" Alandra purposely said it loud enough for Nicholas to hear. As keeper of the ledgers she would be expected to go. "A meeting now?"

Beneath the bed Nicholas cursed softly. Whoever stole that money certainly had rotten timing.

"At this very minute," Murray answered, standing up. For a moment he looked around him. "I could have sworn that I heard a mumble."

Alandra laughed. "My stomach rumbling its hunger."

"Then hurry! Get into your clothes, girl, and I'll get into mine. I smelled some oatmeal brewing. We'll partake of it before we go seek out Will." The very mention of food made Murray smile as he ambled toward the door. "Perhaps I'll even try a bit of sausage, though my stomach is not as immune to spices as it used to be." He opened the door and started to leave, then hung back for a moment. "From the first moment I laid eyes on Christopher, I knew your place was beside him. It's glad I am that there are smiles between you again."

Alandra couldn't quite meet her father's eyes. "Smiles..." she said, wondering what Murray would think if he knew there was so much more.

"I like that young fellow! Indeed, I do. For I know that he loves you. I do not think I could give you up to any other man. But I know you are safe with him."

Murray's eyes darted to the spot on the floor where Nicholas's boots were flung haphazardly. Cocking his head, the old man raised his brows. For a moment he was deep in contemplation as a myriad of expressions flitted over his face.

Though Murray didn't say a word of reproach, Alandra sensed at once that her father knew Christopher was in the room. "Father...." She felt the need to explain, but Murray shook his head.

"I want no explanations, no pretense of shame and remorse," he said, raising his hand. " 'Tis not for me to judge or to scold. Life is all too fleeting, and true love a wonder that few possess. You are happy, daughter. The glow on your face tells me so." He gently tweaked her nose in the same manner he had used when she was a mischievous child. "That is all I want for now."

"I *am* happy!" Alandra let out a long, drawn-out sigh. "Moreso than I ever dreamed possible."

Nicholas heard her impassioned words. Oh, that he always heard such joy from her lips. He didn't ever want Alandra to regret what had passed between them. As to Murray, it was time they had a heart-to-

heart talk. There were things about Nicholas that the
old man had every right to know.

"Alandra...." It was obvious that there were many
things that Murray wanted to say, emotions he wanted
to express, but he said only, "It's my wish that you
will always be happy. You deserve as much, for you
have given me purpose and given my life the most
blessed peace." The old man's eyes moistened with
tears. Hurriedly brushing them away with the sleeve
of his nightshirt, he stepped through the open doorway.

Chapter Thirty-Four

The assemblage of actors was as colorful a group as could ever be imagined—a gathering of multicolored doublets, hosen, and hats that rivaled the flowers in the inn's garden. Even so it was a somber group that met in the inner courtyard to discuss their future, each and every one of them incensed that they had been robbed. Making use of Murray's collection of stools, chairs, benches, and thrones, forming them into a semi-circle, they transformed the stage area into an open-air meeting room.

At the arc of this circle Shakespeare stood while the others seated themselves. With a casualness that belied his importance with the group, he called the meeting to order. Nicholas listened to Will ask the group for suggestions as to their next destination since the London theaters were still closed and under the watchful eyes of the Privy Council and the mayor.

There were arguments both for and against continuing into Bath and Bristol or returning to London. While the players expressed their views, Nicholas had other matters on his mind. Not one to be afraid of any situation, Nicholas nonetheless was nervous and disquieted at the prospect of facing Murray. Not because he feared the jovial old man, for Murray did not look as if he could threaten a rabbit, but because he was apprehensive of disappointing the kind-hearted man. Murray had trusted him, had befriended him, and in return Nicholas had lied to him. He could argue with himself that it had been an act born of a desperation to save himself, but a falsehood had been perpetrated just the same. Alandra knew the truth and Shakespeare. Now Murray must be told. With fierce resolve, Nicholas clenched his jaw. He couldn't base his relationship with Alandra upon a lie, and he would speak to Murray at the first opportunity.

Nicholas turned his attention back to the conversation. William Sly and Richard Burbage unwaveringly stood by their desire to return to London. However, when the votes were taken, the decision to go to Bath had prevailed. Untroubled by any internal dissension, the company made their plans to continue their season on the road. After a few other matters were touched upon, the actors dispersed.

"And so it is decided," Murray exclaimed, bounding to his feet.

He started to leave the stage, but Nicholas grabbed him by the arm. "No, don't go. We have to talk!" Nicholas was not prepared for the tight ball that lodged in his stomach as Murray looked up at him.

"Aye, it seems by the look in your eyes that we do."

Nicholas tensed his jaw again. This was even more difficult than he had imagined. "Then let us go some place where we can talk. Alone!" he emphasized.

"My room? It is at the end of the hall where there are few prying eyes or ears."

"Agreed!" Nicholas followed Murray, running the things he needed to say through his mind as they walked.

"Here we are." Murray opened the thick wooden door, revealing a total state of disarray. The bed was cluttered with costumes, the chairs covered with props of various shapes and sizes. Indeed, it looked much like the play wagon.

"Alandra is forever scolding me for not being of a more tidy nature," he complained good-naturedly, "but in truth I know the exact location of everything that I need."

Uncovering a chair, he bid Nicholas to take a seat, but Nicholas was more comfortable standing.

"Let me begin by telling you that I love your daughter with all my heart," Nicholas said softly. "Of that you must have no doubt."

"Love her. Of course. I know you love her, Christopher. Perhaps I even knew that before you did." Murray's eyes glittered with moisture.

"Murray . . ."

The stage man held up his hand. "Before you think to make a confession to me, I also know that you and my daughter are now lovers."

Nicholas was stunned. "You know? How?"

Murray chuckled. "The next time you take refuge beneath a bed, Christopher, you should remember to hide your boots." He patted the younger man's arm with gentle censure.

"Believe me, I have no intentions of ever acting so foolish again." Nicholas's face flushed, something that rarely happened. "It was just . . . just that I didn't want you to . . ."

"I understand, Christopher." As if he were confiding a secret, Murray lowered his voice. "Besides, I know how impetuous Alandra can be." Taking off his cap, Murray twisted it nervously in his hand. "My only question is, where does your love for my daughter lead you now?"

"I would marry her, Murray, if—"

Throwing his hat up in the air, Murray gave a shout of joy. "And I would be most proud to welcome you as my son."

"Murray!" If only things could be different. If only Nicholas could pretend to himself that he really was Christopher Nicholas. It would be so much easier to go on with the lie. But he had vowed to tell Murray the truth and he would—or be damned. "Believe me when I tell you that my dearest wish is to take Alandra as my wife, but . . ."

"But . . . ?" Murray's voice was choked. "Merry-go-up, don't tell me you are already married!" He looked Christopher straight in the eye, one of his eyebrows rising in mild rebuke as he jumped to that conclusion.

"No!"

"Thank God." Murray sagged his corpulent body into a chair, waiting for Christopher to continue.

"Oh, how do I make you understand?" Nicholas strode up and down. He decided it was prudent to begin at the beginning. "First and foremost, my name is *not* Christopher Nicholas!"

"So? As Will has said, a rose by any other name would smell as sweet . . ."

"It's not only that!" Nicholas took a deep breath. "Everything I told you is a lie, Murray. I am not an actor, never was. I didn't study with Edward Alleyn. Hell, I hardly even know who he is."

Murray shrugged his shoulders. "You are not telling me anything I don't know, Christopher. I suspected as much. I'm afraid that you gave yourself away more than a few times. But I wouldn't be at all surprised to see Will give you a role one of these days. We are all your friends. If you have need of us, you have but to ask and we will give you aid."

"There is much more to my story." Nicholas paused, then blurted out, "I wasn't in your play wagon that night because I was fleeing from the inn for not paying my bill. There was another reason." He stopped pacing to stand in front of Murray, his hands folded in front of his chest.

"Whatever you have done, I assure you that none will chastise you." Murray coughed uncomfortably, as if he didn't really want to hear more about the matter. "With us, with Alandra, you can begin a new life, Christopher. In case you haven't discovered it for yourself, we in the company are not loath to shield those outside the law. Like my friend, Ben."

Though Murray obviously wanted to dismiss the matter, Nicholas pressed on. "I was hiding because the queen's guards were after me." Nicholas's lips were tight as he said, "I am accused of killing Lord Woodcliffe."

"Accused of . . ." Murray gripped the arms of his chair. "But you didn't! On that I would stake my life."

"No, I didn't kill him. Though at first I thought I had." Even now Nicholas was incensed by the memory. "Now I feel of a certainty that I was framed for the deed by my most hated rival at court. A man whose name even now sours my tongue. Owen Stafford."

"Lord Stafford? Rival?" Murray's eyes were as wide as saucers. He knew at once what that meant. "And you . . ."

"My name is Nicholas Leighton. Sir Nicholas Leighton."

"A nobleman!" Murray gasped, drawing back in his chair and recoiling as if he had been slapped. "Oh, no." He covered his face with his hands. "Better that you be a rogue or a thief than a vainglorious popinjay. One of them. Alandra! Oh, my poor, poor girl. I had thought . . . I had hoped . . ."

Nicholas rushed to explain. "That is why I tried so

hard to keep my distance from Alandra, Murray! To avoid hurting her."

"But you will!"

"I won't. You have to trust me. Alandra is more important to me than my life!" The whole story tumbled forth from Nicholas. His infatuation with Morgana, their humiliation at the masque, the meeting at the inn, then the tragedy of her husband's murder. "I was running from Stafford's men with little hope of escape. That's when I spotted your play wagon."

"And got a knock on the noggin."

"At first all I could think about was using the acting company as a haven, somewhere to hide until I could find a way to prove my innocence. It was not in my plans to fall in love with Alandra, but I did."

Since he was making confessions, Nicholas also revealed to Murray the truth about Shakespeare's horse. That he had stolen it and that Alandra had ridden after him to retrieve it. She had also not trusted him and had only agreed to keep his true identity a secret to protect the company. But Alandra had finally told Will who he was and Will had made no move against him.

"And," Nicholas said now, "in spite of my love for her, I vowed to leave her alone. I was afraid that Alandra would have no future with a man in such dire circumstances. I thought we had no hope of happiness so I tried to stay away from her, Murray. I tried, but I couldn't."

"My fault! Mine. I was equally determined to play Cupid for I was so certain . . ."

"That she and I belong together. We do."

Murray threw his arms up in defeat. "You belong together, aye, but you come from two different worlds. Thus it cannot be, Christopher."

"That's what I thought at first, but I have since changed my mind. It can be, Murray. I love her! And saw she believes in my innocence and loves me. What can be more important than that?"

Murray's face was etched with pain. "You sound as if you were reciting lines from one of Will's plays, but life is not as simple as that. There is as much hatred in the world as love. Perhaps more so. If Lord Stafford is intent on ruining you, he will not stop until he has."

Nicholas couldn't admit defeat, not now. He had to believe that right would overpower wrong. Hadn't Alandra told him so? "I won't let Stafford win. I didn't kill Lord Woodcliffe, and I can only hope that someday my name will be cleared."

"And you can return to court." Murray sighed, reflecting his deep, inner anguish. He mumbled to himself, saying, "Actors and playwrights are welcome at court, but only as entertainers. You will never be able to marry Alandra." His full lips quivered. He looked as if at any moment he would break down and cry. "Never!"

"I know. Elizabeth is like a veritable shrew on the subject." Nicholas's eyes were unwavering as he said determinedly, "That is why I do not plan to return, Murray!"

"You mean . . ." Murray lifted his head.

"Whether or not my reputation is restored, I have forsaken my previous life." There would be no turning back now. "Alandra is not only beautiful but everything a man could want in a woman. As long as she wants me by her side, I will stay."

Murray was dubious. "And give up your nobility?"

"The strings that Elizabeth pulls. Aye." As he spoke, he realized that he really did mean it.

Murray jumped to his feet. "I knew I wasn't wrong about you. I knew it, Christopher! I knew it! You and Alandra. It was meant to be."

Frantically, he searched the room, finding a bottle of wine beneath a stack of hats. Two mugs were retrieved from a corner of the room. Filling the two cups, Murray made a toast to the days ahead.

"To the future," Nicholas echoed, not fully certain what awaited him.

Chapter Thirty-Five

Queen Elizabeth strolled in the garden at Greenwich, ignoring the tall man hovering at her side as was her way when she was displeased. Carefully picking up the skirt of her black dress, embroidered with pearls and silver thread, she was obvious in her effort to avoid Lord Owen Stafford as she moved toward the eager-to-please young male courtiers clustered by the yew trees.

But he was not to be thwarted. Picking a large white rose, he blocked her path. "A rose for a rose," he said coyly, offering it to her.

Elizabeth sniffed indignantly. "I do not like yon flower. It makes me sneeze."

Tossing it over his shoulder, Stafford forced a smile to hide his irritation. "Then from this day on I abhor it as well, Your Majesty. I will give orders to my gardener that all the roses in my garden be plucked lest on one of your visits they annoy you."

"On one of my visits?" She toyed with the great rope of pearls around her neck as she looked at him. Dressed in white and black as was she, he looked almost as if he were her consort. "And just what makes you think that I intend to come?" It pleased her that he was so anxious to regain her favor.

"Knowing how fond Your Majesty is of the hunt, I have planned a special surprise," he answered, flashing her the boyish smile that had first won her affection.

"A hunt. How boring." She put her hand up to her mouth as if to stifle a yawn. "That is unless you intend to provide the one quarry I am interested in. That I would find amusing."

"You mean Sir Nicholas Leighton!" His smile quickly faltered.

"I do!" Though he had been making promises proclaiming that he would capture Sir Nicholas any day, Lord Stafford had yet to fulfill his boasts. Elizabeth was quickly losing patience. "With all the time that has passed, I wonder that he is not all the way to Spain by now."

He started to make excuses, but she held up her hand. Turning her back on him, she moved toward the waiting courtiers. "Shall we ride, my lords?"

Not a word was spoken requesting that he come along. It was an intentional slight. "Damn her! And damn him!" Stafford swore. Never had he detested Nicholas Leighton more. Watching as Elizabeth headed off to the stables where her horse would be saddled by several waiting grooms, he wracked his brain as to where his rival could be. Was the queen right? Had he taken a ship and crossed the Channel? Was he in France or Spain, laughing behind his hand at them? It was a question still on his mind as the queen and her entourage thundered past.

"I have to find him and put him where he belongs!"

he muttered under his breath. It had become an all-driving need, an obsession.

"Psssst!"

Stafford turned his head in the direction of the sound. It was coming from behind a tree, but he didn't even seek the source of the rude whisper.

"Psssst, your Lordship!"

A man stepped from his hiding place, the kind of man Stafford usually avoided, but who on some occasions was very necessary. A man who was as much at odds with his elaborate surroundings as was a rat in a highly bred kennel.

"Bloody hell! What on earth are you doing here?"

"Trying to find you."

"Me?" He was incensed. What if someone thought he knew this man, that he was an acquaintance?

"I know where 'e is. I figured it out in my head. Sir Nicholas Leighton."

Stafford's ears pricked up at the name. "Where?"

Will Frizer danced around. "Oh, no. The broadside says there is a reward. First the money, then I'll tell. After all, you are not the only one 'oo wants to know."

With a grumble, Stafford reached in his purse, counting the money out. He was short by a large sum of shillings. "I'll give you this now, but you'll have to come back for the rest."

Frizer shook his head. "Ah, no! I've been burned by that one before. By someone else. And that's why I come to give the information to you instead. It seems to me that you are trustworthy, and it never 'urts to 'ave several patrons, particularly when it is obvious that you are eager to know."

Stafford pulled off one of his rings, choosing the gold one with several diamonds. "Here. This should more than suffice. Now tell me." If the man was just full of hot air, he'd get it back or see him hang.

"Well, sir, you see it's this way. I puzzled it over,

wondering as it was 'ow he could have just melted out of sight. I remembered hearing 'ow 'e and a young woman escaped right out from underneath yer nose when you had set that trap in Bodiam.''

"Don't remind me." Stafford didn't want to hear any more about it.

Frizer rattled on. "Well, now, Will, I says to meself, just 'ow did 'e do it? Then it came to me in a flash. In Bodiam 'e was dressed like an old man, 'e was, but it wasn't the last time he took to that disguise." He revealed to Stafford about being chased in Dover by a gray-haired, bearded man, one amazingly skilled with a sword.

"So?"

"Old men but not really old men at all."

"Not really old." Stafford grunted in disgust and was about to send his unwanted visitor away.

"Actors! Like in the play. That's where 'e is, on that I'll stake my name."

Stafford eyed the ruffian with distaste. "I doubt that you have one."

"Ole Sir Nicholas is with the actors. That, sir, if you will forgive me, is as plain as the nose on yer face. 'E's joined with a traveling troupe. There be no better place to hide then with them."

Stafford was taken aback, but the more he thought about it, the more sense it made. Actors often changed their appearance so drastically when on stage that even their own mothers wouldn't know them. Why hadn't he thought of it?

"With the actors! God's breath!" Well, he wouldn't waste any more time. There were a hundred things to do to prepare for his journey to Dover and beyond.

Chapter Thirty-Six

Nicholas felt at peace with himself and lighter of heart. He had unburdened his conscience to Murray, and for the first time in a long while he really did feel as if he had begun a whole new life. Now instead of court politics, Alandra was the center of his world, the most delightful companion he had ever known.

Each time they were together, he fell more and more under her spell. Thoughts of other women faded into obscurity. There was only room for Alandra in his heart and soul. He had made the decision to start anew, and he would hold to it for her sake. From now on Sir Nicholas Leighton was gone and in his place was a far happier fellow, Christopher Nicholas by name, a prompter by profession. A good one if he did say so himself.

By the time the acting company had moved out of Marlborough, Nicholas had relaxed. Though there was a reward out for his capture, he had not run into any

trouble. None of the actors treated him suspiciously.
Nor had Shakespeare told him he must leave, despite
the predicament Nicholas might create for them. Will
seemed after all to be a man who could be trusted,
one whose opinion was not molded by circumstances.
Perhaps after all Shakespeare too believed him innocent, and Alandra's confidence in him made Nicholas
nearly believe he could have a new life. When a man
was in love, anything was possible.

Love. What a powerful word it was, he thought.
Once he had scoffed at its existence, but he wasn't
dubious now. He showed his romantic passion with
zeal. He besieged Alandra with verses borrowed from
Will, and as he grew braver, sonnets of his own, hoping
they were not more than a little out of rhyme. If love
had turned him into a besotted fool, he didn't care,
this feeling was so new to him.

Strange. Once he would have thought his actions
totally ridiculous. He would have been embarrassed
to make such a show of affection over any woman, yet
now he found that he was relaxing and totally enjoying
himself. Never had he felt so alive. Today the sky was
azure, the leaves an emerald-green, the blossoms of
the flowers so colorful they nearly blinded the eye. The
kind of day to enjoy with someone special. Was it any
wonder then that after arriving in Bath, while the actors settled themselves in at the inn and hurried to
enjoy the warm waters of the baths, he and Alandra
had slipped away? Nestled beneath an old oak tree,
they lay together on the soft grass.

"What are you thinking?" Alandra contented herself
with watching the play of expressions chase over Nicholas's face, hoping that he was even half as contented as she.

"About you and how happy you make me." Alandra
lay soft and warm against him, her breasts pressed
tightly to his chest, tempting him. "And that the days

are moving much too quickly. How I will hate to see summer leave."

"I know," she whispered wistfully. "These weeks have been such a magical time for us."

Nicholas noticed her soulful expression. "And just what are you thinking, my lady love?"

"That we are just too happy. I'm afraid that something might happen to end this contentment." Always at the back of Alandra's mind was the knowledge that Christopher was a nobleman and she but a stageman's daughter. "How long can our happiness last, Christopher?" Despite her hope that perhaps something might happen to aid Christopher in clearing his name, so far nothing had surfaced. Will Frizer had vanished, his last hope, or so Christopher said.

He answered optimistically, "Forever." Drawing her closer as if to assure her, his hands sought the warmth of her slim body.

Alandra was nearly afraid to hope even though all was calm now. One day the past would come back to haunt them, to intrude upon their peace. She gazed around the grove, wanting to engrave its every detail upon her memory. She wanted to remember how the sun streamed through the branches of the trees, casting shadows, making it appear like a nymph's lair. How the wind whispered through the trees. "Forever. You truly believe that?"

In answer he nuzzled her ear. "Mmmm." It was as if some strange madness possessed him, for he was much too happy. Would the day's passing put an end to it? "I wanted to spend at least a part of the daylight hours with you."

Alandra pulled up a blade of grass and ran it over the chiseled contours of his face, pleased that he had made such a commitment. How much she longed to know everything about him, she thought, then suddenly smiled.

"I wish I could have seen you when you were a boy," she teased.

"When I was a lad?" He threw back his head and laughed. "I was tall and gangly, always getting into fights with some boy or other. My mother was incensed that my garments always were in need of cleaning or mending." A faraway look came into his eyes. "I whittled a sword once out of a tree branch. Even then I dreamed of being the greatest swordsman in the land."

She could nearly imagine the scene of a young Christopher fighting valiantly with anyone who dared incure his wrath. "And were you?"

"Aye! If not the best, I came very close," he answered with more than a hint of pride. "Indeed, I did very well for myself."

"And do you miss it?" she asked wistfully.

Did he? Nicholas could truthfully answer no. A subtle change had come over him, a maturity that only life's experiences could bring. "I thought the answer to everything was in being the most powerful, the most skillful. As if life were little more than a test of wills. I was so cocky then, thinking that right would always overpower wrong."

"I have to believe it does," she said sadly. "Just as it will where you are concerned. Surely the queen will find out that it was not you who slew that old lord." Her voice was choked, the words painful as she said, "And you will be restored to favor." *And then we will have to say good-bye,* she thought.

"I would have my good name set to rights, but as to regaining Elizabeth's good will, I have no longing for that. To be one of her peacocks is not what I have planned." His hands wrapped in the tangle of her dark tresses as he kissed her, his tongue parting her lips until she yielded her mouth to him. "For now you are my love and my life, Alandra."

"Are you telling me you have no wish to return to

court?'' She noticed a shadow flicker over his face for an instant.

"My life is here with you," he answered quickly.

He's sacrificing himself for me, Alandra thought. *I cannot raise myself to the rank of noblewoman and thus he thinks to turn his back on the world he knows. For me!*

Nicholas took note of her frown. Hugging her close in reassurance, he touched his lips to her hair. "There is no place else I would rather be than lying here beside you. I tell you truly, Alandra.''

She relaxed, leaning her head against his chest. "Not even at the baths? Father insists that the waters are the closest to heaven we mortals will ever come.''

"Not even there. I would not want to be anywhere else but here with you." Spying a red rose, Nicholas reached out and plucked it, succumbing to his passionate mood. "Take thou this rose, since love's own flower it is, and by that rose thy lover captive is.'' Smiling, he held the flower out for her hand. "Ah, soon I will be able to rival Shakespeare in weaving words.''

Inhaling deeply of the fragrant blossoms, Alandra touched the petals with wonder. It was the first time in her life she had ever been so utterly content. Christopher loved her. Had she ever doubted that, she did not do so now. But if she loved him in return, how could she let him hide from who he really was, from where he belonged?

"Now I ask you. What are you thinking?'' Nicholas whispered. Lying on his back, he rested his head in Alandra's lap.

"I was thinking about how very much I wish you would kiss me again.''

"I would be a cur not to grant such a wish.''

Nicholas pulled her unresisting body beneath him, his muscled length straining against her. Slowly, his mouth made love to hers with mesmerizing kisses that left Alandra weak and dazed. She felt a mounting passion surge through her.

They were lying upon the grass, her hands beneath his doublet, his fingers at her bodice, loosing the lacings. She shivered as he touched her breasts.

"Once I thought lovemaking was only for the nighttime. Oh, but I was a foolish girl . . ."

Her words were smothered by a deep, leisurely kiss as his mouth claimed hers again. His kiss left her weak and filled her with that familiar tingling sensation, a heat that centered from her core and spread all the way down to her toes. It was the kind of kiss she had been so hoping for, the kind that was a prelude to the wonders they had shared in that magical glen near Dover.

Nicholas drew a rasping breath as he lifted his mouth from hers. He realized that what he had always wanted was someone who really cared about him, and Alandra did. Each day they had spent together reaffirmed how important she was to him, how important they were to each other.

"Somehow I feel as if I really do belong here. With you."

"You do!" She drew her head back to look up at him, her eyes shining with a special glow.

His lips traced a fiery path down the curve of her neck to her just bared shoulder. "Mmmmm. Oh, Christopher, don't stop what you are doing . . ." His touch warmed her as surely as did the sunshine.

"You taste good." Deftly, he removed her bodice and brought his head down to kiss her soft breasts, gently taking a rose-tipped peak in his mouth, savoring it.

Soft moans of pleasure floated around them, and Alandra suddenly realized that they came from her own throat. Her hands clutched at his hair as she pressed against him.

Unmindful of the rocks and twigs, they lay side by

side, contenting themselves in the pleasure of touching, of kissing. Weeds tangled in her hair, but she shook them loose with a vibrant toss of her head. Then her arms went around his neck, answering his kisses with sweet, wild abandon.

"Oh, my sweet, sweet Alandra." Rolling her onto her back, he brushed his lips against her hair. "This means I love you." He nuzzled her throat. "And this." His mouth traced a path from her collarbone to the tip of her breast. "And this." He blended their bodies in an intimate caress.

Lifting her arms, she encircled his neck, wound her fingers in his dark hair. For an endless time they clung together, their bodies touching intimately. Nicholas's fingers quested for the secrets of her body, then his probing shaft replaced his hand, slipping hotly against her thighs, teasing the entrance to her softness. He held her to him for endless moments while spasms of exquisite pleasure sent rippling waves through her, a feeling mirrored in Nicholas's expression.

For a timeless moment she stared into the depths of his gray eyes. Glorying in the closeness with him, it seemed to Alandra that at that very moment her heart moved with love. She felt dizzying sensations course through her blood, like the sparks of a radiating fire, consuming her as she felt the firm touch of his hardened flesh inside her. She writhed under his touch, arching up to meet him as he rose over her. She clung to him, her arms around his neck, her legs locked around his waist, answering his movements with her own. Christopher was her mate. The lines of separateness blended. She was incapable of holding any part of herself from him. She had to love him with all the strength of her devotion because she could give him no less than her whole self.

With her hands, her mouth, her body, she demon-

strated the full potency of her love, and he returned
her affection in full measure.

Alandra knew as they lay naked together that she
was indeed a fortunate woman. She had soared above
the clouds and was racing toward the sun, there to
burst into a hundred tiny sparks of flame.

Nicholas gazed down upon her face, gently brushing
back the tangled curls from her eyes. She was his now
as surely as if they had spoken vows. Whispering
words of love, he made gentle love to her once more,
watching her eyes as he brought himself within her
once again. He saw the wonder written upon her face
that anything could be so glorious, and in that moment
he was filled with a complete sense of contentment.
The world was theirs for the taking.

"Alandra! Christopher!" Nicholas and Alandra were
startled out of their passion by the sound of Murray's
voice.

Bemoaning the old man's intrusion, Nicholas
quickly helped Alandra dress, then with his fingers
trembling, feeling as if he had ten thumbs, he clothed
himself. "Your father certainly has not an actor's timing," he grumbled as he brushed the grass from her
hair. Standing, he tried to hide his annoyance. How
had Murray found them?

"Thank God! Thank God!" Still clutching his bath
linen, Murray was in even a worse state of disarray
than the two lovers had been. His hat was in his eyes,
his doublet was unlaced, his stockings fell down
around his ankles. No doubt he had dressed along the
way.

"What is it? What has happened?"

Murray held forth a piece of paper. "This! Oh, Christopher!"

It was a broadside. She stared at it in horror, reality
intruding into her dreams.

"They are tacked up all over Bath. This time with

a sketch of you that clearly gives you away. At the stables. On the door of the inn. Even near the water pumps. Someone has alerted the authorities of your presence among us, Christopher. Somehow they know." Taking off his hat, Murray wrung it in his hands. "Oh dear. Oh dear! What is to become of us all!"

Alandra tugged him down to sit on the grass beside her. "Calm yourself, Father." As if she herself could be composed at the moment, she thought wryly.

"They know, you say. Exactly what do you mean?" Even as he asked, Nicholas knew the answer. Will Frizer had finally put two and two together and realized why he had been chased that day in Dover and by whom. Undoubtedly, the reason Nicholas had been unable to find him in the town was because the weasel had moved on to put his evil lord on Nicholas's tracks.

"Woe is me! Woe is me! Whatever can we do?" Murray rocked back and forth on his heels. "Will is even now being questioned. But he will not say a word, Christopher. Shakespeare is ever a man to be trusted."

"Questioned? By whom?" As if he didn't know.

"Fancily dressed noblemen who looked to be members of the court."

"The queen's guard, no doubt! Or Stafford's men!" Nicholas damned his stupidity in having followed Will Frizer that day. In his bravado, he had given himself away and now the game was up.

Chapter Thirty-Seven

Murray had not exaggerated. Danger hung in the air like the quiet before a storm. Armed men swarmed over Bath like ants to a discarded morsel of food. Cresting the top of the small hill, Nicholas could see them from afar. Worst of all they wore the yellow and brown that were Stafford's colors and not the Tudor green and white. Nicholas was certain that if he were caught he would not live out the day. Stafford would not give him the chance to prove his innocence.

"Christopher, look!" Coming up behind him, Alandra pointed to three guardsmen who were headed in their direction.

"Bloody hell!" He was filled with a compulsion to flee, but shook his head angrily. It would be walking directly into a trap. Intuitively, he knew it would be far better to outwit Owen Stafford than to try to outrun him. Stafford would be expecting him to try and leave the town. Worse yet, were Nicholas captured it would bode ill for the Lord Chamberlain's Men and Alandra. Above all he didn't want that.

"Oh, Christopher, what are we going to do?" Alandra's heart was in her throat as she squeezed Nicholas's hand. "I don't think that pretending to be an old man and his expectant wife will help you this time."

"No, if they suspect I am among actors, they will be prepared for any disguise. I believe my only chance is to become invisible. Oh, that I had magic at my disposal!" He tried to make light of his mounting apprehension. "You don't happen to have an enchanted cloak hidden among your costumes do you, Murray? A garment that will let me walk the streets unobserved."

The old man groaned. "No, I do not. Oh, that I *were* a wizard that I could give you such aid. Nevertheless, you must remain unseen."

"Hide, you mean!" But where? The foliage and shubbery weren't thick enough to conceal him for long, and he certainly couldn't go in to town, not when it was crawling with Stafford's men.

It was a terrible predicament. Owen Stafford would organize a thorough inspection of Bath. He would search out every inn, all the stables, each and every house, look behind every tree, under every rock, and even inspect the bubbling pools of water that had given the town its name. Nor was there much chance that he would believe Shakespeare when he denied Nicholas was with the players.

"What the devil am I to do?" Nicholas aimed his question at Murray and was unnerved when the little man suddenly scurried away. Was it to be every man for himself then?

As quickly as he had run off, Murray returned, with his wagon. "We'll use this! Climb in and I will guide it back toward the inn."

"The wagon," Nicholas scoffed. "Forsooth, do you

really think they would not search it?" Whereas once it had been the perfect hiding place, now it would be far too obvious.

"From back to front and side to side, but"—Murray cleared his throat—"beneath the wagon between the wheels there is a hidden compartment that none save Alandra know about."

"A hidden compartment?"

Reaching under the wagon's tongue, Murray fumbled about for a small latch. "About the size of a coffin. 'Twill be snug and more than a bit uncomfortable, but the perfect place for concealment, at least until the immediate danger is over." Fidgeting to get the trap door open, he confided, "In my younger days I fear there were times when I was not adverse to doing a bit of smuggling now and again."

"Smuggling?" It seemed so out of character for Murray who had proven to Nicholas that he was the most honest of men.

"Aye. Before I turned to the theater, I used this old wagon to carry contraband goods for some of the London merchants. Merchandise whose importation was forbidden." Murray shrugged, the corners of his mouth trembling as he tried to decide whether to frown or smile. " 'Twas in my wilder days. My youth. You see I wasn't always an old man."

"Indeed not!" For a moment Nicholas caught a glimpse of the lad who lived inside the man, an adventurous fellow.

"Now that hidden compartment might very well save you, Christopher," Murray said hopefully, prodding at Nicholas to get him to crawl inside. "We will return to the inn and I warrant you will be safe, even if you are right under their noses."

"That oaf Will Frizer must be daft."
"Or a liar."

"Or both," Nicholas heard three of Stafford's soldiers say as he lay still in his cramped quarters. Luckily for him they had no idea how very close they were to his hiding place, nor did they realize that at this very moment he could see the toes of their boots through the small wooden slats in the wagon.

"All of the actors have been questioned, even threatened with the rack, and not a one of them even blinked an eye. Their voices rang with sincerity when they said they didn't know what we were talking about. Not a one of them knew a man named Sir Nicholas Leighton, or so they insisted."

"They are actors! Did you really expect them to give themselves away, even if they were hiding that fugitive?"

"I say they were telling the truth. If not, then surely at least one of them would have handed him over to us for the money, Edward."

"And yet that Shakespeare fellow did seem to be secretly laughing at us all the while."

"He was good-natured, nothing more. I tell you Frizer made up the whole story he told Stafford in hopes of getting the reward his lordship put on Leighton's carcass. We have come a long way and wasted our time for little or no reason."

"Aye, it is Frizer who should be brought back to London in chains." All three men grumbled their complaints, then when their frustration had been spent, they ambled away.

So, the actors had staunchly defended him, Nicholas thought. Bless them, each and every one, for they surely had recognized Christopher Nicholas as Sir Nicholas Leighton from the broadsides that were all over town. If he hadn't known it before, he now was assured that Will Shakespeare, Will Kempe, Burbage, Lowin, and the others were his friends. Nicholas knew he would never forget such loyalty and vowed that someday he would do them a like favor in return.

His gratitude intensified when he at last came face
to face with the players. Will Shakespeare had called
an emergency meeting in his quarters as soon as the
armed guardsmen had vacated the area. As a precau-
tion, lest the soldiers return, he had posted four of the
younger actors as lookouts in the hallway, at the front
door, back door, and in the loft of the stable. Shroud-
ing all the windows of his room in bedsheets, Shakespeare securely locked his door and windows, then
turned to address those seated in the crowded room.

"You know why I have asked you to come here."
There was a mumble of assent. "One of ours is in trouble and we must decide what to do about it."

"Do?" John Lowin bounded to his feet: "There is
only one thing we can do! Stand behind Christopher.
Give him our aid."

"Stand behind him," Robert Armin cried out, raising his fist above his head as he stood up.

"I do not for one moment believe the charges. Murder a man? Christopher? Ha. It is obviously a blatant
lie!" Lowin added.

"I did *not* kill Lord Woodcliffe," Nicholas cried out
from his seat in the far corner. "I give you my word
as a gentleman on that."

"You see, he is innocent," Shakespeare confirmed,
as if to assure the players. "It is quite clear to me that
our friend and company member is the victim."
Briefly, Will gave an account of what had happened,
based on Alandra's and Murray's explanation of
events. "To put it quite simply, it is a case of jealousy
and ambition. A man of renown was murdered, it is
true, but not by our Christopher. Instead, it would
appear to me that the perpetrator of the deed was none
other than he who cries out for punishment."

"Aye, he is the real culprit," Will Kempe exclaimed,
for once making no attempt at poking fun at the sit-

uation. He was deadly serious as he added his voice
to the decision to defend Christopher.

Only John Heminges seemed to have reservations.
" 'Twould not be the first time a man has been accused
of something he did not do, but think about the re-
percussions our involvement might have if we are
mixed up in this. Our careers will be ruined, nay perhaps our very lives. Lord Owen Stafford is a very powerful man and has much influence with Elizabeth.
After all, we only have Christopher's word that he isn't
a murderer. He has no proof so perhaps then it would
be better for—for Christopher to leave the players!"

"Leave? Leave? And go where, pray tell?" Robert
Armin asked angrily.

"Anywhere but here!" Heminges answered quicky.
"Forsooth, he will bring wrath and ruin down upon
our heads."

"You sound like a coward, Heminges. I tell you 'tis
not our way. We may be only actors, but I would hope
that each and every one of us is courageous in his own
way." John Lowin was incensed and proved it by lunging at the company's business manager.

Heminges drew back, his expression stating that he
knew he had gone too far. "But—but think about our
finances—"

"To the devil with your coffers!" Robert Armin
shouted. "I only know that we must do what is right.
It has always been our policy to protect all the members of Lord Chamberlain's Men as staunchly as if we
were family."

"Aye! We must do whatever it takes." Murray
reached over to pat Nicholas on the shoulder.

Richard Burbage pushed forward to take his place
beside Shakespeare. "Indeed we must!" As if he were
giving a soliloquy, he lapsed into a dramatic mono-
logue enumerating a man's responsibilities to his
friends and companions. "And, were any one of us

faced with the same adversity, I have little doubt but that Christopher, or Sir Nicholas Leighton as we now know him to be, would come at once to our aid." As he spoke, he gestured with an exaggerated theatrical movement that displayed his long-fingered hands. "He would not hesitate! How then can we do other than give him our support and our help to prove he's innocent? Nay, even if it comes to battling this Lord Stafford himself."

William Sly manuevered his stocky form to take his place beside the other actors. "Quoting the words I spoke in *Henry VI*, Will, 'We will fight til the last gasp!'"

In light of the actors' mood Heminges was forced to lay aside his arguments. "Then we are unanimous I suppose." There was a long silence, then he forced a smile in Nicholas's direction. "You heard the decision. You are welcome to stay despite what has happened."

Nicholas stood up, deeply moved by his friends' loyalty. "You will not be sorry! That I vow. When this wrong is righted, I will see that each and every one of you reaps a reward!"

His promise caused Heminges's mood to brighten as if calculating a monetary recompense. "Then by all means let us hope that circumstances dictate a speedy redress of the wrongs done you."

"Which brings me to a point," Shakespeare cut in. "I propose that we do more than give Christopher sanctuary. Let us, each and every one, keep an eye out for this scoundrel Will Frizer. It appears that he is the key to proving Christopher's innocence."

"Of course!" Lowen stroked his mustache. "If we could capture the rascal, we might be able to force a confession from him."

"Aye, if I know human nature," Shakespeare interjected, "and I do, he will haunt our audience in hopes of catching sight of Christopher again. Methinks this

Frizer will have to prove to his patron that he did not lie or imagine he saw Christopher. Ah, yes, he will come to see our performance, on that I have no doubt. And when he does, we will seize *him*. 'Tis then the truth will come to light."

The suggestion caused the actors to lapse into a frenzy of plots and plans, but Shakespeare held up his hand for silence. "I already know exactly what we should do." Elbowing his way through the tightly packed room, he tapped ten of the lesser actors on the shoulder. "I dub you groundlings!"

"Groundlings, of course!" Nicholas knew at once what Shakespeare planned. Those chosen would be disguised as members of the audience and would mingle with the people watching the play. "And since I alone can recognize Frizer in an instant I too will be part of your scheme."

"As will I!" Will Kempe hunkered down, amusing the others with his imitation of the cursing, apple-eating, nut-cracking oafs who so incensed him at times. " 'Twill be our greatest performance of the season."

Chapter Thirty-Eight

Though it appeared that the immediate peril to Nicholas was over, the actors were nonetheless edgy as they prepared for their performance at Bath. Reality had intruded all too harshly in their make-believe sphere, reminding them of just how fragile a man's destiny could be. Beyond the perimeters of the stage was a real world that far surpassed in harshness, deception, and social ambition anything that Shakespeare could create in his tragedies. Thus, despite the bravado of their resolution to aid Nicholas, there was a look of uncertainty in every eye. They all knew that Lord Owen Stafford could return to Bath at any moment with his entourage and drastically alter the ending each and every man wanted for this real-life drama.

Alandra was wary, too, fearing what might happen if the actors' plans went astray. Who was this Will Frizer and could he help Christopher? Christopher had told the troupe that Frizer was a well-known thief and hired murderer, a "cutter." Had he killed Lord Woodcliff? And would he kill Christopher? And what about Lord Stafford? Certainly, he had given up much too easily. Though most of the actors were certain they had seen the last of Christopher's enemy, she and Shakespeare were certain that Stafford would be back. The question that worried her was when?

Even so, Alandra maintained a congenial mood as the members of the company set up for the play. As she aided her father in arranging the costumes and scenery, she tried to keep their spirits light.

"Alandra!"

The voice was familiar, jarring her out of her contemplation. "Christopher!"

Even Alandra would hardly have recognized him in his disguise had she not known already what he had planned to do. Wearing dun-colored baggy breeches, a grotesquely padded doublet to give him a great deal of girth, a long brown wig and matching beard, wrinkled blue hosen, and boots, he did indeed look exactly like a grounding, a cobbler by trade. Clutching a sack of nuts in one hand and an apple in the other, he prepared himself for his "role," strutting about with Will Kempe, who was dressed in equal "splendor" as a tinker.

Screwing up his face, Kempe cupped his hand and put it to his mouth, practicing his role as a heckler. "You whoreson, you simpleton. Do you call that acting? 'Tis more stimulating to watch a tree growing." He punctuated his insult by tossing an orange at Nicholas. "Your turn."

Nicholas cleared his throat. " 'Tis a bungled performance you give us."

Kempe shook his head so vigorously that it sent his hair tumbling into his eyes. "Too polite."

"Too polite?" Nicholas tried again. "You lackwitted,

pie-faced son of a buffoon, you muffed your lines."

"No, no. Your manner is just too lordly," Kempe shot back. "You need to be more oafish, Christopher. Call to mind how you were treated during your first performance."

Nicholas paused for a long moment, remembering how merciless the crowd had turned when something displeased them, then in a loud nasal voice he said, "You call this a play? In truth I've heard better rhyme from a cow." Outrageously, he mimicked Kempe's mannerisms, including spitting on the ground, a most unlordly thing to do.

"Better. Better."

Nicholas practiced hurling insults, competing with his actor friend as to who could act the most churlish. Even his walk came under scrutiny by Kempe, who taught him a bowlegged swagger, a far cry from Nicholas's manly strut.

"By God, you're nearly there," Kempe praised.

Nicholas suppressed his laughter as he slowly transformed himself into a groundling. Trying to be creative, he let his insults fly, becoming more experienced with each taunt. "Actors you call yourselves? Performers? Forsooth, the ants in the dung pile are more worthy of the name."

"Good! Good. But pepper your comments with profanity." A string of swear words flowed freely from Kempe's mouth.

Five of the young actors, also disguised as groundlings, joined in the game. Insult after insult followed, merged with fiendish oaths, each ribald comment and catcall becoming more riotous than before. But in the end Nicholas conceded, proclaiming Kempe the winner.

"Oh?" Playfully, Alandra tugged at Nicholas's beard. "I would definitely say that it is a tie, for in truth I suspect that you will fit right in with the crowd." She held forth a mirror so that he could inspect his disguise, laughing as he turned his head this way and that, while making faces.

"Stafford wouldn't recognize me if I bumped right into him." With a loud guffaw, he gingerly pinched her behind.

"Christopher!" Alandra blushed as she realized that Kempe had witnessed his action.

"Just keeping in character, sweetling! Just keeping in character." Strange, but in spite of the danger, Nicholas was actually having fun. At court such laughter was always tempered with caution. A man never knew, even in the midst of merrymaking, when an enemy would strike, albeit with an air of civility.

"I forgive you as long as I am the only wench that you pinch."

Taking off his cap, Nicholas bowed. "I promise."

"Then away with you. Go throw your apples at the stage." She threw him a kiss for good luck and watched as he zigzagged his now-ample bulk between several support beams of the stage.

As usual there was a goodly crowd in the innyard, perhaps even better than usual. "Due in part to the excitement of the soldiers yesterday," Shakespeare said. "Not only those who love entertainment are elbowing each other for space, but the curious are also here this afternoon."

"Let us only hope that Will Frizer will likewise be here," Alandra whispered, scanning the crowd for a skinny, shaggy-haired scar-faced man.

She played over and over again in her mind the description Christopher had given to the actors, remembering every scar, ever freckle, wondering if Shakespeare was right in his assumptions. In all likelihood Frizer was a long way off, still in Dover, and this charade would be all for naught. And yet if there was even a hint of a chance. She clasped her hands tightly together in a semblance of prayer as the young man with the placard announcing the start of the play made his appearance.

Her optimism dwindled as *The Comedy of Errors* proceeded. Frizer wasn't in the crowd. They had been foolish to think life could be so simple.

"I don't see Frizer, Will, but.... Dear God!" Alandra gasped as she took note of a familiar golden-haired head. Was she seeing things or was Owen Stafford among those seated in the gallery? Squinting her eyes, she looked hard and long at the nobleman, deciding at once that it was he. So, Stafford had come to take a look at the actors for himself. "Will!"

"What is it, Alandra? You look as if you have seen a ghost."

"Oh, that I had, for it would be preferable to seeing the man whom I do see." She pointed. "Owen Stafford!" So, the guardsmen's retreat had not been a victory for Christopher after all.

Unlike her, Shakespeare did not seem in the least bit troubled. "I am not at all surprised, for I had expected as much. 'Twill but make our trap for Frizer a bit harder to spring if he shows his face." He touched her lightly on the tip of her nose. "But do not worry. Your Christopher won't be recognized, on that I would stake my reputation."

Remembering his disguise, Alandra agreed. "Lord Stafford will not be looking for Christopher in the crowd. He'll be watching the actors on the stage."

"Aye. Likewise I would wager that if Frizer is in the audience sniffing about like some huntsman's hound, his eyes will be focused on the performers."

"But if perchance Frizer does show his face and if Christopher calls attention to himself by trying to subdue him, then what?"

"Such an event might well bode ill." Will scowled. "We must make certain that if Frizer is cornered, our dear Lord Stafford's attention is diverted."

"How can I help, Will?"

Alandra knew the answer as soon as she asked. Somehow she had to distract Owen Stafford so that he would not realize what was going on below and have time to alert his guardsmen. There seemed to be only one way to do that. Without another thought, Alandra pushed and shoved her way to the gallery. Moving slowly, she pondered her mode of action.

"Oranges. Get yer ripe juicy oranges," she heard a young woman call out, peddling her wares.

Alandra was struck with an idea. Oranges, yes! Fumbling in her money pouch, she came up with a fistful of coins. "I want all of them." Never mind that the money had been entrusted to her to pay for the company's supper that night.

"All of them?" The woman cocked her head. "All," she asked again.

"Each and every one. And your basket as well." What better way to move freely about the gallery than to masquarade as an orange-seller?

"The basket?" The peddler woman looked at Alandra as if she had suddenly gone mad, but shrugging her shoulders held forth her wares. "It will cost you more coins."

Alandra nodded, giving the woman the requested amount then whisking the basket and oranges from her grip. In order to distract Stafford, she knew she might have to create a scene when the time came. The oranges would be the catalyst.

Purposefully emphasizing the swing of her hips, she made her way to Lord Stafford's side, unnerved more than just a little when she became aware of the envoy of servants and guardsmen he had brought with him. A veritable army. So, he hadn't believed the actors after all. Like some evil ghost he was haunting the acting company with his presence.

Alandra mimicked the peddler's cry as she passed by. "Oranges. Ripe and juicy, oranges." She paused when she was directly in front of the infamous lord.

"By God, girl, move out of the way. You are blocking my view of the stage!" Stafford's tone was peevish.

"Yes, my lord."

Bowing her head in a proper show of deference, Alandra hurried to obey, though she didn't move very far. It was necessary for her to keep Stafford within view and at the same time be able to see what was going on down below in the groundlings' section. So far it was relatively quiet except for the usual good-humored banter between the actors and the crowd.

Alandra's gaze moved from the stage to the audience then to Lord Stafford. For a long time she just stared at him, watching as he lifted a scented gold pomander to his nose with an air of arrogance that left no doubt that he was sure of himself. So, this was Christopher's archenemy, she thought, and thus her enemy as well. In a dark red leather doublet slashed at the sleeves and decorated with gold braid, black leather boots, white ruff, black hosen, and red-and-gold trunk hose, he made a handsome picture. But Alandra knew what deviousness lay behind those almond-shaped blue eyes. This man was responsible for Christopher's ruination and not content with that, now sought his death.

"Let us hope that Frizer was not just telling tales, for I would hate to think that we had wasted the afternoon for little reward," one of Stafford's men exclaimed.

Alandra tensed, attuning her hearing to the grumbling. The name "Frizer" reverberated in her mind.

"I would loathe the idea of spending our time here among this vermin were it not to bring about the fulfillment of my wishes." Stafford raised his hand in a gesture of impatience as one of his companions started to speak. "I know what you are going to say, but my argument stands firm, that I will not leave here until I am certain that Nicholas Leighton is not among the actors. You see, I don't believe a word of what those gypsy devils proclaimed."

Gypsy! Alandra squeezed an orange so tightly that her fingernails brought forth a spurt of juice. Oh, how she wanted to defend her little group, but she dared not. Instead, she merely sauntered up to Owen Stafford again asking, "Are you sure you don't want an orange, your lordship?"

Stafford regarded her with something akin to suspicion as if wondering if they had met before, then as if liking what he saw said, "I will buy one of your oranges if you will sit by me." He patted an empty space beside him as he flashed her a toothy grin.

Alandra was wise enough to know exactly what he had in mind. Pinches, pats, and open fondling, not just conversation, but although abiding his company was the last thing she wanted to do, she knew she must put up with the brash young lord, at least for the moment.

"Maybe I will and then maybe again I won't." She looked up through her lashes at him. "I don't even know your name."

"Lord Stafford!" He emphasized his title as if announcing he were king.

"Ooooh, a lord. Now fancy that."

Pretending to be amply impressed, she started to sit down when suddenly a movement down on the ground caught her eye. Christopher, Will Kempe, and a few of the other actors were quickly encircling another man. Could they have spotted Frizer? It had to be.

"What the devil? Now what are they about?" Stafford craned his neck for a view of what was going on down below.

"Dear God!" Alandra exclaimed. Christopher was unaware of Stafford's presence in the audience. He might give himself away. She had to think fast, had to distract his enemy, before Stafford got wind of what was going on.

"What is it, girl?" Lord Stafford reached to pull her out of his way.

In that moment Alandra was inspired. Taking a step forward, she feigned a stumble, tipping the basket of oranges as she fell against the haughty nobleman. Oranges went everywhere, scattering in a myriad of directions. Most of them were plucked up and confiscated by those of a less-than-honest nature.

"Oh, my oranges! You brute!" Alandra wailed as loudly as she could. "Look what you have done! I'm ruined, I am. 'Tis shame, shame on you, Lord Stafford!"

Surely even Burbage's voice could not have carried as far as Alandra's scolding. Nearly every head in the gallery turned to get a glimpse of the commotion. For the moment it seemed to rival the goings-on in the play.

From his position below, Nicholas also heard Alandra's shriek and knew in an instant that she meant to warn him, but God rot it all, he had Frizer within his grasp. He had to make his move now or never have another chance.

"Kempe, Robert, Edwin, quickly!" he ordered. Obeying, they moved like lightning, closing in on Nicholas's prey.

"God's balls, what is this?" Frizer demanded, reaching for his knife.

Nicholas's quick kick, aimed at the groin, thwarted him. A brutal punch to the jaw followed, then another. It was Kempe, however, who saved the day. Not too proud to use less than sporting means to subdue an enemy, he reached for an empty bottle of ale and broke it over Frizer's head. With a moan, the man sank to the ground.

"Cover his head with your cloak, Edward. Now!" Nicholas's command was instantly carried out. "Hold him up." Nicholas took one side, draping Frizer's left arm over his shoulder, Kempe took the other, supporting his weight. "That's right. Now move toward the outer exit." Like a six-legged caterpillar, they made their way toward the gate where the admission was taken.

"Poor old fellow. Never could hold his ale." Kempe repeated the phrase as he and Nicholas moved along with their human "baggage." "Drunk as a wine-taster, he is. Tut, tut, tut, he will miss such a frolicksome play."

From her place in the gallery Alandra watched with a hammering heart as the "groundlings" and their companion left the innyard. All the while she continued her tirade against the man who she insisted had purposefully upended her orange basket. "Oh, I know you fine lords, I do. You wanted to sample one of my oranges for free."

"For the love of God, shut up!" Unnerved that so many people were staring at them, Stafford hurried to vindicate himself. "It was an accident! Besides, you spilled them yourself, you clumsy little twit. Oh, what matter?" Oblivious now to what was happening down below, Stafford reached in his money pouch, thrusting a handful of coins at Alandra. "Here, take these if it will silence you!"

Alandra made great show of biting each and every coin, as if to ascertain that they were real, then with a wide grin curtsied. "Thank you, my lord."

It was all she could do to contain her joy. It had worked! Christopher had gone about his plan without

being spotted. For the moment at least all was well.
Looking hastily over her shoulder to make certain
none of Stafford's men were following her, she scamp-
ered through the crowd.

Chapter Thirty-Nine

Like a snarling, angry wolf, Will Frizer struggled against the ropes that held him tied securely to a chair. "I'll get loose, I will, and when I do I'll slit somebody's gizzard!" The direction of his gaze targeted Nicholas as the victim.

"I wouldn't be making any threats if I were you." Nicholas's gray eyes flashed as he poked the point of his sword into his enemy's ribs, enough to cause a prick of warning.

Nicholas tensed his shoulders and clenched his teeth, remembering the exhilaration he had felt when he had looked over Will Kempe's head at the crowd of groundlings and caught sight of Frizer's head bobbing up and down. It had been like the answer to a prayer knowing his prey was so close at hand. Raising his arm as if to seek the hawkers in the audience, he had made the signal to the others. Slowly, they had closed in and with an ease that was nearly frightening had caught Frizer. Now the evil man was his prisoner, and yet far from feeling victorious, Nicholas knew only frustration. Where did he go from here?

"You're nothing but gibbet bait, Frizer. A thief, a hackster, a hired murderer." Nicholas threw out the last accusation to see Frizer's reaction.

For just a moment the scoundrel was confused as he looked at his accuser. Though Nicholas had taken off his wig, he was still in his actor's make-up and padding. Then Frizer widened one eye. " 'Tis you!"

"Aye. You had thought to sic Stafford's dogs on me, but I evaded their snapping jaws. The worm has turned, and you are the one who has been cornered. Now, it's only a matter of time before you are dangling from a rope."

"Hang? Me? Hah!" Though the growl sounded confident, Frizer's face paled. The hideous kind of death suffered on the scaffold was brutally painful, as well he knew.

"Yes, hang!" Nicholas countered. The sweetness of his success in capturing the villein was made bitter by the knowledge that the real culprit was Lord Stafford and not this disgusting, pathetic creature. After all, Nicholas was not certain Frizer had even done the foul deed. But the only way to ferret out the truth was to convince this scoundrel that Nicholas believed he had.

"Hang?" For a moment his blustering faltered and Frizer cunningly pleaded innocence. "For what? I be an honest man."

"Honest!" Nicholas addressed the small group gathered in his room to interrogate the prisoner as if to reassure them. "This man is the foremost cutter in all of London. A man who makes quite a good living selling his villainous services, despite the look of him."

Alandra stared at the henchman, thinking him to be a fearsome sight indeed. Scars crisscrossed his face,

one slicing the muscle of his left eye so that it was
frozen in a permanent wink. His auburn hair was long
and unkempt, his dun-colored doublet and hosen in
need of mending. By the looks of him it hardly appeared that being a hired killer was profitable. For a
moment she nearly felt sorry for him, at least until he
turned his heated gaze on her. His eyes revealed an
evil, murderous nature.

"I repeat, I be an honest man!" Again he struggled
with his bonds but found they were much too secure
to enable him to escape.

Nicholas snorted in disgust. "So honest that you
inhabit darkened alleyways and run with rogues."

Ignoring Nicholas, Frizer turned to the others. "You
must listen to me kind people. I have done no wrong.
'Tis naught but a misunderstanding." If he had hoped
to convince the small assemblage that he had been
erroneously accused, the murmur of outrage quieted
him. There seemed to be no question as to whose side
these men were on. "So, I am not only accused but
also found guilty."

There was a mumble as heads were nodded. Only
Heminges disagreed. "Now see here, Christopher! I
don't like this. I don't like this at all. It could bring
the entire countryside down upon our heads."

Seeing that he had at least one sympathetic ear,
Frizer anxiously said, "Aye, t'will make of you all
marked men to so abduct a peaceful man who was
but minding his own business."

"Damn you, Heminges!" Alandra swore angrily before she could even think, yet did not regret her outburst. She knew what Christopher was trying to do,
frighten this evil man into agreeing to testify in his
behalf. "You have not the brains of a simpleton."

"I beg your pardon!"

"Let Christopher handle this," she further admonished.

"Alandra is right." Shakespeare was quick to speak out. "We all agreed to help Christopher and, By God, that means not interferring in what he thinks must be done."

"But—"

"John! On matters of finance I never argue but on this ..."

In the face of Shakespeare's censure Heminges took a step backward.

Nodding his head in Nicholas's direction, Frizer practically shouted, "He is the one wanted for murder, gents. Not I! There be a price on *his* head. He murdered one of the queen's noblemen."

"Save your lies." Nicholas was enraged that he, a nobleman and scion of good family, should have to suffer a thief's condemnation. "They know the true story." His eyes turned to slits of gray fury. "I have told them that you were behind that brave, bold man while he was engaged in a quarrel with me and I suspect that you ruthlessly stabbed him in the back! Then like the coward that you are fled and let me take the blame."

"I didn't!"

"You did! I saw you flee. Upon my oath and as God is my witness, I am sure you did the foul deed." Again Nicholas jabbed his prisoner with the tip of his sword. "Lord Owen Stafford paid you to kill Lord Woodcliffe, didn't he?" When Frizer made no answer, he put the sword point to his neck. "Didn't he?"

"Go ahead and cut my throat, for I will never answer. Never!" Frizer was defiant. "I would have to be a fool to do so. Were I to say to anyone that I laid a finger on that senile old nobleman, my life wouldn't be worth spit!" To emphasize his point, he did just that, aiming his saliva at Nicholas's boot. "And even if I did, no one would give credit to a statement made while a man is threatened with death. So you see, you might as well let me go."

"Oh, Christopher..." Alandra felt nearly as disappointed as Nicholas did. Without this man's confession, he was lost.

"Let you go? I think not! What then? Take you with us? No. You have not the good looks to be an actor among us!" Nicholas turned to Kempe. He could never be a cold-blooded killer, but he knew he had to bluff. "Bring me a rope!"

"A rope?" Heminges was horrified. "Now see here, Christopher, I will not be a party to murder, no matter what sins you say this man has committed."

Once again coming to Nicholas's aid, Shakespeare said, "Silence, John. What Christopher requests makes perfect sense, for I have no desire to feed an extra mouth on our travels." His eyes twinkled mischievously as he too addressed Kempe. "You heard, Christopher. Bring forth a rope."

There was a hushed, mortified silence as Kempe hurried to obey, but Shakespeare's all-knowing look seemed to calm those in the room.

"You wouldn't!" Will Frizer's eyes glinted fear.

"Oh, wouldn't I?" As if to give credence to his threat, Nicholas took the rope from Kempe's hand and slowly, leisurely, tied it in a hangman's knot. He had seen Walsingham, the queen's great spy master, bring forth many a confession by use of fear. "Now, will you tell us all?"

"Never!" Though Frizer was defiant, his voice squeaked.

"Then you are of no use to me." Nicholas slipped the noose around his captive's head. "Alive you pose a danger to me and to my friends. But dead men tell no tales." With a flip of his wrist, Nicholas tossed the loose end of the rope over one of the room's wooden ceiling beams. " 'Tis your choice, Frizer. Do you live or do you die?"

"God's elbows, Christopher has gone quite mad!" William Sly was stunned by what he saw.

"Mad? Perhaps." Alandra turned to Sly, knowing full well that Christopher did not really plan to carry out his threat. "Or perhaps it is just that he seeks to protect all of us. Were we to set this weasel free, he would go running to his master and then where would we all be?" She winked to alert Sly to the ruse Christopher was using.

"Yes ... I suppose ..." Wink or not, William Sly was terribly uneasy.

"Your last chance, Frizer? Will you exonerate me?"

"No!" Frizer's answer was a groan as he suddenly felt the noose tightening.

"Then so be it!"

With a tug on the rope, Nicholas carried out his threat, watching sternly as Frizer choked and gasped, his face turning red.

"All right!" Frizer's voice was a shriek. "I will do as you say."

Relieved that the charade need go no further, Nicholas loosened the noose. "You will be witness to my innocence in the stabbing death of Lord Woodcliff?"

"Yes! Yes!" Frizer sputtered as he fought to catch his breath.

"And you did kill him and will confess to the crime." Fearing Frizer's having a change of heart he amended, "With promise of the queen's mercy." He knew the lighter sentence would mean imprisonment, instead of death and wondered if such a sentence would truly be a blessing.

"I will clear you, but I will not confess to murder!" Frizer said adamantly.

Yet Nicholas was encouraged. It was a beginning.

At least there was now a chance that he might be exonerated of Lord Woodcliffe's murder. He summoned a messenger and hastily scribbled a missive to Elizabeth.

Chapter Forty

For Nicholas and Alandra, it was frustrating to just bide their time in expectation of what was to come, but there was little else they could do. Was it any wonder that with each day that passed it became more and more difficult to display even a semblance of patience? They knew that their whole future hinged on Elizabeth's reaction to the message Nicholas sent to her. Would the queen give her nobleman a chance to clear his name and declare him innocent of the charge of murder, or was Lord Owen Stafford so firmly entrenched in power that all was lost? All they could do was to wait and see, and most importantly guard Will Frizer as diligently as if he were the rarest treasure.

Summer was drawing quickly to a close, but it was more than the approaching days of autumn that puckered Alandra's brow. She marked the on-going time with conflicting emotions. She was relieved and elated now that it appeared Christopher might soon be cleared of the charge of murder, yet she would not have been human had she not selfishly been apprehensive as well. Christopher Nicholas, the prompter, belonged to her but what of the well-born lord? She had a nagging fear that all too soon her happiness and tranquility would be at an end and that Christopher would be forced to go back to his own world as Sir Nicholas Leighton. Thus she held on to the moments they were together, knowing how truly precious and fragile they were.

Despite the uncertainty, however, life had settled into a pleasurable routine. During the day there was always work to be done but the nighttime belonged to them. Christopher visited her every night so that they could sleep together in her bed, and Alandra looked forward to his special signal with a secretive longing. Each time they made love she wondered if it would be the last, treasuring each minute she spent with him, savoring each kiss and caress, and responding ever more passionately. Even so, it was not only passion that bound them together. It was a wanting, a caring, a deep affection, and respect for each other.

Alandra sensed that Christopher really was happy. Now when he smiled, his eyes lit up, when he laughed, there was a ring of sincerity about it. There was a bounce to his step, a soothing tone to his voice, a sense of purpose in everything he did. Loving and being loved in turn most definitely had brought him contentment and his happiness extended into all facets of his life. He took pride in being the prompter and worked hard with the others to make the Lord Chamberlain's Men a success. Now that the truth about him was known to the actors there were no barriers to true friendships. He could be open with them and totally honest, sharing with them his tales of adventure and in return listening to their humorous exploits in the theater world. He was coming to enjoy his infrequent sojourns upon the stage, and if Alandra knew excessive pride to be his weakness, she also knew his strength to be a fierce loyalty to those he cared about, which he displayed in full measure toward all the members of the company.

This morning it really wasn't chilly in her room, yet she lit a fire under the logs in the hearth. She always felt so cold without Christopher's arms around her. Even though she knew he couldn't spend all his time embracing her, she always regretted the hour when they had to get out of bed.

Alandra watched as Christopher went about his morning routine, a ritual she was slowly getting used to. She had become familiar with manly things like shaving but watching him made it more interesting.

Alandra watched him lather his face with white soap then slice through the foam with his razor. He arched his neck backward, tightened his mouth, and turned his face from side to side as he flicked a two-days' growth of whiskers away. Wearing just his hosen and trunk hose, he offered her a pleasant view of broad shoulders and muscles.

"By the by, it's my turn to guard Frizer," he was mumbling. "Care to come?"

"I think I had better. From what Will says, he is proving to be quite a handful."

Frizer was dangerous, demanding, and unruly. Three times he had tried to escape, and three times he had nearly been successful, slightly wounding William Sly and Will Kempe in the process. He had proven himself to be so cunning as a matter of fact that orders had been given that he was to be tied up at all times.

Nicholas sighed deeply. "I will be the happiest man alive when at last he has told the story of what really happened that night and is then out of our hair. Let Elizabeth do with him what she might."

"He has said that he will not confess to the murder. Will you hold to your agreement to keep silent that you think Frizer really killed the old lord, Christopher?"

"Aye. Unless Frizer tries to blame it on another poor hapless soul. I would not see any other man suffer my fate. 'Tis hell to be blamed for that which you did not do." Nicking himself with the razor, he swore beneath his breath.

"It is possible then that Lord Woodcliff's murder will go unpunished." It just didn't seem right to Alandra.

"Unfortunately, that is most likely, unless someone else comes forth to give testimony." He read her thoughts. "It troubles me, too, Alandra, that a man like Frizer will get away with such a deed, but the only way he will clear my name is if I keep silent about my suspecting him. Undoubtedly, he will say that he does not know the identity of the real killer. Nevertheless, I have seen for myself that those who are wrongdoers usually get their due. Frizer will, too. One day!"

Alandra was not so sure. All too many times it seemed that cruelty and violence went unpunished and that those whose only crime was need were the true sufferers. "Let us hope, Christopher. Let us hope."

Picking up a costume that needed mending, she tried to concentrate on her task only to prick her finger with the needle time after time. At last she discarded the garment and just sat staring at the licking orange-and-yellow flames for a long, long time as if to glimpse her destiny there. What did the future hold for her? For Christopher?

"Please let us be together," she whispered, crossing her fingers and closing her eyes to make that wish.

Christopher was everything she wanted, every

dream she'd ever had, every wish she'd ever made. The love they shared was so special. All she could ask of life was to be in his arms, to feel his nearness. To know that he loved her. Christopher was her happiness. How could she give him up? And yet it might come to that.

"If only..." she whispered. So many things were still unanswered. Who was she? Who were her parents? Why had she been abandoned by the roadside? Were her parents still alive? Old or young? Rich or poor? Why had they given her up? Did it really matter? Whoever she was, she wasn't from Christopher's world, though there were times when she fantasized that she was, allowing her dreams to get the better of her.

Her curiosity had doubled of late. She nagged unmercifully at Murray to reveal everything he knew about her parentage. But such proddings only produced her father's nervous mumblings and the blanket that had been wrapped around her when he had found her by the side of the road. Embroidered in fading shades of pink and red were the initials *A.W.*

"What's the matter, Alandra?" Coming up behind her, Nicholas wrapped his arms around her neck. He had witnessed all her moods from tension to tranquility and knew that something was troubling her now.

"Nothing is wrong," she lied.

"Nothing?" He knew better. "What's troubling you, sweetling? Tell me."

Alandra exhaled a long, deep sigh. "I—I was only wondering how long it will be until we hear from Elizabeth," she answered, not wanting to burden him with her doubts and fears.

"Ah, the queen, I fear, takes her own sweet time." How like Elizabeth to play a waiting game. It was her way of reminding him of the power she held in her hands. But then he thought perhaps it was a good sign that she had not marched in at once with her guardsmen to capture him.

"I wish that she would hurry."

"As do I." Nicholas knew that Shakespeare was keeping the players at Bath for an extra long time because of the situation. How he hated to be responsible for the actors' inconvenience. He could sense that they wanted to move on. "We might hear today, and then again it might be a few weeks or more."

It was four days later when Nicholas's message at last was acknowledged. Not by written missive but by messenger. Accompanying that messenger was a tiny entourage. For a moment Nicholas was speechless as he gazed at those who awaited him in the inn's entryway—two guardsmen, dressed in Elizabeth's livery, a nobleman, whom he recognized as being one of the queen's less important diplomats, and a woman dressed in gold and bright blue, a vision of loveliness, whom he recognized all too well.

"Morgana!"

Alandra echoed her lover's words as she came upon the scene. "Morgana...." Her breath caught in her chest. Her heart stabbed with pain. Of all the people in the world this one was the last she wanted to encounter. Now most assuredly her happiness would go flying right out the window.

Pushing past the men accompanying her, ignoring Alandra as if she didn't even exist, Morgana greeted Nicholas with a dazzling smile. "Nicholas." She searched his eyes for only a moment, then reached up to caress his face. "Your beard?"

"My small roles from time to time demand that I remove it," Nicholas said by way of explanation.

To Alandra's consternation, her rival seemed to approve. Her fingers and palm traced his jawline with a familiarity that was delicately bold.

Imposing her importance on those who had accompanied her, Morgana insisted that they go on ahead inside, then turned her attention to Nicholas again. "I like it," she purred.

The unwelcome sting of jealousy welled inside Alandra, despite her attempts to keep it at bay. It didn't help matters that this woman was acting as if she and Nicholas were the only two people in the world.

"How kind of you to approve," Nicholas said dryly, trying to extricate himself from Morgana's caressing hands. It was an awkward situation and he pondered why Elizabeth had sent her. But then wasn't it just like Elizabeth to devise such tests of loyalty and purpose?

"I've missed you. Oh, Nicholas. . . ." As if fearing she might swoon at any moment, the Widow Woodcliff clung to him.

Alandra felt as if she had suddenly been rendered invisible. Though she willed herself not to lose control, it was difficult. Clenching her hands into fists, she willed herself to be calm, forcing her shaky legs to support her.

"The queen," she managed to say, since no one else was addressing the matter. "What is her answer?" Was Nicholas to be brought back to London in chains or as a courtier? The suspense was nearly more than she could bear.

Icy contempt from her rival was the answer. An upraised brow.

Nicholas hurriedly remembered his manners. "Alandra Thatcher, may I present Morgana Woodcliff. Morgana, this is Alandra." Oh, how it made him uneasy for the two women to come face to face.

He feared Morgana would find some way to slight

Alandra when she found out that the pretty young woman had won his heart.

"Alexandra!" Though Nicholas had been quite precise in saying the name, Morgana purposefully seemed to make a mistake in pronunciation. "Alexandra, it is a pleasure."

"Alandra!" she corrected the other woman.

Compared to the elegant blonde, Alandra felt nondescript, colorless. Her simple hairstyle suddenly seemed plain, her garments drab. It was as if she merely blended with the background while the other woman took center stage. It was as if a whirlwind had entered the room, one with whom it was useless to compete.

"Yes, as I said, Elandra."

Alandra shut her mouth against the response that rose to her lips, but she couldn't hide her irritation.

Nicholas could sense that trouble was hovering, and he hastened to avoid a scene by repeating Alandra's question. "Morgana, don't keep me waiting. What is Elizabeth's answer? And why are you here?"

There was a long pause as Morgana made the most of the moment. At last she answered, "Elizabeth has decided to hear you out, despite Lord Stafford's objections. If you are very careful, all may yet be forgiven."

Nicholas scowled. "Forgiven? There is nothing to forgive."

"Not yet, but there will be." Morgana's smile was mysterious.

"Morgana!" What the devil did she mean?

"Hush, Nicholas. There is much that I would tell you and undoubtedly much that you have to reveal. But for the moment I have no other wish than to quench my thirst and relax. It was such a long grueling journey." Leaning forward, she pressed a kiss on his mouth before he could say another word, then looping her arm through his, made her way toward the tap-room of the inn.

Watching them, tears welled in her eyes. All Alandra could think was that her worst nightmare had come true.

Chapter Forty-One

It was a seemingly cordial group that awaited Nicholas at the entrance to the taproom. Had he not known the seriousness of the situation, he might have allowed himself to relax. As it was, all his senses were on alert. He'd learned from experience to be on guard at all times, especially where Elizabeth was concerned. Was the queen really prepared to be fair in her dealings with him, or was this going to prove to be some sort of game for her amusement? The cat cornering the mouse before it sprang? And what of Owen Stafford? How long could he be kept on a leash?

"It was an inordinately tiresome journey. My every muscle aches and my head is pounding," the diplomat was saying, a man Nicholas knew was Thomas Radcliffe, a pliable weak-willed old fool, the perfect pawn for Morgana's wiles. "I guess it is a sign of my age."

"Or poor roads," Nicholas replied politely, remembering his own discomfort while traveling with the actors' caravan. "Perhaps some wine or ale will soothe you."

There was a general murmur of agreement, then without another word Radcliffe and the two guardsmen headed for a table in a corner of the room, ogling the tavern maid as they passed by. The benches squeaked as they sat down.

"Come along, Nicholas. There is much to discuss and plans to be made," Morgana declared in her high-pitched voice. "Then once this tedious business is finished, we can be alone."

Alone. The way the woman said that word there could be no mistaking her meaning, Alandra thought as she stood poised in the archway. She felt miserable as she looked on, as out of place as if she were naught but an eavesdropper. She was certain that Nicholas had forgotten all about her until he tugged at her hand.

"Come, Landra. Anything they have to say you have every right to hear," he said.

Though Morgana protested, Nicholas was staunch in his insistence, thus Alandra followed, making it a threesome as they headed for the table.

As if staking her claim to Nicholas, Morgana positioned herself next to him on his left. She strategically placed Thomas Radcliffe to his right. Alandra sat across the table, sandwiched in between the two guardsmen.

"There, now we are all comfortable," Morgana cooed, though her smiles did not extend to Alandra.

"Aye, comfortable," Nicholas said sarcastically.

He had been so impatient to have done with this matter, had been anxious to have word from Elizabeth, but now that the time was at hand he found himself wishing that he could have just let things stand as they were. There was a certain peacefulness about his life that he knew instinctively was going to end.

Nicholas glanced across the table, scrutinizing the two guardsmen with wary curiosity. One had flaming red hair and a muscular physique, the other was blond and strong but lithe of frame. They were young and virile, the kind of men Morgana and the queen favored. What would they do if he refused to accompany them back to London? For a minute he toyed with the idea but knew the folly of it. He had to return or face Elizabeth's potent anger.

"Girl!" Morgana took it upon herself to summon the tavern maid, a pretty but seemingly clumsy young woman. "Wine for me."

Alandra and Thomas Radcliffe also chose wine while the others were unanimous in wanting ale.

"And do hurry," Morgana ordered with an impatient flick of her wrist. "I have suffered that dusty road for hours, and, I daresay, my mouth is as dry as a bone."

The tavern maid bowed in deference, then slipped quickly away, returning with the beverages, in two blinks of an eye as Murray would have said. The tankards and glasses clanked together as she set them down, and Morgana was quick to chastise the girl for the ale that was spilled, though Alandra knew the reason. Thomas Radcliffe had pinched the poor tavern maid as she passed by. So, that was the type of man with whom Nicholas was dealing. No gentleman he.

"An interesting town, Bath," Radcliffe mumbled, hiding his smile beneath his hand like a mischievous boy. "Very interesting. Pretty wenches. But then I'm sure that you have noticed, Sir Leighton."

Nicholas's eyes touched upon Alandra. "Any place is interesting when one is with the right company."

Oh, how Nicholas wanted to tell them all what was in his heart, to show his affection openly for the woman he loved, but he found himself in a quandry. Morgana was by nature a very jealous woman, and he didn't want her to unleash her malice on Alandra. Thus Nicholas remained subdued, though he couldn't help but caress Alandra visually.

"Ah, yes, I suppose." Thomas Radcliffe looked knowingly from Alandra to Nicholas and back again as if to say "So that is the way it is."

Though pleasantries and formalities were exchanged, there was an underlying sense of uneasiness among the group of people at the table. The real reason for this meeting seemed to be at the back of everyone's minds. For a moment there was tension in the air, broken by Morgana's prattling.

"So, you have become an actor." She turned up her nose at the very thought, a gesture which angered Alandra. "How utterly amusing."

"Not amusing at all," Alandra countered, coming to his defense. "Christopher is not an actor yet, but he is a very good prompter."

"Christopher?" For a moment Morgana looked stunned, then she broke into peals of high-pitched laughter. "So that is what she calls you. Christopher." She spoke lightly and seemed to expect him to stop looking so serious.

"And I have come to favor that name," Nicholas said sincerely. "And my new profession. If I have my way, I will stay among the players after this mess is all sorted out."

Morgana looked at him as if he had suddenly lost his mind. "Stay? Among a group of wanderers? England's foremost swordsman?"

Thomas Radcliffe repeated her amazement. "Stay? By God, you cannot, sir."

Nicholas felt a streak of rebellion against Morgana, against Elizabeth, against his former way of life. "Aye, stay! At least among the actors there is trust and I am not accused of something I did not do." He sipped his ale cautiously, wanting to keep his head clear for what was to come.

Thomas Radcliffe tired of chitchat and came right to the point. "You wrote to Elizabeth in your letter that you have in your custody a witness who will verify your innocence in the matter of Lord Woodcliff's death. Is that correct?"

Nicholas turned his head so that he was looking directly at Morgana. "Two witnesses," he answered.

"Two?" Radcliffe was taken aback. "You did not speak of other than a man by the name of Will Frizer in your letter."

So, it is just as I suspected, Nicholas thought. Morgana had kept silent about being at The Black Unicorn that night, though her testimony might well have saved him. Well, they would have it out now. "Frizer's testimony coupled with that of Lord Woodcliff's widow. She was at the inn."

"Lady Woodcliff was there?" Thomas Radcliff's jaw dropped open in disbelief.

Though Nicholas could be gentle, there was no tenderness in his hand as he gripped her arm. She had to speak the truth. "Tell him, Morgana. Tell him you were there."

Morgana's eyes were wide pools of feigned innocence. "Why should I tell him that, Nicholas?" She pried his fingers away. "I wish to help you, but I dare not lie. In truth I was with my uncle that night."

A muscle tightened in Nicholas's jaw, knowing once and for all how things stood. "You lying bitch!" he swore beneath his breath, just loudly enough for Morgana to hear. There was a tense silence as he took a draught of his ale, pondering his next move.

Morgana's face paled, but she managed to maintain her poise. "I fear all the excitement has addled Sir Leighton's wits, or perhaps there is some misunderstanding. I would never go to such a dangerous area of London."

Nicholas studied Morgana. She looked like a lovely, fragile doll, but he was not at all deceived. Beneath the creamy white skin, the jewels, the velvet, and her smiles, was a conniving woman.

"Ah, yes, there is a misunderstanding, *Lady* Woodcliff," he said between clenched teeth. Once they were nearly lovers, now her deceit had made him her enemy. "A purposeful misunderstanding. You asked me to meet you there so that we could run away *together*." There, he had said it.

Ignoring Nicholas's accusation, Morgana hastened to tell her version of the story, one where she was pursued and not pursuer. "I would be untruthful if I did not admit to being attracted to Sir Leighton, to Nicholas. We did share a kiss or two. He is an extremely handsome man with a charm that is nearly impossible to resist, but though he most obviously had it in mind to seduce me, I insisted that we maintain a chaste relationship."

"You, madame?" Nicholas was furious, remembering all the times she had so willfully tantalized him. He had been the one to back away.

"But what about the inn?" Radcliffe seemed anxious to hear that story. "He says you met him there."

Morgana nodded. "It is true Sir Leighton asked me to meet him at The Black Unicorn that night."

Nicholas grimaced. "*You* asked me." What a magnificent liar.

Suspicion inched its way up Alandra's spine as she listened. Why would this woman so blatantly tell such a falsehood? The answer was clear to Alandra, though she had to admit that her dislike for the woman prejudiced her viewpoint.

In a dramatic gesture that could well have rivaled Richard Burbage, Morgana told her version of what

had happened the night of the masque and of her humiliation at Lord Stafford's "little joke." She acknowledged the fierce rivalry between the two young
noblemen, pitifully related how she had been caught
in the middle. Dramatically, she put her hands over
her eyes as she did admit to having cried on Nicholas's
shoulder.

"But, I repeat, Sir Leighton issued the invitation. I
was tempted, but my loyalty to my husband kept me
from going to the inn."

By God! She was nearly skilled enough to convince
him, Nicholas thought.

Morgana made a great show of weeping. "Oh, that
I had. Perhaps had I been there, I might have been
able to save my poor husband's life. But I did not go,
and for that I will never forgive myself."

Nicholas winced at the twist she gave the tale.
Whether she meant to or not, in her hurry to vindicate
herself she had thrown suspicion on him anew.

"Bloody hell!" he exclaimed. He swallowed and visibly regained control of his anger.

Alandra clenched her fingers in her lap, trying to
ignore the tightening in her stomach, the voice that
whispered in her ear that things could not be going
worse for Christopher. Ah, but there was always Will
Frizer. Thank God for him. He would soon reveal this
scheming blonde for what she was.

Nicholas seemed to sense her thoughts, for as he
raised his eyes to hers, he mouthed the name. "So be
it . . ." he whispered.

He held tightly to his tankard and scrutinized the
reaction of Thomas Radcliffe and the guards to Morgana's words. He was not surprised to see that she had
won their sympathy, nor could he blame them. The
poor bereaved widow. Once he too might have been
taken in by such artful deception but not now, not
after basking in the warmth of Alandra's sincerity.

Thomas Radcliffe was obviously deeply troubled. "Is it perhaps possible that you mistook another woman to be Lady Woodcliff, another lady with yellow hair?"

Nicholas groaned, dragging his fingers through his thick dark hair. "I made no mistake!"

"But it was dark, you might have drunk a bit too much ale . . ." Radcliffe raised his brows.

"Not so much that I would not know what I was doing." Nicholas realized fully now that he must tread very carefully. "Let me reiterate one major point. Lord Woodcliff was stabbed from behind. Such a cowardly deed I would never do!"

"Of course Sir Leighton did not kill my husband. I never for a moment believed Lord Stafford's story." Morgana tried to make some amends. "I said as much to Elizabeth, but she wouldn't believe me." Her voice was calm. Morgana's only show of agitation was that she drummed her fingers on the table as she spoke.

"Well, at least you give me that." Nicholas dragged the conversation back to the matter at hand. "I think it best that you question Will Frizer as to what happened that night. Let him do his part as an eyewitness. That is all that I can say."

And let this blond-haired witch beware, lest she be shown for the liar that she is, Alandra thought.

Radcliffe seemed as anxious as Nicholas to put end to this matter. "Indeed, we will speak with this Frizer at once."

Satisfied, Nicholas nodded. From under the table, he felt Alandra take his hand and give it a gentle squeeze. The loving gesture calmed him, and he couldn't help thinking that with a woman like Alandra believing in him all had to be well in the end. It had to be. Confidently, he stood up to lead the way to the room where Frizer was being held prisoner.

"Frizer will tell you of Christopher's innocence, you

will see," Alandra said to Radcliffe. She was certain, for she too believed that all would be well.

Triumphantly, she put her hand on the door latch and opened the portal wide. She gasped when she saw Robert Armin slumped upon the floor. "Robert!"

Fearing the worst, Alandra hurried to his side, relieved to see that he was only out cold and not dead. The same, however, could not be said for the man he had been guarding. Not five feet away, lying face down in a pool of blood, was Will Frizer.

"God's thunder!" At first having thought Frizer the culprit of Armin's cracked head, Nicholas was stunned. Hoping beyond hope, he bent down and sought a heartbeat. There was none. Frizer had been stabbed in the heart by someone who had aimed well. "Who could have done this?" Nicholas asked in despair.

"And why?" Alandra wailed. They had been so careful, had guarded the rogue night and day. How could this have happened? Who would want Frizer dead?

Thomas Radcliffe eyed Nicholas with undisguised suspicion. "So one witness denies what you insist and the other ends up dead. We shall see what the queen has to say of this."

"The queen..." Nicholas muttered.

Alandra recognized a pained resignation in his expression, as if he realized there was no use in arguing.

"Shall we go?" Radcliffe nodded his head, and the two guardsmen who had been as silent as bookends during the conversation moved toward Nicholas. They grabbed hold of his arms, leaving no doubt as to his status. He was their prisoner.

Will Frizer was dead and Morgana steadfast in her falsehood of being nowhere near the inn. Nicholas was on his way to see Elizabeth but for what purpose? With no witnesses from the Black Unicorn to corroborate his story, Alandra knew very well how perilous was his fate. And though she and the others had heard Frizer's confession, would Elizabeth believe them?

Chapter Forty-Two

Tension engulfed Nicholas. Suspicion rose up like a stone wall. He could see that in Thomas Radcliffe's eyes he was already tried and condemned. Yet he made a last attempt to proclaim his innocence as he struggled against the iron-fisted hands that held him. "I did not commit murder! Not this man's and not Lord Woodcliff's."

Radcliffe cleared his throat then proclaimed loudly, "I arrest you in the name of the queen."

Nicholas stood deathly quiet but when he was dragged toward the door, he came back to life. "Just a moment alone with Alandra to say good-bye," Nicholas pleaded.

"To say good-bye. To her?" Morgana's usually beautiful face turned ugly with her anger. "No, I will not allow it."

Radcliffe looked as though he wanted to deny such a privilege but reluctantly nodded, and the guardsmen released Nicholas. "A few minutes only! And just remember that we are right outside the door. An attempt at escape will be construed as a confession of your guilt, not only in Woodcliff's murder but this man's murder as well."

With a grimace of disgust, Thomas Radcliffe pulled a sheet from the bed and draped it over Will Frizer, then for once ignoring Morgana's protestations, he led the small group from the room, leaving the two people alone.

Nicholas slid his arms around Alandra's waist and pulled her close against his heart. "And so I am right back where I began. An accused murderer." Threading his fingers through her dark brown hair, tilting up her face, he shook his head. "No, not where I began, for then I did not know you, love you."

"Oh, Christopher . . ." Her eyes glittered with tears. "There must be something we can do. We'll come to London. To The Black Unicorn. There were witnesses. I'll find them somehow, make them give testimony in your name. And we all heard Frizer confess. Perhaps we can convince Elizabeth of your innocence." Her lips quivered, and she bit them to fight against crying.

"No! You will stay here." He didn't want her or the players to have anything to do with all of this, for to do so would put her life and theirs in danger. Will Frizer's murderer was on the loose, and Nicholas knew very well that were Alandra and the players to interfere all their lives might be forfeit. That he could never bear.

"But I must. I can't let you face this all alone."

Steadfast in her loyalty she looked radiant to Nicholas. Her large copper-colored eyes and the slant of her brows gave an impish quality to her face, emphasizing her youth. Her full lips, the sensuous curve of her mouth, and the depth of emotions churning in her eyes, however, left no doubt that she was a woman. His woman.

Never had she been more beautiful to Nicholas's eyes, never had he wanted to cling to her as fervently as he did now. Deep down he wanted to be with her, wanted her to come with him, to soothe him in his darkest hour of need, but he knew with a heavy heart he would have to set her free. Unselfishly, he knew it to be the best thing for *her*.

"I must go alone and you must stay here!"

"I won't, nor will the others." Alandra was indignant. "We'll all come back to London and—"

Nicholas bent his head and kissed her, silencing her tirade. Sliding his hands down then cupping her bottom, he crushed her intimately against him. Alandra responded with a fervor that tormented him. Oh, if only they had time, how passionately he would have made love to her, he thought. But Nicholas knew his time had run out.

Alandra longed for his arms again the moment he set her free, but when she reached out to him, he eluded her embrace.

"We must not make this harder than it already is. Good-bye, Alandra. May God in his mercy be with you all the days of your life."

"Good-bye?" Just like that. One kiss and then *adieu*?

He looked down into her determined face and felt a fierce surging of love, but answered, "There is nothing else to say."

Oh, God, he thought, if only she knew how this was tearing him up inside. It was only with the greatest of self-control that he kept his sanity, lest he fall to his knees blubbering like a child. He loved her. Had he not known it before, he knew it now. Leaving her was going to be the most difficult thing he had ever done.

"Don't forget me, Christopher." Morgana's beauty

loomed in her mind. A cat who would find a chance to pounce now that he was at her mercy. The very thought made her miserable. "Alas, but I know you will."

Forget her? Nicholas knew that as long as he lived Alandra Thatcher would be in his heart. He'd remember her pert prettiness, her spunk, her gentleness, her giving nature. He'd remember her smile and the bright sound of her laughter. The days she so patiently taught him, the time they had spent together would be implanted in his mind. Forget her? Never. She was a part of his very soul. The memory of the love they had shared would fill the gloomy corners of his soul in days to come. Even so, he forced himself to be gruff for her sake.

"It would be for the best. One day you will meet another man...."

"Nay, do not speak of it!" No man could ever take Christopher's place. The very idea made her shudder. Far better to die alone. "We were too happy for me even to think about it."

Nicholas closed his eyes to his pain. "Aye, we were happy, but happiness does not last forever. We loved each other, aye, but we knew one day we would have to part. We entered into our love with open eyes. Now the time has come to say good-bye and to wish each other well."

She was taken aback, stung by his words. "Just like that. I'm to watch you leave and wave a fond good-bye? No, Christopher, if you think I can do that, then you never really knew me at all."

He looked away from her, for it was the only way he could control his emotions. "Nicholas. My name is Nicholas." *Don't touch her*, he thought, *or else you are lost*. "Sir Nicholas Leighton. The moment I walk out that door, Christopher Nicholas is dead and my time among the players is no more."

The sound of Alandra's sobbing broke through his resolve, such a mournful keening he could not ignore. "Alandra, love. Don't. . . ." But her tears fell like rain. "Alandra. . . ." How could he do else but pull her into his arms again? Nicholas wiped away her tears with a gentle hand, his fingers lingering on her flushed cheek.

Alandra wound her arms around his neck, nestling her soft breasts against his chest. "I adore you, Christopher. We will be together again. This I swear. God couldn't be so cruel as to keep us apart."

She kissed him then, ravishing him with her lips, teeth, and tongue. They held each other close until Radcliffe and the guardsman intruded.

"Come, you must make yourself ready. It is still light, and Lady Woodcliff is anxious to get back on the road for the return journey," Radcliffe stated with authority.

At Radcliffe's nod, the two guardsmen grabbed hold of Nicholas again. He was marched away, put upon a horse with his hands tied behind his back, to ride for London at the head of the tiny caravan.

As they traveled down the road, the inn got smaller and smaller, still as he looked back, Nicholas could see the outline of Alandra's head and shoulders leaning from the window as she bravely watched him ride away. Her wave seemed to emphasize her promise that they would be together again. Then as the entourage rounded a bend in the road, he could see her no more.

Act Three: A Surprising Revelation

"And when love speaks the voice of all the gods,
Makes heaven drowsy with the harmony."
Shakespeare, *LOVE'S LABOR LOST* act 4, scene 2

Chapter Forty-Three

It was a lonely world for Alandra without Nicholas, just as she knew it would be. There was an ache inside her, a void that nothing and no one could fill. Yet she knew that Murray and Shakespeare were right when they said that life must go on. And it did tediously. The only thing that kept Alandra going, however, was Shakespeare's promise that as soon as they were finished with the tour, the players would head straight-away to London and there do what they could to aid in clearing their friend, Christopher. Robert Armin had seen his assailant and could at least clear Christopher of Frizer's murder.

Shakespeare had concluded that whoever killed Will Frizer was behind Lord Woodcliff's murder and feared to be exposed. But who had killed the actors' captive? How had the culprit taken Robert Armin unaware? Was the murderer still on the prowl? Those questions deeply troubled Alandra.

The answer to one question at least had been answered when Robert Armin had been revived after Nicholas and the entourage had left the inn. Robert had sheepishly confided that he had opened the door when the tavern maid had called out that she had brought him some ale. Wanting the beverage, he had thought there would be no harm in opening the door to her. Instead of getting a drink, he had gotten a bump on the head that had rendered him senseless, but he seemed to remember a woman's voice calling out a name, Tom. Before he had succumbed to the black whirling before his eyes, he had also caught sight of a face—a man with coal black hair, bushy brows, and a crooked nose. A man missing an ear.

Alandra had inquired after the tavern maid, hoping to learn the whole story, only to find that she had been thrown out by the innkeeper because of Morgana's complaint about the young woman's clumsiness. As to the man with the thick brows, misshapen nose, and missing ear, it was as if he were but a figment of Armin's imagination. No one recalled having seen him at the inn.

"And thus it is hopeless," Alandra had dejectedly announced to Shakespeare. "Will Frizer was killed before he was given a chance to speak up on Christopher's behalf."

The brown eyes of the playwright were gentle as he looked at her. "We'll get your Christopher out of trouble. I promise. Somehow we'll find the real murderer and expose him to the queen." And once they had discovered the killer's identity, Will had a remarkable idea for making certain that Elizabeth was told directly. "A masque began Christopher's problems. It seems only fitting that a play likewise get him out of the noose, so to speak."

"We'll act out the murderer's identity when we give

our play before the queen!'' Alandra threw back her
head and laughed.

"Precisely!"

"Oh, I can hardly wait!'' she exclaimed. Imagine
Christopher's surprise when he learned that the Lord
Chamberlain's Men had come to his rescue, she
thought. He would be free, and then they could be
together again.

Instead of that hope calming her as they set out
again upon the road, it made her more impatient to
have done with the tour and return to the city on the
Thames. Suddenly London and Christopher seemed
so far away.

The last stop on the players' journey was Bristol, a
city upon Will's beloved Avon, England's busiest west
coast port for hundreds of years. One of the chief cities
of England, the second city of the realm, it stood north-
west of Bath, on a hill that afforded a clear view of its
cathedral and the beautiful houses that had been built
by the town's merchants. It was a city that loved the
theater, thus the players looked forward to a successful
week of playacting, but as soon as the Lord Chamberlain's Men arrived, they said at once that the city
was not at its best. Years of depression and bad har-
vests had hit Bristol. Hardly an atmosphere that guar-
anteed replenishing the company's coffers. Even so, it
was decided that they would stay. Alandra, however,
doubted that the play Will had chosen, *The Merchant
of Venice*, had any chance of being a success, not
amidst such turmoil.

But it was! Longing to forget their troubles, if only
for a little while, the common folk of Bristol and the
elite as well flocked to see the players.

"They loved us,'' Richard Burbage exclaimed at the
play's end, coming off the stage after his twentieth
bow.

"And what is more, they didn't throw even one apple

or orange," William Sly said with a purposeful wink.

"That's because they didn't want to waste anything edible," William Kempe quipped. "For once I had hoped that they would, considering our meager circumstances and all."

Playfully the actors engaged in cheerful and witty joking. "Banter," as Murray called it. Good-humored fun.

"Banter," Alandra repeated. There was something about the word that tugged at the tendrils of her brain. "Banter."

"A word meaning to tease, Alandra," Shakespeare informed her, mistaking her wide-eyed expression. "Banter."

"Banter!" The word tripped off her tongue as she repeated it over and over, until the actors were staring at her, thinking she must surely have lost her mind. "Tom. Banter. Tom Banter. Of course!" Her face grew pale as she suddenly put it all together, remembering the name. "That's who killed Will Frizer. It all makes sense."

"It does?" Murray looked at her quizzically, whispering behind his hand that he was going to take her at once to the inn and put her to bed. "I fear she has always been of a choleric humor."

"No!" Alandra pulled away from her father's outstretched arms. She needed no doctoring. "You don't understand." Thus she hurried to explain that Christopher had mentioned that one of the rogues who had been with Frizer at the Black Unicorn had been named Banter. *Tom* Banter. "Don't you see, it all fits together."

"The Tom who hit me over the head," Robert Armin exclaimed.

It made sense, Alandra thought. Will Frizer and Tom Banter had killed Lord Woodcliff. Tom Banter had killed Will Frizer. But what about the woman Robert

Armin had heard calling to Banter? Who was she? The answer hit Alandra like a physical blow. Morgana! Who else? It all added up and explained so many things.

Rushing over to Shakespeare, Alandra tugged at his sleeve. "We have to go to London. Not at week's end but as soon as we can. Early tomorrow!"

"Tomorrow?" Will shook his head. "We can't. We promised another four days' worth of performances."

"We have to. If you and the others won't go with me, then I'll go alone. I swear it." Even if she had to steal a horse or walk all the way, she had to hurry to London. The truth of the matter was clear to her now. Christopher was in more danger than he could ever have suspected.

Chapter Forty-Four

Dark walls rose high about Nicholas, so high that the ceiling seemed to be shrouded in gloom. Bars on the window blocked his view of the sky. Ominous silence surrounded him, except for an occasional drip, drip, drip. It was damp in the stone room because of a recent rain. The little bit of air that drifted through the window was musty and held the unwelcome stench of the Thames.

Nicholas was being kept in a cell in the Tower of London, which at least was better than the damp, dismal smell of Newgate. At least Nicholas had that—the illustrious Tower where many other noble prisoners had been confined. To pass the time, he tediously counted them off—Catherine Howard, Sir Thomas More, Lady Jane Grey, Edmund Nevill, even the queen's own mother, Anne Boleyn. In such scheming dangerous times, the list was endless and the fate of the prisoners was nearly always the same—death.

Nicholas stared around him with burning, angry eyes. Someday he'd get away from here and woe be to Owen Stafford for masterminding this. Oh, yes, he had figured it out. It had to be Stafford. Somehow he had intercepted the message Nicholas had sent, and he had read it before giving it to the queen. While Nicholas had been chattering with the fools Elizabeth had sent to bring him back, Stafford had located Will Frizer and had paid to have him murdered. It all made sense.

Nicholas laughed at himself and his own stupidity. He had all along held a ray of hope that Elizabeth would at least give him a fighting chance, if he ever returned to court. He had spent several years in the queen's employ, using his sword to save England from her enemies. That should merit him some consideration, he had thought. As it turned out, the joke was on him, for Thomas Radcliffe had told Nicholas during their journey to London that Owen Stafford had wormed his way even more strongly into Elizabeth's favor.

But worse was the news that there were changes at court. Nicholas's only hope had been to make use of his other friendship with the Earl of Essex, but Radcliffe had said that earl's unsuccessful expedition to the Azores during the summer had been a turning point for the worse in his fortunes. He was in disfavor and his precarious position had caused the court to split into factions.

Radcliffe added that Lord Burghley too was absent from court. An old man wracked with a severe illness, his son, Robert Cecil, had taken his place as Elizabeth's foremost councilor and had secured the secretaryship and the chancellorship of the Duchy of Lancaster. He had used his position to build a strong following in Parliament.

Knowing that the odds were against him, Nicholas

had faced a bitter "homecoming". Without benefit of audience with Elizabeth, Nicholas had been thrown into the Tower of London.

He remembered being brought in through the river entrance, Traitors' Gate, looking around in sick despair as the full realization of his fate hit him. Never had he imagined that he would be within the Tower's walls as a prisoner. Hustled by his gaolers, the yeoman warders, he had been taken to the lieutenant's lodgings, the headquarters of the officer in command. There he was "booked in" and assigned a prison room.

Nicholas had not been brought to trial, however. He was released just long enough to be questioned twice by Robert Cecil, then taken back to the Tower. As the days dragged by he had begun to fear that this was to be his prison for many years to come, day following day, month following month. Forgotten by the outside world.

Now as he paced in his cell, he wondered if there was sufficient evidence to convict him. He doubted it. Not unless false evidence or bribed witnesses were used against him. At the back of his mind was the suspicion that whoever had murdered Will Frizer would be in no hurry to have him talk with the queen. He would be kept cooped up in the Tower until he was old and gray.

At least he was not suffering. Tedium and boredom were perhaps the worst thing about being imprisoned. That and his loneliness and his longing for Alandra. Any time his eyes closed, it was of her that he dreamed.

If only he hadn't sent that message. If only he had said to hell with his honor. He would have forgotten about Elizabeth, about England, and grabbed happiness while he had the chance. If only he had truly become Christopher Nicholas. But his fierce pride had been his downfall, his determination to clear his good name. Now the only thing that soothed him was that at least Alandra was safe, far away in Bristol with the Lord Chamberlain's Men.

Alandra stared at the great stone walls of the fearsome fortress. "The Tower," she whispered, feeling a twinge of fear and foreboding. She shuddered as she saw it looming in the distance, guarding the city. It looked forbidding and frightening. Moreso now that she knew Christopher was inside.

"The full title of the Tower is the Ancient Palace and Fortress of Her Majesty's Tower of London," Heminges was saying, pointing it out to her as if there was any possibility that she could miss seeing its giant limestone towers and turrets. Built on the orders of William the Conqueror to subdue the turbulent Saxons who were the former inhabitants of London, the Tower dominated the landscape.

Looking at the white tower, she remembered the many stories she had heard about it in her childhood, for it had a somber history. It was a symbol not of beauty but of power. For whoever challenged the authority of the queen the prison cells awaited.

Clutching her hands together as the play wagon rolled down the road, Alandra blurted out her naive hope. "Somehow we will help Christopher escape!"

"Break him out of there?" Murray shook his head sadly. "There is no way we could even attempt it. The walls are at least eight feet thick. To enter the castle from the landward side, there are three drawbridges to be crossed. There are guards at four checkpoints, porcullises, heavy wooden drop gates. No, that is not the way to come to his aid."

"Then how?" Even as she asked the question, Alandra fantasized in her mind what she would like to do. Kidnap that witch Morgana and have her put on the rack until she confessed to the murder of her husband.

Or better yet boil her in hot water such as had once been done to all those who tried to breach the Tower's walls.

Murray pulled at the reins, slowing the play wagon down. "You, Will Kempe, Shakespeare, Armin, and I are going to take lodgings at The Black Unicorn. Keeping our ears and eyes open, doing a bit of spying, we should soon pick up a few leads that might turn up Tom Banter."

"Or the woman I heard talking that night through the door." Alandra thought a moment, remembering that the woman's name had been Bessie.

"Somehow. Some way, we'll discover something." Murray reached over to tug at her hair. "Get the frown off your face, girl. We'll soon have Christopher free. I've got it in mind to see the two of you back together."

As Shakespeare joined them, he too seemed optimistic. "Truth has a strange way of coming to light. If we are stealthful, I do believe we can find out what really happened that night and who is to blame. Then we can get back one of our most valuable members."

"Who was to blame?" Alandra screwed her face up with disgust. "I know full well. That blond witch!"

"Or Lord Owen Stafford," Murray countered. "I fully believe 'twas he. Ambition goads a man to do many evil things."

Shakespeare loosened his hold on his horse's reins and put up his hand. "It doesn't really matter who was at fault, only that we prove it was not Christopher."

To that end, Shakespeare devised a plot, one that would make good use of the actors' expertise with make-up and costuming. He would put on finery fit for one of noble birth and have it whispered about that he was in search of a "cutter." A rogue who would sell his villainous services. He would make inquiry about a specific "hackster," Tom Banter by name, and hope the ploy was successful.

Chapter Forty-Five

Alandra crouched near the inn's window in the chill of the dawn, her brown eyes peering through a crack in the shutters. The innyard was shrouded in the white mist that threatened rain, thus she could see little more than shadows. Coils of fog drifted about like ghosts, silhouettes ambled about as the workers of the inn tended to their daily chores.

It was Will Kempe's, Robert Armin's, and Shakespeare's assignment to find Tom Banter. To her had been given the task of keeping watch on the courtyard and to try to locate Bessie, which was proving to be difficult at best. For some reason, be it fear or stubbornness, the woman was keeping well out of sight. The more Alandra inquired concerning her whereabouts, the more she was met with stern silence. But Alandra was not one to give up.

Alandra's nightgown was crumpled, her dark brown hair hung loose and in tangles around her shoulders, but she hardly noticed. All she could think about was Christopher. All of London chattered about his fall. To such a proud man, the disgrace must surely wring his soul, Alandra thought. He was shut up in that cold, damp tower like the animals in the queen's private zoo with only Alandra and his actor friends to save him. And they would! God's nightgown, they would convince Elizabeth to free him. Somehow.

But Alandra could not help wonder at what price his freedom would be paid. She knew that despite his promise to remain with the company, he would more than likely return to the court and Elizabeth.

"Merry-go-up, daughter, you are going to turn into a statue if you kneel by that window much longer," Murray gently chided her. "I don't think you even got a wink of sleep. All night long you flitted back and forth from your bed to that window like a little moth."

"And I'll stay by this window all day if it means accomplishing my goal," Alandra answered with great sadness. She shivered. It was cold in the room, but she was much too involved in spying to go and get a robe.

"Ah young love. I wonder if Christopher has any idea just what a loyal little kitten you are." Striding to where she crouched, Murray knelt beside her and stroked her long dark hair.

"Oh, Father, we just have to find Bessie. Her testimony could be so valuable." She sighed deeply. "Do you suppose that we will? Or is it as John Heminges says, like looking for a pin in a straw stack?"

Murray's smile was as mischievous as an elf's. "I've been doing a bit of spying myself, listening about in the kitchens. I heard the cook talking about one of the chambermaids, a woman by the name of Elizabeth Herbert. A widow in the prime years of her life." To Murray, that meant she was in her fifties.

Alandra whirled around, hope glowing in her eyes.

"Elizabeth! Bessie is often used as a nickname." It was certainly worth pursuing. "It might be the woman we are seeking."

"That's what I be thinking which is why I intend to corner that lady. She can't hide forever. This morning I'm going to haunt the halls and hope that I can come upon her when she is making up the rooms."

"She might run from you. You might frighten her away if you start asking her any questions." It was a disturbing thought. Alandra supposed that the woman's reluctance to be located was because she had undoubtedly heard the gossip about the nobleman housed in the Tower for Lord Woodcliff's murder and was determined not to be involved in any way. "Be careful, Father."

"She will never guess why I am seeking her out. Knowing that the cook is a woman who loves to chatter, I gave it out that I am a lonely man who is looking for a wife. I've heard that this Elizabeth is quite stunning."

"A wife!" Alandra was so stunned that she lost her balance and had to steady herself with her hand.

"Chitchat only," Murray insisted, though there was a shadow of loneliness in his eyes. "I've found from experience that there are very few widows who aren't hoping to find another husband. Most of them make it a practice to go 'fishing' as I call it. I intend to turn the tables and be the one who initiates the courtship."

"Fishing? And you think this Elizabeth Herbert will take the bait?"

Alandra studied Murray, coming to the conclusion that he was actually looking forward to meeting the mysterious widow. And why not? For the first time she suddenly realized how lonely her father must be. Oh, he had her love and affection to be sure, but it wasn't the same thing. She realized that fully now.

Murray deserved the same happiness she had with Christopher.

"Take the bait!" Murray affected a swagger as he walked around the room. "And why not? I was quite a charmer in my day."

"And still are, you old dear!" Rising to her feet, Alandra gave him an affectionate kiss on the cheek.

Murray flushed, dimpling as he said, "We'll soon see. Ah, yes. Time will be the judge of me."

Murray was true to his word of coming face to face with the Widow Herbert, a petite and attractive woman with gray-streaked auburn hair and a cheerful smile. With the zeal of a man half his age he wooed her, taking her on moonlight walks in the garden, picking flowers for her to wear in her hair, reciting colorful poems that enumerated her charms, confiding in her and in turn being a patient listener. It did not take long before he earned the widow's trust and affection.

"Elizabeth is the Bessie we have been looking for," Murray at last announced to Shakespeare and Alandra one evening as they sat at the small table in Shakespeare's room, partaking of dinner.

"Are you certain?" Alandra asked, thinking it seemed too good to be true.

"As certain as I am of being an Englishman!" Murray toyed with his blackbird pie, obviously deeply troubled. "She told me about having witnessed the murder of a nobleman."

"Lord Woodcliff?" Shakespeare asked.

"She did not mention him by name, but the description that she gave me leaves little doubt. Killed by a fiendish rogue, or so she says." Murray clucked his tongue, his expression pained. "But woe is me. How can I betray her so when she trusted me?"

"Will she bear witness that Christopher is innocent?"

Murray answered Alandra with a nod. "I am more than certain that I can convince her to do so. But God help me, if she comes to any harm." The thought of Will Frizer's fate seemed to haunt him. "I wouldn't be able to forgive myself."

"If she speaks up, she might very well be in danger. You must realize that, Murray. 'Tis the chance that we take."

"Aye, I know. I know."

Alandra saw the look of sadness on Murray's face, giving away the depth of his·affections. There could be no question that he was coming to have a great regard for the Widow Herbert in the brief time they had been together. But it was also evident by the look he gave Alandra that he put her happiness above his own, above everything.

"Somehow I'll convince her to tell what she knows," Murray added softly.

The matter of Tom Banter's whereabouts was not so easily accomplished. Despite Shakespeare's carefully laid out plan, one week passed, then two, and Alandra in her impatience grew tired of listening to Shakespeare and her father telling her that there was no choice but to wait. She wanted to act and act now. They had Will Frizer's testimony, which they'd all witnessed, and Bessie Herbert had agreed to speak up on the matter.

Then something happened that made action imperative. While walking about in the inner courtyard, Alandra overheard some disturbing gossip. Robert Cecil had called for the execution of Sir Nicholas Leighton.

The very thought of Christopher dying chilled Alandra's blood. She couldn't live without him! But what could she do? She didn't know anyone at court, had no connections. And yet if she waited, if Christopher was judged and found guilty, what then? She could not allow that! Even if she had to throw herself on the mercy of the queen, she would not let that happen.

The queen! Of course, that was it. Alandra's eyes opened wide as she realized what she had to do. She'd go at once to Whitehall to seek an audience with Elizabeth Tudor in the name of the players. On the pretense of arranging the upcoming play and seeing to the scenery, she'd take advantage of that one moment to plead with the queen and to tell her all. Surely when Elizabeth heard all that Alandra had to say, she would at least give Christopher a chance. Dear God, she must!

Chapter Forty-Six

Through the tiny window of his cell Nicholas could hear the sounds of London, the clatter of the cart and coach wheels on the cobbles, the barking of hounds, the yells of traders, the brawling of apprentices, the din of pedestrians as they wound their way past the shops and stalls. And the bells. They tolled the hours of the day, reminding Nicholas of the tediousness of his existence.

"All too familiar sounds," he grumbled, not even bothering to get up from his bed. He just lay there lethargically. What did it matter? He wasn't going anywhere. The Tower was by now becoming much too well known to him. Was it any wonder he was in a foul mood? Until Elizabeth saw fit to release him, he was "her guest."

Not that he was being mistreated. He lived in comparative comfort because of his status as a nobleman. His room was well furnished, with Turkish carpets adorning the floors, fine wooden chairs, tables, and a comfortable bed. He was even given a certain amount of freedom, as he was allowed to take walks accompanied by several guards. He was well fed and given enough water. It was just that he was disheartened and bored.

He was an active man and there was nothing to do. He was not allowed any visitors, nor was he allowed to write letters. Except for the guards and the warder, he saw and talked to no one. Minutes, hours, even days passed by without any change in his routine until Nicholas seemed to lose all track of time.

He felt betrayed, and the bitterness showed plainly upon his face. He had risked his very life for Elizabeth's safety many times. Now he was angered that she couldn't even take the time to pay him a visit, even if it was for naught but to scold him. She had seemingly turned her back upon him who was ever her loyal servant. She had given him a taste of power and then snatched it back violently because of another's false witness. The queen's displeasure seemed absolute and all because of one man. Stafford! He had poisoned Elizabeth's mind against Nicholas.

Two conflicting emotions took control of Nicholas's heart. The first was hatred, and he spent long hours thinking of ways to get even with his enemy. Oh, how he detested that bastard. Behind Stafford's smiles and the velvets he wore lurked a savage beast looking for a chance to kill. Nicholas was certain that Stafford had instigated the murders of two men and had blamed them on Nicholas.

Oh, what he wouldn't give to have his hands around that devil's neck! Or a sword at his throat. Closing his eyes, Nicholas fantasized about the different tortures he would bring to his rival, but his hatred melted away to be replaced by an emotion of a gentler sort. His love for Alandra.

"Alandra. Alandra. Alandra." Even just saying her name brought him a sense of peace. His mind was haunted by the memory of her sweet smile, the shadow-darkness of her hair, the way her cheeks dimpled when she smiled, her large flashing eyes. Stretching himself out upon the bed, he willed himself to sleep so that he might conjure up his dreams of her.

The pressure of hands on his shoulders awakened him, and instinctively, he lashed out with his fists.

"Nicholas, what on earth are you doing?" Morgana shrieked as she struggled against his flailing hands.

"Morgana!" His eyes flew open and he bolted upright. "Have you come here to gloat?"

"No, of course not!" She moved toward him with feline grace.

Nicholas shrugged her away. "Get out of here. I have nothing to say to you." She was the last person in the world he wanted to see. "Leave me. I would have some peace," he declared loudly.

"Shh," she scolded, laying a solicitous hand on his arm. "I am here to help you. Be quiet or you will bring the guards."

His mood was grim as he asked, "What are you doing here?" Though he had not had any company since arriving, he was definitely not in a mood to see her.

"I have come to help you escape!" she whispered.

She immediately got his attention. "Escape!" Freedom after three weeks in prison was a heady thought. Nicholas hardly dared to breathe, his heart thundered in his chest. Above all freedom was what he wanted, but he was loathe to trust her.

"Perhaps I have it in mind to stay here," he said testily. "The accommodations are so appealing. There is a great deal that can be said for solitude."

"Stay? You can't!" she squealed. "Robert Cecil is calling for your head, telling all who will listen that the court cannot condone unwarranted murder."

"Robert Cecil," he grumbled. With the exception of Lord Stafford, Cecil was the man Nicholas detested the most. An ambitious little dwarf who thought to build himself up by tearing others down. He lacked public graces and had manners befitting a blacksmith. He was an upstart who just happened to have an influential father in Lord Burghley.

"He has been goaded on by Lord Owen Stafford—"

"Stafford!" The very name infuriated Nicholas. In a gesture that was anything but gentlemanly he grasped her hair, winding it around his wrist like a rope, forcing her to meet him eye to eye. "Speaking of Lord Stafford, just how do you and he fit together in all of this?" For a moment Nicholas wondered if Stafford too had been ensnared by Morgana's charms, then threw the notion aside.

"I abhor the man!" Morgana gasped. "How could you forget what he did to me?"

It had been Stafford who had exposed her whorish nature to the court. Hardly the act of a lover. With a mumbled oath, Nicholas released her. "If this talk of aiding me is some sort of joke. . . . If it is I swear I'll—"

" 'Tis no joke, Nicholas." She ran a hand over his chest with a familiarity that used to stir him. "I have it all arranged."

Quickly, she explained to him that he was to sit by his window, motionless and silent, as if brooding over his misfortune, so that the warder would get used to seeing his still figure against the light of the window. In three days' time Morgana would smuggle in an exact duplicate set of the garments he was wearing, the midnight-blue doublet trimmed in gold braid, gold hosen, and blue trunk hose, and a cap.

"I seldom wear a cap!" he interjected.

"You will now!" she declared.

Morgana then told him that he was to assemble the dummy using the straw that she would also bring to him, and then dress it in the clothes. The dummy would be positioned by the window seat so that when the warder made his rounds he would think Nicholas was at the window, sullenly thinking about his confinement.

"I will come to you with the key and unlock your door. There will be a boat..." She pressed her face against his chest, feeling his warmth and strength.

"So, I'm to go by waterway. But to where?" he asked stiffly, not even making an effort to touch her.

"Across the Channel. We'll go together."

"No." Even though she held his fate in her hands, he couldn't lie to her or to himself.

She was stunned. "What do you mean? Oh, Nicholas, I had to lie to Radcliffe. You know what Elizabeth would have done if she knew I planned to run away with you that night. My presence at the inn would have only strengthened the case they have against you. I knew what I was doing."

"Morgana..." How did you tell a woman you had found someone else, that you didn't want her? "I—"

"It's that girl!"

Did he imagine it, or was there a hiss in her voice?

"Yes." He'd get free of the Tower and head straight-away to Bristol, take Alandra in his arms, and carry her away. To the ends of the earth if need be. "It's only once in a lifetime that a person finds true love. I did and am blessed for it." He was sincere when he said, "And you will find such happiness, too. One day."

Morgana refused to be defeated. "You only think you are in love." She threw herself into his arms, hugging him tight. "I love you, Nicholas. You're all I ever dreamed about, all I've ever really wanted. While you were away, I was so lonely, so desolate."

He sincerely doubted it. "You'll find someone else."

He wanted to say that the truth of the matter was that she loved only herself but held his tongue.

"Never. I wanted you the moment I first saw you at court, striding across the room to greet Elizabeth. You seemed taller than other men, braver. Magnificent!"

"I was cocky. Nothing more."

She traced the hard-muscled lines of his chest. "You were, are, splendid!"

His fingers caught her wrist, pushing her probing fingers away. "Don't." His voice held the tone of a father's with an errant child.

She raised her haughty head, her eyes blazing anger, but she controlled herself, tossing her well-coiffed blond hair. "So that's the way it is to be."

"Aye. I won't pretend just to escape." Knowing the fury a woman scorned often exhibited, he expected her to change her mind about helping to free him, to rant and to rave, but strangely she didn't.

"Is she your mistress?" she asked instead, cocking her head to one side as she looked up at him.

"We love each other," he answered, "yes!"

She thrust back her shoulders and held her head high as she made her way toward the door.

Nicholas was resigned to the fact that now he would languish in the Tower. Morgana was a spoiled, vain woman who would never forgive him for rejecting her. "I'm sorry, Morgana," he said softly. In a strange way he was. Had she possessed a heart to match her beauty, they might have been happy together. Certainly, he had thought they could be once.

"Don't be." Her look was haughty. Reaching down her bodice, she withdrew the key to his door, and he could only imagine how she had obtained it. "Just be ready to enact our plan when the time comes. In three days' time."

He repeated her words, knowing complete euphoria

t the thought of escape. "Three days' time. I'll be
eady."

He watched as she opened the door, wishing he
ould take advantage of the moment and flee, but held
ack. He had to be patient.

"Good-bye, Morgana. And thank you."

Chapter Forty-Seven

London was a seething mass of noise and motion. The city was a crammed commercial huddle, swarming with people. Open carts, coaches, drays, horses, and wagons clogged the streets. The waterways too were crowded with various types of boats and barges. Alandra felt a keen affection for the city in which she had grown up. The voices of the vendors hawking their wares, the church bells, the grumbling of shoppers haggling over the prices of their purchases were as welcome to her as a familiar melody.

Elbowing her way through the crowd, she crossed the street carefully so as not to be run over by the carts and wagons. Church spires, steeply pitched roofs of three-storied, gabled houses, turreted towers, and trees formed a jagged landscape against the sky. Chimneys billowed dark gray smoke from the forges and furnaces in the workshops below.

Alandra took advantage of her walk to enjoy the

scenery and was in high spirits as she made the long
trek to Whitehall Palace to see Elizabeth. She could
see the square tower of St. Paul's Church reaching
toward the heavens, and imagined that it was saying
a prayer that she would be successful in getting Christopher free.

She made her way by foot and by barge beyond Fleet
Street, through Temple Bar to the Strand, the tho-
roughfare that led to the palace where the queen was
now in residence. It was only when she saw the walls
of Whitehall that she began to lose her new-found confidence. Perhaps she should have told her father and
Will of her plan, but why endanger them if she failed?

Putting her hand up to her hair, she brushed back
the stray curl that had fallen loose from her coiled
braid. She had attired herself in one of her better
gowns for the journey, for it would not do well to look
the pauper. Her spring-green gown with bell-shaped
sleeves was a copy of those worn at court. The green-
and-gold brocade underdress was one of the costumes
used by the players but added just the right sophis-
tication. As always she wore her skirts over a stiff
farthingale.

"You cannot back out now," she scolded herself as
she approached the palace. Even so, her feet seemed
to have a will of their own and wanted to take her
back along the pathway.

She announced herself to the guard at the front gate
and was admitted. Hearing the gate click shut, she
swallowed hard, but now was not the time to become
queasy. She was Christopher's only hope.

Stepping inside the crowded anteroom, she looked
about her. It was a bright world she had entered. She
was aware of the ladies in their silk, brocade, and
velvet gowns, looking like bright peacocks, their hair
piled high, their faces painted. Gems sparkled like
stars as they moved, making them look unearthly, as

though they came from another sphere. All around her their eyes were staring, hostile, amused, mocking, and curious. Each and every look they gave her emphasized that she was an outsider, alien to their world of pomp and glitter.

Such attractive people, Alandra thought, *with a surface beauty that dazzles the eye, yet beneath lurks hatred, envy, jealousy, and greed.* Christopher had revealed all these flaws to her, assuring her over and over again that he had no intention or desire to return to this way of life.

Alandra walked slowly through the room, hardly even noticing the splendor of the furnishings. Her attention was fixed on the woman in the ornate chair at the end of the chamber, under a canopy of the royal colors of green and white. The crest of the Tudors was above her head.

Around the queen, like planets revolving around the sun, stood a circle of men, their faces turned toward the queen with expressions of mock adoration. Their jabbered flattery held a jarring tone of insincerity. As Alandra entered, these men showed a faint flicker of interest, darting furtive glances at her.

One man stood out from the others. His golden hair looked like the sun. It was Lord Stafford. Alandra shot a quick, furtive glance at him from under her lowered lashes, hoping against hope that he wouldn't recognize her. She was relieved that he, unlike the others, was not looking at her at all. He ignored her as if she wasn't worth even one peek. Standing tall and erect, his attention was focused on Elizabeth.

Suddenly two of the queen's guards crossed their pikes in front of her face, halting her before she had a chance to get within forty feet of the queen.

"What is your business?" one of them snarled, looking scrutinizingly at her clothes and thereby deciding she did not belong within.

Alandra stated her purpose, then watched as the reason for her visit was announced to the queen by one of the young pages.

"She says she will see you," the boy dutifully reported. Seeming to take a liking to Alandra, he confided, "She usually turns away all those without an appointment. You are most fortunate."

"Yes, most fortunate indeed," she agreed.

Outwardly, Alandra was calm, but inside she was trembling as she somehow forced her feet to carry her to where Elizabeth sat. The queen was attired in a dress of silver, white, and crimson. The dress had slashed sleeves lined with red taffeta. She had a chain of rubies and pearls around her neck.

"Ah, so you are from the Lord Chamberlain's Men, a friend of Will Shakespeare." Seeming to tire of the fawning attention of her male courtiers, Elizabeth motioned them away.

"I am," Alandra said with respect then halted. Her heart hammered in her chest until she was certain it would burst. Remembering her manners, she dipped a curtsy, spreading her green skirts like a fan.

The queen smiled. "His plays amuse me."

Alandra moved closer. "He is a true genius with a gift few men have for revealing both the majesty and tragedy of humanity." There was a pause. Alandra wasn't sure whether to breach the silence or to wait for the queen to speak again. She waited.

"Indeed. It appears that you greatly admire him."

"I do. More than I can say." Alandra couldn't help but stare. She had never imagined she would be this close to the queen. The very thought was awe-inspiring.

"Come closer!" Elizabeth motioned with her ring-bedecked hand. "I promise I will not bite, child. I've already had my dinner."

Alandra did as the queen bid and was taken by surprise as she came to within an arm's length of the imposing monarch. Far away Elizabeth had appeared to be beautiful, but up close it was obvious that she had lost whatever beauty she might have possessed. Her face was thin and full of wrinkles, her bright red hair most obviously a wig. She had gone to great lengths to foster the illusion of a young woman.

The long, thin fingers fastened on Alandra's chin, raising her face. Elizabeth looked long and hard into Alandra's eyes, her face growing as pale as her dress.

"Anne!" she croaked. "It can't be." The queen raised a trembling hand to her brow.

Alandra shook her head. "Not Anne, Your Majesty. My name is Alandra. Alandra Thatcher."

Make-up coated the queen's face like a gruesome mask, yet the mask collapsed now. "Yes, of course. But that dark hair, those pretty eyes ..." She was visibly upset. Her hand kept going to her throat. "You must forgive me. For a moment I thought ... But, of course, that is quite impossible. Anne is dead. Has been for many years...."

For a moment Alandra feared the queen might faint. "Are you well, Your Majesty?" She was genuinely concerned. *Why, she's more to be pitied than feared,* Alandra thought. Beneath all the paint and finery she was much the same as any other aging woman.

The queen quickly recovered. "Yes. Yes. It is just that for a moment you looked like a young woman from the past. Perhaps the only woman I might have called my friend."

"Her name was Anne?" Alandra was interested in hearing about this woman who had looked so much like her.

"Yes. She was one of my ladies-in-waiting. A vibrant young thing who brought sunshine with her wherever she went." A few of the queen's teeth were missing, most likely from sweets, so that it was difficult to understand her when she spoke quickly.

"What happened to her?"

"No one really knows. She disappeared for a few months from the court, and when she returned, it was as if her soul had died. She just wasted away and then one day she died." For a moment her eyes seemed dull as if they reflected the tragedy, but Elizabeth suddenly brightened. "But we will not talk of it and make our mood melancholy. We must make arrangements for this play Master Shakespeare plans to give."

Alandra hurried over the details, describing the size of the area needed to put up the stage, then taking a deep breath revealed the true purpose of her visit. "But that is not why I am here. Will Shakespeare, or my father, or any of the others, could have taken my place. I am here to make a plea on behalf of Christopher." Without thinking, Alandra called him by the wrong name.

"Christopher?"

Alandra realized her mistake. She could not fail, she would not. Her voice seemed to come from someone other than herself. "Sir Nicholas Leighton, Your Majesty. He has been dealt a great wrong, and I am here to ask for your help."

"Sir Nicholas Leighton?" The queen was taken aback. "What have you to do with him?"

The story tumbled from Alandra's lips, as many details as she could elaborate upon. She told of finding him in the play wagon and hitting him over the head. She told of his fib about being an actor, his theft of Shakespeare's horse, her wild ride after him, his attempt to clear his name, and his disappointment when he was thwarted in the attempt.

"Nicholas claiming to be an actor?" The queen smiled at the very idea. Instead of being angered or fretful, she was interested in his escapades. "How per-

fectly thrilling." Her voice lowered to a whisper. "So
that was how he has eluded Lord Stafford's pursuit of
him. Very, very clever."

"Aye, he is most clever." Alandra fell to her knees.
"And a most loyal subject to Your Majesty. That is
why it shatters him so that you have thrown him in
the Tower without benefit of a trial."

"Thrown him in the Tower?" The queen seemed genuinely surprised. "Why was I not told of this?"

"But—but I...He thought that you knew."

Alandra told the queen about the message Nicholas
had sent to the queen about having at last cornered
the suspected murderer of Lord Woodcliff, his visit by
the guardsman, Radcliffe, and Morgana, about Will
Frizer's death. She wanted to voice her suspicions
about why and who had been behind the murders, but
the queen did not give her the chance.

Alandra was unnerved by Elizabeth's hawklike
countenance. Her eyes seemed to skewer her as she
looked directly into Alandra's face. "There is something foul here. But I will get to the bottom of it. Of
that I can assure you."

"Thank you, Your Majesty." Never had Alandra felt
so relieved.

"I like you!" Elizabeth patted Alandra on the head
like a puppy. "Your honesty, sincerity, and passion
remind me of myself when I was young. I wish for you
to come back tomorrow."

"Come back?" Alandra was astounded.

"It is a command. Yes, come back tomorrow and we
will talk more about Sir Leighton's difficulties."

"You will free him?"

The queen did not respond. The interview was over,
and Elizabeth bid her gentlemen return. Without even
saying good-bye to Alandra, she began flirting with
them again.

Alandra felt deserted and confused as she walked back toward the entranceway. Yet she knew it was a start. Somehow she would convince the queen to let Christopher out of that dreadful Tower.

Chapter Forty-Eight

"Justice." That was the word Nicholas pondered as he lounged on the bed in his cell. When he had first been imprisoned he had thought he would not be convicted but he realized now that his chances for justice waned the longer he was kept in the Tower. He had no doubt that he would be found guilty. Perjury and bribery were all too common among juries. Stafford would win his guilty verdict by such measures. Hadn't he already convinced the queen?

And what of Elizabeth? Ah, that was the most unsettling thing of all. By her denial to hear him out, she had practically condemned Nicholas. *There is no other way. I must escape*, he thought for the hundredth time.

Yet Nicholas loathed having to trust Morgana after all that she had done. The moment she had left his cell, he had been assailed by doubts. But what choice did he have? She was his only contact with the world outside these walls. And perhaps when all was said and done, she really would try to make amends for her former actions.

It didn't take Nicholas long to convince himself of the wisdom of Morgana's plan, thus he began to implement his part of the scheme. Every time his warder, Henry Abbott, entered, he found the prisoner sitting at the small barred window, motionless and silent. A tall, gangly sort of fellow, whose doublet sleeves rose well above his wrists, he had one eye that tugged inward, giving his eyes the appearance of being crossed when he looked down from his lofty height. The warder had been fairly congenial to Nicholas, he couldn't fault him on that. Therefore, it was difficult for Nicholas not to answer the well-meaning Abbott.

So when his cell door clanged open now, Nicholas had to force himself to hold his tongue.

"Do you play chess?" Abbott asked, trying to draw his sullen prisoner out of his gloom. "No, huh? Pity. We might be a good match."

Nicholas was tempted. Chess was his favorite game, and he realized how it would help pass the hours. Still, he had to keep silent.

"Don't want to talk, don't want to play chess. How about food? Are you hungry sir?"

The tangy smell of freshly caught fish pervaded Nicholas's nostrils from the tray the warder had brought in. It made him realize he was hungry, but he forced himself to keep his back turned. Once he was free, he would be able to have as many fish as he could eat.

"The dampness and cold are coming in. They say there is going to be a storm. I could be persuaded to bring you some extra blankets if you but say the word."

It *was* growing cold within the chamber, Nicholas thought. A blanket would be a luxury he could well make use of during the coldest part of the night.

"Hmm! If I had not heard you talking when you first

came here, I would be thinkin' that you are a mute!"
Nicholas's refusal to speak seemed to be getting the
best of Henry. "Well, it doesn't matter. I brought something for you. Even if you won't say thank you, I'll
give it to you anyway." From under his doublet he
procured a leather-bound book. With a shrug, he held
it toward Nicholas.

"If you won't show your gratitude, I'll say thank you
anyway."

The warder's hand was long-fingered and freckled,
the back tufted with dark brown hair, Nicholas noted.

"It's a book by some ancient Greek or other. Heady
reading, if you ask me. I thought you might enjoy it.
It will help you while away the hours, doing something
besides just lying there."

The warder jabbered on, trying to make conversation, to say anything that would bring Nicholas out
of his shell, but Nicholas was a master of stubbornness. He didn't even sneeze. In the end the warder gave
up.

Once the warder had left, Nicholas paced back and
forth in his cell, wearing a path in the floor with his
boot heels.

A rattle of keys announced that once again Nicholas
was not alone. Looking up, he expected to see the warder's face at the grate, making another offering. Instead, he was surprised to see Morgana.

"I have a present for you," she said, detaching a key
from the ring at her belt. She slid the key into the lock.
"The straw and your clothing. I have it all in a bundle.
I paid the tailor extra to make your garments to my
specifications and to complete them in a timely manner."

Pushing through the door, she handed the sack to
Nicholas. He opened it and pushing the straw aside
found the cloak, hat, doublet, and trunk hose that she
had promised. Digging deeper, he also found a ruff.

"You didn't desert me," he whispered. Untying the cord that held the garments together, he held each one up. "They look to be perfect for our little plan. Exactly like the garments I am wearing."

"With one difference." Morgana took the doublet from him and turned it inside out. "It is reversible." A red doublet showed when she tugged at it just right. "It will make it easy for a quick change when you must get past the guards."

"Amazing."

Morgana didn't stay. It was obvious to Nicholas that she didn't want to be found within the cell, thus without even so much as a blink, she hurried away. Even so, her visit was appreciated. Nicholas filled his lungs with air, ignoring the dank smell of the moat's water, feeling a new vigor, a renewed stirring of hope. He would escape. Now he had outside help. Friends, if one used the term loosely.

Alandra, would see him sooner than she knew. With that thought he deftly assembled the dummy figure, stuffing it with the straw and any spare clothing that he had.

Putting his hand on its shoulder, he dubbed it Nicholas. "The day I walk out of here, Sir Nicholas Leighton will be gone forever. You'll be my symbol of rebirth, good sir." He bowed, showing the dummy proper respect, then quickly, before the warder passed by on his rounds, Nicholas shoved the "other Nicholas" under the bed.

Chapter Forty-Nine

The day was clear with a hint that soon Jack Frost would come with his magic paintbrushes to decorate the windows of the London shops, churches, and houses. The slight chill in the air made Alandra wish she had brought a cloak to warm her on this early-morning journey. Goosebumps tickled her arms and shoulders, though if it was from the cold or her nervousness, she didn't really know.

Looking at the tall structure ahead, she was glad that on this second visit to Whitehall she had reached it in good time. The journey had not seemed as long perhaps because her familiarity with the route had quickened her steps.

"Good morning." The guards at the gate recognized her, allowing her to enter without a pause.

The maze of corridors at the palace were crowded with courtiers and servants, passing each other as if in mock procession. All eyes turned toward Alandra as she walked by. She felt her cheeks burn under their scrutiny and wished for a moment that she was back at The Black Unicorn with the players. Smoothing the full skirts of her gown, and fiddling with her ruff, she tried to compose herself, swallowing the rising lump in her throat. Though she was clothed in a borrowed dress and the best of her finery, she couldn't compete. Even the servants were garbed in elegant styles and fabrics.

"But that doesn't mean I can't hold my head up," she whispered to herself. She squared her shoulders, lifted her chin, and sweeping past the gawkers, made as grand an entrance as any of the players had ever managed upon the stage.

The antechamber was packed. The buzz of voices sounded like a beehive. Swarming around the queen's secretary, several of the courtiers were acting quite bold as they sought to petition the queen for this or that. Alandra was surprised to see Lord Stafford among them, arguing that he should have immediate entrance. Even though she saw him in profile, the tightness of his mouth and the flare of his nostrils revealed his anger all too plainly. Was he being turned away because of what she had said to the queen yesterday? She could only wonder.

"Come this way," the secretary said to Alandra, noticing her at once.

Alandra followed obediently, her skirts swishing so loudly she was certain all around her could hear them. As she walked, she took note of things she hadn't noticed before. The walls were of dark wood paneling. At either end of the room were tall windows draped with lustrous brocade curtains. Lifting her eyes to the ceiling, she could see swirls of ornately carved wood. Row upon row of royal portraits adorned the walls.

"The queen will see you now," her escort said, then

opening the door to the presence room, quickly left her.

Inside strolling musicians idled about, singing vibrant melodies. There were dozens of servants in attendance as if pampering the queen was the most important business of the realm. Elizabeth was seated in her carved chair in the chamber, clothed in white again, as if she really took seriously her claim as the virgin queen. The dress looked to be dusted with moonbeams. Diamonds sparkled around her throat and dripped from her ears. From a distance she looked like a shimmering, shining deity, but Alandra knew a closer study would reveal her many flaws.

This morning the queen was angry. Her long pale fingers moved restlessly, clasping and unclasping in her lap, plucking at the material of her skirt, then beating the arms of her gilded chair as she talked with a rotund little man in brown doublet and hosen.

"God's nightgown, but he has no lack of balls in asking that of me," she was saying. "Tell that young puppy that I will decide when I want to see him."

"Yes, Your Majesty."

Alandra couldn't help wonder if it was Stafford the queen scorned, and thought how it would serve him right if it was. Pausing in the doorway, she waited until the tirade was over, then walked slowly toward the queen. This time she was not as nervous as before, until she took note that Morgana was in the room.

Reaching the queen, Alandra sank into a low curtsy, expecting to hear Morgana's shrill squeal of protest. But to her surprise, none came.

"So, you are here again, child. Good. Good."

As if anyone would dare to refuse the queen's commands, Alandra thought. "Yes, Your Majesty." Alandra kept her knees bent, holding her pose, waiting until Elizabeth nodded that she could stand up.

"Hmm. Let me look at you."

Elizabeth's keen eyes moved over Alandra slowly, taking in the details of her dress. One of the actor's wives, a woman of means, had loaned Alandra a pale blue satin dress embroidered with flowers and swirls for the occasion. Her low bodice tapered to a point below the waist. The ruff she wore was enormous and gave Alandra the feeling that her head was a separate entity, suspended above the stiff pleats. Her hair was worn in cascades of dark curls over her shoulders, emphasing the slim length of her neck.

"You look particularly pretty this morning. Charmingly subdued, like a country girl. Are you?"

"Am I what, Your Majesty?"

"From the country?"

Alandra shook her head. "No. I grew up in London. A mascot to the players you might say." Her farthingale pinched her as she moved, and seeking comfort, she tried to position it more favorably.

"Bothersome, aren't they," the queen exclaimed.

"A bit like wearing a carriage wheel around one's hips," Alandra said truthfully much to the queen's mirth.

"Oh, it is. It is. But very, very stylish and all the rage." Once again the queen studied her, long and hard. " 'Tis a pity you aren't of noble birth or even a merchant's kitten. You would make a fine lady-in-waiting."

Alandra shrugged. "I am what I am and for that I am happy."

"Exactly what are you?" Had anyone else asked such a question, it would have seemed rude, but a queen had every right to inquire.

"A simple, happy girl. I have always found that life is what you make of it."

"And just what have you made of your life, child?" Elizabeth really seemed interested.

"I am a good daughter and help my father with his

costumes, sets, and scenery. I am honest, try to be understanding, and always try to appreciate the simple things. 'Tis the things we sometimes take for granted that truly make life worthwhile."

"Perhaps. I wouldn't really know." Elizabeth looked down her long nose. "Ah, but you are pretty. And surprisingly enough it does not pique my jealousy. Yours is an innocent prettiness. And you are quite likeable."

Alandra smiled. "I hope so, Your Majesty."

The queen studied her narrowly, asking bluntly, "What do you think of my courtiers?"

For a moment the question startled Alandra. "Truthfully?" she asked.

"Of course."

"I—I don't think I would want them as my friends," Alandra answered humbly.

"What!" she said angrily.

The queen had obviously expected Alandra to display awe and admiration.

"Explain," Elizabeth demanded.

"From what little I have seen of them," she said, thinking of Morgana and Stafford, "I think they care only about themselves. Their smiles do not extend to their hearts, or their beauty to their souls."

"I see . . ."

For just a moment Alandra thought she had overstepped her bounds. "But then perhaps I should not judge."

Elizabeth waved her hand. "No, no. I want you to be truthful. Honesty is at a premium here."

"Murray, my father, has said often that a man has only enough true friends in his lifetime to count on one hand," Alandra continued thoughtfully. " 'Tis true I think, except among the players. When Christopher needed them, they flocked to his side without hesitation. Even facing a dangerous man like Will Frizer."

"They came to Sir Leighton's aid? Undoubtedly, he paid them."

"Not a farthing!" Alandra insisted.

She quickly told how Will Kempe, Christopher, and a few of the other actors had dressed as groundlings, heckling their own fellow players. She told of her own part in pretending to be an orange-seller, and her ploy to divert Lord Stafford's attention by spilling her oranges. She revealed the humor of the clever manner in which Will Frizer was hit on the head with a bottle of ale and thus apprehended.

"Ah, I can almost see it before my eyes." The queen threw back her head and laughed with the rough guffaw of a man. "God's elbows, but I think I could have made use of such a ploy several times when dealing with the damnable Spanish!"

There was a long pause. As quickly as she had laughed, Elizabeth grew solemn again. "I have decided that I want to know all about you. Thus can I determine your sincerity regarding Sir Nicholas."

At the mention of Christopher, Alandra's heart lurched. She must quickly come to the point, lest like yesterday the queen grow tired of her and issue her out the door without making a decision on his fate.

"Please, Your Majesty." She went down on bended knee. "He is a good man, a most loyal subject. He didn't kill Lord Woodcliff. As I told you, there is a witness, and myself and the players heard Will Frizer's declaration of Christopher's innocence. Frizer more than likely did the deed. Nor did he kill Will Frizer. You have but to crook your finger and we will give you the needed evidence."

"Oh, do get up!" Elizabeth waved at her with impatience.

Alandra rose but said, "Won't you free him from the Tower?"

"In good time." The queen's voice was icy. "Since

he is there, I will let him do a bit of pondering." Her eyes darted toward Morgana who was engaged in conversation with four men, forming a circle around her. "I do not tolerate lewd behavior, nor do I look kindly on flirtations. Man-hunting little fools disgust me."

So, it was Nicholas's attention to Morgana and not the queen's suspicion that he was a murderer that kept Christopher confined, Alandra thought. Then her trip to Whitehall had been in vain. And all their efforts at finding Bessie and Tom Banter a waste of time. The queen was a horrible woman!

"Oh, don't look so grim." Elizabeth tapped her on the shoulder with her fan. "I never did think Nicholas to be the one who killed Lord Woodcliff or this Will Frizer. He does not have such villainy in him."

"You never thought him guilty?" Alandra was stunned. "Then why was he made the object of a hunt for Lord Woodcliff's murder?"

Elizabeth pursed her lips. "Stafford's doings and not mine. There are times when he can be a most insolent pup. Besides, the thought of Nicholas being on the run was exciting."

Exciting, Alandra thought. A man had run for his life, might have been killed, had been arrested for another murder, and this woman thought of it as a game. Oh, how she wanted to scold Elizabeth, but she dared not say a thing. Yet it was only by biting her tongue that she maintained her silence.

The queen changed the subject, returning to her questioning. "You told me yesterday a little bit about yourself. Refresh my memory. Who are you?"

Alandra's anger melted away and was replaced by sadness. "More than anything in this world I want to know who I am," she answered honestly. "To not know troubles me more than you could ever know. I have never known the comfort of a mother, you see."

"Nor have I..." The queen's eyes were sad. "My

mother was killed when I was little more than a babe. Thus I know your feelings, child." She called for one of the pages to bring forth the miniature she had of Anne Boleyn and displayed it to Alandra.

"She was beautiful!" Alandra thought how terrible it must be for Elizabeth to know that her father had ordered her mother to be beheaded, supposedly for adultery, though it was whispered the real reason was to make way for his marriage to Jane Seymour.

"Beautiful and intelligent. Both traits that I inherited."

"Of course!"

Elizabeth was pleased that Alandra agreed. "Now, I seem to remember that you told me yesterday that the players have been like family to you. Explain."

Alandra went into detail, telling Elizabeth about how Murray Thatcher had been driving his wagon along the road when he had found the basket and his surprise when he found a baby inside. Her eyes shone with love as she explained how he had decided right then and there that she was to be his.

"He didn't make an effort to find your real parents?" Elizabeth's tone was stern.

"No," Alandra answered, then quickly added, "they had left no clue as to who they were. And, besides, they must not have wanted me if they abandoned me by the side of the road."

"There might have been reasons. No one can judge." The queen drummed her fingers on the arm of her chair, revealing her agitation, though at what or at whom Alandra didn't know.

"And you say there were no clues as to your identity?"

"Only a blanket, Your Majesty."

Elizabeth's eyes gleamed with interest. "A blanket?"

"One of fine linen. It gives me hope that my heritage

is not that of a pauper." Alandra gave a deep sigh. "But then I will never really know."

"No, I suppose that you won't. And 'tis a shame. Your story intrigues me. How I do love a mystery."

One of the queen's spaniels playfully tugged at the hem of her dress, diverting her attention as she scratched him behind the ears. Picking up a ball, she playfully threw it across the room, watching as he padded after it.

"Alandra is a very pretty name. How did you come by it, child?" she asked at last.

"Murray told me that he gave me that name because of the initials on the blanket. Alandra for the *A* stitched there, Wilona for the *W*. He thought that it went very well with Thatcher. Very well indeed." She held up her chin proudly.

"*A! W!*" Elizabeth cocked her head. Shrewd eyes surveyed Alandra. "How strange..." For a long moment she stared at her, appraising Alandra with the same haunted look she had held when first they met.

"Strange?" Alandra didn't understand what the queen meant. All she knew was that Elizabeth was studying her again and that it was unnerving. God help her, if she had said anything that might have gotten Murray into trouble.

"I want you to come back again. Tomorrow afternoon."

Alandra had feared she might not please Elizabeth. Now it seemed she needed to have more fear of having been far too entertaining. "As you please, Your Majesty."

There were no good-byes, no formal dismisal. Elizabeth's attention had shifted to a young man garbed in deep red. She motioned him to take Alandra's place at her side.

Without looking back, Alandra hurried across the shiny marble floor and swept through the doorway.

The queen turned to the man and whispered, "Do you see that young woman?"

"Aye, Your Grace!"

"I want you to leave no stone unturned in your quest. I want you to find out more about this girl."

His brows shot up in surprise. "About her?"

"She pleases me and her story is deeply moving." The queen snapped her fan in his face. "Do as I bid. I must know if what she tells me is true." She bit her lip, her eyes glazed as her thoughts dipped back in time. "For if what I suspect is true and perhaps even if it *isn't*..." She didn't finish her statement, but as her eyes touched on Morgana, she laughed.

Chapter Fifty

Clouds hovered low over the city as Alandra made her way back to The Black Unicorn. In order to save time, she hailed a boatman and traveled part of the way by barge, while pondering over the queen and what had been said today. So all this time Elizabeth had known in her heart that Christopher was innocent of Lord Woodcliff's and Will Frizer's murders and still had refused to lift a finger to help him. It seemed a most heartless thing to do, yet after listening to the monarch, Alandra realized it was not a bit out of character. The question was what to do now.

"Get him out of the Tower by force if necessary," she whispered to herself, letting her daydreams conjure up visions of a daring rescue. In the end she gave such fantasies up. Shakespeare and her father were right. There was no way to beat the Tower. Moreover, such an act would only get Nicholas into more trouble than he was already in. It seemed, therefore, that the only answer lay in changing Elizabeth's mind and making her see how wrong it was to punish a man just for succumbing to the charms of Morgana's beauty and being a womanizer. Alandra knew although she had disliked his behavior, that he had changed and of that she would have to convince Elizabeth.

Alandra felt cold drops on the back of her neck and glanced up at the clouds. Turning up the collar of her cloak, she paid the boatman, then ran down the cobbled streets, ducking in and out of shelter, as she made her way to the inn. She was greeted at the front door by an inquisitive group of actors whom the innkeeper told her had spent the better part of the morning just looking out the window to catch sight of her when she returned. Happy to see their warm, welcoming faces, she was glad that she had finally confessed about her first visit to the queen and the second invitation for her to return to court.

"Well, monkey, what did old carrot top have to say?" Will Kempe playfully tweaked her nose. "Is she going to give Christopher a chance to defend himself?"

"Is she going to let him out of the Tower and put Lord Stafford in his place?" William Sly inquired anxiously.

Alandra's dejected look answered for her.

"No?" Robert Armin slammed his fist against the wall. "Why?"

"She's toying with Christopher," Alandra answered. Rain dripped from her sodden cloak, and she hurried to hang it on the nearest peg.

Two of the actors spoke at the same time. "Toying with him?"

Alandra gave vent to a long sigh. "She knows he didn't kill Lord Woodcliff or Will Frizer. All this time she has known. Christopher is in the Tower because he angered the queen by showering that yellow-haired witch with his affections. She told me so."

Will Kempe blew a long whistle. "I don't envy him then. Anyone will tell you how vindictive she can be when it comes to her slighted pride. I fear our Christopher is in for a long stay."

"Aye," William Sly agreed, "and there is little we can do to help him. Sorry, Alandra."

"Not half as sorry as I . . ." Her voice trailed off.

Following them into the main room, she told the same story to her father, Shakespeare, Burbage, and Heminges. Her news did little to brighten the already-dreary day. Worse yet, the actors had their own troubles. It was true that the Privy Council was promising to open the theaters again, but also true that the land lease on the theater occupied by the Lord Chamberlain's Men was running out. The landlord, Giles Alleyn, was not anxious to renew it. The players would have to look elsewhere for a building that housed a stage.

"And thus we are homeless." Robert Armin sighed.

"We might as well go back on tour. At least we had a place to hang our hats," William Sly mumbled.

"No! Most definitely not that." Now that the theaters had been allowed to exhibit plays again, Richard Burbage was of a mind to stay in London where he could gain further acclaim for his acting prowess. "You forget there is still The Curtain."

Burbage's father had acquired the neighboring theater, The Curtain, ten years before. Though the Lord Chamberlain's Men had acted there, they were not in a hurry to make it a permanent home. It was a building in poor repair and lacking in amenities.

"Perhaps for a time," Shakespeare conceded, trying his best not to hurt Burbage's feelings.

"We can entertain the rats," Kempe chortled, mocking the rodents' squeaks. "But then perhaps they might be a better audience than those damnable groundlings at that."

"We need our own theater," Heminges grumbled. "The Lord Admiral's Men have their permanent theater in The Rose."

"But where can we go to establish our own permanent home?" William Sly inquired. "The Swan has been closed. We don't want to go back to playing innyards."

"We'll build our own theater," Shakespeare suggested, obviously liking the idea the moment he proposed it.

"Build our own?" Heminges seemed to be calculating the cost in his head. By the expression on his face, he clearly thought it a dream that was totally unreasonable.

"And make it a globe of dramatic excellence. A theater-in-the round patterned after the innyards. Yes, we'll call it The Globe."

The topic of conversation changed from Alandra's visit to the queen to the matter of building the new theater, with everyone enthusiastically giving suggestions, then Murray brought the subject back to Alandra's summons to the palace again.

"It seems you were gone a long, long time. Surely the queen must have had more to say for herself than just no. What did you talk about?"

"She wanted to know all about me. She said that she liked me."

"Wanted to know about you?" Murray's brows shot up, then wrinkled in a frown. "As to what?"

"Who I am and where I come from. I told her about your having found me in a basket by the side of the road and how—"

"Alandra! You didn't!" Murray exclaimed as he exchanged a wary glance with Shakespeare. Wringing his hands, Murray started to pace back and forth. "You shouldn't have done that. Oh, woe is me! You shouldn't have revealed it to her. 'Twas none of her business.''

"But why? It's true...."

She really didn't understand her father's reaction, but later on when a messenger came from Elizabeth bidding Murray to come to Whitehall and to bring the monogrammed blanket, she understood his fear. Nor was the matter put easily to rest. Heminges, Sly, and Burbage were likewise summoned, as were several of the other actors who had been with Murray and Shakespeare in the early years.

Alandra was certain that she was living a nightmare as she once more faced Elizabeth in the presence room. She was pale and shaken, certain that she had voiced information that was now going to endanger the very man who had been so good to her. Her eyes pleaded with Murray to forgive her as she stood beside him awaiting the queen's utterance. Her hand rested on her father's arm, but though she tried to remain calm, her poise shattered with one look at the queen's frown.

"Oh, please, Your Majesty..." Alandra dipped low in a curtsy and held the pose, hoping that a show of humility might somehow elicit Elizabeth's mercy.

"Rise," the queen promptly told her, "and, for the love of God, wipe off that woebegone expression. I've brought you here for some happy news, child."

"Happy news?" Alandra gripped Murray's arm.

"What would you do if I told you that I know who you are?"

Murray gasped.

"Who I am?" The feeling that her world was about to be shattered overcame Alandra. Her fingers went numb, and she found herself saying, "I'm—I'm not certain that I really want to know."

"Of course you do," Elizabeth snorted. "I suspected as much, but I had to make certain before I revealed it to you, thus I have questioned several people who have ascertained your identity."

All sorts of thoughts whirled around in Alandra's head. What if her real parents had been enemies of the queen and had been executed at Elizabeth's command? What then? What if her mother had "pleaded her belly" to escape being sent to the scaffold, only to meet her death once her baby was born? Wouldn't that explain why Alandra had been found by the side of the road? And if her parents were Elizabeth's enemies, what of her? Would the queen consider her an enemy as well? Or what if her parents had been from foreign shores? Spanish perhaps? Would she then be sent away from the homeland she had so come to love?

"You are a member of a most honored family."

"What?" Alandra had become so immersed in her own thoughts that for a moment she didn't understand.

"I said that you come from noble lineage, child. A Woodcliff, albeit one of illegitimate birth, I'm afraid." Elizabeth shrugged apologetically. "Even so, there are many rewards."

"A Woodcliff?" Alandra was certain that Elizabeth was making fun of her, playing another one of her games. But how cruel to mock her with the name of that poor murdered old lord.

"The initial *W* on your blanket stands for Woodcliff."

"How could you!" Alandra couldn't control her anger. "How could you, an anointed queen, perpetrate such a jest? Well, have your laugh and have done with it. Then please allow my father and myself to go where we belong."

Elizabeth drew in her breath in a rasp. She sputtered like a pistol about to misfire, but instead of raging, she chuckled. "So, you are no milksop. You will speak your mind and do it with fire. A bit like your grandfather in his younger days. But you are tempered also with your mother's gentleness. A good combination.''

Alandra was in shock; Murray was speechless.

"Then you are serious? You aren't making fun of me?" Alandra asked, finally finding her voice. For a moment she feared she might faint, but struggled against doing such a humiliating thing.

"Most emphatically no!" the queen declared.

Elizabeth ordered two brocaded chairs to be brought beside her so that Murray and Alandra could have a seat as she elaborated on the details. Alandra was no simple maid at all, but the illegitimate daughter of the old lord's only child, a young lady-in-waiting named Anne.

"Anne Woodcliff!" Alandra exclaimed. Now she knew why Elizabeth had stared at her that first day they had met. She had seen Anne Woodcliff's image emblazoned in Alandra's features.

"A sweet and lovely young woman, but one, I fear, who was deplorably naive. She listened to the sweet, but lying words of a scoundrel and found herself with child." Elizabeth clasped her hands together. "Oh, if only I'd known, then I would have helped her. But she feared my anger and her father's wrath and thus kept it secret." The queen revealed that Anne had left the court to hide away on one of her father's estates and there had given birth to her daughter.

Alandra remembered the queen saying that Anne was dead. "Did she—did she die giving birth to me?" She wanted to understand how she could have been abandoned.

"No, though I'm told she had a hellish time." Elizabeth told how the young woman had entrusted her secret to the woman she had hired as a nurse. She had hoped that she could somehow make a home for the baby. "And she might have had her father not found out."

Alandra could well imagine the scene. "And so she gave me up."

"No. For one so gentle she put up a terrible fight. One that in the end she lost." The queen told of how Lord Woodcliff had had the baby abducted in order to save his daughter's good name. "He reasoned that she could have other children."

" 'Twas he who put me by the roadside," Alandra said softly as the pieces of the puzzle were slowly coming into place for her.

Elizabeth nodded. "I knew him well. He was a kind man, an honorable man. He loved his daughter to distraction. He meant well. Had he known that she would be so overtaken with melancholy that she would just fade away, he would never have done it."

"And so my mother grieved..."

"She tried to find out where you had been taken. She searched far and wide but to no avail. There are those who insist that she died of a broken heart and having witnessed her decline, I think it possible." Elizabeth was devilishly pleased with herself. If everything she said wasn't exactly the truth, at least it could be said that she could fabricate a story to rival any other.

Alandra's eyes burned with tears. Her mother had loved her so much that she had let her unhappiness consume her. It was a tragic story. "And what of my father?"

"Richard Pembroke was his name. I'd like to tell you that he deserved your mother's love, but he was a rogue. He was married at the time of their liaison, though he didn't tell her. Nor from what I heard did he grieve for long but moved on to another conquest."

"Is he—is he alive?"

Elizabeth shook her head. "No. He was killed during

the attack on the Armada. A rare show of courage ended his life, though it does not vindicate him of what he did." In a rare display of emotion, the queen's eyes misted with tears, though she hurriedly brushed them away. She had woven such a sad tale that she was overcome.

"But there is a bright side to all of this." Snapping her fingers, she summoned a page and instructed him to bring forth a rolled-up piece of parchment. "At last I have found Lord Woodcliff's heir." And Morgana Woodcliff be damned. At last Elizabeth had it within her grasp to reap her revenge upon that woman in the most tantalizing of ways.

"Me?" Of all the things in the world she might have expected, Alandra had never foreseen this.

"Of course. You are of his blood. I could see that in your face, even if I didn't know your story. And there is the blanket. Besides, my spies did a thorough job of locating witnesses who will corroborate that you are indeed Allison Catherine Woodcliff."

"Allison Catherine Woodcliff," she repeated. But no, Alandra thought, no matter what happened she would always be Alandra Thatcher. A person couldn't just cast away so many years of love. Murray was her father, she wanted no other.

"As Lord Woodcliff's only grandchild you are entitled to his country estate, his house in London, and a considerable amount of money and jewels. What do you say to that, child." Without giving Alandra a chance to answer, she guffawed. "Imagine that. Morgana Woodcliff is your step-grandmother. What a fine joke indeed! Oh, I can hardly wait to tell her." She could hardly wait indeed!

So that was it, Alandra thought. That was the reason for all of this. It was to take revenge on the woman the queen hated. Undoubtedly, Elizabeth would get great delight in announcing to Morgana that she was going to have to share her late husband's fortune. More than anything in the world Alandra wanted to turn her back, walk out, and never see the queen again, but she knew the futility of such a scheme. Thus she listened in silence as Elizabeth gave orders that Alandra was to become a lady-in-waiting. Christopher had lived in her world for a time. Now she was going to live in his.

Chapter Fifty-One

Nicholas was roused from a fitful slumber with a violent shake so forceful that it rattled his teeth. "Wake up! Nicholas, do open your eyes!"

Sitting up against the pillows, he tried to recapture the fading image of his dreams. Alandra. As usual he had dreamed of her. Perhaps that was why seeing Morgana staring back at him was all the more unsettling.

"What is it now? God's nose, but you have a lot of brute strength for a woman." She had already fulfilled her promise of bringing him the straw and the clothes for the dummy. What was her purpose in coming again?

"I have brought you a length of rope. Just in case it is needed." Morgana's smile looked anything but sincere.

"Rope?" She could have slipped it through the bars of the door. Undoubtedly, this was just an excuse to see him, he thought, not liking the idea. He didn't want her to have any hope that because she was helping him out of his cage he owed her anything.

"What's it for? Can't climb out the window."

"It's not for that. It's for use in case the warder comes upon you unexpectantly. It would then be needed to keep him confined so as not to sound the alarm. That is unless you think it better to kill him," she said sweetly.

"Kill him! Nay. He has done me no harm. It is not his fault that I am here."

Taking the rope from her hand, he accepted it grudgingly. "Let us hope that I have no need of it and that your plan works smoothly."

There was a strange glitter in Morgana's eyes. "Oh, it will. My plan will most definitely go exactly as I intend. It has up to now."

"So I would suppose," Nicholas said beneath his breath.

For a moment a strange feeling of danger tickled his spine, but he hurriedly pushed it away. It was either trust Morgana or languish here until Elizabeth felt the benevolent urge to set him free.

"Everything is set for tonight."

"Tonight?" It seemed too soon. Nicholas had always believed that a well worked-out plan took some time.

"Are you having second thoughts?" Morgana leaned against him, touching him on the shoulder. "Perhaps you like the living arrangements here."

"I don't! Not at all. Every man values his freedom." He meant that as a *double entendre*, but she pretended not to understand.

His tone softened as he asked, "Aren't your visits to me going to arouse suspicion? After all, there aren't many golden-haired women as lovely as you roaming about the Tower."

She beamed at the compliment. "I took care of that from the first. If enough money changes hands, it can silence the most tattling of tongues." Slowly, seductively, she removed her cloak, as if to say her visit was going to be lengthy. "Besides, I like coming to see you."

"See me?" Nicholas waited warily, knowing what was to come. She still hadn't gotten it into her head that any attraction he had once held for her was dead.

"It's not too late for us, Nicholas!"

She walked toward the door, covering the grille with her cloak. Deftly, she unfastened the bindings of her gown. Pulling the fabric down to her waist, she gave him a view of her breasts, firm, perfectly molded mounds tipped with rosy crests. A sight that would have tempted any other man.

"Nicholas..."

He reached out to her, but not to take her in his arms. Instead, he plucked at the cloth of her bodice and covered her. "Morgana, don't embarrass yourself. I've told you before and I'll say it again. I am taken."

Nicholas heard the sound of her slap before he felt it. Then the whole side of his face burned.

"I hate you for this, Nicholas. You will never know just how much!"

He did. It showed in her eyes. Yet he knew he couldn't have reacted any other way. Alandra deserved his faithfulness. "Perhaps you had better go."

She made no move to leave. "I saw her, by the way."

Nicholas stiffened, every nerve in his body on alert to trouble. "Saw who?"

"Your little peasant girl." Putting her hands on her waist, she laughed softly as she eyed him up and down. "Oh, *now* I have your attention. You should see your face. Your mouth is hanging open." Purposely, she let the silence stretch out before she said, "She was at court. To see the queen."

"Alandra at court?" Nicholas didn't like that at all. He didn't want Alandra anywhere near Elizabeth. She was an innocent to the kind of intrigue and skullduggery that went on at court.

"She didn't think I saw her, but she was very, very noticeable in her quaint little gown." Walking toward the door, she tugged at her cloak, putting it back on her shoulders. "Undoubtedly, she was asking the queen to pardon you, but, as you see, you are still here. At least for now."

"Morgana! Is she safe? The queen . . . She treated her well didn't she? Where is Alandra? You must take her a message." Though he had been anxious to get rid of her, now Nicholas was loathe to see Morgana go. He wanted to know more, but Morgana had it in mind to tease him.

"So many questions. Why, I do think I'll just let you wonder about your little lover's fate." The door clicked as she slipped out.

"Morgana!" Frantically, Nicholas pushed against the door, peering out at Morgana's retreating form. "Come back. There are things I must know." She ignored him, soon disappearing out of sight.

Damn! Nicholas looked down at the rope he clutched in his fist. It was a reminder now not only of his own danger but of Alandra's as well.

Chapter Fifty-Two

The inn's shutters were closed to keep out what little day's sunlight was left. Only a few glowing embers sparked in the fire's hearth. Lying face down in the middle of the small four-poster bed, the covers drawn over her head, Alandra shuddered with sobs as she relived the events that had taken place not an hour before. Lord Woodcliff's granddaughter, his heir, how was that possible? What ghastly joke was fate playing on her? And yet it was true. The nurse that Anne Woodcliff had taken with her to the country had verified each and every detail.

"Be careful what you wish for," the phrase ran through her mind. Alandra moaned, remembering all the times she had so wanted to be a lady, to mingle with those glittering nobles at Whitehall, and how often she had wanted to know who her parents were. Now her wishes had been granted, she had been summoned to court, and she wanted with all her heart to take those wishes back. She knew now that all she really wanted to be was Alandra Thatcher, but that matter had been taken out of her hands by a prying old woman.

She wouldn't go to court. She wouldn't! She was no match for those sharks. They'd tear her to pieces. She'd not ruin her whole life just because of that selfish, vengeful queen. She'd not be made a puppet just so Elizabeth could laugh behind her hand at Morgana. She'd stand firm and utter the word the queen had never heard before—no.

And send Christopher and all your friends into ruin by crossing the queen? Alandra laughed bitterly at the very idea. No, she would do as she was bid, dutifully and politely.

Oh, how galling it all was! Yet Alandra knew she was helpless. She who had always spoken her mind would now be forced to play the politics of the court or end up like Christopher in the Tower. The truth of the matter was she had lost control of her life, her destiny. But then perhaps no one ever really was the captain of his own fate. Certainly, Christopher hadn't been. He, like she, was the queen's victim.

"Merry-go-up!" she moaned, flinging herself over on her back. How could she have ever been so silly as to think life could be simple? Or really believe that happiness was so easy to obtain? How could she have deluded herself when all around her was misery?

London wasn't really a city of rainbows. It was crowded, dirty, full of poverty, suffering and hunger, and it stank. Just ambling through the city, one walked literally through death and pain. But Alandra had preferred to see the sun behind the clouds, to smell the fragrance from the countryside that floated in, had preferred to believe that people were really kind at heart. At least until ambition got in the way. Or family reputation.

She swallowed hard. Her own grandfather had put her in a basket and left her beside the road as if she were little more than rubbish. He'd discarded her with little care of what would happen to her. He'd broken her mother's heart with little conscience. And all because of his lofty position at court and the family name. And what of her father? A married man who had willfully seduced a young, naive woman for his own sport. A troublesome story, yet true. Oh, if only she hadn't been told. But she had been. Now how was she going to live with it?

They would know. Everyone at court would know that she was bastard born, albeit of lordly parentage. All the country homes, fine London houses, gold coins, diamonds, and velvets couldn't wipe that stigma away. She would be the object of gossip. Worse yet was the stunning reality that Morgana Woodcliff was her step-grandmother and as such would have Alandra under her thumb. Morgana, a woman she had grown to hate. Was it any wonder she felt so much like running away?

But she couldn't. She would suffer her fate in silence and hope beyond hope that there was still a chance for a happy ending. At least there was one silver lining to her cloud. At least now she was acceptable for betrothal to Christopher, if and when he got out of the Tower. If only Elizabeth would set him free.

Alandra rose from the bed and slowly changed into garments that matched her mood, a black velvet dress that had been designed for mourning. Having to leave soon for the court, she then began packing her belongings in trunks and boxes, smoothing the wrinkles from her gowns, as she examined each and every one, brushing off her leather shoes, dusting her gloves, rolling up her pairs of stockings. She had few possessions worthy of the court, no precious rings, bracelets, ropes of beads, fans, or gold chains. She had only items that would be ridiculed by the lords and ladies: the first flower Christopher had given her pressed between the pages of a book; a handwritten copy of Shakespeare's *A Midsummer-Night's Dream;* a dried four-leaf clover; a hand-carved wooden toy Murray had given her; and a crown made out of paste that Murray had created when she had laughingly wished that she were a princess, if only for a day. Things of value to her if to no one else. She stubbornly boxed up each and every one, then taking a deep breath she made her way down the narrow stairs.

Alandra choked back her tears as she bid the actors good-bye. "I'll never forget you. Never!" she said, kissing Robert Armin, William Kempe, William Sly, and John Lowin on the cheek. The lump in her throat threatened to strangle her. Strange how one's life could so suddenly be turned upside down, she thought.

"Alandra, words can never reveal how much we will miss you." Though he had spoken several times of leaving her behind, the usually pompous Heminges was warm and emotional in his farewell.

"Imagine, our dear little girl a lady of the nobility." Richard Burbage took her hand and bowed, kissing her soft flesh reverently.

"A lady," she scoffed. "I have no desire to be such, but I fear they will try to change me into an ambitious, vain, fawning monkey, as my father calls them."

She smiled through her tears at Murray, then threw herself into his arms, the sprinkle of her tears turning into a torrent. "I'll never fit in at court. Never."

"Hush, hush, dearling. There, there! It's all right ..." He patted her on the back, succumbing to his own sobs, a sound much like a puppy whimpering. "Aye, you will! You will. You'll become the finest lady at court and shall make me very, very proud."

"I don't want to go!" she mumbled against his shoulder. "I want to stay here with you." Who would take care of him now? He was growing old, his eyesight failing. Who would help him with his sets and costumes? Drive the wagon? See that he didn't work himself into fatigue?

"And I would have you do just that, but it isn't possible, daughter. You heard with your own ears the queen's command." Murray tried to sound stern. "And perhaps in truth it is where you should go. Being a lady is what you were born to be. And a lady like a precious gem needs a proper setting." She would never know how much that statement pained him, nor that it wrenched his heart to contemplate the loneliness her absence would bring. She was the light in his world, and now that light was going to be dimmed.

"You'll come to visit me?" Though she had begged Elizabeth on bended knee to allow Murray to live at court, her request had been denied.

He held her at arm's length, his misted eyes appraising her. "Aye."

"Often?"

"I'll come, as often as the queen will let me," Murray declared, wiping his nose on his sleeve. "That is a promise."

"We all will," Will Kempe piped up. "It will take the entire queen's guards to keep us away."

"Aye, we'll come," William Sly added. "You've always brought us good luck, Alandra."

Alandra knew they wouldn't break their vow, and yet it wouldn't be the same. Once she left here, the past would be ended and her future would begin. A future she was not certain of. Was it any wonder that already she was lonely? Oh, how she hated good-byes, moreso now as the rest of the company lined up to bid her farewell. Only one face was missing—Shakespeare's.

"Father, where is Will?"

"He had an appointment in the seedier part of town,

where the bull-and-bear-baiting arenas are. Bankside to be precise. There is a theater there that we might perchance use, at least until better quarters are located." Murray drew her aside, lest unwanted ears hear what he said next. "But his visit was for a dual purpose. It seems the man who runs the bull-baiting establishment, Harry Sackerson, has seen Tom Banter."

"Tom Banter!" Alandra had given up hope that he would ever be found.

"Shh!" Murray cautioned her, for there were others besides the actors wandering in and out of the inn. "He was seen meeting with a lady there. One who fits the description of your yellow-haired rival."

"Morgana!" Alandra laughed bitterly. "My step-*grandmother*, you mean." What evil was she planning now?

As Alandra watched her trunks being carried downstairs and loaded in a cart, she pondered the question, imagining all sorts of plots. She stepped up into the curtained litter that was to take her to Whitehall, then looked across the inn's courtyard. Shakespeare was running toward her, his hand clutched at a rope. At the end of the rope, securely bound at the wrists, was a violently cursing boy, a skinny young thing with hair like straw. The blue eyes were hardened, angry, old beyond his years.

"Tell her what you told me, you young gibbet bait," Shakespeare scolded, giving the boy a push that landed him on the ground. "Christopher is in severe danger!"

"Christopher?" Alandra felt a shiver of fear. "Dear God, what do you mean?"

"We must hurry, there is little time!" Frantically, Shakespeare waved his hands in the air, signaling the other actors to come.

Ignoring the men who manned the litter, he blurted

out what he had learned from the young scoundrel he held in tow. "Christopher is to be freed from the Tower tonight. The plot is already afoot."

"Christopher. Freed?" That news was a blessing to Alandra not a curse. Why then was Shakespeare so worried? "By whom?"

"Morgana Woodcliff has masterminded the scheme."

"Morgana!" Alandra digested that bit of information with mixed feelings, and yet as long as Christopher was freed, what did it matter who freed him? "But you speak of danger."

"Aye, of the darkest kind." Though usually a man of calm temperament, Shakespeare nudged the young rogue none too gently with his boot. "Talk or I swear I'll take you to the queen to hang from the gallows," he said, much in the same manner Nicholas had once threatened Will Frizer. "Speak, or by God...."

A tight circle was forming around the boy. Hunching himself forward, his eyes downcast, the boy began to mumble.

"Talk clearly. Tell us the villainy of what is planned!" Shakespeare chanted.

Raising his head, the boy revealed eyes that held stark terror. His skinny body went rigid, his voice broke into a squeak of pure terror. "I can't! E'll kill me if I do. Tom Banter is the devil incarnate!"

"Then I'll tell the tale." Shakespeare's eyes were filled with pity as he looked at the boy. "Tom Banter has been hired by Morgana Woodcliff to commit another murder!"

"No!" Alandra clutched at her throat, knowing without asking who was to be the victim.

"I overheard Banter talking to this young scoundrel."

Rapidly, Shakespeare told how he had spotted Tom Banter, recognizing him at once because of his long black hair, crooked nose, and missing ear. Positioning himself behind a post, he had eavesdropped on the conversation the "cutter" was having with the boy.

"Christopher is walking right into a trap. He wrongly places trust in those who are to free him, little knowing that once he is free of the Tower's walls he is to be murdered and thrown in the Thames. In what manner or at what time only this young ruffian knows, though he will not tell."

"Christopher is to be murdered!" Alandra blinked hard to dispel the vision that suddenly danced before her eyes. Feeling dizzy, she clutched at the curtain.

"I didn't want ter do it! I didn't!" As if seeking mercy, the boy extended his hands toward Alandra. "Have mercy, mistress!"

"Mercy?" Alandra stared at the convulsively sobbing boy. He seemed more victim than villain. Therefore her voice was gentle. "Tell me, please. You have my word that if you help us we'll let you go and no one will ever know that you spoke out. Please!"

"The laidy has used bribery, she 'as. She's gotten the key to the bloke's cell and learned the routine of the warder by 'eart. The bloke will walk right out the doors of the Tower right after sundown, 'e will, leaving behind a straw-and-cloth dummy, just so's the warder won't be suspicious. My part was ter lead him to the boat where Tom Banter will be waiting. Once clear of the Tower's guards Banter will slash 'im through and through, put his corpse in a sack, and throw him over the side. The laidy who 'ired the deed done wants the queen to think he flew the coop and that he sailed for far off lands...."

Shakespeare didn't wait to hear more. With all the valor of the heroes of his plays, he shouted out his commands. Forgetting about her summons to Elizabeth's court, Alandra hurried down from the cart to join the actors as they scurried from the courtyard.

Chapter Fifty-Three

Nicholas stared out the tiny barred window through the gathering gloom. Although the fortress seemed impenetrable, he would soon be leaving here with Morgana's help. That thought gave him a heady feeling, the deepest satisfaction. In preparation for the evening's events, he had studied the pattern of the warder's comings and goings for days, noting that there was at least a three-quarters of an hour's stretch between his third and fourth rounds when he visited an influential prisoner to play chess. More than enough time for Nicholas to be well clear of these walls.

But that was just the beginning. There were four checkpoints in all, and each had to be passed without his being seen. Bulwark Gate and the Lion, Middle, and Byward towers. The night was particularly dark without a moon, thus he hoped that with the aid of his dark cloak he would have at least a chance. Morgana had informed him that a young lad would be waiting for them by the wall to lead them toward a boat. It sounded so simple, so foolproof, that he really thought with proper timing his escape could be accomplished.

He walked to the grille of the wooden door and looked out. The warder had finished his third round, now it was time for the countdown. Nicholas counted to ten before he moved to the bed. Casting a final cautious look toward the window, he reached underneath the mattress and pulled out the dummy. He positioned it at just the right angle in the chair, bending it slightly forward, and stepped back, marveling at how truly human it looked when viewed in the shadows. Just as he would look.

"Time to take my place, my good man," he said, with a mock bow, feeling light of heart for the first time since his arrival at the Tower.

Nicholas knelt in the shadows, waiting for the sound that would herald the beginning of his escape, growing more and more impatient as the time passed on. Where was Morgana? What was taking her so long? Frustration coiled in his belly as he began to think she had changed her mind. He heard footsteps and nearly called out her name until he realized the thudding trod was much too heavy for a woman's footfall.

The warder! He was early! With a mumbled oath, Nicholas scrambled to find a hiding place, choosing to duck behind a large leather chair. The door swung open as he concealed himself, revealing the warder bearing a tray.

"I've come to ask again if you'd like a game of chess. I've brought you a glass of ale to cheer you up." The warder waited for a response from the prisoner, but, of course, heard not a word from the still figure by the window.

The door was ajar, and the warder's back was to Nicholas as the man advanced toward the table. A perfect set up for escape. A chance Nicholas couldn't deny himself, particularly since it was all too probable that the warder would discover the dummy. Taking a deep breath, Nicholas bounded from his concealment, rounded the door, and silently sped down the stairs.

The Tower was a maze of stairs and doors. Nicholas ran down one hall, frantically searching for a way out, only to find he was going in circles. Cursing, mumbling, he tried to quell his panic, retracing his steps, trying another door, then another. At last he was successful and emerged into the glorious fresh air. The feel of freedom momentarily made his senses reel.

But his feeling of euphoria was short-lived. The sentries paced nearby, guarding gateways and walls, preventing a quick dash for freedom. One cry and the whole tower would be swarming with guardsman.

Approaching the Byward archway, Nicholas tried to recall the layout of the Tower as best he could from his school days. Guardrooms were on each side within the thickness of the archway, and beyond the right-hand one was a side entrance leading out on to the wharf. Sally Port, traditionally the royal entrance. Persons of importance disembarked at the King's Steps and then, crossing the wharf, entered via the Sally Port, thus bypassing the gates and main drawbridges. But it was always guarded.

Unable to grab his cloak as he had run from his cell, Nicholas needed one to shield him. He picked up a large, loose stone then hid in the shadows. By now the warder would have discovered the dummy. Every minute counted now, nay every second. Then as if in answer to his prayers, he heard the sound of boots. A workman passed where Nicholas was concealed. The stone descended, the man collapsed on the ground, and Nicholas had his cloak. Added to his good fortune was the fact that the guard to Sally Port was nowhere to be seen.

With the greatest self-control, Nicholas forced himself to maintain a leisurely pace. Hardly daring to breathe, he turned right, and passing through the two ancient doorways, traversed the little drawbridge, and emerged on to the wharf. His every sense was on edge, waiting for a sudden shout, a pounding of feet. But none came.

"Nicholas, you old dog, you've done it!" he whispered.

But elation was befouled, when he heard a woman's voice ask, "Who is there?"

Nicholas turned around, coming face to face with a woman swathed in black. Only the eyes showed. Blue eyes that were staring at him in astonishment.

"Thank God, it is you!" He nearly felt like hugging Morgana he was so glad to see her face. Now he would no longer have to complete his escape alone.

"Nicholas!" She was rightfully astounded. "How on earth—"

"I couldn't wait."

"Obviously." She sounded annoyed. "I couldn't help being late. That damnable boy! He never showed up. Just wait until I see him. I'll box his ears." Taking Nicholas by the arm, she tried to calm her anger. "But never mind. His absence won't upset our plans. I know right where the boat is waiting. I'll take you there."

It was ridiculously easy, made moreso because of Morgana's being by his side. Neither of the two guards they passed even stopped to question them.

"I hope the boat is waiting," Nicholas whispered, giving Morgana's hand a fond squeeze.

"It is."

As they passed by the last obstacle, Nicholas could see the outline of the stern and prow. A boat rocked in the water.

"Morgana, I'll never know how to thank you," Nicholas said, expressing his gratitude.

"A kiss for old times," she said softly.

How could he refuse? Smoothing back her veil, Nicholas pressed a kiss against her lips, one more of fondness than of passion.

Morgana clung to him, her mouth seeking and demanding as it closed over his. It was a long caress of lips and tongue that she seemed reluctant to break. She was breathless as she pulled away. "Oh, Nicholas."

Was there regret in her voice? Nicholas assumed it to be because of what might have been.

"We'll meet again, Morgana. I'll find a way to make Elizabeth listen to my explanation and to clear you of any wrongdoing, as well. In the meantime I sincerely make a wish for your happiness. I want you to find the right man, I really do."

Then as he moved toward the boat, Morgana disappeared into the Tower. For a moment he hesitated as he watched her go, then continued his path down the steps, but a gut-wrenching scream halted him.

"Christopher! Step back!" Alandra shouted. "It's a trap. The man in the boat is Tom Banter. He's here to kill you!"

A large dark, hulking figure emerged from the shadows as the boat pulled alongside the quay. Hurling through the air like a demon from the boat and landing on the wharf, the man lunged at Nicholas with a knife. Nicholas staggered back but did not fall. He maintained his balance, cursing beneath his breath that he was unarmed. It would be far from a well-matched fight, yet he remembered a trick or two.

"Christopher, can we help?" One, two, three, then four silhouettes materialized out of the darkness—Shakespeare, Kempe, Murray, and Armin.

"Just stay out of my way, or better yet give me something to fight this brute with," he demanded.

From the corner of his eye, Nicholas saw the men

hurriedly pulling out their weapons. In the meantime he took off his cloak, wound it around his arm, and used it as a shield against his opponent's slashing knife. Sidestepping Tom Banter again and again, he waited for a chance to turn the other man's lack of wits against him and was rewarded, hearing the knife clatter to the ground as he snapped his coat at his adversary's wrist. But even unarmed, Tom Banter was ruthless. Like a mad dog he sprang forward, catching Nicholas on the chin with a punishing blow. It gave Banter enough time to retrieve his knife.

Sweeping forward in a graceful move, Shakespeare attacked Tom Banter from behind. His unexpected action spoiled the murderer's aim, thereby saving Nicholas from suffering a mortal wound. Hastily, Shakespeare pushed a rapier into Nicholas's hands, the kind the actors used for fencing. It was not the sharpest or sturdiest of rapiers but it was a formidable weapon when wielded with Nicholas's skill.

It was a furious battle, a test of strength and prowess. Nicholas did not dare take his eyes from the quick-moving blade. Again and again Tom Banter lunged, his anger at having been thwarted making him careless. Reacting to the warning of his senses, using his perfect timing, Nicholas blocked each thrust, once more knocking his assailant's knife to the ground. Will Kempe and Murray scrambled for it, with Murray winning the prize. He held it up like a trophy of battle, as if he and not Nicholas had vanquished the enemy.

But Banter, undaunted, came forward with his fists flailing. Like a baited bull he struck out, connecting once again with Nicholas's chin.

Then Kempe and Armin got into the act, gathering anything at all that they could lay their hands on. Stones were thrown, blades slashed the air, large sticks were used as clubs. The distraction worked to Nicholas's advantage. Getting the jump on the snarling rogue, he smashed the pommel of his rapier into his opponent's teeth. The dark-haired man staggered back, his right hand going to his bloodied mouth.

"Get him!" Shakespeare's cry unleashed the full potency of the actors' fury.

Surrounding Tom Banter, they soon had him subdued.

"Try to kill Christopher, will you?" Will Kempe asked, sweeping off his belt to use it as a rope. While Shakespeare and Murray held the man's hands behind his back, Kempe tied his wrists.

"I owe you this." Coming up behind Tom Banter with a stone, Robert Armin thought it justifiably sporting to hit him over the head. "Now we are even."

Moving away from the wall where she had remained during the fight, Alandra felt the exhilaration of the moment, experienced the joy at seeing Nicholas triumph. While Shakespeare, her father, Kempe, and Armin guarded Tom Banter, she had only one thought in mind. She flew into Nicholas's arms. Her mouth ached to feel his lips, her body burned to have him hold her again. Blinking back tears, she looked into his face. Every fiber of her being cried out that she loved him, would always love him.

"Landra!" Nicholas gazed down at her face, gently brushing back the tangled dark hair from her eyes. "You will never know how very much I missed you."

"I do! Oh, Christopher, I do. For truly I felt the same." She wanted to tell him everything, about the queen, her real identity, her summons to court, but now didn't seem to be the proper time, thus all she did was hold him. He was free and they were together, that was all that mattered. There would be time later for explanations. "We'll find a ship, sail away, go across the Channel. Oh, Christopher . . ."

"No, I'll not run away. Not now," he vowed.

Though the ugliness of what nearly happened to him

was tempered by being reunited with the woman he loved, Nicholas was deeply troubled. All that had happened tonight haunted him, for he realized clearly now that Morgana had meant to have him killed. Was it therefore surprising that she had disappeared?

" 'Tis the coward's way to flee," he said, looking into Alandra's beautiful eyes. "Nay, I've gotten free of the Tower, but instead of running away from Elizabeth, I believe it's time I went to her. It is the only way we can hope for any happiness, Alandra."

She trembled in his arms, even so she did not argue. Perhaps it was the only way. "All right," she said, "but I will be beside you."

"And I," Shakespeare exclaimed.

"And me," Murray added, his declaration echoed by Armin and Kempe.

"If they put you in the Tower again, they'll have to put us there, too," Kempe said staunchly.

Thus it was decided that at the first crack of dawn the actors would pay a visit to the queen.

"But in the meantime"—Nicholas nuzzled Alandra's neck—"let us go home . . ."

"Home. I can't. I'm expected at court."

"Elizabeth can wait another day. Tonight belongs to us."

So much had happened that Alandra was in a daze on the journey back to the inn. She hardly even remembered walking through the door or climbing the stairs, but suddenly she was standing by the hearth, slowly removing her clothes before Nicholas's appreciative eyes.

"So lovely. So very, very lovely." He could see the soft curves of her body through the sheer material of her undergown and whistled. Her hair formed a thick shawl of silk, loose and gleaming. Her eyes were wide, her mouth soft and alluring. At that moment she was the most beautiful vision he had ever seen.

"Oh, Christopher, I love you so!"

Her rich, husky voice was like hands upon his skin, doing more to arouse him than any caress.

"Alandra..." He came to her, enfolding her, kissing her mouth and hair, her cheeks, her brow, and her chin, driven beyond endurance by her softness.

Fitting her body to his in a sensuous dancelike motion, Alandra responded.

"My mother once told me that when a person is thinking about a loved one their ears burned. If that is true, then you must have felt my thoughts, my longing. I thought about you, dreamed about you," Nicholas muttered against her mouth.

He cupped her breast in his hand then ran his hard hands over her, stroking, searching out her most sensitive places. Alandra writhed under his touch. Without any trace of modesty, she tugged at her thin gown. It floated in a whisper to the floor.

Nicholas stepped away to strip off his own garments. When he came to her again, he was all naked power and throbbing strength. He lifted her and carried her to the bed. All the days of anguish, of searching, of wanting drifted into oblivion as they made love.

He was gentle, remarkably so, savoring her body, touching her in a manner that spoke of his love. Alandra made a small, wondering sound in her throat and opened up to him like a blossoming flower. In turn he groaned as she explored, stroked, and made love to him. Alandra was caught in a trance of wondrous delight. She had been starved without his love but now being with him was like savoring a banquet. He molded her, shaped her, made her rediscover the appetite she had for passion. When he entered her, she felt her heart move with love. Clinging to him, she called out his name.

Later she snuggled up against him, burying her face in the warmth of his chest, breathing in his manly scent. They needed to talk. He had to be told so many things, and yet she couldn't bare to break the spell. Her eyes felt heavy, she was relaxed, and she felt content for the first time in such a long, long time. She didn't want to sleep. Not yet. She wanted to relish this moment of joy, but as he caressed her back, tracing his fingers along her spine, she drifted off.

Chapter Fifty-Four

Whitehall was a noisy mass of confusion. It was the queen's "dancing" day, thus the great hall was filled to the brim not only with musicians but all those with a penchant for revelry as well. Lords and ladies alike had to shout to be heard over the loud din of instrument. Alandra and Nicholas couldn't have picked a worse time for an audience with the queen. And yet there was nothing that could be done now, thus addressing the guard, they entered.

At the hub of nobles was Elizabeth in a gown of oyster, embroidered with brown and gold, an interesting design that looked as if a thousand eyes were staring out from her bodice and the folds of the skirt. Elizabeth walked, ignoring the murmuring knot of courtiers clustered around her. She pretended to be oblivious to Nicholas's presence as well, as if it were every day that a man escaped from the Tower. But if Elizabeth ignored him, the courtiers did not. They openly stared, for the daily gossip had preceded him. "Shall we approach the queen, Christopher?" As if to prod him on, Alandra took a few halting steps.

Nicholas hesitated. Alandra could sense the struggle going on within him, then he captitulated and walked beside her without a word. They were followed by the entourage of actors, flamboyantly attired in their costumes, and Bessie who looked pertly pretty in her Sunday-best dress. The stately music gave dignity to the group as it entered the hall.

Alandra and Nicholas made a striking sight. He was dressed all in black and gold, his white ruff a startling contrast to the dark of his hair. For the occasion he had hastily procured a new dress for Alandra of gold velvet to match his gold lacings. As they approached Elizabeth, he clasped Alandra's hand to give her reassurance, hiding his own apprehension beneath a smile.

Nicholas, Alandra, and their party elbowed their way through the gawking crowd with a cool poise that belied the nervousness they all felt. Only once did Nicholas give pause and that was at the sight of an all too well-known profile. Clad in an outfit of red and silver was his old nemesis.

Stafford was busy ingratiating himself with the queen, yet Nicholas knew full well that Stafford was aware of him. Nicholas surveyed the golden-haired man, yet his hatred had been tempered into severe dislike now that he knew that at least the man was innocent of Woodcliff's and Frizer's murders. Undoubtedly, he too had been naught but Morgana's pawn. Perhaps Stafford had even believed that Nicholas was guilty. Well, soon he would know, and it would all be over. Even so, they would always be rivals. That was just the way it was.

Nor was Stafford his only adversary. Morgana's eyes met Nicholas's across the distance of the room and

Nicholas knew that she realized the moment of truth had come. Yet she held her ground and didn't try to leave the hall. She laughed, but the sound was hollow, and her head kept turning in the entourage's direction again and again.

"If looks could kill, I know I would be dead," Alandra whispered in Nicholas's ear.

Undoubtedly, Morgana had already heard the gossip of Alandra's lineage and feared she'd have to share the spoils she had won so evilly. As her eyes focused on Alandra, they glittered with undisguised hatred.

The music changed from one of slow tempo to that of a frenzied pace. It was a dance of Spanish origin, one of turning and bowing and stepping quite lively. Elizabeth changed partners frequently, but at last she tired and paused for a rest. In that moment her eyes met Nicholas's. From across the room he bowed, daring her to continue to treat him as if he were invisible.

"Very well I see you." The queen lifted her voice so that it carried throughout the hall. The music broke off, the dancers stopped, and everyone just stared. "I was not aware you had been summoned to court, Sir Leighton."

"I wasn't. I came of my own volition to tell you something that you must know."

"Don't waste your breath, Sir Leighton," Elizabeth chided. "I know all about it. Guards, remove him and take him to the Tower." She was incensed, seeing his escape as a public affront to her importance and power.

"Majesty, I will gladly return to prison but I beg you to listen to me. You don't know how or why I was unjustly accused," Nicholas responded. "The wise and thoughtful monarch whom I know would give me a chance to reveal the truth of all that has gone on. Gloriana would give me a chance to explain so that I might obtain her mercy."

Elizabeth eyed him thoughtfully. "Speak then, tell
s why the realm's foremost swordsman has paid us
n impromptu visit."

"I have come to accuse Morgana Woodcliff of will-
lly and cold-bloodedly hiring an assassin, Tom Ban-
r, to kill me, and Will Frizer as well as paying Frizer
kill her husband, Lord Woodcliff."

There was an outcry from those assembled. The
rds decried the accusations as blatant falsehoods,
ut the ladies seemed of a different mind.

Elizabeth exclaimed bitterly, "You had best know
hat you are saying or be guilty of slander amongst
our other crimes."

"I have witnesses, including Tom Banter who was
ired to kill Will Frizer and me. One witness is present
ow"—Nicholas pointed to Bessie—"and Banter and
young boy are at this moment lodged in a locked
om of this palace." Looking behind him, Nicholas
otioned for the actors—Kempe, Sly, Heminges,
owin, Armin, Murray, and Shakespeare—to take
heir places beside him.

Shakespeare's presence impressed the queen, for she
ade it a point to address him. "Master Playwright,
welcome you to this hall, though were it up to me,
e would set aside such serious matters for a delight-
l comedy. Have you any new treasures?"

Shakespeare bowed. "Several, Your Majesty, based
n yon nobleman's escapades."

"Ah, yes, while he was fleeing from my supposed
rath, he hid among your theater company." Her jaw
lenched warningly. "Do you always shield fugitives,
ven when they are wanted by your queen?"

"Nay. But in this case I perceived the man to be
nnocent and thus I sought to guard him *for* Your Maj-
sty."

"I see!" Sensing that Will Shakespeare might well
e her match, Elizabeth dropped the issue. "Then by

all means let this matter proceed so that I may return to my dancing."

Regal, humorless, and unsmiling, she conducted the audience with her usual competence and little display of emotion, that is until the details of the plots were revealed. Shakespeare, Nicholas, Alandra, Murray, Armin, and Kempe spoke so eloquently as they told the story from the beginning including Will Frizer's attesting to Nicholas's innocence in Lord Woodcliff's death and Armin's identifying Tom Banter as Frizer's murderer, and hearing a woman calling to the killer. Bessie gave her testimony and the young boy was summoned, and their evidence was further damning.

Dismissing the young boy from court, Elizabeth's eyes blazed with rage as she summoned Morgana. In the queen's eyes the Widow Woodcliff was already condemned. "Woman, what do you have to say to all of this?"

"Lies! All lies. 'Twas Nicholas who killed my husband...He...he..." Morgana fell to her knees, knowing Tom Banter's testimony alone would be enough to hang her. Elizabeth had always hated her and would lust for this victory. "Mercy, Your Majesty."

"Mercy?" The queen guffawed, delighting in the chance to bring about this haughty beauty's downfall. "I should give you just as much mercy as you gave your husband, that loyal and brave old man, and your other victim, or that you were prepared to give Nicholas Leighton." Her eyes squinted dangerously. "Black should be your only color, madame, for you are like the spider that devours its mate."

"He—he was old and I was young—"

"With eyes for other men. Whore! I will not abide such deviltry in my court." Elizabeth stamped her foot. "Take her away. She is banished to the western counties, and all of her properties are to be given up to the Crown, to do with as I will. While she is in exile

she would be wise to thank God for a merciful queen
who loathes to shed a noblewoman's blood. But if she
causes any further trouble, or if there is any further
plotting, I will forget my leniency and part that
painted head from her slender shoulders. Do I make
myself clear?"

Lord Stafford, visibly shaken, quietly retreated from
the room as everyone in the hall shook their heads
fearfully. All eyes watched as Morgana was dragged
forcibly from the hall, and as the door slammed shut
behind her, everyone shuddered.

Alandra quickly recovered. "And what about Tom
Banter, Your Majesty?"

Elizabeth waved her hand and eyed Alandra with
impatience. "Justice will be done. He will be turned
over to the magistrate."

Elizabeth then turned her attention to Nicholas.
"You have served me well, Sir Leighton. Exposing that
he-cat before all has gladdened my heart more than
you will ever know."

"My duty as always is to my queen and to justice.
Now perhaps truly Lord Woodcliff will be at rest."

"Perhaps." Elizabeth's eyes lit upon Alandra, and
there was mischief in her eyes. "I draw great delight
in banishing that witch, however, I was looking forward to an interesting time watching you and your
step-grandmother getting acquainted."

Fighting over Lord Woodcliff's inheritance, Alandra
thought sourly. The queen would have to find another
game to amuse her. "I was looking forward to it, too,
Your Majesty," she lied. In truth Morgana was not
being sent far away enough to suit her.

Elizabeth placed her hand on Nicholas's shoulder.
"I pardon you your escape and I take great delight in
welcoming you back to court. Lord Stafford is amusing, but frankly, his ego can sometimes be a bore. I
believe he needs to have you here just so his head does

not get too puffed up! With a bit of competition, he may learn to be more humble and to remember that I have raised him up and I can bring him down."

"Your power is absolute, Your Majesty," Nicholas said, barely hiding a smile.

"Yes. And I can grant any wish." Elizabeth's mood was gradually improving, and her fond smiles clearly affirmed that Nicholas was in her good graces again. "Knowing that, what is it you would wish for, Sir Nicholas?"

Nicholas squeezed Alandra's hand. "Truthfully, Your Majesty?"

"Of course truthfully."

"I wish to marry Alandra Thatcher, nay Woodcliff."

Elizabeth eyed him coolly. "Marry?" Her disdain for the idea was not disguised.

"I want her to be my wife."

"Indeed." Elizabeth reached out with her fan, touching Alandra's chin, turning her face this way and that with the soft feathers. "I had rather been fond of the idea of marrying her off to Lord Stafford. He is so fair and she so dark."

Was she joking or was she serious? Alandra didn't know.

"What think you of that, Sir Leighton?" Elizabeth demanded.

"Over my dead body!" Nicholas replied, then bowed to temper his show of anger. "Your Majesty."

"So, I see. That is the way it is." Elizabeth's eyes darted back and forth between the two young people, taking note of the glow in their eyes whenever they looked at each other. She sighed regretfully. "True love I suppose you would call it."

"True love it is," Nicholas answered.

He knew that he might have grown enormously wealthy, might have become even more powerful, had

he been content like Stafford to let the queen love him
as she loved the lap dogs that hovered at her knee. But
he wanted no part of the queen's game. He saw how
Elizabeth's eyes glowed with suppressed passion as
she looked at him, and it was obvious that she favored
him, yet Nicholas had to be honest.

"And I suppose were I to deny you this request you
would do as Sir Walter Raleigh did and marry her
anyway."

Nicholas knew the queen could be most unforgiving
where matters of the heart were concerned. Raleigh
and his bride had been condemned to the Tower when
they had married secretly. But he wouldn't lie. He
wanted Alandra more than life itself.

"I must confess that I would elope with her at the
very first chance, Your Majesty."

Nicholas's confession was met by stern silence. For
a moment he was certain that he would end up back
in the Tower.

"Such an impetuous man! But then I have always
liked men of daring." Elizabeth put her hand to her
temple and pondered the matter for a long, long time.
"You know how much I favor you. Of all the lords,
you are among those I hold most dear."

"Your Majesty does me too much honor. I am overcome," Nicholas whispered. Cautiously, he waited,
crossing his fingers behind his back.

"I had plans for you!" Again there was a long drawn-
out silence. "Even so, I do not see how I can do otherwise than say yes. You have already spent time in
the Tower, and I must confess that I have no desire to
see you escape again. 'Tis an embarrassment."

"Yes, Your Majesty." Nicholas could barely contain
his joy. The queen had consented to their marriage!
"Sweet love, did you hear that?" he whispered in Alandra's ear.

Fearing that the queen might change her mind as

she was wont to do on occasion, he hurriedly and politely took his leave, dragging Alandra behind him. Bessie and the actors followed them quickly. Only when they were beyond the palace doors did Nicholas dare let out a thunderous shout.

"What a wedding it will be. As splended as any of my plays," Shakespeare added, kissing Alandra fondly on the cheek.

The other actors greeted the idea of the marriage with equal enthusiasm. "We'll give a performance of *A Midsummer-Night's Dream*. 'Tis a perfect play for a wedding," Kempe stated.

"Seeing as how it was written to celebrate just such an occasion," Armin confided.

Murray took Bessie by the hand, thinking to himself that there might be *two* weddings in the near future. Looking into Bessie's twinkling eyes, he smiled, knowing she'd make a lovely wife.

Then he turned to Shakespeare. "All's well that end's well, eh, Will?" Murray cocked his head and winked in Alandra's direction, only to see that she was oblivious to their chatter, kissing Nicholas with abandon.

Shakespeare nodded, and without a backward glance, the players departed, leaving the two lovers locked in each other's arms.

About The Author

Under her own name or the pseudonym Katherine Vickery, Kathryn Kramer has published with Dell, Berkley, and Pocket Books. A past winner of the *Romantic Times* Reviewers' Choice Award, Ms. Kramer has written thirteen bestselling historical romances, including *Lady Rogue* and *Siren Song*.

Cassie Edwards

Enjoy torrid passion and romance from bestselling author Cassie Edwards!

"Cassie Edwards is a shinning talent!"

—*Romantic Times*

TOUCH THE WILD WIND. Sasha Seymour hoped to carve out a sheep station from the untamed Australian Outback. All that stood between her and the forces of man and nature was the strength of her partner Ashton York — for in his tawny arms she found a haven from the storm.
_3059-4 $4.95 US/$5.95 CAN

ROSES AFTER RAIN. Rugged Ian Lavery thought he could survive all the dangers that vast and untamed Australia had to offer — until he met Thalia. Wild and sweet, their passion went beyond the bounds of propriety.
_2982-0 $4.50 US/$4.95 CAN

WHEN PASSION CALLS. Lovely Melanie Stanton had been promised to Josh Brennan for as long as she could remember. But marriage was the last thing on her mind until Josh's long-lost brother returned to his family's vast spread to claim her.
_3265-1 $4.99 US/$5.99 CAN